The
Brazen
Bride

He was startlingly, heartbreakingly, breathtakingly beautiful.

His face, all clean, angular lines and sculpted planes, embodied the very essence of masculine beauty—there was not a soft note anywhere. Combined with the muscled hardness of his body, that face promised virility, passion—and direct, unadorned, unadulterated sin.

Such a face did not belong to a man given to sweetness but to action, command, and demand.

Chiseled lips, firm and fine, sent a seductive shiver down her spine. The line of his jaw made her fingertips throb. He had winged black brows, a wide forehead, and lashes so black and thick and long she was instantly jealous.

As usual her instincts had been right. This man was—would be—dangerous. To her peace of mind, if nothing else.

Men like this—who looked like he did, who had bodies like his—led women into sin.

And into stupidity.

STEPHANIE LAURENS

The Brazen Bride

THE BLACK COBRA QUARTET

AVON

An Imprint of HarperCollins*Publishers*

AVON BOOKS
An Imprint of HarperCollins*Publishers*
10 East 53rd Street
New York, New York 10022-5299

One

December 10, 1822
One o'clock in the morning
On the deck of the Heloise Leger, *the English Channel*

Hell hath no greater fury than the cataclysmic storms that raked the English Channel in winter.

With elemental tempest raging about him, Major Logan Monteith leapt back from the slashing blade of a Black Cobra cult assassin. Raising his saber to counter the second assassin's strike, using his dirk, clutched in his left fist, to fend off the first attacker's probing knife, Logan suspected he'd be learning about the afterlife all too soon.

Winds howled; waves crashed. Water sluiced across the deck in a hissing spate.

The night was blacker than Hades, the driving rain a blurring veil. Falling back a step, Logan swiped water from his eyes.

As one, the assassins surged, beating him back toward the prow. Blades met, steel ringing on steel, sparks flaring, pinpricks of brightness in the engulfing dark. Abruptly, the deck canted—all three combatants desperately fought for balance.

The ship, a Portuguese merchantman bound for Portsmouth, was in trouble. Logan had been forced to join its crew five days before, when, on reaching Lisbon, he'd discovered the town crawling with cultists. Battered by pounding waves, buffetted and tossed on the storm-wracked sea, as the deck leveled, the ship wallowed and swung, no longer held into the wind. Whether the rudder had broken or the captain had abandoned the wheel, Logan couldn't tell. He couldn't spare the time to squint through the rain-drenched dark at the bridge.

Instinct and experience kept his eyes locked on the men facing him. There'd been a third, but Logan had accounted for him in the first rush. The body was gone, claimed by the ravening waves.

Saber swinging, Logan struck, but immediately was forced to block and counter, then retreat yet another step into the narrowing prow. Further confining his movements, reducing his options. Didn't matter; two against one in the icy, pelting rain, with his grips on his dirk and his saber cramping, leather-soled boots slipping and sliding—the assassins were barefoot, giving them even that advantage—he couldn't effectively go on the offensive.

He wasn't going to survive.

As he met and deflected another vicious blow, he acknowledged that, yet even as he did his innate stubbornness rose. He'd been a cavalry officer for more than a decade, fought in wars over half the globe, been through hell more than once, and survived.

He'd faced assassins before, and lived.

Miracles happened.

He told himself that even as, teeth gritted, he angled his saber up to block a slash at his head—and his feet went from under him, pitching him back against the railing.

The wooden scroll-holder strapped to his back slammed into his spine.

From the corner of his eye, he saw white teeth flash in a dark face—a feral grin as the second assassin swung and slashed. Logan hissed as the blade sliced down his left side, cutting through coat and shirt into muscle, grazing bone, before angling across his stomach to disembowel him. Instinct had him flattening against the railing; the blade cut, but not deep enough.

Not that that would save him.

Lightning cracked, a jagged tear of brilliant white splitting the black sky. In the instant's illumination, Logan saw the two assassins, dark eyes fanatically gleaming, triumph in their faces, gather themselves to spring and bring him down.

He was bleeding, badly.

He saw Death, felt it—tasted ashes as icy fingers pierced his body, reaching for his soul.

He dragged in a last gasp, braced himself. Given his mission, given his occupation for the last several years, Saint Peter ought at least consider letting him into Heaven.

A long-forgotten prayer formed on his lips.

The assassins sprang.

Crack!!

Impact—sudden, sharp, catastrophic—flung him and the assassins overboard. The plunge into turbulent depths, into the churning fury of the sea, separated them.

Tumbling in the icy dark, instinct took hold; righting himself, Logan struck upward. His dirk was still in his left fist; he'd released his saber, but it was tied to his belt by its lanyard—he felt the reassuring tap of the hilt against his leg.

He was a strong swimmer. The assassins almost certainly weren't—it would be a wonder if they could swim at all. Dismissing them—he had more pressing concerns—he broke the surface and hauled in a huge breath. He shook his head, then peered through the water weighing down his lashes.

The storm was at its height, the seas mountainous. He couldn't see beyond the next towering wave, while with elemental rage the wind whipped and strafed, shrieking worse than a thousand banshees.

The ship had been in open water in the middle of the Channel when the storm had hit, but he had no idea how far the tempest had tossed them, nor any clear idea of direction. No idea if land was close, or . . .

He'd been losing blood when he'd hit the water. How long he would last in the cauldron of icy waves, how soon his already depleted strength would fail—

His hand struck something—wood, a plank. No, even better, a section of planking. Desperate, Logan grabbed it, grimly hung on as the next wave tried to slap him away, then, gritting his teeth, he hauled himself up and onto the makeshift raft.

The cold had numbed his flesh, yet the cut down his side sent burning pain lancing through his entire body.

For a long moment, he lay prone on the planks, gasping, then, gathering his ebbing strength, steeling himself, he inched and edged further onto the planks until he could lock his right hand over the ragged front edge. His feet still dangled in the water, but his body was supported to his knees; it was the best he could do.

The waves surged. His raft pitched, but rode the swell.

Beneath the lashing roar of the storm, waves crashed. Cheek to the wet wood, he listened, concentrating, and confirmed that the waves were smashing against something nearby.

The ship was, he thought, wallowing in the unrelieved blackness to his right. Breaking up. Sinking. Given how he and the assassins had been flung, the impact must have been midship. Whipping up his failing strength, he lifted his head, searched, saw debris but no bodies—no other survivors—but only he and the assassins had been so far forward in the prow.

Lightning cracked again, and showed him the ship's bare masts silhouetted against the inky sky.

As the simultaneous clap of thunder faded, he heard a sucking, rushing sound. Recognizing the portent, he peered at the ship.

The listing, tipping, capsizing ship.

Out of the night, the main mast came swinging down. . . .

He didn't even have time to swear before the top of the mast thumped down across him and the world went black.

"Linnet! *Linnet!* Come quickly! Come *see!*"

Linnet Trevission looked up from the old flagstones of the path that ran from the stable to the kitchen door. She'd left the stable and was nearing the kichen garden; directly ahead, the solid bulk of her home, Mon Coeur, sat snug and serene, anchored within the protective embrace of stands of elm and fir bent and twisted into outlandish shapes by the incessant sea winds.

At present, however, in the aftermath of the storm that had raged for half the night, the winds were mild, coyly coquettish, the winter sun casting a honey glow over the house's pale stone.

"Linnet! *Linnet!*"

She smiled as Chester, one of her wards—a tow-headed scamp of just seven—came pelting around the side of the house, heading for the back door. "Chester! I'm here."

The boy looked up, then veered onto the stable path.

"You have to come!" Skidding to a halt, he grabbed her hand and tugged. "There's been a wreck!" His face alight, excitement and tension straining his voice, he looked up into her eyes. "There are bodies! And Will says one of the men is *alive*! You have to come!"

Linnet's smile fell from her face. "Yes, of course." Swiping up her skirts—wishing she'd worn her breeches instead—she strode quickly toward the back door, inwardly reviewing the necessary tasks, tasks she'd dealt with often before.

On the southwest tip of Guernsey, dealing with ship-wrecks was an inescapable part of life.

Chester trotted at her side, his hand gripping hers—too tightly, but then his father had been lost at sea three years ago. As they neared the kitchen door, it opened to reveal Linnet's aunt, Muriel.

"Did I hear aright? A wreck?"

Linnet nodded. "Will sent Chester—there's at least one

survivor. I'll go straightaway—can you find Edgar and the others? Tell them to bring the old gate, and the pack of bandages and splints."

"Yes, of course. But where?"

Linnet looked at Chester. "Which cove?"

"West one."

Grimacing, Linnet met Muriel's eyes. Of course it would be that one—the rockiest and most dangerous. Especially for whoever had been washed up. "Broken bones, almost certainly."

Nodding briskly, Muriel waved her off. "Go. I'll have everything ready here when you get back."

Linnet met Chester's eyes. "Let's race."

Chester flashed a grin, let go of her hand, turned and ran back around the house.

Both hands now free, Linnet gathered her skirts and set out in pursuit; with her longer legs, she was soon on Chester's heels. The path cut through the surrounding trees, then out across the rocky expanse that bordered the edge of the low cliffs.

"Hold up!" Linnet called as they rounded the southern headland of the long northwestern side of the island and the west cove opened up below them.

Chester halted at the top of the path—little more than a goat track—that led down to a strip of coarse sand. Beyond the sand lay rocks, exposed now that the tide was mostly out, a tumbled jumble of granite from fist-sized to small boulders that formed the floor of the cove. The cove wasn't all that wide; two promontories of larger, jagged rocks enclosed it, marching out into the lashing gray waves.

Looking down, Linnet saw three bodies, two flung as if carelessly discarded on the rocks. Those two were dead—had to be, given the contortions of limbs, heads, and spines. The third she could only catch glimpses of; Will and Brandon—another two of her wards—were crouched over the man.

Aware of Chester's pleading look, Linnet nodded. "All right—let's go."

He was off like a hare. Linnet kilted her skirts, then followed, leaping down the familiar path with an abandon almost Chester's equal. As she descended, she scanned the cove again, noting the flotsam thrown up by the storm; to her educated eyes the evidence suggested that a good-sized merchantman had broken up on the razor-sharp rocks that lurked beneath the waves out to the northwest.

Reaching the sand, Chester bounded toward Will and Brandon. Suppressing the urge to follow, Linnet carefully made her way out onto the rocks and confirmed that the other two men were indeed dead, beyond her help. Two sailors, by the look of them, both swarthy. Spanish?

Leaving them where they lay, she picked her way through the rocks back onto the sand, then walked to where the third body lay close to the cliff.

His back to her, Will looked up and around as she neared, his fifteen-year-old face unusually sober. "He was on the planking, so we lifted it and carried him here."

Halting, she dropped a hand on Will's shoulder and answered the question he hadn't asked. "It was safe to move him if he was already on the planks."

Shifting her gaze from Will's face, she got her first look at their survivor. He was lying on his stomach on the section of planking, a wet tangle of black hair screening his face.

He was large. Big. Not a giant, but in any company he would rank as impressive. Broad shoulders, long, heavy limbs. Running her gaze down his spine, she frowned at the bulge distorting his sodden coat. Bending, she reached out and touched it, felt the hardness, traced the odd shape.

"It's a wooden cylinder in oilskins," Will told her. "It's slung in a leather holder with a loop around his belt. We think his arms must go through other loops to hold it in place."

Linnet nodded. "Curious." Had he been carrying the cylinder secretly? With it nestled between the muscles bracketing his spine, if he'd been upright, the fall of his coat would have concealed it.

Straightening, she ran her gaze down his legs, but saw no evidence of breaks or wounds. He was wearing breeches and a loose coat, the sort many sailors wore. His right arm was extended, the fingers of his large hand curled around the front edge of a plank. His other hand, however, lay level with his face, fingers locked in a death grip about the hilt of a dagger.

That seemed a trifle odd for a shipwreck.

Conscious of her pulse thudding—the run to the cliffs shouldn't have made her heart beat so rapidly—she bent to look at the dagger. Not just a dagger, she realized—a dirk. The fine scrollwork on the blade was exquisite, the hilt larger than that of most knives, with a rounded stone set in the crosspiece. Reaching down, she pried long, hard, ice-cold fingers away from the hilt, then handed the dirk to Will. "Hold that for me."

The man hadn't stirred; not a single muscle had so much as tensed. Linnet drew back, aware of her instincts twitching, flickering in definite warning, yet for the life of her she couldn't make sense of the message.

The stranger was all but dead—indeed, she wasn't sure he wasn't—so how could he be dangerous?

From his position kneeling on the other side of the planking, Brandon said, "He's got a sword, too. On this side."

Linnet circled the man, looked where Brandon pointed, then crouched and unhooked the lanyard that attached the weapon to the man's belt. Drawing the blade carefully from under the man's leg, she straightened, studied it. "It's a saber—a cavalry sword." She'd seen enough of them during the war, but the war was long over, the cavalry largely disbanded. Perhaps this man had been a trooper, and after the war had turned to sailing?

"We *think* he's alive," Brandon said, "but we can't find any pulse, and he's not breathing—well, not so you can tell."

Leaving the saber with Brandon, Linnet returned to Will's side. The man's head lay turned that way.

"He must be alive because he's bleeding," Will said. "See?"

He lifted the clothes along the man's side, and a rent parted, exposing pale flesh and a long, nasty cut. A recent cut.

Crouching beside Will, Linnet looked, and recognized a sword slash. That explained the dirk and saber. While Will held the clothes, she leaned closer, examining the wound, following it up—to the side of the man's breast. Thick muscle had been sliced through. Tracing the wound down, she sucked in a breath when she saw bone—a rib. But that was lower, where there wasn't so much muscle between taut skin and rib cage.

"He's bleeding," Will insisted. "See there?"

Linnet had noted the pale pinkish liquid seeping from the cut. She nodded, not yet ready to explain that that might simply be seawater oozing back out of the wound, tinged with blood that had bled out before. Before the man had died.

Yet it was possible he still lived. The sea had all but frozen his flesh; any bleeding would be extremely slow, even were he alive.

Continuing to trace the wound, she discovered that it curved inward, angling down and across the man's stomach. She couldn't see further than the side of his waist, but a gut wound . . . if he had one, he was almost certainly dead, whether he'd already died or not.

Lying as he was, the pressure of his body combined with the effects of the icy sea might have held the wound closed, inhibited the usual bleeding.

She glanced at Brandon's face, then at Will, alongside her. Chester was hovering at her shoulder. "I need to check the wound across his stomach. I need you to help me ease this side of him up—enough for me to look."

The boys eagerly reached for the man's left shoulder, his side. Settling on her knees, Linnet placed Brandon's hands on the man's shoulder, positioned Will's hands beneath the left hip, set Chester ready to help support the shoulder Brandon would lift. "All together, then." Linnet licked her lips, said a little prayer. She was too experienced in matters of life, death, and the sea to allow herself to become invested in a stranger's survival; she told herself it was for the boys' sake that she hoped this stranger lived. "Now."

The boys heaved, pushed, propped. As soon as they had the man angled up and steady, Linnet ducked down, close to the heavy body, peered beneath to trace and follow the wound—then exhaled the breath she hadn't realized she'd held. Easing back, she nodded. "Let him down."

"Will he be all right?" Chester asked.

She couldn't yet promise. "The wound is less deep over his stomach—no real danger. He was lucky." A scenario was taking shape in her mind—a picture of how the man had received such a wound. It should have been a killing, or at least incapacitating, slash. He'd escaped death by less than an inch, just before his ship had wrecked.

"But he's still not really breathing," Brandon said.

And she still wasn't sure if he was alive. Linnet checked for a pulse in the man's wrist, then in his strong throat. There was none she could detect, nor any discernible rise and fall of his chest, but all that could be due to being close to frozen. There was no help for it; shuffling nearer, with one hand she brushed back the fall of black hair hiding his face, bent close, focused—and stopped breathing.

He was startlingly, heartbreakingly, breathtakingly beautiful. His face, all clean, angular lines and sculpted planes, embodied the very essence of masculine beauty—there was not a soft note anywhere. Combined with the muscled hardness of his body, that face promised virility, passion, and direct, unadorned, unadulterated sin.

Such a face did not belong to a man given to sweetness, but to action, command, and demand.

Chiseled lips, firm and fine, sent a seductive shiver down her spine. The line of his jaw made her fingertips throb. He had winged black brows, a wide forehead, and lashes so black and thick and long she was instantly jealous.

She'd frozen.

The boys shifted uneasily, watching, waiting for her verdict.

As usual her instincts had been right. This man was—

would be—dangerous. To her peace of mind, if nothing else.

Men like this—who looked like he did, who had bodies like his—led women into sin.

And into stupidity.

Dragging in a breath, she forced her eyes to stop drinking him in, forced her mind to stop mentally swooning. She hesitated, needing to get nearer—and too rattled to lightly risk it.

Maintaining her current, already too-close distance, she held her fingers beneath his nose. And felt nothing.

Turning her hand, she held the sensitive skin on the inside of her wrist close, but could detect not the smallest waft of air.

Lips thinning, mentally muttering an imprecation against fallen angels, she leaned down, close, in—angled her cheek so that it was a whisker away from his lips . . .

And felt the merest brush of air, a breath, an exhalation.

She eased back, straightening on her knees, and stared at the man's face. Then she turned to the wound in his side, checked again. And yes, that was blood, not just seepage. "He's alive."

Chester whooped. The other two grinned.

She didn't. Getting back to her feet, she looked down at trouble. "We need to get him up to the house."

"*Oof!* He's so damned heavy!" Easing the stranger's shoulders down—resisting the urge to just drop him—Linnet settled him against her pillows. Of course, he had to have *her* bed; it was the only one in the house long enough, big enough, and, very likely, strong enough to be sure of supporting him.

Stepping back, she planted her hands on her hips and all but glared at him, unconscious though he was.

Muriel tucked the covers in on the bed's other side. "Now to thaw him out. I'll send the children up with the hot bricks."

Linnet nodded, her gaze locked on the comatose figure in her bed. She heard Muriel go out, the door shutting behind her. Folding her arms, Linnet swapped her glare for a scowl as she battled to wrench her mind and her senses from their preoccupation with the body in her bed—with the idea of all that muscle, naked, washed, dried, and with his wound stitched, salved, and well-bound, denting her mattress.

She'd seen more naked men, of all descriptions, than she could count—inevitable given a childhood spent largely on her father's ship. It certainly wasn't any degree of novelty, nor attack of missish sensibility, that had left her nerves fluttering, jittery, her breathing tight and shallow, her stomach feeling peculiarly hollow. She would have said, and been certain of it, that seeing another naked male would barely register—would have no effect on her, make no real impression.

Instead . . . there was a naked fallen angel in her bed, and her pulse was still hammering.

Of course, after Edgar, John, and the other men had arrived on the beach and carried the stranger up to the house, to her bedroom, then heaved him onto her bed, she'd had to help Muriel tend him. Had to help her aunt peel off his clothes, uncovering all that solid, muscled flesh. Had to help bathe and dry him, then stitch and bind his wound. It was hardly surprising if she still felt hot after all that exertion.

She hoped her aunt put the uncharacteristic flush in her cheeks down to that.

Between them, she and Muriel had stitched and bandaged thoroughly. As he thawed and his blood started to flow normally, he'd bleed as usual; his immersion in icy water had been an advantage in that respect. They hadn't been able to put a nightshirt on him; not even one of her father's would fit, and the difficulty in manhandling the stranger's heavy arms and body . . . Muriel had fetched extra blankets instead.

"Here's the bricks." Will pushed the door open with his shoulder and came in, bearing two flannel-wrapped bricks that had been heated on the kitchen hearth.

The others—Brandon, at thirteen nearly as tall as Will, Jennifer, twelve, Gillyflower, eight, and Chester—followed Will in, each carrying at least one brick.

Lifting the down-filled quilt, Linnet took each brick and

nestled it on the sheet covering the stranger's body, working her way around so that eventually he lay cradled in a heated horseshoe that ran from his chest down and around his very large feet. Once the last brick had been set in place, she tucked the quilt in.

Stepping back, she looked down at their patient. "That's the best we can do. Now we wait."

The children stayed for a little while, but when the man showed no hint of stirring, they drifted out. Linnet remained.

Restless, wary, strangely on her guard, she had no idea what it was about the man that kept her pacing the floor, her eyes, almost always, trained on his fallen angel face while inwardly, silently, she willed him to live.

Every now and then, she would pause beside the bed and lay a hand across his brow.

It remained icy cold.

Deathly cold.

Despite all they'd done, it was entirely possible he would never wake, much less recover.

Why, in this instance, a stranger's life mattered so much she couldn't fathom, but she wanted him to live. Actively and continually *willed* him to live.

To have a fallen angel fall into her life only to die before she even learned the color of his eyes was simply unacceptable. Fallen angels did not fall from the sky—or get washed up in her cove—every day; she'd never laid eyes on a man like him, awake or comatose, in all her twenty-six years, and she wanted, yearned, to learn more.

A dangerous want, perhaps, but when had she ever shied away from danger?

The afternoon waned, but brought no change in her patient. As evening closed in, she sighed. The children came up with another set of warmed bricks. She helped them switch the hot bricks for the cool, then, with the children clattering down the stairs, eager for their dinner, she drew the curtains over the window, checked the man one more time, and headed for the door.

Her gaze fell on the objects she'd left on the tallboy by the door. She paused, glanced back at the figure so still in her bed, then picked up the three items—the only things other than his clothes he'd been carrying.

The dirk—a fine piece, far finer than one would expect a sailor to own.

The saber—definitely a cavalryman's sword, well used and lovingly honed.

She'd get the boys to polish both blades. The saber's scabbard might yet be salvageable.

The third object, the wooden cylinder, was the most curious. As Will had guessed, the man had been carrying it wrapped in oilskins in a leather sling; with him unable to shrug the sling off, they'd had to cut the shoulder straps to remove it. The wood was foreign; she thought it was rosewood. The brass fittings that held the wooden strips together, and locked one end closed, smacked of somewhere far away, some alien shore.

Gathering all three items, Linnet glanced back at her bed, at the dark head on her pillows, silent and still, then she turned, went out of the door, and closed it quietly behind her.

Logan woke to a dark room.

To a soft bed, and the scent of woman.

That he recognized instantly. All the rest, however . . .

Where the devil was he?

Very carefully, he opened his eyes and looked around. His head hurt—throbbed, ached. So badly he could barely squint through the pain. Doing so, he located a hearth across the room, the fire within it a pile of glowing coals.

Where in all hell was he?

He tried to think, but couldn't. The pain intensified when he tried, when he frowned. Shifting fractionally, he realized there was no bandage about his head, but there was one—a large and long one—winding about his torso.

So he'd been wounded.

How? Where? Why?

The questions lined up in his brain, but no answers came.

Then he heard voices—from a distance, through walls and doors, but his hearing seemed as acute as usual. . . .

Children. The voices belonged to children. Youthful, too high-pitched to be anything but.

He couldn't recall anything about children.

Disturbed, uncertain, he moved his arms, then his legs. All his limbs were functioning, under his control. It was only his head that ached so fiercely. Gingerly, pushing aside lumps he recognized as wrapped bricks, he eased to the side of the bed.

Some primal memory kept insisting there were enemies about, even though he couldn't remember anything specific. Had he been captured? Was he in some enemy camp?

Very carefully, he pulled himself up in the bed, then swung his legs over the side and sat up. The room swam sickeningly, but then steadied.

Encouraged, he stood.

The blood rushed from his head.

He collapsed.

Hit the floor with a hideous *thump*, almost cried out—might have cried out—when his head hit the floorboards. He groaned, then, hearing footsteps pounding up some stairs, he slowly tried to push himself up.

The door swung open.

Propped on one elbow, he turned his head and looked, knowing he was too weak and helpless to defend himself, but it wasn't any enemy who came charging in.

It was an angel with red-gold hair, bright and fiery as a flame, who scanned the room, saw him, then came racing to his side.

Perhaps he'd died and gone to Heaven?

"You *dolt*! What the devil are you doing trying to get up? You're *wounded*, you imbecile!"

Not an angel, then. Not Heaven, either. She continued to berate him, increasingly irate as she checked his bandages, then small hands, surprisingly strong, gripped his arm and

she braced to haul him up—an impossibility, he knew—
but then two strapping lads who had followed her in came
around his other side. The not-an-angel snapped orders, and
one lad ducked under his other arm, the second coming to
help her as on a count of three they hoisted him up—
    It *hurt*.
    Everywhere.
    He groaned as they turned him and, surprisingly gently,
angled him back onto the bed, setting him down on his left
side, then rolling him carefully onto his back.
    The not-an-angel fussed, drawing down the tangled
covers, removing bricks, then lifting and shaking. Logan
watched her lips form words—a string of increasingly
pointed epithets; as the worst of the violent pain receded, he
felt himself smiling.
    She saw, glared, then flicked the covers over him. He con-
tinued to smile, probably foolishly; he was still in so much
pain that he couldn't really tell. But he had noticed one
thing—he was naked. Stripped-to-the-skin, not-a-stitch-
except-his-bandage naked—and his not-an-angel hadn't
turned a hair.
    And although most of his body had wilted, one part
hadn't—and she had to have noticed; she couldn't have
missed it as she'd looked down when she'd steered him to
the bed, then laid him down, stretched him out.
    Which surely meant he and she were lovers. What else
could it mean?
    He couldn't remember her, not even her name—couldn't
remember sinking his hands in all that rich, warm hair,
pressing his mouth to her sinful lips . . . lips he could imagine
doing wicked things . . . none of which he could remember,
but then he couldn't remember anything through the crush-
ing pain.
    An older lady came in, spoke, and frowned at him. She
came to the bed as his lover tried to shift him further into
the center of the wide mattress. Thinking he should help, he
rolled to his right—

Pain erupted. His world turned black.

Linnet winced at the gasp that exploded from the stranger's lips—saw his body go lax, boneless, and knew he was unconscious again.

"Damn! I didn't get a chance to ask who he was." Leaning against the side of the mattress, she peered into his face. "But what caused that?"

Muriel, too, was frowning. "Did you check for head wounds?"

"There weren't any . . . well, not to see." Linnet knelt beside him and reached for his head. "But his hair is so thick, perhaps . . ." Infinitely gently, she took his skull between her hands. Fingers spread, she searched, felt. . . . "Oh, my God! There's a *huge* contusion." Drawing back her hand, she studied her fingertips. "Blood, so the skin's broken."

The observation led to another round of careful tending, of warm water in basins, towels, salves, and eventually stacks of bandages as between them she and Muriel cleansed, then dried, padded and bandaged the wound. "Looks like he was hit over the head with a spar."

In order to properly pad the area so that, once bandaged, their patient would be able to turn on the pillows without excruciating pain, they had to get Edgar and John to come and hold him upright, taking extra care not to dislodge the bandages around his chest and abdomen.

Examining the wound, Edgar opined, "Hard head, he must have, to have survived that."

John nodded. "Lucky beggar all around, what with that slash and the shipwreck and storm. Charmed life, you might say."

Linnet thanked them and let them go back to their dinners. Muriel, too; after closing the door behind her aunt, Linnet turned back into the room. Folding her arms, gripping her elbows, she halted by the bed and stared down at her patient.

He'd been a fighting man—in one or other of the services at one time was her guess. He had numerous scars—small and old, most of them—scattered over his body. A charmed life? Not in the literal sense. But she really, really wanted to know who he was.

Given her position in this corner of the world, she needed to know who he was.

Retreating to the armchair by the window, she sat and watched him for a while. When he showed no signs of stirring, let alone waking and doing something stupid like trying to get up, she rose and went downstairs. To finish her dinner and organize another round of hot bricks.

Three hours later, Linnet stood once more by her bed, arms folded, and frowned at her comatose fallen angel. By the dim light thrown by the lamp she'd left on the small table nearby, she studied his face and struggled to tamp down her concern.

His color wasn't bad, but his face was tanned, so that might be misleading. His breathing, however, was deep and even, and his pulse, when she'd checked it mere minutes ago, had been steady and strong.

Yet he showed no signs of waking.

After his ill-advised excursion, he'd lapsed back into unconsciousness, if anything deeper than before. Bad enough, but what was truly worrying was his still chilled flesh. Even the spots that should by now have warmed remained icy cold.

At least she now knew his eyes were dark blue. So dark she'd originally thought they were black, but then he'd looked directly into her eyes and she'd seen the blue flames in the darkness.

So he was a fallen angel with black hair and midnight eyes—and despite the four changes of hot bricks they'd applied, he was still too damned cold for her comfort. Too unresponsive, too close to death. And she couldn't shake the absolute conviction that it was, somehow, vitally important that he lived. That, somehow, it was up to her to ensure he did.

It was ridiculous, but it felt as if this were some God-sent test. She rescued people all the time—it was what she did, a part of her role. So could she rescue a fallen angel?

She paced, scowled, and paced some more while about her the house, her house, her home, slid into comfortable slumber. Edgar and John both helped about the manor house; after dinner, after the usual sitting and chatting in the parlor—tonight mostly speculating about the wreck and their survivor—the pair had retired to the cottage they shared with Vincent, the head stableman, and Bright, the gardener. Mrs. Pennyweather, the cook, and Molly and Prue, the two maids-of-all-work, would by now be snug in their beds in the staff quarters on the ground floor.

Muriel and Buttons—Miss Lillian Buttons, the children's governess—had rooms on the first floor, in the opposite wing to Linnet's large bedchamber. The children had rooms in the extensive attic, on either side of the playroom and schoolroom.

As the manor house of the estate encompassing the south-western tip of Guernsey, Mon Coeur was a small community in its own right, with Linnet, Miss Trevission, its unquestioned leader. Indeed, she was more a liege lord, a hereditary ruler; that was certainly how her people saw her.

Perhaps noblesse oblige, that sense of responsibility for those in her care, was what so drove her to ensure the stranger lived.

Halting by the bed, Linnet looked down at his face. Willed his lashes to flutter, willed him to open his eyes and look at her again. She wanted to see his lips curve again; they had before, in a wholly seductive way, but she suspected he'd been delirious at the time.

Of course, he just lay there. Placing a hand on his brow, then sliding it down to the curve of his throat, she confirmed he was still far too cold. He was literally comatose, and nothing they'd yet done had succeeded in warming him sufficiently.

Drawing back her hand, she huffed out a breath. She'd intended to sleep on the daybed before the windows, but . . .

her bed, the manor's master's bed, was wide—designed for a couple where the man was large. Of course, if she was going to warm him up, she'd need to sleep close, rather than apart.

Swinging away, she crossed to her chest and hunted out her thickest flannel nightgown. One eye on the bed, she stripped out of her warm gown, her woollen shift and fine chemise, then pulled the nightgown over her head.

Her patient hadn't stirred, hadn't cracked an eyelid.

Quickly letting down her hair, she slid her splayed fingers through the mass, shaking the long tresses loose. Lifting her woollen robe from its hook on the side of her armoire, she donned and belted it—another layer of armor against any attack, however feeble, on her modesty.

Approaching the bed, she inwardly scoffed. No matter who he proved to be, she'd been managing men all her life; she harbored no doubt whatsoever that she could and would manage him. Just like the others, he would learn. She ordered, they obeyed. That was, and always would be, the way of her world.

Lifting the covers, she checked the bricks and, as she'd suspected, found them already cooled. She removed them, stacked them by the door, then returned to the bed.

Calmly lifting the covers, she slid into the familiar softness, to the left of her fallen angel. Laying her hands along his bandaged side, she gently pushed, persevered until he rolled over on his undamaged right side. Quickly shifting nearer, she spooned around him, using her body to prop his in that position.

Reaching over and under him, she wrapped her arms about as much of him as she could. Then, because his back was there and convenient, she laid her cheek against the smooth, cool skin. She doubted she would sleep, but she closed her eyes.

She woke to a sensation of floating. Her wits were slow, reluctant to surface from the pleasurable sea in which they were submerged. A curious warmth suffused her, tempting her to simply relax and let the tide of tactile sensation sweep her on. . . .

It took many long minutes before her mind assembled enough coherency to sound any alarm, and even then some part of her questioned, unable to believe, unable to perceive any danger—not in this.

Not in the long, rolling swells of pleasure that something, some being, sent smoothly sliding through her.

But then a hard palm and long, hard fingers closed about her bare breast—and she came awake on a shocked gasp of sensual delight.

Wits reeling, waltzing to a tune she had never before encountered, she had to open her eyes to orient herself. To convince herself that yes, somehow their positions had changed, that both she and her fallen angel had turned, and now he was spooned about her, his chest to her back.

His hands on her body.

His erection nudging between her thighs.

She knew perfectly well she should leap from the bed— now, right now, before his wandering hand and the pleasure his touch wrought laid seige to her wits again.

But . . . his hand, his fingers, stroked and caressed, played and teased, and she closed her eyes on a sigh.

Damn—he knew what he was doing. Knew better than any other man she'd ever met how to do this. She bit her lip on a moan as his questing hand shifted and closed again, then settled to pay homage to her other breast.

He was clearly experienced, and she was no wilting virgin, no paragon of missish modesty, yet . . .

She couldn't allow this.

She'd be disgusted with herself in the morning if she did. Not least because, as she well knew, letting her fallen angel have her so easily, without even having exchanged one word, would give him too much power over her.

Or at least lead him to think he had power over her, and that would lead to unnecessary battles. She was queen in this realm, and such things happened at her command— only at her command.

Accepting she would have to end this now, she sighed, opened her eyes, and took stock—which only resulted in sending a wholly unfamiliar shiver down her spine.

Her robe was undone, the halves spread wide. Her night-gown was rucked up, above her breasts in the front, to the middle of her back behind her, which was why she could feel . . .

She had to end this *now*, but she was too wise to try to wriggle away, even leap away. Either move left it up to him to let her go. And he might not. Not readily. He might try to make her plead.

Used to playing power games, chess of a sort, with men, she mentally girded her loins—dragged her senses in and shackled them—then stretched her arms up over her head, sinuously straightening her long body and turning within his hold to face him.

It didn't go as she'd planned.

Instead of finding him smiling at her in lazy masculine triumph, ready to accept her surrender, she barely had time to register that his eyes were shut, his expression still blank—that even if she'd woken, he had not—before one hard hand slid into her unbound hair, palming her skull, and his bandaged head shifted and his lips closed on hers.

Ravenously.

Greedily.

As if he were a man starved and she all his succor.

Heat hit her in a crashing wave, passion and hunger and want and need all churning in that burning kiss. An instant conflagration erupted between them. She felt like she was melting, muscles taut yet turning passive, fluid and giving, emptiness—a hollow ache—burgeoning at her core, yearn-ing to be filled.

Primal. Urgent. Demanding.

He was all that—and he made her feel the same.

Her hands skimmed his shoulders. Even as she battled to regain her mental feet, she registered the warmth spreading beneath his still cool skin.

If nothing else, the exchange was heating him up.

If he'd been awake, her turning would have made him pause long enough for her to douse his flame. Instead, his unconscious, his dream-mind, had read that sinuous slide to face him as encouragement and agreement. As surrender.

By the time she'd realized that, he'd laid claim to her mouth and every one of her senses with a primitive passion that curled her toes.

He plundered, his tongue mating with hers, and her body came alive as it never had before. Yet he was . . . dreaming?

Even as she wrestled with that conclusion—tried to think what it meant, what she should do—he tore his lips from hers, ducked his head, and set his mouth to her breasts.

Took a furled nipple into his mouth and suckled.

Hard.

Her body bowed; she fought to stifle a scream—the first of pure pleasure she'd ever uttered. He pushed her onto her back and loomed over her in the dark. She gripped his shoulders, gasps tangling in her throat as, head bowed, he continued to feast, to lave and suckle her breasts.

Even asleep, he knew exactly how to make her body come quickly, rapidly, roaringly alive. Make it sing, make it burn.

She'd had three lovers—had "made love" precisely three times, once with each. Those experiences had convinced her that the activity was not for her, not something she was suited for.

As she was never going to marry, she'd seen no reason to learn more.

Now she faced a choice she hadn't expected. Even as pleasure lanced through her again and her body arched beneath him, evocatively into him, she knew she could stop him, her fallen angel, but she'd have to wake him up to do it. Even wounded and weakened, he was too damned strong for her to simply push him back and soothe him deeper into sleep. Yet her reasons for not indulging with him didn't apply if he remained asleep. If he didn't know—wouldn't recall when he awoke . . .

His lips drifted down, his hands firmed about her sides, and her body thrummed—enthrallingly alive, hungry and needy. His hands, hard and callused, sculpted, shaped her curves, slid down and around to cradle the globes of her bottom, long fingers kneading, stroking, caressing.

For the first time in her life, she felt . . . overwhelmed. Just a touch helpless. Not truly so—not frighteningly so—but the strength of him surrounded her, managed her, controlled her . . . as far as she allowed.

And then he moved over her, fully atop her, his hard, muscled thighs spreading hers wide so he could settle his hips between.

Her breath hitched. She had to decide *now*. The heavy length of his erection brushed her inner thigh, sensation and promise, evoking a flaring curiosity, splintering and fracturing her earlier resolution.

Would it be different with a fallen angel?

Every nerve, every inch of her, wanted to know.

But would he wake? Was it possible for him to reach the inevitable end without breaking free of Morpheus's hold?

Finding out . . . what a risk! But all her life she'd thrived on challenge—on taking calculated risks and winning.

He lifted his head, body surging over hers, and locked his lips on hers.

Invaded her mouth, reclaimed, reconquered—and she raised her hands, closed them about his bandaged head and kissed him back.

Deliberately plunging into the heat, into the fray, seizing the moment, taking the risk.

She kissed him as ravenously as he'd kissed her—as she'd never kissed any other man. No man before had dared to devour her, nor invited her to devour him.

For heated, frantic moments they dueled, then he shifted,

his spine flexed, all reined power, and she felt the marble-hard head of his erection part her folds. He pressed inexorably in, through the slickness of an instinctive welcome.

He hadn't even touched her there, yet she was ready—ready, willing, and wantonly eager to feel the length of him, to experience the strength of him, the sheer power and weight of him as he forged steadily into her, then, at the last, thrust deep to her core.

Stretching her, filling her as she never had been before. She'd never felt so invaded, so utterly posssessed.

So complete.

Then he moved, deep, sure thrusts that rocked her beneath him . . . within seconds, she'd never felt so taken, never felt taken before at all, yet he unquestionably took, took all she would give, could scramble to give, and give she did—he gave her no choice.

Then somehow the scales tipped, and it was she who sank her fingertips into his buttocks, gripped and clung, urgent and demanding. And he who gave, unstintingly lavishing all his power, his passion, driving sensation into her, through her, building the glory higher, and yet higher—forcefully riding deep within her until she shattered.

Until the glory imploded and sensation fractured into glimmering shards and she broke apart on a muted scream.

Logan heard it, that inexpressibly evocative sound of female completion, and let his reins fall. Let the dream sweep him on into the familiar heat and fire, surrendering to the primitive driving urge, jettisoning all hope of lingering to further savor the heated clasp of his lover's slick sheath, the ripples of her release barely fading as he drove harder and harder into her body—his dream lover who clearly knew him so well.

Who had let him ride her, then ridden him. Who had met his demands, and matched them, countered them.

Who had led him to this—the pinnacle of erotic dreams.

He sensed release nearing, felt it catch him, sweep up and over him. With one last thrust, he sank deep within her, and surrendered. Let it take him.

Rake him.

Until, at the last, he shuddered, and sleep thickened and closed about him again, and pulled him down into a deeper realm, one where satisfaction and content blended and soothed, cradling him in earthly bliss.

Linnet lay beneath her fallen angel, his dead weight an odd comfort as she struggled, battled, to regain the use of anything—wits or limbs. Even her senses seemed frazzled beyond recall, as if she'd drawn too close to some flame and they'd singed.

Oh. My. God was her first coherent thought, the only one she could manage for several long minutes. Finally, when she'd regained sufficient control of her limbs and sufficient mental acuity, she gently nudged, eased, prodded, and managed to stir him into shifting enough to let her slide from beneath him.

He slumped, heavy and boneless, beside her, but she no longer feared waking him up. If their recent exertions hadn't, nothing would, not soon. And he hadn't woken, of that she was sure. She'd seized the moment, taken the risk— and it had paid off.

Magnificently.

At last able to fill her lungs, she drew in a huge breath, let it out long and slow.

Staring up at the ceiling, she whispered, "Damn—that was good."

Then she glanced sideways at the man—her fallen angel—lying facedown in the bed beside her. "I might have to rethink my policy on men."

Two

December 11, 1822
Mon Coeur, Torteval, Guernsey

*L*innet woke when she usually did, which in December meant an hour before dawn. Oddly relaxed, unusually refreshed, she stretched, savoring the unexpected inner glow, then raised her lids—and found herself staring at a stranger's throat.

Tanned. Male. Incipient alarm was drowned by wariness as full memory of the previous day, and the night, flooded her mind.

She jerked her gaze upward.

To a pair of midnight blue eyes.

Propped on one elbow, he was looking down at her, his regard shrewd, assessing, and curious.

"Where am I?"

His voice matched the rest of him—disturbing and deep. Just a little gravelly, with the hint of an underlying burr.

"More importantly," he went on, "what are you doing in my bed?"

She struggled to sit up, thanking her stars that before she'd fallen asleep the second time, she'd had the sense to pull down her nightgown, tie her robe tight, and stuff the extra blanket down between them, a barrier between his body and hers. "Actually, you're in my bed."

When his winged black brows flew high, she hurriedly added, a touch waspishly, "You were injured, unconscious, and it's the only bed in this house long enough, and judged sturdy enough, to accommodate you."

For a moment, he said nothing, then murmured, "So there are other beds?"

She was tempted to lie, but instead nodded curtly. "I was worried by your continuing chill, and decided it was wisest to . . . do what I could to keep you warm through the night."

Flicking the covers aside, she slid out of the bed, tugging her robe and gown firmly down as she stood.

He watched her like a predator watched prey. "In that case, I suppose I should thank you."

"Yes, you should." And she should go down on her knees and thank him—not that she ever would. Cutting off the distracting memories, she glanced at the bandage around his skull. "How's your head?"

He frowned, as if her question had reminded him. "Throbbing . . . but not, I think, incapacitating."

"You'll feel better after you eat." Crossing to her armoire, she opened it and looked in, ignoring the weight of his steady blue gaze. He hadn't remembered—she felt sure he hadn't. He wasn't the sort of man to hold back if he had.

As she pulled out a gown, he said, "You haven't yet told me where I am."

"Guernsey." She glanced back at him. "The southwestern tip—Parish of Torteval, if that means anything to you."

His frown darkened. "It doesn't." His gaze drifted from her.

Shutting the armoire, she opened a drawer and drew out a fresh shift. Turned back to him. "What's your name?"

"Logan." He looked at her, after the barest hesitation asked, "Yours?"

"Linnet Trevission. This house is Mon Coeur." Turning back to her chest of drawers, she added stockings and chemise to the pile in her arms, then crossed to where she'd left her half boots. Picking them up, she glanced at the bed. "So—Logan who?"

He looked at her, looked at her, then he softly swore. Swinging his legs from beneath the covers, he sat up on the edge of the bed.

Well-shaped feet, long, muscled calves dusted with black hair, broad knees, taut, heavily muscled thighs. Linnet gave thanks for the corner of the sheet that draped across his lap. Unconscious, with half his torso hidden by bandages, he'd been an impressive sight; awake and active, his impact was mind-scrambling.

She needed to get out of the room, but . . . she frowned as he dropped his head into his hands, fingers gripping tight.

"I can't remember." The words were ground out. Then he looked down, at the bandages about his chest and abdomen. Lowered a hand to trace them.

"You were on a ship—most likely a merchantman. There was a storm the night before last, a bad one, and the ship wrecked on the reefs not far from here." Linnet caught his dark eyes as they rose, as if in hope, to her face. "Do you remember the name of your ship?"

Logan tried—tried to dredge some glimmer of a memory up from the void in his brain, but nothing came. Nothing at all. "I don't even remember being on a ship."

Even he heard the panic in his tone.

"Don't worry." His gorgeous erstwhile bedmate—and wasn't that a terrible fate, to have slept like a log with all those mouthwatering curves within easy reach, and not have known?—studied him through pale emerald eyes. "You've a nasty head wound—most likely from a falling spar. You were incredibly lucky to have got onto a broken-off section of the ship's side before you lost consciousness. You had a firm grip on the planks—that's what got you to shore and into the cove, and stopped you getting smashed up on the rocks. More smashed up." She nodded at his bandaged head. "The blow to your skull would have rattled your brains. Most likely your memory will come back in a day or two."

"A day or two?" He watched her cross to a dressing table against the far wall and pick up a brush and comb. His gaze shifted to the rippling fall of her red-gold hair. Even in the dim light of predawn, it looked like fire; his fingers and palms tingled, as if recalling the silky warmth. He frowned. " 'Most likely'? What if I don't remember?" The thought horrified him.

"You will. Almost certainly." She headed for the door but paused, glanced at him, then detoured back to the large armoire. "But you shouldn't try to bludgeon your brain into remembering. Best to just let it be, let your memory slide back of its own accord."

He narrowed his eyes at her. "You're a doctor?"

She arched brown brows at him, gaze distinctly haughty, then turned to look into the armoire. "No, but I've been around enough men who've had their heads thumped to know. If you're alive, and can walk, your memories will return."

Logan frowned at her. Not even a healer, but she'd been around enough men. . . . "Miss Linnet Trevission of Mon Couer—who's she?"

Closing the armoire, taking a few steps his way, she flung a quilted woollen robe at him. He caught it. She nodded at it. "That was my father's—my late father's." She met his gaze. "So among other things, I'm your hostess."

Before he could respond, she swung to the door. "There's a water closet at the end of the corridor." She pointed left. "There's a bathing chamber next to it. I'll have shaving gear sent up for you, and whatever clothes we can find—my aunt is seeing what she can salvage of your things, but until then, some of my father's might fit."

Linnet paused with her hand on the door and looked back. Grasped an instant to drink in the sight of the gorgeous naked male sitting on her bed. "You can rest here as long as you wish, then when you feel up to it, you can join us downstairs."

Opening the door, she went through, then reached back

and drew the door shut behind her. She paused, staring at the panels but seeing him . . . feeling him . . .

Exasperated, she shook free of the recollection, blew a strand of hair from her face, then continued down the corridor.

She'd been right. He was going to be trouble.

More than an hour later, Logan made his way down a long oak staircase, looking around as he slowly descended. *Mon Coeur.* What kind of man named his house "my heart"?

Regardless, Linnet Trevission's father had been no puny weakling; his clothes fitted Logan well enough to get by. The shirt and coat were a trifle tight across his shoulders, and he'd had to button the breeches one button wider at the waist, but the length of sleeve and leg were almost right. Linnet herself was tall for a female, so it was no great surprise her father had been tall.

He'd found the clothes waiting in a neat pile on the bed when he'd returned from shaving. After using the water closet—its existence an indication that Mon Coeur wasn't some small farmhouse—he'd looked into the bathing chamber and found a shaving kit neatly laid out. He'd availed himself of it. He'd been halfway through removing several days' growth before he'd realized he knew what he was doing.

He'd lathered chin and cheeks, then picked up the sharp razor and applied it as he had countless times before, in a pattern he'd worked out a presently unknown number of years ago.

His panic over not being able to remember things—lots of things—had receded as the fact that he remembered lots of other things, like what *Mon Coeur* meant, as well as things he did by rote, had sunk in.

When Linnet had informed him he was on Guernsey, he'd known instantly what that was—had known it was an island in the Gulf of St. Malo, that it enjoyed special privileges as a property of the English Crown. He didn't think he'd been there before, even elsewhere on the island. As he recalled—

and he savored the fact he could—Guernsey wasn't large.

All of which he took as a sign that his memory lapse would indeed prove temporary.

He knew how to dress himself; he knew how to shave. He knew he—whoever he was—hadn't entirely appreciated his hostess's haughty superiority.

But he didn't yet know *who* he was. Didn't know what sort of man he was, or what he'd been doing on the ship.

Reaching the bottom of the stairs, and having seen enough to confirm that the Trevissions were, at the least, the Guernsey equivalent of landed gentry, he made his way down a corridor toward the sound of voices.

Children's voices. The sound tweaked a memory, but the instant he halted and tried to bring it into focus, it slid away, back into the void. Suppressing a grimace, he continued on—to a long, comfortable parlor running down one side of the house. Although a fire was burning in the hearth, there was no one in the parlor, but on walking in, he saw a pair of open double doors in the rear wall and a bright, airy dining room beyond.

The chatter filling his ears was coming from there. It sounded as if half a small army was gathered about the long table.

He paused on the threshold. Seated at the head of the table, Linnet looked up, saw him, and beckoned. "Good. You're on your feet." Her gaze passed, critically assessing, over his face. "Come and sit down, and have some breakfast."

She waved to an empty chair beside her. He moved forward, scanning the other occupants. Children, as he'd thought—two lasses, three lads—and a middle-aged gentlewoman, plus an older lady seated at the table's foot. Recalling Linnet mentioning an aunt, he inclined his head politely. "Ma'am."

The older lady smiled. "I'm Muriel Barclay, Linnet's father's sister. Do sit down and break your fast, Mr. . . . ?"

Closing his hand on the back of the chair beside Linnet's,

Logan smiled, a touch tightly. "Just Logan at the moment, ma'am. I'm afraid I can't remember the rest."

Drawing out the chair, he glanced at Linnet. Her lips had thinned a fraction, but clearly she hadn't informed her household of his lack of recall.

"Don't you know all your name?"

The question, in a loud, childish voice, drew Logan's gaze down to the small girlchild seated to his other side. Wide cornflower blue eyes looked up at him. Subsiding into his chair, he let his smile soften. "Not at the moment, poppet."

"Not to worry." Mrs. Barclay's brisk tone was a more moderate, less autocratic version of her niece's. "I'm sure it'll all come back to you shortly. Now I expect you'd like some ham and eggs, and perhaps a few sausages?"

Logan nodded. "Thank you, ma'am."

"I'll let Mrs. Pennyweather know you're here." Mrs. Barclay rose and headed out of another door.

Now that he noticed it, Logan heard, distantly, the clang of pans and other kitchen sounds. Manor house, his mind decided. Which presumably made his hostess the lady of the manor.

He glanced at her to find her waiting to catch his eye. Having done so, she directed it around the table. "This is Will, and that's Brandon beside him." The two older lads bobbed their heads and smiled. "They found you yesterday morning, and Chester"—she indicated the youngest of the three boys—"came running here to fetch me."

Logan nodded to all three boys. "Thank you—I'm grateful."

"And beside Chester," Linnet continued, "is Miss Buttons—Buttons to us all. She endeavors to teach this horde their letters and numbers."

Logan inclined his head to the middle-aged woman, who smiled back. "Welcome to Mon Coeur, sir," she said, "although I daresay you would have preferred to arrive in a less painful way." She nodded at his head. "Does it hurt very much?"

"Not as much as it did."

"It'll fade through the day." Mrs. Barclay returned in the wake of a little maid, who smiled shyly as she set a plate piled high with succulent eggs, bacon, sausages, and ham before Logan.

He thanked her and shook out the napkin he found beside his plate.

"Jen—please pass Logan the toast rack." Linnet waved at the last two at the table. "These two young ladies are Jennifer and Gillyflower—Gilly."

Logan smiled and thanked them both as they passed him the toast. There was a curious dearth of men about the table, but there were four plates already used before four vacant chairs. Will, the oldest boy, looked to be about fifteen years old. As the others all returned to their meals, Logan buttered a slice of toast, crunched, and realized he was ravenous.

Picking up his knife and fork, he cut a piece of thick ham, chewed, and almost groaned in appreciation. Opening his eyes, he glanced across the table.

Will caught his eye. "We searched all yesterday, up and down the coves, but we didn't find any other survivors."

"Just the two dead bodies we found near you," Chester added.

"Two dead?" Logan glanced at Linnet.

"The bodies are here, in the icehouse. Two sailors. The boys will take you to view them later, in case you know them."

If he remembered them. She didn't say it, but he saw the thought in her eyes. He merely nodded and attacked the ham. It tasted like the food of the gods.

The boys chattered on. Apparently no one had yet gleaned any clue as to the name of the ship, where she'd been from, or whither she'd been bound.

Jennifer started talking to Buttons. Linnet spoke to Gilly about some chicks. Conversation rose around Logan, gradually returning to its earlier pitch, with many conversations running all at once, voices interweaving, an underlying warmth blossoming in a laugh here, a smile and a teasing comment there.

This wasn't a standard family, yet a family it was—Logan recognized the dynamics, felt inexpressibly comfortable, comforted, within its warm embrace. As he set down his knife and fork and reached for the cup of coffee Linnet had—without asking—poured for him, he wondered what this pervasive sense of feeling so much at home here said of his life, of the life he was used to.

The boys had finished their meals and were eagerly waiting on him. He drained his mug, then nodded to them. "All right. Let's go."

They grinned; poised to leap to their feet, they glanced at Linnet.

She nodded, but said, "After showing Logan to the icehouse, I want you back to do your chores."

With promises of obedience, Will and Brandon leapt up. Chester had already been reminded he had a lesson with Buttons. He'd pulled a disappointed face, but, Logan noticed, didn't argue, or even grouse.

Linnet looked up at him as he rose. "I left a heavy cloak for you by the back door." She studied his face. "Nothing more's returned?"

He met her green eyes, shook his head. "Not yet."

Will and Brandon led Logan past the kitchen. He looked in to thank and compliment Mrs. Pennyweather, a bright-eyed, flushed, but jovial woman, then followed the boys to a short hall by the back door. While the boys donned coats, Logan found the cloak Linnet had left and swung it about his shoulders, then they stepped out into the winter morning. The air was chill, crisp; their breaths fogged as they followed a path through what he assumed was the kitchen garden. The neat beds lay largely fallow under a white lacing of frost, with berry and currant canes cut back and tied.

Beyond the garden, a stand of trees screened what proved to be a large stable, with a barn flanking it, a cottage to the side, and numerous outbuildings arranged around a sizeable yard. Beside the boys, Logan walked into the yard and was immediately hailed.

Halting, he waited as a heavily built man of middle years and average height came forward. His gaze shrewdly assessing, carefully measuring, the man offered his hand.

"Edgar Johnson—estate foreman."

Logan gripped, shook. "Logan—I'm not sure of the rest yet."

"Aye, well, you took a nasty knock, and you've that gash, too. How's it healing?"

"As long as I don't reach too far with my left arm, the gash isn't a great problem. The head's still throbbing, but I have it on good authority that that will fade." Logan smiled easily as three other men and two older lads, who had emerged from various buildings, came to join them.

Edgar made the introductions. The men shook Logan's hand or nodded deferentially. All made appropriate noises when he mentioned his lack of memory. John, a tall, weedy, lugubrious soul, was, Logan learned, the man-of-all-work about the house, while Vincent, a grizzled veteran, was the head stableman. Bright, not as old as the other three, was the gardener. The two lads—Matt and Young Henry—worked under Vincent, caring for various horses and carts; they were about to depart for the nearest village with cabbages for the market.

Logan asked the two lads to keep their ears open for any word about the wrecked ship. Touching their caps, they vowed they would, then they crossed the yard, clambered up into the cart, and sent the heavy horses lumbering out, onto a track that wended away across a relatively flat plateau.

From the moment Logan had walked into the yard, the older men had been measuring, weighing, and assessing him, a fact of which he was well aware. Now, as if agreeing, for the moment at least, to accept him as they found him, they all nodded and returned to their chores, leaving Will and Brandon to lead him on.

"It's not far." Brandon pointed to a narrow path leading away from the main yard.

Flanked by the boys, Logan trudged along, juggling impressions against what he thought should have been, what he thought he should have encountered from the older men.

Mostly buried under a mound of piled earth, in this season the icehouse was empty, yet decidedly chilly. Later in winter, the stocks of ice would be replenished, but for now there was plenty of space for the two bodies laid out on old farm gates balanced on trestles.

The bodies proved uninformative; Logan had no recollection of either man.

The boys had halted in the doorway. They shifted, perhaps uncomfortable with the taint of death.

It was a smell Logan realized he knew well.

What that meant . . . he couldn't tell.

Glancing back at the boys, he let his lips curve. "Why don't you two head back to your chores. I know the way back."

Brandon flashed him a grin. "You could hardly miss it."

Smile widening, Logan inclined his head. Both boys raised their hands in waves . . . salutes? Logan didn't frown until they'd disappeared, but, again, the instant he tried to pin the memory down, it fled.

Turning back to the dead sailors, he studied their faces, their clothes, but felt not the smallest stirring of recognition. "Poor souls," he eventually murmured. "What happens to you next, I wonder?"

"I can answer that."

Logan swung to see a man—a gentleman from his dress—silhouetted in the doorway. As the man stepped inside, Logan saw the white collar around his neck.

"Hello." Brown-haired, brown-eyed, and of medium height, the man smiled and offered his hand. "You must be our survivor."

Logan gripped the man's hand firmly. "Logan. I'm afraid I can't remember more at present." He indicated his bandaged head. "I took a crack over the head, but I've been assured my memories will eventually return."

"Oh, I see." Behind his overt cheeriness, the vicar, as Edgar and company before him, was measuring Logan. "Geoffrey Montrose, Vicar of Torteval Parish."

Logan shifted his gaze to the dead men. "So these are now yours."

"Sadly, yes. I came to say what prayers I can for them." He looked more closely at the men, then grimaced. "Although I suspect my prayers will be the wrong sort."

"I'm not sure they're Spanish—they could be Portuguese, in which case your prayers might be appropriate." How he knew that, Logan had no idea, but he knew it was so.

Apparently Montrose knew it, too, for he nodded. "True—very true." He glanced at Logan. "Do you know who they are?"

Logan shook his head. "I don't know that I ever knew."

Montrose drew his vicar's embroidered scarf from his pocket and draped it about his neck. He looked at Logan. "Will you stay?"

Logan considered the men. "They were on the same ship. They died, I didn't. The least I can do is be here to note their passing."

Montrose nodded. In a solemn, cultured voice, he commenced a prayer.

Head bowed, Logan followed the words, but although they were familiar, the cadences more so, they stirred no major memories.

After Montrose had performed the rites he thought fitting, Logan followed him back into the weak sunshine.

"Are you heading back to the house?" Montrose asked.

"Yes." Falling into step beside the vicar, Logan added, "I'm not sure I'm allowed further afield yet." Lips twisting, he continued, "Truth be told, I'm not sure I wouldn't lose my way—no telling how damaged my memory is."

"Well, you've fallen into the right hands if you need to heal and convalesce." Montrose shot him a sharp glance.

"Linnet—Miss Trevission—is famous for taking in strays and . . . I suppose you could say nurturing them back to full health."

Logan wasn't sure he hadn't been insulted, albeit subtlely, but let the comment slide. He was fairly certain he had a thick skin, and besides, he'd wanted to ask, "The children?"

"And the men, too. And then there's the animals."

Logan's lips twitched, but he held to his purpose. "I had thought the children might be relatives." Not all of them, but Gilly had similar coloring to Linnet . . . it was possible.

Montrose blushed faintly, clearly understanding what sort of relationship Logan had imagined. "No—not at all. They're orphans whose fathers died in the family's employ. Linnet—Miss Trevission—insists on taking all such in and raising them at Mon Coeur."

Logan's brows rose in sincere surprise. "A laudable undertaking." As they emerged from the trees, he looked at the house. Definitely of manor house proportions, solid and well-tended. "Especially with no husband."

"Indeed." The single word was sharp. An instant later, Montrose sought to soften it. "We all help as we can. In such a small community, the children would otherwise have to move away, possibly even leave Guernsey."

Logan merely nodded. His most urgent questions answered, he paced beside Montrose up the garden path. And continued to dwell on the connundrum posed by Linnet—Miss Trevission. The strangeness of her household derived from her; the entire household was centered on her, anchored by her. Possibly, he was starting to suspect, *governed* by her.

From all he'd thus far gleaned, thus far seen, she was a highly eligible, apparently reasonably wealthy, extraordinarily attractive gently bred lady in her midtwenties, and yet, for all that, she remained unwed.

More, Montrose was a passably handsome gentleman and was, Logan judged, of similar age to the lovely Miss Trevission. The good vicar surely must harbor some hopes in her direction. The population of Guernsey, especially this remote corner, wouldn't be large, the eligible females few and far between. Yet although he'd detected a similar degree of male protectiveness in Montrose as he had in the other men—the ones old enough to consider him a potential threat to Miss Trevission's virtue—from neither Montrose nor the others had he picked up any suggestion that they had any intention of broaching the matter with either Miss Trevission or him.

Which, in his admittedly possibly erroneous view, seemed odd. Men like Montrose and the others were usually more vocal about who the females they cared about allowed to reside under their roof. Usually more challenging. Indeed, he wouldn't have been surprised to have received a subtle, or even an unsubtle, warning. Yet although they'd assessed him, not one had made any direct comment—not even Montrose.

Neither Edgar nor any of the other men slept in the manor house itself, a telling point. At present, he, a complete stranger, was the only adult male in residence at night—and he was occupying Miss Trevission's bed.

While that point appeared to be common knowledge— apparently Edgar and John had helped tend him—Logan seriously doubted the associated fact—that Miss Trevission had shared her bed with him—was similarly widely known.

As they neared the back door, he glanced at Montrose, and wondered what the vicar would say if he knew.

But that reminded him. . . .

Waving Montrose ahead, he followed the vicar past the kitchen and dining room, and into the parlor. Mrs. Barclay was there; she welcomed the vicar warmly. They settled to chat about the local church services leading to Christmas. The children, presently with Miss Buttons in the schoolroom, were, Logan gathered, a significant part of the choir.

He sat quietly in an armchair letting the comments flow over him—they didn't stir any memories, didn't seem to connect with him at all. He suspected he was no churchgoer. Given the subject occupying his mind, he was content to have the vicar distracted while he wrestled with his recollections.

His problem was that he didn't know, couldn't tell, whether his recollection of the previous night was a memory or a dream. When he'd woken that morning, he'd assumed he'd had an amazing, richly detailed, highly erotically charged dream, with predictable consequences. He hadn't had such a dream in decades; the question of why now had at first puzzled him. But then he'd found Linnet asleep beside him and hadn't known what to think. To imagine. Yet she'd been covered and trussed like a nun, with a bolster of blanket between them. He'd concluded his first thought had been correct—all he recalled had been a dream.

But then she'd woken. Opened her eyes, looked at him, spoken. From that moment on, he hadn't been so sure. And the more he learned of her, her strange household, her unusual status, only further made him question whether his increasingly clear recollections were truly a dream, or . . .

He was still in two minds when Linnet walked into the room.

Although Logan didn't move a muscle, his attention sharpened as his gaze locked on her. Linnet knew it. She didn't so much as glance his way, yet she felt the weight, the piercing quality of his dark blue gaze.

Had he remembered? Did he *know*?

She'd imagined that, with her usual high-handed authority, she would have no trouble carrying off the pretense that nothing had occurred between them, but to her irritation, her very real chagrin, she discovered herself caught on the horns of a totally unforeseen dilemma.

If he thought it all a dream, and remained convinced of that, then nothing more would happen. There would be no further interludes, and he and she would part as mere acquaintances once he remembered who he was.

And she would never again experience what she had last night.

Therein lay the rub.

But if he remembered, if he realized that all those heated moments had been real . . . she could have more. Lots more, for however many nights remained before he recalled who he was, and where he was supposed to be.

Yet she didn't want to go down that road, either. It had taken no more than a few exchanges to realize he was a sort of man who didn't "manage" well. When faced with her natural flair for command, most men fell into line easily enough—but he wouldn't. The vision of him sitting, mostly naked, on the side of her bed was blazoned on her brain. Easily led he wasn't, and would never be.

To hint him toward realizing, or not? That was her dilemma. And while her wise and sensible self voted strongly not to risk tangling with him again, her wild side wanted to embrace the chance, risk or not. As far as her wild side was concerned, risks were for taking—which was what had led her to this point.

Even as she smiled and gave Geoffrey her hands, she knew Logan was watching, noting, assessing, considering— and she felt the temptation to give him some sign. Quashing it, she asked Geoffrey, "How is Mrs. Corbett? Have you seen her recently?"

Geoffrey nodded. "She's improving, but she's determined to stay in her cottage, and who can blame her? It's been her home since . . . before I can remember."

"She was there when we were children, but her husband was alive then, and her sons were there, too." Linnet paused, then said, "I'll keep an eye on her—I ride past often enough."

She sat and continued to talk with Geoffrey about local affairs, about the people on the Trevission estate and matters further afield. Logan listened closely, but said nothing, asked no questions. For such a large, vigorous man, he could sit very still, could make one forget he was there.

Keeping her gaze locked on Geoffrey, she ignored Logan entirely. Geoffrey noticed, was puzzled by it, but she didn't want to engage with Logan, not even in outwardly innocent exchanges; she didn't trust that nothing of the tension between them would show. And while Geoffrey might not understand it, or recognize it for what it was, he would see enough to grow concerned, and she didn't need that.

Especially not if she opted to take a risk—a further risk— with Logan.

By the time she rose to walk Geoffrey to the stable, she was increasingly inclined to take that risk. Talking to Geoffrey had underscored the reality of her life. Geoffrey was a childhood friend. During her earlier years, those she'd spent mostly on the island, he and she had run wild. She loved him—like a brother.

Yet he was the only eligible male around. If she traveled to the island's capital, she might find one or two others, but what use was that to her? Locally, there was no male with whom she could indulge, and while until last night she hadn't realized what she'd been missing, now she knew.

Now she wanted more—at least a little more.

Logan could give her that.

In front of the stable, Geoffrey turned to her while Vincent went to fetch his horse. "Your latest stray—you will be careful, won't you? I know he seems perfectly gentlemanly, but he's . . . well, you only have to look at him to know he's . . ."

Linnet let her lips curve. "Dangerous?"

"Well, not necessarily *that* . . . I was thinking more of him not being meek and mild. I have to say it's difficult to judge a man when he doesn't know who he is, but, well, you know what I mean."

"I do, Geoffrey dear, and you know better than to worry."

"You could send him to St. Peter Port, to the castle."

"No, I couldn't. You know I couldn't."

Geoffrey sighed. "I know you won't worry over what others may think, or say—how it will look that he's staying in the house, but—"

"Geoffrey, answer me this—who is there to see? Who will ever know where he slept?"

Geoffrey frowned at her. "What you mean is that no one anywhere around here will argue with whatever you decree."

"Exactly." Smiling, Linnet stretched up and bussed his cheek. "Take care of yourself, and I'll see you next time I get to church."

Vincent appeared with Geoffrey's mount. Linnet stepped back as, capitulating, Geoffrey swung up to the saddle. After waving him off, she remained in the yard, watching him ride away.

Then she turned and strolled back to the house. Clearing the line of screening trees, she paused and looked up. And saw Logan in the window of her bedroom looking down at her.

Brazenly, she gazed back at him, drinking in the sight of his broad shoulders, his height, the sense of innate virility in his powerful frame, then, unhurriedly, she resumed her journey to the house.

She wouldn't, couldn't, send Logan on his way—not until he remembered who he was. And if that gave her time to experience more of the singular pleasure he could show her . . . so be it.

After luncheon, she suggested he should rest. Logan thought otherwise. "I'll come with you and the girls." He held her gaze. "Montrose mentioned you tended animals, but he didn't say what sort."

"All sorts!" Gaily, Gilly grabbed his hand. "Lots of sorts. You can help us—we'll show you how."

Getting to his feet, Logan smiled—as innocently as he could—at Linnet.

She narrowed her eyes, but didn't argue further. They donned coats and cloaks, then, with Jen, she followed him and Gilly from the house.

"The pens are this way." Turning left from the back door, Gilly towed him along a path running along the back of the house and on toward another line of trees. Glancing around, Logan noted that the house was more or less encircled by trees, all old and gnarled, but affording excellent protection from the prevailing winds. The path led them through an archway formed by living branches, out onto a wider, more open expanse—pastures and enclosures protected by more trees.

"We have to feed the babies." Gilly tugged him to a large wooden bin with a slanting wooden lid. Releasing his hand, she looked up at him expectantly. "You have to open it."

He smiled and did, remembering at the last minute to push up with his right arm and not lift his left.

"Careful of your stitches." Linnet was suddenly beside him, helping to set back the lid. When he raised his brows at her, faintly amused, she waspishly informed him, "Muriel and I spent more than an hour sewing you up—I don't want our handiwork damaged."

"Ah." He continued to smile, continued to be tickled by her irritation; he'd noticed that none of the others dared bait her temper.

Then again, she had red hair.

And gorgeous green eyes, which she narrowed at him, then she reached into the bin, lifted a sack, and thrust it at him. "You and Gilly can feed the baby goats."

Taking the sack, he turned to find Gilly jigging with impatience. With a grin, she whirled and dashed off. He followed her to one of the further enclosures and consented to be instructed in how to feed young goats.

By the time they'd done the rounds of all the pens, feeding calves, donkeys, fawns, even a few foals as well as the rambunctious kids, he'd realized what the vicar had meant about Linnet's strays. Strays, orphans—those without family. She took them all in, and did her best to care for them.

With daylight waning before what looked to be a storm blowing in, they returned the sacks of grains, carrots, and turnips to the bin, then between them, he and Linnet lowered the lid and secured it. They'd exchanged barely a word since beginning the feeding. Falling into step alongside her, behind Jen and Gilly, who skipped ahead comparing notes on their favorite "pets," he glanced at Linnet's face, smiled, and looked ahead.

Deciding she was unlikely to do more than wither him for his presumption, he murmured, "You're not exactly the usual run of gently bred female."

He felt the green glance she sent him.

"Do you know so many gently bred females, then?"

He considered the question. "I suppose I must, given my comment."

She made a scoffing sound. "If you can't remember details, how can you know what gently bred females are like—what the limits of behavior are?"

"I know they wouldn't share a bed with a stranger—not under any circumstances." He caught her eyes—her wide green eyes—as she glanced at him. "I remember that much."

How much did he remember?

He could see the question in her eyes—and could think of only one reason it would be there. His pulse leapt, but before he could press further and wring an admission from her, she looked forward and said, "Thank you for helping—you're very good with children. Perhaps you've spent time with others at some point—can you remember? Perhaps you have some of your own?"

The idea rocked him. But . . . "No—I don't think so." But he couldn't be sure. The notion left him with a hollow feeling; the idea he might have children and had forgotten them, however temporarily, chilled him—and in some stirring corner of his brain, he knew there was a reason for the feeling.

When he continued silent, keeping pace beside her, cloak pushed back, his hands in his breeches pockets, head bent, a frown tangling his black brows, Linnet tried to congratulate herself on having so successfully deflected him, but his continued silence nagged at her. Almost as if she'd landed a low blow.

She suspected she had.

She'd noticed how well he interacted with the boys; they'd only known him a day, yet they'd instantly taken to him. That wasn't, perhaps, surprising; even bandaged, he cut a dashing figure with his peculiar aura of danger hanging about him almost as tangibly as her father's old cloak. But the girls were usually much more reserved, yet even quiet Jen had smiled and chatted to him as if she'd known him for months, if not years.

He'd been attentive, responsive, engaged, yet utterly dictatorial. He'd stopped Gilly from climbing too high on a fence with the simple words, "No—get down."

The order had been utterly absolute; he'd expected to be obeyed—and he had been.

That moment, above all, had bothered her; she knew all there was to know about command, and she liked, indeed insisted on, being the one who wielded it.

Logan—whoever he was—was a born leader; now she'd started looking, she could see the telltale signs. And all her instincts were telling her it wasn't his size or his strength she should be wary of. In personality and character they were very much alike. Giving him any reason to consider her one of those it was his duty, indeed, his right, to protect—and to therefore issue orders to, ones he would expect to be obeyed—would only result in battles, battles he wouldn't win, but she didn't need those sort of clashes in her life.

She didn't need, didn't want, a man who expected to control her, to bend her to his will, anywhere near.

Especially not if he might succeed.

Her saner side had come to the fore. Despite her brazen self still wanting to spend as many nights as possible in his arms, self-protection trumped her newfound desire for sexual satisfaction.

Which had resulted in her instinctive, and it seemed perfectly gauged, deflection.

She glanced at him, saw him still brooding, and inwardly grimaced. Felt a touch guilty.

But at least she'd had time to slow her heartbeat. He'd evoked a moment of uncharacteristic panic, but she was over that now. No matter how much he might suspect, no matter how much he might hint, he couldn't actually know—not for certain. Unless she told him, or in some way gave herself away, he couldn't be sure he truly had made her sob and moan last night.

They entered the house in the girls' wake. When they paused to hang up their cloaks in the hall, she glanced at him again.

He was still looking inward, his expression shuttered.

She grasped the moment to look—to study him again, and let her senses inform her mind of all they could detect.

What she saw made her shiver.

Abruptly turning, she led the way to the parlor.

He, whoever he was, was too much—too large, too strong, too powerful, too virile, altogether too commanding. And while there was, undeniably, a challenge in the prospect of engaging in a wild liaison with such a man, a wise woman would keep her distance.

She could, when so moved, be very, very wise.

❧ Three ❧

With the exception of the other men, who were continuing with their duties about the estate, the household gathered about the dining table for afternoon tea—for scones, raspberrry jam, and clotted cream.

"I know I like scones and jam," Logan said in reply to Muriel's query, "but for some reason . . ." After a moment, he grimaced. "I don't think I've had any for a considerable time."

"Well, have another." Buttons passed him the tray. "There's plenty."

Linnet watched as he helped himself to two more, yet while the children chatted and Buttons and Muriel swapped local gossip, once again, although physically present, Logan became so still that he seemed no longer there.

He was wrestling with his memory again. She longed to tell him that no good would come of it, that bludgeoning his brain wasn't going to help.

She hadn't helped with her comment about children.

She studied his face. His color was good, his eyes clear. She would have liked to check the wound in his side, but didn't want to lift the dressings yet—tomorrow, maybe. Meanwhile . . . his physical condition had improved considerably and he'd shown no sign of developing a fever. Perhaps it was time to risk prodding his memory.

Rising, she went into the parlor, to the drawer in the sideboard where she'd placed the three items he'd had on him when they'd found him. Her hand hovered over the saber, but in the end she picked up the dirk and carried it back to the table.

Logan blinked back to the world when Linnet appeared by his side and placed a dirk on the white cloth before him.

"You had this when we found you—you were clutching it so tightly I had to pry your fingers from the hilt. Presumably it's important to you."

She said nothing more, simply slipped into her chair at the head of the table to his left.

He picked up the dirk.

He knew it was a dirk. Knew it was his. Holding it in his left hand, he stroked the fingers of his right over the ornately wrought hilt, over the polished stone embedded in it. . . .

And remembered.

He closed his eyes as the years flooded back.

His childhood. Glenluce. The little cottage above the town. His mother, sweet-faced and gentle. His uncle, her brother, who had raised him, taught him, counseled him so wisely. His father . . . oh, yes, his father.

"Monteith." Opening his eyes, he met Linnet's. "My name is Logan Monteith." The chatter about the table ceased. Into the ensuing silence, he recited the bare facts—that he'd been born and raised in Glenluce, in Galloway, a small country town on the river, The Water of Luce, just above where it ran into Luce Bay.

He remembered much more—the light slanting off the water, the wind in his hair. His first pony, the first time he'd gone with his uncle sailing and fishing in Luce Bay. The scent of heather on the moors, the smell of fish by the wharves. The cries of the gulls wheeling high above.

And his father—above all, his father.

He glossed over the fact that his father hadn't lived with

his mother, had appeared only irregularly in that little cottage above the town. Omitted to mention that his father hadn't married his mother, and even on her deathbed, his mother hadn't cared.

But he, Logan, had.

Even when he'd been young, too young to truly comprehend the situation, he'd cared enough for them both.

"Later, I went to Hexham Grammar School." Those memories were vivid—the chill of the stone buildings, the small fires, the echoes of dozens of feet pounding along corridors. The shouts of boys, the roughhousing, the camaraderie. The masters in their black gowns. "I remember my years there. I was a passable student." Scholastically, he'd done well enough, a sharp eye, native wit, and a ready tongue enough to get him over all the hurdles. "I remember it all, to the last year. When I returned home, I . . ."

Abruptly, the memories ended. He frowned. Try as he might, he couldn't see further, couldn't push further; it was as if he'd reached a black stone wall. He stared unseeing across the table. "I can't remember anything more."

Linnet exchanged a swift look with Muriel. "Don't worry—the fog will clear if you give it time." She glanced at the dirk, still in his large hands. "Who gave you the dagger?"

He looked down, turned it in his hands. "My father." After a moment, he went on, "It's been in his family for centuries."

"An heirloom, then," Muriel said.

Slowly, his gaze still on the blade, Logan nodded.

Gently, Linnet asked, "Your mother, your father. Are they alive?"

Logan lifted his head, met her eyes. "Waiting for me to come home?" When she nodded, he stared at her, then frowned. "I don't think—*feel*—that they are, but . . ." After a moment, he shook his head. "I can't be sure. I can't *remember*. They were alive, both of them, when I finished at Hexham."

Linnet resisted the impulse to tell him to let the matter rest, let his mind rest after the sudden influx of memories, let it catch its breath, at it were. "Now you've started remembering, the rest will surely come."

"Indeed." Muriel briskly nodded. "It often comes back like that—in fits and starts."

The children had been commendably silent, listening and watching, but Brandon couldn't hold back any longer. "What sort of boat did you sail with your uncle?"

The question pulled Logan from his absorption. Linnet mentally blessed Brandon as Logan, clearly thinking back, answered.

That was the signal for the others to put their questions, peppering him with queries on pets—numerous, siblings—none, and for details of Glenluce and Scottish ways.

The distraction gave Linnet a chance to refine her view of Logan in light of what he'd recalled. Even in Guernsey, they knew of Hexham Grammar School. As Winchester Grammar School was to the south of England, Hexham was to the far north. The boys who attended were gentry, overwhelmingly of the higher orders—the aristocracy and even the nobility. Many noble houses of the Border regions sent their sons to Hexham.

Logan's ingrained manners, his air of command, and his protectiveness toward those he considered weaker, combined with his having attended such a school, painted a picture of a gentleman very much Linnet's equal—born to good family, gentry at least, brought up in the country, by the sea.

The children's questions faded. Logan fell silent, a frown once again knitting his black brows.

Finally, he let the dirk he still held between his hands fall the few inches to the table. Folding his hands atop it, he looked at Linnet. Lips thin, he shook his head. "I still can't remember anything more." Frustration etched his face, darkened his eyes. "What did I do next? What did I become?"

She dropped her gaze to his hands, then on impulse reached out and took them in hers.

Memory of a different sort struck.

She nearly jerked at the jolt of remembered sensation.

Of excitement—pure, unadulterated, lancing-sharp—that flashed across her senses. Heat, sensual and potent, unfurled in its wake . . . mentally gritting her teeth, locking her gaze on his fingers, his palms, she ignored it. Ignored the unprecedented *thump-thump* of her heart, and focused.

Examined.

Managed to draw enough breath to say, in a level, passably unaffected tone, "You don't have the right calluses to be a sailor." She released his hands, resisting the urge to run her fingertips over the calluses that were there.

To her relief, when she glanced up, he was staring at his hands. "I do have calluses, though."

"Yes, but you didn't get them sailing."

He nodded, accepting. "Something else repetitive. Reins?" He looked at her. "Perhaps I was a driver?"

"Or a rider." She thought of the saber in the sideboard drawer.

She was about to rise and fetch it when he dropped his head in his hands, for an instant gripped, held still, then started massaging his temples. Linnet hesitated, then looked down the table at Muriel.

Concern in her eyes, Muriel shook her head.

Looking back at Logan just as he scrubbed his hands over his face, then rubbed the back of his neck, Linnet had to agree. He might be physically strong, but he looked mentally exhausted. Pushing too hard all at once might not help.

Turning to Will, she asked, "Which way did you go on your ride?"

Later, after dinner, Logan followed the children into the parlor and, sprawling with them on the floor before the fire, taught them a card game he'd remembered from his childhood.

The children were quickly enthralled, calling out, laughing, and crowing triumphantly as they swapped cards and won tricks.

It was a game he could play without thinking—he'd

spent many long winters' evenings playing with his mother and uncle. The activity gave him time and mental space to review all he'd recalled. His own childhood, the memories he hadn't shared.

He understood, now, why he felt so much at home here, amid the warmth and joy of a house full of children, a large house of comfort, of quiet, unadorned elegance, and a vital, almost tangible, sense of family. This was the antithesis of his own childhood—one of a lone child, the bastard son of a distant earl living quietly estranged from all family with his unwed mother on the earl's pension. His uncle had been his only anchor, the only member of his mother's well-connected English family who had not cut all ties.

With an easy smile fixed on his lips, he watched the children play, helped little Gilly select her cards, and inwardly acknowledged that the reason he felt so wonderfully at peace here at Mon Coeur was not because it was in any way like his home but because this large house encapsulated and embodied the childhood home of his dreams.

This was all he'd ever wanted—even better than, as child or man, he'd been able to imagine. Mon Coeur had it all, everything a lonely soul could want: lots of children, adult women of both the necessary generations—mother and grandmother—needed for complete care, for that all-embracing feminine nurturing. It even had older men to provide the essential male influence; Edgar and John had joined the household about the table, then followed them into the parlor. The two sat in what was clearly their usual armchairs, set in one corner back from the hearth, and quietly chatted about this and that. Male talk, discussions Will and Brandon, and even sometimes Chester, paused to listen to and take in.

Mentally sitting back, seeing it all, absorbing it, Logan was tempted to tell Will, Brandon, Chester, Jen, and Gilly just how lucky they were. But they wouldn't understand—wouldn't be able to see as he could, through eyes that had always, until now, looked on this world from the outside.

It was human nature not to value what one had until one no longer had it. He hoped for their sakes it would never come to that, not for them.

He glanced at Linnet, felt oddly reassured. She would never allow any of them to lose this, to lose Mon Coeur.

Mon Coeur. A name he now understood.

"Logan!" Gilly tugged his sleeve. "Pay 'tention. Which card should I put down?"

He focused on the five cards she held tightly in both hands. Pointed. "That one."

"All right."

He watched as she whipped it out and laid it down.

The others looked, and groaned.

"Did I win?"

Logan laughed, lightly tousled her bright head. "Yes, poppet. You did."

From the other side of the parlor, Muriel watched Gilly beam and bounce on her knees, watched Logan gather the cards and reshuffle them. Saw the interest in the other children's eyes, the boys' eyes especially, as they watched and learned.

Much of her earlier wariness toward Linnet's latest stray had dissipated. Yet looking at Linnet as she sat in an armchair and watched the group before the fire, Muriel wondered if her niece had ever before looked at any man as she was looking at Logan Monteith. Certainly not that Muriel knew.

There was interest, clear as day, in Linnet's green eyes—not a calculating interest, but a fascinated one. An intrigued attraction.

Then Linnet stirred. Uncrossing her legs, she rose. "That'll have to be the last game tonight."

The children and Logan looked up; the children all waited—looking hopefully from Logan to Linnet—but Logan merely inclined his head and turned back to deal the cards. "Last hand."

The children pulled faces, but no one moaned.

Turning, Linnet walked to where Muriel sat, Buttons beside her.

Viewing the subtle smile curving her niece's lips, Muriel felt compelled to ask, as Linnet reached her, "What about the sleeping arrangements?"

Logan might be a gentleman born and bred, nevertheless . . .

Linnet didn't pretend not to understand. She grimaced lightly. "Logan will have to continue in my bed—his head's still causing him considerable pain, and there's nowhere else he'd be comfortable. I doubt the cot in the box room would support his weight, but it'll do for me, at least for a few nights."

Muriel nodded, her gaze going to Logan. "I suspect that's the best arrangement in the circumstances. The better rested he is, the more likely he is to regain his memory." Rising, she said, "I'll have Pennyweather bring in the tea."

Linnet remained where she was, her gaze returning to Logan—skating over his shoulders, the long, strong legs stretched out before him, the clean, harsh planes of his face, his firm lips.

She let her gaze drink him in—and thought of the small cot in the box room.

As usual, Linnet was the last to go upstairs. Once everyone else had retired, she did her rounds; in the calming stillness, the soft, enfolding shadows, she walked the ground-floor rooms of her home, checking every window, securing every door. Mon Coeur might stand in a sparsely populated neighborhood, yet by that very fact the house was isolated, far removed from the communal safety of town or village, and was within a few hundred yards of the coast—a coast that in the past had been an occasional haunt of pirates, and was also frequently raked by ferocious and unpredictable storms.

There was, she considered, sufficient reason for vigilance.

Once all was secure, she climbed to the attics, looked in

on all the children. Tucked Chester's blankets in again, then did the same for Gilly in the room she shared with Jen.

Finally assured that all was as it should be, she descended to the first floor. The lighted candle she carried casting a warm glow on the polished wood of floor and paneled walls, she walked to the closed door of her room.

There, she hesitated, for the first time that evening not quite sure of herself.

The feeling, the realization, irritated. Squaring her shoulders, she reminded herself of her resolution to be wise, then raised a hand and tapped on the door. She waited, then, hearing nothing, reached for the knob, turned it, opened the door, and looked in.

Logan wasn't in the bed. No lamp was burning, but the curtains were open; faint moonlight laid a swath of pale silver across the untrammeled counterpane. The candle flame didn't illuminate much of the large room; stepping inside, she set the candlestick on the nearby tallboy, turned, and saw him silhouetted against the window. He'd been looking out to sea, but had turned his head to watch her.

Eyes adjusting, she saw he was still fully dressed. Closing the door, she frowned at him. "I thought you'd be in bed. You should be by now."

He regarded her for a silent moment. "Are you going to join me?"

He couldn't know. He *didn't* know. She told herself that, again reminded herself of her resolution. "I was just going to get my robe and nightgown. I'll sleep in the box room next door."

He stirred, then with long, prowling strides closed the distance between them. "You'd rather sleep with boxes than with me?"

She fought the urge to step back as the space between them shrank. He halted with less than a foot between them, forcing her to tip up her head to meet his eyes. The candlelight cast them in deep and dangerous shadows. She held his gaze, levelly stated, "Sharing a bed with you would, in the circumstances, be unwise."

"Unwise?" One devilish winged brow arched. He held her gaze for an instant, then stepped closer.

Her nerves leapt; instinctively she stepped back—and came up against the panels of the door.

Temper sparking, she opened her mouth to berate him.

His head swooped and he covered her lips with his.

Kissed her. A full, open-mouthed, lips-to-lips kiss that stole her breath and left her giddy.

He drew back a fraction—enough for her to feel her lips clinging to his, to the taste of him, to the promise in the kiss—then he growled deep in his throat and returned, this time voraciously. His tongue plunged in with no by-your-leave, stroking, claiming, then settling to plunder. He leaned in, commanded, demanded—and she discovered it was impossible *not* to kiss him back, impossible to let such flagrant, blatant demands go unmet, unchallenged.

And suddenly they were there again, where they'd been last night, feeding and taking, giving and seizing.

Wanting.

It was he who, eventually, pulled back.

Just an inch, enough to meet her eyes through the candle-glow. His were narrowed; she would swear they burned blue.

"Last night you didn't think sleeping with me unwise."

She struggled to catch her breath, to find a way to distract, to deflect. To redirect.

His gaze dropped to her breasts as they swelled, flicked up in time to fix on her mouth as she moistened her suddenly dry lips. "That—"

"Was you last night—the houri beneath me. The one I rode to oblivion, the houri who took me in and rode with me. I remember your taste."

Her brazen self was fascinated that he could, that he would; against her will, her gaze lowered to his lips. Focused on them as they curved in a blatantly masculine way.

"It was an excellent way to warm me up. Exceedingly noble. I feel I should be . . . unreservedly grateful." He'd braced his big hands, splayed, on the door to either side of her shoulders, caging her within arms she knew were corded steel. He shifted one hand, fingers catching a strand of hair that had come loose from the careless knot atop her head. He sifted the tress between his fingertips. "I remember this, too—soft as silk, warm as flames."

She dragged her eyes from the mesmerizing sight of him caressing her hair, fell into his eyes as he smiled, then he looked at her lips again.

They throbbed. She fought the urge to run her tongue along the lower. Managed to haul enough breath into her lungs to say, "That—last night—was an impulsive act."

"So be impulsive again." His hand shifted, drifted; he slid his long fingers between her arm and her side, hooked them in the side-laces of her gown.

Let his thumb cruise, brushing, impossibly lightly, over her breast.

She sucked in a tight breath as her flesh reacted, as her nipple pebbled and a wash of seductive heat swept through her.

"I was thinking," he said, his voice a deep, gravelly murmur, the faintest of burrs underscoring the purring quality, "that tonight I should go out of my way to thank you."

Out of his way?

She stared into his eyes from a distance of mere inches, breathed in the warmth of him, sensed the latent heat of him, the muscled power, reaching for her. . . .

No, no, no, no.

But . . .

Locked in his eyes, she gave in and licked her lip. "I shouldn't."

He held her gaze, his eyes searching hers, then his lips slowly curved. "But you will."

He took one long step back. With the fingers crooked in

her laces, he drew her with him, then to him. Against him and into his arms, then he bent his head and kissed her again.

Kissed her until she forgot every jot of wisdom she'd ever known.

Until she melted.

Until she wrapped her arms about his neck and surrendered.

Four

*S*he wasn't surrendering to him but to herself—to that brazen self who wanted to know what more of the magic he could show her. Last night had been a revelation, but if there was more to know, more to experience, she needed to know, to learn of it.

Knowledge, experience, understanding—she'd realized from her earliest years how important those were, how crucial to leadership. Taking risks to achieve them was, to her, second nature, simply a part of who she was.

Once she sank against Logan, wound her arms about his neck and kissed him back—as fearless as he was ravenous— her decision was made. Made and communicated; there was no going back. She never even considered it. Stepping back from a challenge wasn't her style.

And his kiss—this kiss, his mouth and hers joined—was the first fascination. The first flare of heat, the first taste of passion. It was more, so much more, than any kiss she'd ever shared with any of her earlier lovers; they'd been boys, mere learners, dilettantes.

This kiss, his kiss, was one of claiming—of challenge, of blatant promise. Of sensual threat. A statement of intention, certainly—of domination. As with lips and tongue he ravaged and sent her senses spinning, she clung and fought to return the pleasure, to match and meet his educated assault, while inwardly her brazen self rejoiced.

Titillated, expectant, glorying in the moment.

His arms had closed around her, his hard hands holding her, then they moved and he sculpted her curves—possessively, predatorially.

Excitement sparked; her nerves came alive—aware, awake, as they never had been. Tense and waiting, anticipating.

The next touch, the next flagrantly possessive caress.

It came, his hard hand closing about one globe of her bottom, the firm curve filling his palm; his fingers kneaded as he held her to him, lifted her to her toes—then he moved, hips suggestively thrusting, the ridge of his erection riding against her mons, the hard length impressing strength, intention, and erotic promise against her taut belly.

Setting greedy flames flaring low, swelling the hollow emptiness that had opened there.

The emptiness she needed him to fill.

Yet . . .

She felt a tug—realized he'd undone her laces. Felt her bodice sag. In mere seconds he had her out of it, had drawn her arms free, pushed the gown down to her hips, leaving it to slide as it would to the floor, and his hand closed, hard and demanding, about her breast, screened only by her thin shift and even finer chemise.

On a gasp, she pulled back from the kiss. Eyes closed, stretched up on her toes, her fingertips sinking into the heavy muscles of his shoulders as his wicked fingers found her nipple and tweaked. "*Slowly*," she gasped.

And immediately felt his touch ease.

And what a thrill that was—a shiver of knowledge, of understanding, skated down her spine. She lifted her heavy lids and looked into his eyes.

They glittered through his dark lashes, his own lids low. "Just as long as slow doesn't mean stop."

The words were deep, almost guttural. They made her

smile. "No—just slow. Slow so I can . . ." Feel everything, every little nuance. So I can learn of myself, and even more of you. Her smile deepened. "Savor."

His eyes searched hers. "With that," he murmured, "I'll be happy to comply."

His hand hadn't stopped caressing her breast, had been toying firmly, definitely, yet without the urgency she'd sensed had been about to sweep them both away.

He bent his head and kissed her again, took her lips again, engaged with her again, and instantly she sensed, all but felt, the rein he'd imposed on his passions.

That he maintained as, slowly, he stripped her gown, her shift, then her chemise away, and laid her on the bed, stripped off his own clothes—slowly, so she had the chance to catch her breath and admire the lines of the most magnificent male body she'd ever laid eyes on, bandages and all—then he joined her.

Unhurriedly propped on one elbow beside her, and ran one hard, callused hand *slowly* over her body from her throat to her calves.

She let herself respond instinctively, found herself arching lightly into the caress, her body, already heated and yearning, wanting more—blatantly, uninhibitedly.

If she wanted this—wanted to know, to learn, to experience—she saw no point in inhibitions. They had no place here, no purpose between her and him.

Something in his eyes as he looked down at her, for a moment studied her face, gave her the impression he somehow understood that, that he'd seen, taken note, and would use the knowledge, would respond accordingly.

Then he bent his head and set his lips to her breast.

First one, then the other, sampling, tasting, then feasting. Slowly.

Even as she writhed, as she gasped, then softly moaned, as her fingers tangled in his thick hair and she held him to her, helplessly offering her flesh, her body, for his delectation, she knew she'd been inspired in insisting on slow.

Slow. The word became a heartbeat, a pulse of this loving. This seduction he waged on her flesh, on her mind.

On her senses, on every inch of her skin.

She came alive beneath his hands in a way she never had before—and this time she knew it, felt the change to her bones, reveled in the inexpressible pleasure, in the freedom and joy of knowing this could be hers.

That she could have this, be this, the houri he'd called her.

He opened her senses, and she rose to the challenge— waited eagerly to experience what next would come as he lazily—slowly—wended his way down her body, placing hot, wet kisses here, there, past her navel, over the swell of her stomach.

Resting his head on her waist, he looked down, watching as he sent his fingers circling through the tight red-gold curls at the apex of her thighs, then he pushed past, down, and touched her.

Parted her already slick folds and caressed her.

Slowly. Blatantly.

As if he had all the time in the world to feel her, touch her, stroke and caress her.

Urgency slammed into her. She caught her breath; instinctively her thighs eased, parted—inviting, wanting.

She felt more than heard his deep chuckle.

"Slowly, remember?"

"Yes, *but*—" She broke off on a strangled gasp as another far-too-knowing caress had her arching beneath him, fingers digging into his shoulders.

"Ah—perhaps this is what you want?"

Before she could gather her whirling wits, his hand shifted between her thighs and he sank one long finger—slowly— into her, deeper and deeper into her sheath, until he could reach no further.

The breath she'd drawn in and held gushed out, halfsigh, halfmoan. "Yes. Oh . . . yes." Her head was spinning.

"Good." He stroked, *slowly*, deep inside her, then again, and her nerves tightened.

Tightened.

He continued his slow stroking until heat beat in swelling waves through her veins, pulsing and spreading beneath her skin.

Until she was wet, and helpless, and needy.

Until she was one stroke away from wantonly begging.

Until she was so taut that with the next stroke she was sure she'd fracture.

That next stroke never came. He slid lower in the bed; his finger left her. He pushed her thighs wider apart, one trapped by his shoulder, the other held wide with one strong hand.

She cracked open her lids, looked down her body at him— saw him looking down at her—at her swollen, throbbing flesh.

Then he ducked his head and set his mouth to her there.

She came off the bed with a shriek.

He paused, looked up at her. "Is anyone likely to hear you?"

"What?" It took a moment to process the question, to think of the answer. "No. Even the attic rooms aren't directly above us."

"Good." With that, he set his other hand across her belly, holding her down, lowered his head, took her soft, most intimate flesh into his mouth, and suckled.

She screamed, fought to mute the sound, fought to breathe, hands scrabbling for some purchase that would hold her to reality as he played on her senses for all he was worth.

In this arena, he was worth quite a lot. Knew a lot—so much more than she. Her skin was dewed, flushed, her heart pounding, long before he eased back from the exquisite torment.

Panting, mind racing to catch up, she felt his gaze on her, gauging, but couldn't find the strength to lift her lids— couldn't cope with what she knew she would feel at the sight of him supping at her there.

Once he'd thoroughly—*slowly*—consumed her, reducing her to a mass of excruciatingly alive nerves, tense, knotted, and desperately aware, he shifted, licked, laved, then with his tongue probed.

Plunged her into passion unlike any she'd ever known. Her hands clenched, helplessly gripping, in his hair, all she could do was hang on as he drove her, shuddering, quivering, to the brink of ecstasy.

Then he drew back.

He surged over her, and she felt his heat, despite the bandages felt the inexpressible pleasure of his hard body hovering inches above hers as he wedged his hips between her widespread thighs, as he fitted himself to her—then sank home.

Her body arched. She clung, desperately held on—desperately wanted to feel every fraction of an inch of him as he thrust deep and hard into her heated, helplessly willing, mindlessly needy body.

As she felt her sheath stretch, greedily taking him in, all the hard length of him as he forged deep, she hungrily clutched, held him to her. With her arms, with her body, she wrapped herself around him and held tight.

Heard his guttural groan as he came to rest deep within her, then he lowered his head, found her lips—and she tasted her nectar on his lips and tongue as he kissed her ferociously. Then his spine flexed, powerful and sure, and his erection pumped within her, his hips driving in a steady, pounding rhythm. . . .

She couldn't hold on. Couldn't hold back the tide that rose up and crashed over her, surging again before barreling through her.

Ecstasy smashed into her, a tidal wave of sensation that streaked down every vein, down every nerve, to explode in brilliant glory.

Shattering her, emptying her, draining her, then filling the void with glory-tinged bliss.

A bliss that only deepened, only strengthened when he stiffened, then she felt the warm rush deep within, and he groaned and slumped in her arms.

She held him close and marveled, drifting in the aftermath—one deeper, more profound, than she'd previously known. Hands weakly shifting in his hair in an instinctive caress, she lay relaxed and boneless beneath him, beyond amazed at the depth and intensity, the sheer vibrancy of feeling that with him the act had encompassed, had contained.

Never, ever, not in any of her three previous attempts, had the act been anything like this. Not even a weak echo of this.

Logan knew he should shift, that he was pressing her into the bed and she probably couldn't breathe, but . . . he could feel her hand in his hair, gently stroking, and some part of him didn't want to let the moment go. Not yet.

She'd wanted slowly, so he'd gone as slow as he could. Not so easy given that the instant she'd melted into his arms, he'd known he would have her again—that her body was his to take again—and his baser self had been fixated on that, on achieving that as quickly and as blatantly as possible.

Why that last was so important—why some part of him had been so urgent to reimpose, reenact, reiterate his possession of her—he didn't know. He liked women, liked indulging with them, yet never before had he wanted to do more than physically enjoy them. Possess them? No. Not him.

He wasn't a possessive lover—or at least he never had been . . . for a moment, he wondered how he knew, yet consulting his deeper feelings, he knew he was right. He'd never before felt the need to mark a woman as his.

Yet he felt that way with Linnet Trevission.

Perhaps being clouted over the head had changed him?

Yet . . . why her?

Admittedly she felt better beneath him—fitted him better, suited him better—than any other woman he'd ever known. Still . . .

Perhaps when his memory fully returned, he'd lose this primitive urge to tighten his hold on her and never let her go.

Perhaps.

Dragging in a breath, he managed to lift his body from hers—reluctantly separating skin from slick skin—then he left himself down gently on his back beside her. He was well aware the gash on his side had not yet mended; he'd felt the stitches pull during his recent exertions, but was fairly certain none had popped.

Chill air played over his cooling skin. He hadn't noticed the temperature before. Reaching down, he snagged the covers and flicked them up over them both. She lifted a hand weakly to help.

Grinning to himself, he lay back and simply rested. Sensed that it was a long time since he'd just lain back afterward like this, and let the warmth of aftermath lap, then gently recede.

He couldn't raise his left arm and gather her in, not without stretching his wound. Eventually, even though he sensed she was awake, he turned carefully onto his side and slid his right arm over her waist. Felt insensibly comforted by having her beneath his arm, within his hold.

She shot him a quick glance, but immediately looked away, confirming she was wide awake. He knew why he was—he was basking, savoring the moment too much to succumb to slumber and miss it—but he knew he'd satisfied her, thoroughly, deeply, and utterly completely, so by rights she should be comatose . . . except she was thinking. Pondering.

He suspected he knew about what. Weak light from the distant candle played over them, well enough for eyes adjusted to the dimness to see reasonably well. Keeping his lips straight, his expression blank, letting his lids fall so he could only just see through his lashes, he murmured, "Your other lovers—I take they weren't as . . . inventive as I."

The look she shot him was faintly shocked, but even as he watched, that faded. Clearly assuming his eyes were closed, she studied his face, frowned. "I wouldn't have said inventive. I suspect experienced is closer to the mark."

He could smile without giving away that he was watching her. "I see. How many were there?"

Why he wanted to know was a mystery—he never had

with any other lover. But with her . . . he wanted to know.

She continued to frown. "Three."

"Only three?"

"Three before you." Folding her arms over the covers, snugging them beneath her breasts, she acerbically added, "Three was enough to convince me that there was little in the activity to recommend it to me."

That had him opening his eyes wide to stare at her. Directly into her pale emerald eyes. She couldn't possibly mean . . . "Three lovers—three times?" That would explain why he'd found her so incredibly, arousingly tight.

"I wasn't about to further indulge them if I got nothing from the event."

"Nothing?" His mind boggled; she'd been gloriously, uninhibitedly responsive. "They must have been clods."

"They weren't." She shrugged. "Just . . . not as imaginative as you."

He held her gaze, inwardly held his breath. "Am I to take it, inventive, imaginative, and experienced as I am, that you won't be averse to indulging with me again?"

She hesitated, but now he was piecing her situation together, he wasn't all that surprised. He knew well enough not to push, but merely wait; she was, after all, a gently bred female, so that she'd indulged at all with anyone . . .

He narrowed his eyes. "How old are you?"

She narrowed her eyes fractionally back. "Twenty-six."

When his expression relaxed, she frowned. "Why? What does it matter?"

"It doesn't, but it does explain why you've indulged at all—twenty-six is getting a trifle long in the tooth."

"Indeed. As you can clearly remember, twenty-six is more or less on the shelf."

"And they—local society—expect you to marry."

"Yes, but that's not why I decided to take a lover. We weren't courting—there was never any question of that."

He inwardly frowned. Either customs had changed radically, or he was missing some relevant fact.

Before he could think of what question to ask, she said, "I'd already decided I would never marry."

He let his frown materialize. "Why not?"

She arched her brows, haughty again. Even naked, she could pull it off. "For the same reason Queen Elizabeth didn't."

Oddly, that made perfect sense. "Ah. I see."

Linnet was surprised. Indeed, she doubted he truly had, but then he confirmed it.

"The question of power."

"Yes. My position here is essentially that of liege-lord, a hereditary position I've been bred to fill, and I have no inclination whatever to give it up."

He held her gaze for a long moment—so long she wondered what was passing through his mind. Then he said, "You haven't answered my question."

She frowned. "What question?"

"Whether, given my expertise, you're agreeable to indulging with me again."

She couldn't see any reason why she shouldn't. Could formulate several reasons why she should. "Ask me again later, when you're able."

Something hot—that sense of blue flame—shifted behind his dark eyes. The sight made her breath hitch, made parts of her tingle. Made her seize on a distraction. "Could you really tell from kissing me that it was me with you last night?" Aside from all else, she wanted to know.

He smiled, slowly. "That, and other things."

"What things?"

The heavy arm across her waist lifted, raising the covers. "Let me show you."

Before she'd realized what he was about, he'd lifted over her, spread her thighs with his long legs, and settled his hips between—proving that, contrary to her expectations, he was very much able already.

He looked down between their bodies, shifted, and she felt the broad head of his erection nudge past her folds—

instantly setting her nerves jangling, her body tightening in expectation, in anticipation. Pausing, he raised his head, caught her eyes as he settled on his elbows above her.

From a distance of mere inches, his gaze burned into hers. "This—how you feel when I'm pushing inside you"—he demonstrated, forging slowly but steadily in—"how you close so tightly around me when I fill you— " With a powerful thrust he filled her completely, making her gasp, making her arch beneath him, making her already furled nipples brush against the coarse bandages circling his chest—making her cry out.

Making her sheath contract tightly around him—making him hiss and close his eyes.

But then he opened them again, pinned her as she lay beneath him. "This," he said, his voice gravelly and low as he withdrew and then thrust deep and hard again, "was the final proof."

She'd thought her nerves were shattered, wrung out, unable to respond, not again, not so soon. But they were already sparking, tensing, tightening. As for him . . . "I didn't think . . ." That was all she could manage to say as he filled her again.

"Don't think." He lowered his head to rest alongside hers. "Stop thinking. Just feel."

She didn't take orders well, but this time she complied.

His breathing harsh by her ear, her own breath coming in panting gasps, his heavy body moving over hers, her own responding, his hips and legs pinning her, spread and open, beneath him, she really had no choice as he settled into a driving, pounding rhythm that rescripted all she'd ever known about what could pass between a man and a woman.

Flames rose and enveloped them. Cindered all thought, any lingering inhibition. When she felt him tug one of her knees, she responded, raising her legs and wrapping them around his hips, opening herself even more.

For him to take. To fill. To ravish.

Logan didn't hold back. She'd given him a telling piece of

information—her comment about Queen Elizabeth. About her position here. Her other lovers would have known it and bowed to it—and so failed. She was too strong a woman to be made love to gently, reverently, at least not at first. She didn't need a man to bow to her but to take her, possess her—to show her what it was like, how it felt, to be desired and possessed.

So he took, gave desire and predatory hunger free rein and unrestrainedly possessed. He demanded, commanded, and took all she had to give, savoring her moans, her gasps, her surrender, until her ulitmate climax brought on his own.

The ensuing cataclysm rocked even him.

As he hung above her, gasping, waiting for his thundering heart to slow, his sawing breathing to ease, he looked down, and watched as, this time sated well beyond thought, she slipped, boneless and relaxed, into sleep beneath him.

He felt a satisfaction deeper than any he'd ever known as he withdrew from the clinging clasp of her body, then slumped beside her.

For however long he remained here, for however long this odd hiatus in his life lasted, she would be his. His to possess whenever he wished.

Whenever he could persuade her to it.

December 12, 1822
Mon Coeur, Torteval, Guernsey

Logan woke to dawn seeping through the room, and an empty space in the bed beside him. As the events of the night replayed in his brain, he found himself grinning, but as the reality of the situation impinged, his sense of euphoria faded.

He didn't yet know who he—Logan Monteith—was, not as an adult, not now. He didn't know what he did, how he made his living—didn't know where he lived, nor where he'd been going. He needed to jog his memory and remember, but regardless, one fact stood crystal clear.

Despite his lack of memory, he had to have a life he needed to return to. Ergo, his time here, with Linnet, was limited.

He'd known that, and she knew it, too. Indeed, in a way she was counting on it, knowing that, regardless of whatever grew between them, he would eventually leave. The critical point being that she and her position stood in no danger from him.

Pushing back the covers, swinging his legs from the bed, he frowned. The knowledge that their liaison was already slated to be temporary, fleeting, sat poorly . . . as if he'd endured many such meaningless encounters in the past and no longer found succor in them.

That might well be true. Grimacing, he stood, crossed to the armchair by the window, and lifted the robe Linnet had given him. Shrugging into it, belting it, he decided he needed to do all he could to bring his memory back.

Going along the corridor, he washed, shaved. Twisting before the small mirror, he tried to unpick the knot securing the bandage around his chest, but couldn't. He wanted to take a look at the wound, but would need help to do so. Turning his attention to the bandage about his head, he started unwinding it, only to discover it had stuck to his scalp and he couldn't get it loose. Frustrated, he rewound it as best he could.

Returning along the corridor to Linnet's room, he saw one of the little maids standing outside the door trying to balance a pile of clothes well enough to knock.

Hearing his footsteps, she turned, brightened. "There you are, sir—I've brought these up for you." She offered the pile. "These are what you was washed up in. We've done the best we can with them, but Miss Trevission says that if you find anything unwearable to please continue to use the clothes she gave you."

"Thank you." He took the pile of neatly laundered clothes.

The maid bobbed a curtsy, turned, and clattered away. Logan entered the bedchamber, closed the door, then laid the clothes out on the bed. He studied them—the plain coat and linen shirt, the black breeches—tried to recall anything about them—where he'd bought them, even when or why he had—but they told him nothing. He didn't even feel any sense of ownership. Perhaps he was the sort of man who cared nothing for his clothes.

That didn't sound right, didn't feel right.

Inwardly shrugging, he donned the clothes, discovering slashes in the shirt and coat corresponding to his wound neatly mended. The breeches were a better fit than Linnet's father's had been. He continued using the stockings Linnet had given him, and her father's boots—wearable, if a touch tight. His own had yet to reappear.

Feeling oddly more himself, he went downstairs and headed for the dining room and the babel therein. Today he was early enough to catch the other men at the table. Exchanging nods and greetings, he slid into the vacant chair next to Linnet's.

Brandon reached over the table, holding out a belt. "This is yours. We reoiled it and it came up well, but we couldn't save your boots."

"Thank you." Logan took the belt. Uncoiling it, he saw the buckle was . . . something he should remember, but didn't. Shifting in his chair, he slid the belt through the loops on his breeches, cinched and buckled it.

As the other men rose and left for their work, Linnet caught his eye. "Your boots were Hobys."

When he blinked at her, she asked, "Do you know what that means?"

He nodded, but couldn't work it out. A gentleman's boots were usually made to measure and therefore not readily transferrable—witness the current pinching of his toes. So the boots he'd been washed up in were almost certainly his own, and Hoby was one of the ton's foremost bootmakers.

The other little maid—Molly, he thought her name was— brought him a plate piled even higher than the day before. He thanked her and absentmindedly fell to eating while he tried to solve the riddle.

In case he hadn't seen it, Linnet murmured, "Your expensive boots don't match your ordinary clothes."

He glanced at her, but said nothing.

Linnet left him to his thoughts. The children finished, and she dispatched them to their various chores and lessons. Buttons followed Jen, Chester, and Gilly out, shooing them ahead of her to the schoolroom.

With only herself, Muriel, and Logan left in the room, Linnet transferred her gaze to Logan, and waited.

Eventually he looked up and met her eyes. Grimaced. "I have no idea what the discrepancy between my clothes and boots means."

He fell silent again, his forehead—what showed beneath the now lopsided bandage—deeply furrowed. Linnet looked down the table at Muriel, sipping her last cup of tea, and arched a brow. Her aunt saw, considered, then nodded.

Linnet rose, went into the parlor, retrieved both the scabbarded saber and the wooden cylinder, returned to her chair, then placed both items on the table before Logan. "These were the only other things you had with you, other than your clothes and boots, and the dirk."

He glanced sharply at her and reached for the saber.

Unperturbed, she responded, "As I believe I mentioned, we've"—with her head she indicated Muriel, watching from the table's foot—"had significant experience with temporary loss of memory. It never pays to push, to try to recall too much at once." She watched curiously as he withdrew the saber and examined the blade. "Regardless, I was going to give you the saber yesterday, after the dirk had been so helpful in bringing so much back to you, but, if you recall, you were tired after that, so pushing again then didn't seem wise."

He glanced at her, grimaced, then looked back at the

saber. "Despite your solicitousness, this isn't having the same effect as the dirk."

"Perhaps it isn't yours," Muriel said.

Logan slid his hand into the saber's guard, grasped the hilt. Hefted it, rolled his wrist a little, gauging the weight. "No—I think it is mine. It feels . . . familiar. But . . ." Frustrated, he shook his head. "I just can't remember what it means, what it tells me."

Setting it back on the table, he picked up the wooden cylinder. Examining the strips of wood that formed it, held together by brass clasps, he frowned. "This tells me even less. I'm fairly certain it's not mine." He tried to open what appeared to be the top, secured by a combination of brass levers, but nothing he did seemed to release the lid.

"It has to be important to you," Linnet said. "You were carrying it, wrapped in oilskins, in a specially designed leather sling—the cylinder rested along your spine, secured by a belt loop and two other straps that went over your shoulders. We had to cut the sling off you to tend to your wound."

"I can't open it—I'm not sure I ever could." Setting it down, he stared at it. "I must have been a courier—presumably taking that to someone, somewhere. But why? And to whom? And where was I heading?"

No answers came.

After a moment, Linnet rose. "Never mind that now—my advice is to leave it and it'll come to you. However, as you're clearly going to puzzle over it anyway, come and let me take a look at your head while you think. That bandage needs retying."

As the loosened bandage had developed a tendency to slip down over one of his eyebrows, Logan grunted and rose. Muriel rose, too, and headed for the kitchen. Logan followed Linnet into the corridor leading to the back door, then she turned off it, down a narrower corridor. Stopping outside a door, she opened it and went through, into a small bathing chamber.

"Sit there." She pointed to a bench beside a sink.

Noting that her voice of authority had returned in full measure, Logan somewhat grumpily sat.

Linnet ignored his frowning, undid the sloppily tied knot—one he had clearly fashioned—and carefully unwound the bandage, removing the various lumps of padding they'd included to protect the wound.

"It's stuck," Logan informed her, just as she reached that point. "That's why I couldn't take it off myself."

"You shouldn't have tried." She looked, then humphed. "I'll need to moisten it, dampen it to remove it. Wait here while I fetch some warm water."

She went out and to the kitchen. When she returned minutes later carrying a basin with warm water, Logan was sitting exactly as he had been, hands braced on his knees, his gaze fixed in the distance, his brows drawn down in a distinctly black frown.

"If you keep on like that, you'll give yourself a brain fever." Setting down the basin, she squeezed out the cloth she'd dropped in the water, then drew his head forward, and gently, carefully, wet the patch where the bandage had stuck.

He shifted, but she kept hold of his head. "Does that hurt?"

"Not of itself—only when you press."

"Good." The bandage finally came free. She lifted it away. "Lean further forward so I can check the wound—you might not need another bandage."

He obliged. Lifting the thick locks of his hair, she inspected the contusion. Although still raised, it looked nowhere near as angry as it had two evenings before, and the break in the scalp was closing nicely.

She straightened. "Let's leave it unbandaged through the day. The air will help it heal. But you might need padding to sleep comfortably—we'll see."

"I sleep on my side or stomach mostly."

She recalled that he'd tended to sleep draped over her—more on his stomach than not.

Sitting up, he caught her gaze. "I need to check the wound in my side—it's itching, but until I look at it I can't tell if that's good or bad, but I couldn't untie the knot."

"Just as well. That's my handiwork—*I'll* untie it and check the dressings and the wound."

He shrugged. "As you like." He eased out of his coat. She helped him free his hands, then turned away to lay the coat aside.

When she turned back, he had his shirt half over his head. She leapt to help him draw it off and down his left arm. Pulling it free, she shook it out, then laid it on the coat and turned back to him once more.

Inwardly frowned as her mouth went dry at the sight of him. She wondered how he could possibly seem larger—broader, harder, more powerfully muscled—than he had in her bed last night. He'd seemed more than big enough, powerful enough, then. Of course, then, the bleak winter daylight hadn't been washing over him, highlighting every line, every curve, every sleek bulge.

And she hadn't, then, had time to stare.

Realizing, she gave herself a mental shake and briskly walked closer, waving him to swivel so she could reach the knot in the middle of his broad back.

As she reached around him to pick the knot apart, the scent of him—a definable scent that screamed *male*—teased her senses.

She held her breath and concentrated on the knot.

It came apart before she expired.

Straightening, surreptitiously dragging in a deep breath, she started unwinding the long bandage. Series of bandages. He had to help, but eventually, after she once again applied her damp cloth, the bandages and the dressings were stripped away, and he sat naked to his waist on the bench.

"Here." Grabbing his left wrist, she lifted it. "Lean on the sink. I'll need to check the stitches—you might have pulled some."

His dark eyes watched her, but he said nothing, simply complied.

Ducking under his raised arm, she followed the line of the wound down, inch by inch checking each stitch, running her finger along the side of the gash—still angry but healing, and with no sign of infection, thank God. She worked her way down the side of his chest, bending to examine the spot where his rib had been exposed, then continuing her inspection down to his waist.

As she neared the point where the wound disappeared beneath his breeches, his right hand moved to the buttons securing the waistband, but then paused. "Do you want to check the rest?"

The lower part of the wound, the part that swept across his belly, hadn't needed stitches, but she and Muriel had applied a salve. "I should check it for infection. Just in case."

He could have checked that section, but she preferred to see for herself.

"As you wish."

There was something in his tone that made her look up at his face as he obliged, his hand shifting as he freed the two buttons, but when her eyes met his, he merely arched his brows.

She frowned, then looked down.

Leapt up and back. "Oh!"

Color flooded her cheeks. Her gaze remained immovably locked on the head of his fully erect penis. She hadn't thought . . . hadn't expected him to be standing to attention quite like that.

Hauling in a breath, she wrenched her gaze upward, narrowed her eyes on his. "You did that on purpose!"

He laughed. It was such a lovely, rolling sound that she was caught, blinked. Then his eyes returned to hers. "I assure you it doesn't respond to commands."

She'd known that, but . . . the sight of him like that had temporarily scrambled her brain. Beyond her control, her gaze slid down again, to where he stood, if anything even more rampant. That part of him looked a lot bigger than she'd imagined . . . had she really taken all that inside her?

"From the look on your face, I take it your previous experiences all occurred at night, or at least in a bed."

She managed to haul her gaze up to frown at him. "Where else . . . oh."

She'd never get her color back to normal if she kept thinking. . . .

"Clearly there's a lot you've yet to experience. I'll be happy to show you . . . but did you want to check my wound first, or not?"

She blinked at him, gathered her wits. "Yes."

"In that case"—he waved with his left hand, the one propped on the sink—"be my guest."

His other hand was splayed on the bench beside him. She suspected he could, if he wished, use it to help her, but from the gleam in his eye, the damn man was baiting her. Challenging her.

She'd never refused a challenge in her life.

Steeling herself, she stepped closer. His knees were wide spread; she halted between. Then she looked down. Boldly reached for his erection, closed the fingers of her left hand about it, and tilted it to the side.

She couldn't see the gash well enough while standing. Fluidly dropping to a crouch, she slid her fingers down his length, keeping the head tipped aside so she could focus on what was now a red, healing welt. The salve had helped seal it. As far as she could see, the seal had withstood his exertions of the night.

Satisfied, she tensed to rise, but beyond her control her eyes shifted left. To the solid rod she held between her fingers, more or less level with her face. The flaring rim caught her eye, as did the dark color, more purple than red. The skin beneath her fingertips, fine as a baby's cheek, seemed odd in contrast to the rigid, steely strength. Fascinated, she shifted her fingers, stroked.

Realized he'd grown not just silent but still.

Totally, utterly still—like a massive cat about to pounce.

Before she could react, his hands closed about her shoulders. She rose as he drew her up.

"Don't let go."

The words were bitten off, a command—after one glance at his face, one she deigned to obey. Excitement slithered through her, anticipation streaked down her spine.

One large hand rose to slide around her nape, drawing her to him. Into a kiss.

His lips closed over hers, just as she felt his other hand close about hers, locking her fingers around his erection. She tightened her grip—and sensed the hitch in his breathing. Sensed that, with her touch, she held his attention, his entire focus, absolutely.

She drew back from the kiss enough to breathe across his lips, "So teach me. Show me."

A command of her own, one with which he complied.

He kissed her, all hot tongue and ravenous lips, while he guided her hand, showed her how to please him.

His hand drifted from her nape, down her back, to her waist. Then further to cup her bottom and knead. Then he urged her closer.

He was raising her skirt, and she was curious and eager to learn what it would be like to indulge in broad daylight, when a knock fell on the door.

Releasing him, she whirled to face the door as Molly called, "Miss, are you done with that basin yet?"

"Ah . . . almost." She swallowed desperately, fought to strengthen her voice. "I'll be finished in a moment. I'll bring it to the kitchen when we're done."

"All right, miss."

Soft footsteps receded down the corridor. Linnet breathed freely again.

Then she whirled—and discovered Logan reaching for his shirt.

She looked down. His breeches were closed. For one

crazed moment, she didn't know if she was grateful or not.

Then she looked him in the eye. "Just as well—I have to work with the donkeys this morning."

He arched a brow, then pulled his shirt over his head. His expression when his head emerged was harder, bleaker. "I have to remember—if I'm a courier, then there's some place I'm supposed to be, and no doubt people waiting for me to arrive."

She frowned, then backed a step so he could stand and tuck in his shirt. "You can't force your memory—you need to stop trying."

He said nothing, just shrugged on his coat.

She stifled an irritated humph, then reached for the basin and lifted it. Cast him a deliberately challenging glance. "I could use some help, if you're up to it."

He looked at her—directly enough for her to wonder what she'd said—but then his lips thinned and he waved her to the door. "Donkeys. Lead the way."

She did, waiting by the door for him to open it, then carried the basin back to the kitchen.

❧ Five ❧

onkeys, Logan learned, were integral to life on Guernsey. They were the favored beasts of burden, better than horses on the rougher island lanes, more agile than bullocks, and, so he was informed, essential for transporting goods up and down the steep streets of St. Peter Port, the island's main deepwater port, capital, and center of commerce.

Wrapped in Linnet's father's cloak, he trudged with Linnet and Vincent across frost-crisped fields, counting the shaggy brown-gray beasts.

When they finally returned to the stable yard, Vincent clapped his gloved hands, his breath fogging around his face. "I make that twenty—maybe twenty-two—we can send to the fair."

Linnet had been making notes in a small ledger. "Let's send the twenty-two. We'll sell them for certain, which is better than us having to carry any extra through to next spring. Our breeding stock's sound—we don't need to adjust this year."

Vincent nodded. "I'll get the boys to bring them in to the holding pens next week—spend the weeks after that making sure they're in prime shape and looking their best for the fair."

Linnet grinned. "You do that." Shutting her book, she glanced at Logan. Her eyes scanned his face. "Now we're out and about, we may as well check the goats."

He merely arched a brow and, resignedly saluting Vincent, who grinned in reply, trudged obediently in her wake as she headed back out of the yard, taking the track along which the boys had driven the wagon to market.

Lengthening his stride, he drew level with his bossy hostess. "Where does this track go?"

"A little way along, it joins the main road that runs along the south coast, then turns up to St. Peter Port." She stopped at a gate in the fence, unlatched it, then led the way through.

He followed, relatching the gate before tramping after her. The paddock was rougher, more rocky. A wooden-beamed structure, a long, low, open-sided shed, nestled in a dip ahead, a stand of trees behind it. "So you breed goats, too?"

"Not so much breed as husband." She halted on a low rise and pointed to a herd grazing some distance away. "Goats have always run wild on the island, and in large part still do. Most fences aren't high enough to keep them in. But in winter they come down from the heights for feed and shelter."

"They're golden." Logan studied the unusual coat color displayed by most members of the small herd.

"Most of that lot are Golden Guernseys." Linnet had her book out again. She looked down as she made a note. "The color comes and goes depending on how much they breed with the other goats—there are several varieties on the island."

"Do you send goats to market, too?"

"Some, but usually not as many in a year as donkeys. We take what we need, and then whatever seems appropriate to cull goes to market in St. Peter Port. Given there's so many goats about, it's only in the larger towns that there's any real demand."

They walked a number of the rougher paddocks, counting numbers. In one field, Linnet wanted to get a closer look at some kids.

Hanging back and watching as she coaxed the young ones to her, Logan heard a snort, looked, and saw a buck lower his head, paw the ground.

Linnet fell back as Logan abruptly appeared beside her, startling the kids away, but then she saw that his right hand was wrapped about the horns of a twisting, irate buck—who had been about to butt her.

She blew out a breath as Logan shoved the animal away. The buck snorted, eyed him evilly, but then harrumphed and turned away.

"Thank you." She caught Logan's eye. "I'd forgotten about him."

He frowned. "I take it you usually do this—checking the animals—on your own."

"Generally."

"So what happens if one of them mows you down?"

"I pick myself up, brush myself down, and put salve on the bruises later."

Falling into step beside her, he shook his head. "Gently bred ladies aren't supposed to land on their arses in goat shit."

"Gently bred ladies aren't supposed to sleep with strangers, either."

That shut him up. Head high, she led the way on and around to the pastures where the dairy herd grazed.

While she walked among the animals, checking their condition, noting which calves were showing most promise, he stood to one side, watched.

"I didn't see a dairy among the outbuildings."

"It's a separate building." She waved to the north. "It's on the other side of that hill."

"All part of your estate?"

When she nodded, he asked, "How many people does the estate employ?"

"Outside the house, fifty-three."

Logan knew that was a significant number—fifty-three outside employees would translate to forty or more families dependent on the estate. Not a small number. "That must make the estate the biggest employer in this region, if not on all of Guernsey."

"Both." She looked up, smiled pointedly. "Hence my comment about Queen Elizabeth."

He inclined his head. She saw herself as responsible for the welfare of a large number of people, and in fact she was. Logan didn't know why, but he understood that—the concept of duty.

Letting his eye rove over the cows, placid and large, he said, "The cows and cattle around Glenluce are different breeds—Ayrshire for dairy, Black Galloway and Belted Galloway for beef."

"I've seen Ayrshires, and the Blacks. Are the Belted much different?"

"Other than the white band, not that I ever heard."

Eventually they trudged back to the house. It was the smells that stayed with him the longest, that teased his memory the most. He'd been familiar with the scents of donkey, goat, and cow, but . . . his memories suggested much drier, dustier versions, but that made no sense, not if those memories came from Scotland.

He felt Linnet's gaze on his face, glanced up and met it.

She searched his eyes, then looked toward the house. "At least you've had some fresh air."

Luncheon was being served as they walked in. Logan spent the meal chatting with the men, mostly about land and farming.

When the meal ended and the other men rose and left, Linnet cocked a brow at him. "You're not a farmer."

Although she'd been talking with the children, she'd lent an ear to his conversations with the men.

He grimaced. "I know only the general things one knows from growing up in the country—the rhythm of the seasons, the weather. But I don't feel any connection to farming itself, the mechanisms, the details."

"Your hands aren't the hands of a farmer." Linnet pushed

back her chair and rose. "I'm going to go out riding." She met his gaze as he got to his feet. "Given the distance you walked this morning, you should probably rest."

One black brow arched. "On your bed?"

She ignored the suggestion in his eyes. "Riding might jar your head, and it will stress the wound in your side. It's healing nicely—no need to tempt fate."

He held her gaze, the midnight blue of his eyes pronounced as a frown formed in the dark depths. "I want to ride." He shook his head slightly. "Don't argue—I'm fairly sure I ride. A lot."

Not a little exasperated, she held his gaze, searched his eyes . . . read his determination and the underlying need to remember. "All right." She blew out a breath. "But first you have to let me rebandage your chest."

Logan suffered through the rebandaging—anything to get on a horse. The more he thought of riding, the more he wondered that he hadn't thought of it before.

He felt as eager as a child anticipating a treat when, finally, he strode beside Linnet down the long central aisle of the stable.

"We've plenty of hacks—we all ride. You can—"

"This one." Logan halted before the door to a large stall containing a massive gray stallion.

Linnet backtracked to halt beside him. "That's Storm. My father bought him as a colt, but never got to ride him. We use him mostly for breeding."

"But he's been broken to the saddle." Logan unlatched the stall door, pushed it open.

"Yes, but he's not been ridden much. He's so damned strong, even Vincent has to wrestle with him." Linnet frowned as Logan walked straight to the big stallion's head, placed a hand on the horse's long nose, then reached up to scratch between his ears.

Logan flung her a glance. "In case you hadn't noticed, I'm damned strong, too."

Not a point she could argue. Resisting the urge to waste her breath lecturing him, trying to get him to choose a safer mount, she shook her head and stepped back. "The saddles are through here."

Vincent was busy saddling her roan mare, Gypsy. Before she could stop him, Logan selected bridle and saddle and carried them back to Storm's stall.

She leaned on the stall door and watched as he readied the big horse—who gave every sign of cooperating, almost certainly eager to run—and gave thanks she'd insisted on bandaging Logan's chest again. Yet his movements as he settled the bridle, then hefted the saddle to the gray's broad back, were practised and economical; he'd clearly performed the task countless times.

Vincent came up, leading Gypsy. He raised his brows when he saw Storm saddled. "That'll be interesting."

"Indeed." She hoped it wouldn't prove *too* interesting. Logan getting thrown wouldn't help at all.

But as he led Storm out of the stall and into the yard, and she followed with Gypsy, she sensed in him nothing but supreme confidence. Then he planted his boot in the stirrup, swung up to Storm's back, gathered the reins as the big stallion shifted under his weight—and even she ceased to doubt.

He grinned at her. Grinned like a boy.

Blowing an errant strand of hair from her face, she climbed the mounting block and clambered into her sidesaddle. She preferred to wear breeches and ride astride, but increasingly no longer did. She missed the freedom. Leading the way out of the yard, she was conscious of a spurt of envy.

Storm and his rider easily kept pace as she headed out along the track. Storm tried a number of his usual tricks, but each time was immediately brought into line; encountering an invincible hand on his reins, he quickly desisted and settled to the steady pace.

She glanced at Logan, found him riding easily. "We'll be able to gallop once we turn into the fields."

Expectation lit his face. "Lead on."

She did, through the soft light of the winter afternoon, with pewter clouds scudding across the gray sky. Following her usual circuit around the estate's perimeter, checking the fences and gates, they galloped several times, cantered for most of the rest.

He grew more and more silent, more clearly absorbed with his memories.

When, with the light fading around them, they clattered into the stable yard, and Vincent and Young Henry came running to take the horses, he halted Storm and, for the first time in over an hour, met her gaze. "I was in the cavalry."

She nodded, then wriggled and slid down from her saddle. He dismounted, handed over Storm's reins, then fell in beside her as she walked to the house.

When she glanced at him, arched a brow, he frowned. "It's not like with the dirk—this time it's coming in bits and pieces, lots of snippets. Like bits of a jigsaw that I have to arrange to see the whole picture."

She looked ahead at the house. "Just let it come. And if you can't make sense of one piece now, set it aside for later, when you'll have more pieces to work with."

He grunted, and followed her into the house.

When, washed and in a fresh gown, she came down to dinner, she found him in the parlor, standing before the sideboard where they'd left his dirk, the saber, and the wooden cylinder. He had the saber in his hand, was experimentally wielding it. He looked up, met her eyes. "This *is* mine."

She merely smiled, and with her head directed him into the dining room.

He remained quiet and withdrawn during dinner, stirring himself only to apologize to Gilly for not hearing her question. The others understood he was wrestling with his memory and largely left him to it.

But at the end of the meal, when they all rose to repair to the parlor, he halted behind his chair, blinked.

She paused beside him, laid a hand on his arm. "What is it?"

He looked at her, refocused on her face. "The mess—I remember. I used to be in the officers' mess."

"You're a cavalry officer." She didn't make it a question; the guise fitted him all too well.

Slowly, he nodded. "In the Guards—I'm not sure what regiment."

She patted his arm. "Come and sit by the fire, and tell us what you can."

Somewhat to her surprise, he fell in with that plan. He sat in the armchair to one side of the hearth, the one opposite hers, with the children sprawled on the floor between them.

Logan looked at the eager, innocently inquiring faces looking up at him. "I'm a cavalry officer in the Guards." Or was, yet he felt the occupation was still his. "I don't know what my current rank is, but I was a captain during the Peninsula Wars."

"Did you fight at Waterloo?" Will asked.

He nodded. He could remember that terrible day, still hear the screams of men and horses, the obliterating roar of cannon. "I can't remember all the details yet." He felt sure he eventually would. "We were, at one point, caught up in the defense of Hougomont, but otherwise . . . it was a very . . . messy day. Most major battles like that are."

"Were you in Spain?" Brandon's eyes were huge.

Logan nodded. "Both early on—before the retreat from Corunna—and later, when we returned."

Linnet stirred. "My father captained one of the ships that helped with the evacuation at Corunna."

Logan glanced at her. "It took a lot of ships to get the army—what was left of it, at any rate—away." Without prompting, he drew them a word sketch of what it had been like—the panic and confusion, the horses that had had to be left behind.

Recalling and retelling it embedded the memory more firmly in his mind—back into the slot where it belonged. Encouraged, he told them of subsequent battles, after they'd returned to hold Portugal, then fight their way across

Spain—Talavera, Cuidad Rodrigo, Badajos, Salamanca, Vittoria, the crossing of the Pyrenees, the battle outside Toulouse. "We returned home after that, but then went back for Waterloo."

He frowned, then shifted as Muriel handed him a cup of tea. Thanking her, he sat back and, grateful, let Linnet, who had noticed his sudden halt, distract the children.

Once the children had gone upstairs, and Muriel and Buttons had followed Edgar's and John's lead and left, too, Linnet arched a brow at him.

He grimaced. "I don't know if it's simply that Waterloo was a hellish nightmare—that the day was disjointed, with us being sent first here, then there—but . . ." He drew in a breath, let it out in a frustrated sigh. "I can't see the faces. I know I fought alongside men I knew—who I knew well, comrades for years—yet I can't see their faces, not clearly. And I can't remember any names."

Linnet studied him for a moment, then rose. "As you've just proved, your memory is returning. The details may be hazy and incomplete, but with time they'll come clear."

When he didn't respond, just frowned at the floor, she inwardly sighed. "I'm going to do my rounds. I'll be back in a moment."

She headed for the dining room.

When she returned from checking the windows and doors on the ground floor, he was sitting where she'd left him, but was now turning the wooden cylinder over and over in his hands.

He glanced up, then returned to studying the cylinder. "I've run into another black wall. What the devil does this thing mean? What have I been doing since Waterloo? And with whom? For whom am I carrying this"—he waved it—"and what does it contain? Or is it just mine, for storing valuable papers?"

He was like a dog worrying a bone. And the intensity driving him was starting to worry her.

"Nagging at things rarely helps."

When he sent her a black look, she laughed. "Yes, I know, easier said than done, but it's time to go upstairs. After all our riding, you'll need your rest." *Or at least distraction.*

Grudgingly, he rose, carried the cylinder back to the sideboard, then followed her from the room.

At the top of the stairs, she paused, through the shadows met his eyes. "I'm going up to check on the children. I'll join you shortly."

He nodded. As she climbed the next flight of stairs, he walked slowly toward her room.

Logan stood by the window looking out on the wintry dark. A gap between two of the encircling trees offered a glimpse of moon-silvered sea rippling beneath an obsidian sky.

The more he remembered, the more he recalled of himself, of his past, the better he sensed what manner of man he was. Which, here and now, left him in a quandary. He was an honorable man—tried to live his life by that overriding precept—so was sleeping with his hostess, a beautiful, gently bred female with no effective protector—taking advantage of her, as most would deem it—the action of an honorable man?

To the man he now knew himself to be, the answer was a clear-cut no.

Last night . . . he didn't know what he'd been thinking. In truth, he hadn't been thinking; he'd responded to the challenge, the intrigue, the necessity of learning whether the night before had been dream or reality. But in satisfying his curiosity, he'd started something else—something he didn't understand—for Linnet wasn't just any woman, not to anyone, but most especially not to him.

The door opened. He turned. He hadn't bothered to light the lamp.

The soft glow of the candle Linnet carried preceded her into the room. She entered, looked around and saw him, turned to set the candlestick on the tallboy and close the door. Then she walked toward him, the skirts of the fine green woollen gown she'd donned for the evening swaying enticingly about her long legs. The fabric clung lovingly to the sleek curves of breast and hip, reminding him of how those firm curves felt undulating beneath him.

Fisting one hand, he pushed the tantalizing memory aside. She'd made up her mind to be unattainable and, bastard-born, he had his own road to follow—wherever it might lead. There was no benefit to either of them in allowing whatever it was that had flared between them to deepen, to evolve.

He knew that, recognized and acknowledged that, knew that simply ending the budding liaison here and now was the honorable thing to do, yet . . .

She halted, close, too close to pretend that they hadn't been—weren't—lovers. Despite the nearness, she was tall enough to meet his gaze easily. She studied his eyes, then said, "I've a proposition for you."

He arched his brows. Felt immediately wary, but whether of her, himself, or what might be coming he couldn't have said.

Her lips curved. "I don't believe it will hurt." She paused, then went on, "I want you to educate me in the ways of the flesh. In every erotic, sinful pleasure."

Lustful anticipation slammed through him.

Equally instinctive, the honorable part of him held firm. He tightened his jaw, tightened his hold on his baser impulses. "It might, perhaps, be wiser if we didn't further indulge."

Linnet's brows flew high. So he could spend all night obsessing about what he couldn't remember? "Hmm . . . no. That won't do. It occurs to me that you are presently without coin or other material means to repay my hospitality."

His lips firmed. "I'll help you with your donkeys. And the goats."

She laughed, her eyes never leaving his. "Not enough—not nearly enough."

"Throw in the cows—and I'm a dab hand with horses."

"Now you're getting desperate—and, if you think about

it, just a touch insulting." She shifted nearer, held his gaze unrelentingly. "Stop arguing."

His eyes narrowed on hers.

Holding his gaze, she lowered one hand and boldly closed it about the solid rod of his erection.

He hissed in a breath, closed his eyes.

"Tell me," she purred, "why is it you don't want to fall in with my plan?"

She knew the answer: Because he was the sort of man the last days had shown him to be, and he would therefore feel compelled to retreat to a position of conventional honor. She'd seen that coming and, discerning no benefit to either of them in his taking that tack, had devised a way around it by making his falling in with her plan an equally mandated act. He would want to repay her; she'd shown him the way.

His lips grimly set, he opened his eyes, looked into hers. "Do you really want that? To be taken, possessed, your body used in ways you've never even imagined?" His voice lowered. "Do you truly want to put yourself in my hands, in such a way, to that extent?"

Primitive threat underscored his tone, smoldered in the midnight embers of his eyes, and sent an evocative shiver down her spine. Sadly for him, that had the opposite effect to what he'd intended.

She thrived on challenges, the riskier, the more exciting, the more tantalizing the better. Smile deepening, she tipped up her face, and closed what little distance remained between them. "Yes. Take me." Her eyes on his, she categorically stated, "However you want, however you wish—take me *now.*"

Logan's lips were on hers, his tongue plundering her mouth, his hands fisted in her hair before he'd thought. And then . . . he couldn't.

Think.

All he could hear were the words of her taunting order.

Take me now.

Indeed he would.

However you want, however you wish . . .

As he held her face steady and ravaged her mouth, he remembered he was supposed to teach her, to repay her . . . by opening her eyes to all that could be within the realm of sensual pleasure.

She'd tied his honor in knots, so not even that could excuse him denying her.

So yes, he would do as she commanded. But how?

As per her sultry order, he consulted his fantasies, swiftly rejecting this one, that—those he couldn't envision her in. Couldn't imagine placing her in; she might have agreed to every erotic and sinful way, but she was a relative innocent with no real idea of what that encompassed.

But . . . yes, *that* one. He immediately knew it would work—that she would enjoy being taken, possessed, like that.

Wrenching his mouth free, he looked down at her face for a brief instant, then grabbed the hand still cradling his erection and towed her—dragged her—across the room. After one shocked gasp, she caught up her skirts and kept up easily enough.

Reaching the end of the bed, he yanked her to him, raised his arm over her head, and twirled her, twirled her—then brought her to an abrupt halt before the cheval glass in the corner.

He looked over her head at the reflection revealed in the glow from the candle she'd left burning on the tallboy.

The light washed over her, enough for them both to see her wide eyes and the soft flush tinting her alabaster skin, while he, in dark coat, black breeches, and black boots, with his black hair and tanned skin, appeared as little more than a dark presence behind her.

Perfect.

"This is a performance." Closing his hands about her shoulders, he bent his head and pressed a hot, open-mouthed kiss to the point where her exposed nape met her shoulder.

Head still lowered, he lifted his gaze to the mirror, trapped her eyes. "An erotic performance, and you are the one who'll perform."

She drew in a huge breath, breasts swelling beneath her dinner gown. As she opened her lips, he laid a finger across them. "First rule of this classroom—no talking from you. I will give orders, and you will obey. Other than that, you may moan, sob, even scream—and believe me, you will—but at no point will any word pass your lips. Not even my name." He held her gaze, then softly asked, "Do you understand?"

She opened her mouth, saw his rising brow, closed her lips and nodded.

"Excellent. So let's begin."

The first thing he did was pull pins from her hair. Linnet expected him to take all of them, but no—he picked out one pin here, one there, concentrating on laying first this tress, then that, over her shoulders, trailing yet others to drape her neck. She stood and watched him in the mirror; she could only see what he was doing, where his darkly tanned hands were heading, once they came forward of her shoulders. Only then did the light reach them well enough for her to see.

She was wishing she'd brought up a candelabra rather than a single candle when he lost interest in her hair and focused on her breasts. She felt the shift in his gaze, felt the heat on her breasts—felt them tightening, peaking.

In the mirror she watched her nipples pebble beneath the fine wool of her gown.

"Undo your bodice."

This is a performance, an erotic performance, and you are the one who'll perform.

She finally understood. Even as her hands rose to do his bidding, she wondered what she would learn from this lesson. Her green gown fastened down the front, a row of pearl buttons closing the bodice; she slipped the first free, eager to find out.

His gaze followed her fingers as they worked steadily

lower. She paused when she reached the raised waist—looked at him.

"Keep going."

She could feel the heat of him down her back, sense the solidity, the strength, the masculine power, all held in check mere inches behind her. Primed, ready for action, but utterly controlled. She wouldn't mind breaking that control, splintering it, fracturing it, but that, she suspected, was a lesson for another day. Tonight . . .

Reaching the end of the row of buttons, level with the line of her hips, she halted. Went to ask *"What now?"* but remembered in time.

"Slide the gown off your shoulders, free your arms and hands, and let it fall to the floor."

She did as she was told; as the gown slid to puddle about her feet, she realized why he'd let only a few tresses of her hair free. Her hair was long, nearly reaching her waist, and thick and wavy; if he'd let it all down, it would have screened her upper body from his sight.

Merely having her naked clearly wasn't his aim.

His next order came. "Take off your shift, and hand it to me."

Her shift reached below her knees. She bent to grasp the hem and her bottom met his groin. He didn't shift away. Losing the contact as she straightened and drew the shift off over her head, a strange frisson of awareness streaked through her.

Her arms free of the garment, with one hand she offered it back, over her shoulder. He took it, his fingers brushing over hers as he did.

Another odd shiver threatened.

She expected to be told to remove her chemise in the same way, but instead, he drawled, "Now, let's see. . . ."

Her breasts were already swollen, achy, even though he hadn't touched them, not even brushed them. Her nipples were furled so tight they hurt.

"Open the buttons."

The chemise had a front placket that reached to her navel, closed by tiny flat buttons she never bothered undoing. One by one, she slipped them free. The placket gaped as her hands descended, revealing the creamy whiteness of her skin, the valley between her breasts.

By the time she reached the end of the line, her nerves had tightened, expectation gripping.

"Draw the sides apart and show me your breasts. I'm your audience—display them for me."

Curling her fingers in the fine material, she boldly, brazenly, drew the sides wide, baring her breasts to his hot gaze. She could feel it moving over her exposed flesh.

"Keep your eyes on your body, not on me."

She obeyed, shifting her gaze from the darkness behind her to the white glow of her breasts—and found the peculiarity of seeing and feeling simultaneously strangely arousing. She saw the light flush spread beneath her white skin, felt the telltale warmth spread, saw her nipples tighten even more as sensation heightened and her breasts grew heavy.

"Very good." The raspy murmur washed over her ear. "Keep watching."

His hands came around her and lightly cupped her breasts. Too lightly at first, but within a minute his touch had changed—to one of flagrant possession. His tanned hands and fingers stood out in stark contrast against her white skin as they surrounded her breasts, as he captured her nipples, rolled, then squeezed—and her knees went weak.

"Stand straight—don't lean back."

She swallowed and tried to comply. His body was close behind her—mere inches away, given the heat bathing her back. His strong arms reached around her, a steely cage, yet only his hands—those wicked, hungry hands—were touching her.

She wanted more, her body burned for more, yet for long minutes his hands remained on her breasts, kneading, increasingly explicitly claiming, spreading fire beneath her skin, turning the taut, swollen mounds rosy—until, head tipping back, she moaned, careful nevertheless to keep her eyes on the mirror. In truth, it would have been hard to wrench her gaze away; a fascination she'd never imagined might exist kept her eyes locked on her body.

On his hands making free with it.

A shiver slithered down her spine.

"It's time to show me what else you're hiding beneath your chemise." The gravelly whisper tickled her ear. Briefly, his lips cruised the delicate whorl, a trickle of fire, a promise of more. "Use both hands and lift the hem. Show me."

Her heart thudding heavily, she did. Drew the fine fabric up, exposing her upper thighs, then higher, revealing the red-gold fire of the curls at the apex of her thighs.

Dragging in a breath, she raised the hem still higher, to the curve of her belly.

"Excellent." His purr was almost guttural.

She still had on her garters, stockings, and slippers, but he didn't seem concerned with those, and in truth, neither was she. She couldn't tear her gaze from his hands. While one continued to play, firmly and possessively, with her breasts, the other skated down, over the rucked edge of the chemise, to stroke her curls.

He touched them, ruffled them, played until she hauled in a tight breath and shifted. Then he chuckled and said, "Let's see."

He angled his hand so she could watch as he pressed one long finger into the shadowed hollow beneath her curls.

She dragged in a quick, too-shallow breath, held it as the sensation of his touch, of each successive deliberate caress, married with the vision in the mirror.

The impact only escalated as she instinctively eased her feet wider apart, and he reached further, deeper, and the combined stimulation rolled in wave after wave through her.

She bit her lip against another moan, saw the flush of arousal deepen and spread until her skin glowed rosy in the candlelight. Felt the dew of desire break like a fever across her exposed skin.

And still his hands worked her flesh—her breasts, the swollen slickness between her thighs. And still she watched, unable to look away as the fires inside grew, as he stoked them relentlessly.

"Put your hands on mine." The gravelly command was barely comprehensible. "One on each—close your palms over the backs of my hands and *feel* what I'm doing to you."

She obeyed—because she had to. Because she couldn't stand not to, not to know what might come.

She wasn't prepared for the instantaneous heightening of her senses—through his hands, their tensing movements, she knew what would come an instant before it happened. Now she knew, saw, felt; anticipation was added to the sensual tumult burgeoning inside her.

Gasping, panting, barely able to remain upright, she couldn't take much more . . .

His hands slowed. "Tsk, tsk—you still have your stockings and slippers on."

Because he hadn't told her to remove them yet. She bit her lip against the tart rejoinder she suspected he was waiting for.

His chuckle said she'd guessed aright, but then he said, "Release my hands."

She did. To her dismay, he drew his hands from her. She felt bereft to have lost the contact.

"Pull your chemise off over your head."

She rushed to do so, realizing as she did that he'd moved. Even as she refocused on the shadows behind her, he set the straight-backed chair that had stood beside her dressing table down on her left, its seat toward her.

She stared at it. Before she could figure out what he would have her do, he rapped out, "Face forward. Keep your eyes on your body."

Yes, he'd been a cavalry officer. She snapped her gaze back—and felt something inside quiver. She rarely used her mirror, had never used it to view herself naked.

"Drop the chemise."

Realizing she was still holding the garment in her right hand, she released it, forgot it as it floated to the floor.

Forgot everything as she looked at herself—naked and on display—as the knowledge he was doing the same washed over her. A shiver she couldn't hide racked her.

"Are you cold?"

Despite the fire burning in the nearby hearth, she should have felt the air's chill, but the heat in his gaze, the warmth suffusing her skin, left her immune. She opened her mouth, then remembered and shook her head.

"I didn't think you would be." Experience, knowledge, rang in the words.

His hands appeared on her shoulders, lightly touching. Then they moved.

Over her. He touched, caressed, stroked, explored—every inch of her skin, all he could reach.

She was reeling, senses drowning in the tactile pleasure of his too-knowing touch when, largely out of sight behind her, he caressed her derriere, explored, stroked, weighed, then kneaded—knowingly, firmly, openly possessively.

In keeping with his orders, she'd kept her eyes on herself—startled, then mesmerized by what she'd seen in her face. Had she always been this wanton, this sexually abandoned?

Had she just been waiting for him to be herself? For him to show her herself?

He shifted closer, his dark head dipping by her ear, even though his strong hands continued to fondle her bottom. "Put your left leg up on the chair, bend over, and slowly roll down your garter and your stocking. Leave them and your slipper on the chair, and wait for my next order."

Breathing had grown difficult; she felt giddy as she complied, couldn't think as she lifted her left foot to balance it on the wooden chair, then, grasping her garter, she slowly rolled it down, bending over as she did.

Two long, hard fingers slid into her sheath. Her hands on her calf, she froze, bent over, inwardly shuddering as one callused hand caressed her bottom while the fingers of his other hand explored her intimately.

Recalling his order, she struggled to roll her garter and stocking all the way down, to slide off her slipper, then, bent over her knee, hands on the chair seat, wait, wait . . .

She was panting, all but sobbing, nerves excruciatingly alive, aware to her bones of every touch inside and out, when he gave her the order to straighten, then he shifted the chair to her right, and instructed her to repeat the exercise with her other garter, stocking, and slipper.

It took every ounce of control she possessed to comply— to give herself up to such intimate exploration.

But she wanted every touch, gloried in every deft stroke of his hard fingers inside her.

She knew he could make her shatter with just his fingers, expected him to do so, yet even as she felt herself inexorably tightening, he drew back. Drew his hands from her.

"Stand up."

Lowering her right leg, she did, blinking as she focused on her reflection in the mirror.

More of her hair had tumbled down, a river of fire lacing over her flushed skin. Her lips were parted; her tongue came out to moisten them. Even in the dim light, her eyes glittered emerald green. And her body . . .

Was that her?

"Time for the rest of tonight's lesson."

Before she could think, he gripped her waist, spun her to face him, then lifted her, turned, and tossed her on the bed.

She landed with her head almost on the pillows, bounced once. He reached around her, dragging the pillows down to either side of her.

"Wait." He stripped off his coat, unknotted the neckerchief he'd worn about his throat. Tossed both aside, sat to haul off her father's boots, strip off his stockings.

Then he came up on the bed on his knees, walked himself

closer. His gaze had locked on her lower body. Reaching out, he grasped her calves and spread her legs wide apart.

She couldn't breathe, couldn't move. Nearly sobbed with resurging need.

He looked down at what he'd revealed. His face was a harsh mask of stark male desire. Releasing one leg, he reached down, trailed one long finger up through the sopping wetness. His lips curved in pure masculine anticipation.

He reached for the pillows, scooped her hips up in one arm, and stuffed the soft padding beneath her, raising her hips as he slid down to lie between her spread legs.

His shoulders kept her legs forced wide as he brought his mouth down on her, as he sucked, suckled, and she shrieked.

In seconds he'd reduced her to a writhing mass of wanting. Within a minute she needed—*needed*—release.

Yet no matter how much she moaned and sobbed, how much she thrashed and wordlessly pleaded, even when she sank her hands in his hair and tugged, he kept pushing her tighter only to let her fall back again, up and back, up and back, until she thought she'd go mad.

Then he took her with his tongue and she soared over the precipice, straight over that indefinable edge.

She'd thought she'd known what he could do to her, but this time she saw stars. This time she felt the cataclysmic shock all the way to her soul.

By the time her senses, drowning in glory, had resurfaced enough to be aware, he'd stripped out of his shirt, out of his breeches. Naked but for the bandages she'd wrapped tightly about his torso, he looked like a wounded god as he returned to kneel between her legs again, hooked his arms beneath her thighs so the back of her knees lay across his bent elbows, then closed his large hands about her hips.

And lifted her, drew her hips up and to him.

He set the head of his erection at her entrance, looked up and caught her gaze, then thrust powerfully in, hard and deep.

Looking down, he withdrew and repeated the process.

Helpless to do otherwise, she watched as he held her hips immobile and thrust himself into her, relentlessly plunging deep to her core, harder, faster, hotter, deeper.

The friction was shattering.

She came apart on a wild cry, but he continued to use her—use her, fill her, take her, possess her—until she shattered again, more completely and deeply and soul-wrenchingly than she ever had.

This time he followed her.

Unable to resist any longer, to hold out against the powerful, milking contractions of her sheath, Logan gasped, closed his eyes, dropped forward to prop on one braced arm above her as his hips bucked helplessly, and he pounded into her, then with a muted roar, he thrust one last time and spilled his seed deep within her.

Her body clutched, clung.

Held him.

As the bright nova faded, he became aware of small hands weakly stroking his body, gently tugging. Dredging up the last of his strength, he pushed aside the pillows, then let himself down. Onto the one female body that cradled his perfectly. He let himself slump into her embrace.

Later, much, much later, when he finally stirred enough to lift from her and, pulling up the covers, settle beside her, Logan had a moment of not unaccustomed crystal-clear clarity; in most situations, this would be the point when he left the lady's bed.

He wasn't leaving Linnet's bed.

The determination behind the thought, the innate stubbornness, stood in direct contradiction to what rational thought suggested the eventual outcome would be.

At that moment, the notion that any future between them was doomed didn't seem able to impinge. The knowledge, the certainty, that him remaining in her bed like this would inevitably lead to emotional difficulties didn't seem to matter.

The only thing that did matter was that he was there, and she lay beside him, taken, possessed, and sated to her toes.

He couldn't think beyond that, beyond the wonder he'd felt in her body, the completeness, the triumph he'd found in possessing it. In drawing so much closer to her.

That last was dangerous, but he no longer cared.

If she demanded, he would give, and would keep giving until she no longer wanted him.

Regardless of honor, of safety, of danger, that was his new reality.

Sleep tugged. Confident there was no point in further thought, he gave in and let it drag him under.

December 12, 1822
Close to midnight
Shrewton House, London

"This really is a beautiful room." With a negligent wave, Alex indicated the delicate white-and-gilt moldings, the pale blue silk wallpaper, the French Imperial-style chairs upholstered in the same blue silk. Turning to the large bed, Alex raised approving brows. "The counterpane, too. Nothing but the best for our dear sire's offspring." Regarding Daniel Thurgood as he shut the door, Alex added, "Even if we were born on the wrong side of the blanket."

Daniel's lips curved. "It was a nice thought to use Shrewton House as our London base. Might as well enjoy our sire's hospitality, even if he never knows."

"How fortuitous that he winters at Wymondham."

"Indeed." Shrugging off his coat, Daniel laid it over a chair, then bent to warm his hands at the fire in the hearth. The room had been chosen and readied by his man, Creighton, and Alex's houseman, M'wallah. Watching Alex circle the room examining the various expensive trinkets placed here and there, Daniel mentally blessed Creighton. A pleasantly distracted Alex made life much less stressful.

And their lives, unexpectedly, had taken a stressful turn.

He, Alex, and their half brother Roderick had formed a close—indeed, closed—circle years before. While Roderick was the present Earl of Shrewton's legitimate son, he and Alex were illegitimate, yet both were of decent birth and thus able to pass in society. London had been their playground for some years, but when Roderick's position at the Foreign Office had resulted in the chance to visit India, all three of them had jumped at the opportunity—and what an opportunity it had proved to be.

Roderick had requested and been granted a posting to the Governor of Bombay's staff, a position that had made him privy to the details of many of the trade caravans. Once Alex and Daniel had joined him, they'd quickly set about exploiting the situation.

The outcome had been the Black Cobra cult—a creation of their own making that had satisfied the vicious appetites the three of them shared in ways not even they had dared dream. For the last several years, the Black Cobra cult had delivered to them a steady diet of money, sex, sadistic pleasure, and, above all, power.

All three had grown adept at manipulating and exploiting the cult members—hardly innocents—to shore up, then steadily expand, the cult's activities. For several years, they'd pursued their hedonistic purposes without any serious hindrance from the authorities, represented by the Honorable East India Company. As the Earl of Shrewton, their dear father, was a member of the board, and as the Governor of India, the Marquess of Hastings, was beholden to the Prince Regent—who in turn was deeply indebted to the earl—there had seemed no reason to fear any threat from that quarter, or at least none they couldn't easily see off.

That had all changed one day in late August, when a letter written by Roderick as the Black Cobra, signed with the Black Cobra's distinctive mark but, by unfortunate ill luck, sealed with Roderick's personal family seal, had fallen into the hands of a cadre of officers Hastings had, months before, dispatched from Calcutta with specific orders to expose the Black Cobra.

Roderick, Daniel, and Alex had laughed off the officers' efforts until then, but the realization that the letter could, if it reached the right hands in England, bring Roderick down—thus compromising the ability of the Black Cobra cult to prey on the caravans, the primary source of Daniel's and Alex's wealth—had sobered them. Even though it was Roderick alone at risk, Alex had agreed that to safeguard the cult's continuing prosperity, Daniel and Alex should return to England with Roderick, to assist in seizing the letter and dealing appropriately with the officers responsible.

Such threats to the Black Cobra couldn't be allowed to go unpunished.

Unfortunately, by the time they'd learned of the letter and the threat it posed, the four officers had copied the letter, then separated and fled Bombay. Which of the four was carrying the real letter—the original with Roderick's incriminating seal, the only letter they needed to regain—was anyone's guess.

By luck and good management, they'd reached England before any of the officers.

Annoyingly, an attempt two days ago to kill the senior officer, Colonel Derek Delborough, when he'd landed at Southampton had been foiled by some interfering female.

Daniel and Alex had just parted from Roderick after a short conference during which their efforts, past and present, to stop the officers and regain the letter had been discussed and reviewed.

Straightening from the fire, Daniel turned as Alex drew near. "Now that Delborough's here, in London, and holed up at Grillon's, how do you see our campaign progressing? Can we rely on Larkins to get the job done?"

Larkins was Roderick's man—an Englishman with a sadistic streak. He had managed to infiltrate a thief into the colonel's household with the express purpose of stealing the letter—copy or original—that the good colonel was carrying.

Alex halted beside Daniel, smiled into his eyes. Whereas Daniel had his mother's coloring—dark hair and brown eyes—Alex and Roderick had inherited the earl's distinctive pale blond hair and pale blue eyes. In Alex's case, ice-blue eyes. "Larkins knows the price of failure—I'm sure he'll manage, one way or another. I'm more concerned with the others—while I've allowed Roderick to think he's in charge, M'wallah is, as usual, receiving all communication from cult members first. So while what Roderick just told us is correct, and we've men and assassins on the trail of the other three with strict orders to inform us the instant any of them successfully reach one of the embarkation ports on the Continent, the very latest news as of an hour ago is that Hamilton has reached Boulogne."

"I take it the Major remains in possession of his customary rude health?" Daniel started to undo his cuffs.

"Sadly, yes. However, Uncle—you know the man, the sycophant always happy to slit the nearest throat 'to the glory and the delight of the Black Cobra'?" When Daniel nodded, Alex went on, "Uncle and his men are already in Boulogne. At this point, we must rely on them to ensure Hamilton gets no further."

"Any word on the other two?" Daniel wasn't surprised to learn that Alex had withheld information from Roderick. It was common practice between them, keeping their dear half brother sufficiently in the dark so that they controlled the cult. In truth, they were the power behind Roderick's façade.

"The story with Monteith is rather better. Our men in Lisbon spotted him the instant he set foot on the dock there. He'd signed on as crew on a Portuguese merchantman out of Diu—that's why we missed picking up his trail at that end. He'd gone from Bombay overland to Diu and was too far ahead of our trackers. But he saw our men on the Lisbon docks. Although he was alone, he managed to fight his way out of an ambush, creating such a stir that he was able to get away. He immediately grabbed passage on another merchantman bound for Portsmouth. That was on the fourth of December, more than a week ago. What the dear major didn't know is that three assassins slipped onto the ship before it sailed. With any luck, Monteith is dead by now.

"As for Carstairs, I told you we had word he'd passed through Budapest and was headed for Vienna?"

Pulling his shirt free of his trousers, Daniel nodded.

"Since then, we've heard nothing, but he seems to be the slowest of the four, the furthest away. We can put off dealing with him for the moment." Alex smiled as Daniel stripped off his shirt. "Indeed," Alex murmured, "I believe we can put off all further discussion of the tiresome subject of Roderick's lost letter—at least for now."

Taking Daniel's hand, Alex led him to the bed. "Time for dwelling on other things, my dear."

Halting by the side of the sumptuous bed, Alex turned and went into Daniel's arms.

Six

December 13, 1822
Mon Coeur, Torteval, Guernsey

He'd tried to do the right thing, but Linnet had turned the tables on him.

The next morning, Logan sat at the breakfast table outwardly listening to a general discussion of the day's planned activities while inwardly brooding on his reversal of the night.

His foxy hostess—she of the fiery hair, peridot eyes, and incredibly fine white skin—had neatly manipulated him with her demand—one he couldn't very well decline, given it was entirely within his ability to comply—to repay her by teaching her more about the pleasures to be had when a man and a woman joined.

If it had been nothing more than physical pleasure—the giving and the taking—he wouldn't be so . . . uneasy. But he was too good a commander not to see the problems looming. They were who they were, yet . . . she might come to mean, might even have already started to mean, too much to him.

He'd known she was different from the very first instant he'd laid eyes on her—his angel who was no angel. From the moment he'd slid into her willing body in his dream that had been no dream, he'd known she was special, that she held the promise, the chance, the hope of more—that she, somehow, resonated with some need buried deep within him, one he hadn't yet articulated but that somehow instinctively she fulfilled.

All well and good, but until he recalled who he was, what he was doing, and where he was supposed to be, any relationship between her and him was . . . stifled. For all he knew, it might be strangled at birth.

She might not want him even if he wanted her.

"Stop frowning."

The words from his left, in typical bossy vein, had him changing his absentminded frown to a scowl and bending it on her.

Linnet pulled a face at him. He'd been in a strange mood ever since he'd come downstairs. "I've been thinking about where you might have come from—where you might have been in recent months."

He raised his brows, listening. At least his scowl was dissipating.

She looked up as the other men rose. She acknowledged their salutes with a nod, waited until they'd passed out of hearing before looking again at Logan. "Your hands are very tanned."

He looked at them, then slanted her a midnight blue glance, no doubt realizing why the darkness of his hands had stuck in her mind. She could still see those strong hands traveling over her very white body.

Shifting, disguising the movement as turning to face him, she pointed out the obvious. "You've been in the tropics—somewhere hotter, much sunnier. You're a cavalry officer. Perhaps if you look at maps, something might strike you." Rising, she touched his shoulder. "Wait there—I'll fetch our map book."

The Trevission map book contained an excellent collection of maps of all the countries, coasts, and shipping routes around the globe—all those involved in trade. Linnet set it on the table and opened it to a map of the western Channel. "Here's Guernsey." She pointed. "Here's where the ship wrecked, and that particular storm blew from the northwest." With her finger she drew a line from the western cove out to sea. "Your ship was traveling somewhere on that line, which means it was most likely headed for Plymouth, Weymouth, Portsmouth, or Southampton. Given it was a merchantman, and looked to have been of reasonable size, Plymouth or Southampton are the more likely, with Southampton most likely."

The children leaned across the table, looking. Geography was the one subject in which Buttons never had to work to hold their interest.

"Plymouth or Southampton—if either was the destination, where was the ship coming from?" Logan glanced up at her.

Linnet turned to the front of the book, to a huge map that folded out, showing all the major countries and shipping routes. She pointed to the relevant ones, of which there were many. "Southampton's England's busiest port. Your ship could have come from the Americas, but given the current situation there, more likely that it came from the West Indies." She looked down at Logan. "There are British soldiers there, aren't there?"

Logan looked at the map, grimly nodded. The information was there, in his brain. "But we have troops over half the globe—in many countries from which ships would pass Guernsey to Plymouth or Southampton." He pointed to the map. "Aside from the West Indies, even though the war's long over we still have troops in Portugal, and even some in Spain, and there's detachments through North Africa, and whole regiments in India."

He stared at the map, then sat back and looked up at her. "There's another possibility. I *was* a cavalry commander— I'm sure of that—but I might not be one now. I might be a mercenary." He waved to the map, indicating a broad swath across the middle. "And there's mercenaries fighting over much of the world."

When he looked down again, frowning at the map, Linnet inwardly grimaced. She gave her attention to the children, seeing them off to chores or lessons, then looked back at Logan—still wracking his brains.

Reaching out, she folded the large map, then shut the book.

Met his dark eyes as they lifted to her face. "Come and help me with the pigs. You haven't met them yet. Who knows? Perhaps they'll inspire you."

Rising, she waited pointedly until he rose, too, then she led the way out.

Later that morning, certain that no other occupation would suit him as well, Linnet had Gypsy and Storm saddled, and with Logan rode out toward the hills, then cut back to the coast above Roquaine Bay.

Her destination was a small stone fisherman's cottage nestled in a hollow at the top of a cliff, looking out to sea. Old Mrs. Corbett, a longtime fisherman's widow, lived there alone.

"She had a bad fall last month, but she won't leave here, even though she could live with her son in L'Eree, further north." Linnet drew rein at the top of the cliff; the rocky descent to the cottage was too steep for horses. "I suppose we all understand, so we try to keep a neighborly eye on her."

Already on the ground, Logan halted by Gypsy's side; before Linnet realized his intention, he reached up, grasped her waist, and lifted her down. Being held, trapped, between his strong hands, that instant of helplessness sent memories of the night surging through her mind.

When he set her on her feet, she had to haul in a breath, quiet her thudding heart.

He looked down at her, but then released her. "I'll wait here with the horses. She might feel imposed upon, overwhelmed, if I come in."

Just the thought of Mrs. Corbett coping with such a large masculine presence in her small house . . . the old woman would be thoroughly distracted. With a nod, Linnet handed him her reins and started down the steep path.

The cottage door opened. Mrs. Corbett came out, wiping her hands on a cloth. "Good morning, missy—and as there's no storms brewing, it is a good morning, too."

"Good morning, Mrs. Corbett. How's the hip?"

"Aching some, but I can manage." Mrs. Corbett's gaze had fixed on Logan, now seated on a large rock at the head of the path and looking out to sea. Glancing back, Linnet saw the sea breeeze ruffling his black hair, the pale glow of the sun playing over his chiseled features.

"Be he the one who washed up in your cove?"

"Yes, that's him. His memory hasn't yet fully returned."

"No doubt it will in time. But come you in and have a sit down—I've griddle cakes made this morning."

Linnet followed the old woman indoors. She sat and they chatted about the little things, the mundane things that made up Mrs. Corbett's world, then moved on to local gossip. As many locals looked in on the widow, she often had the latest news.

Eventually satisfied Mrs. Corbett was coping, Linnet rose. "I must be going. Thank you for the cakes."

Seizing a cane that rested by the door, Mrs. Corbett followed her outside. "Always a pleasure to have you drop by."

Linnet paused at the foot of the steep upward climb.

Halting beside her and looking up at Logan, the widow murmured, "Could he possibly be as good as he looks?"

Lips twitching, Linnet followed her gaze. Felt forced to reply, "Very likely, I should think."

Mrs. Corbett humphed. "You might want to think about hanging onto him, then. A lady your age, with your responsibilities, needs something to look forward to at night."

Linnet laughed and started up the path. As much as she appreciated Logan, especially at night, she wasn't about to forget that when his memory returned fully, he would leave. Would have to leave, because clearly there was somewhere he was supposed to be, something he was supposed to be doing.

Behind her, Mrs. Corbett leaned on her cane and raised her voice to call to Logan. "You're not a sailor, are you?"

Logan rose to his feet, politely inclined his head. "No, ma'am. I can sail, but I'm not a sailor."

"Good."

Reaching the top of the path, Linnet allowed Logan to lift her to Gypsy's saddle. Gathering the reins, she watched him fluidly mount, then looked back to salute Mrs. Corbett.

Hands folded over the top of her cane, the old woman looked up at her. "You remember what I said, missy. Sometimes life drops apples in your lap, and it never does to just toss them away."

Linnet grinned, waved, and turned Gypsy's head for home.

"What was that about?"

"Nothing." She kicked Gypsy to a gallop, sensed Storm surge, coming up alongside. She glanced briefly at Logan, then looked ahead.

Much as she might wish it, hanging on to him—holding on to a man like him—wasn't a viable option.

On the way back to Mon Coeur, they fell in with Gerry Taft, her chief herdsman, and his crew, who were rounding up the cattle and driving them down from the low hills to the more protected winter pastures. Logan hadn't met the herdsmen before; she performed the introductions, then she and Logan joined the effort to keep the normally wide-ranging herd together and moving in the desired direction.

With the fields so large, with so few fences and the ground broken by rocky outcrops and the occasional stand of wind-twisted trees, what should have been a simple matter wasn't easy at all.

They rode and checked, constantly shifting direction, patroling and enforcing the perimeter of the loosely congregated herd, urging them with shouts and yells to keep moving. And within five minutes, apparently unable to help himself, Logan was giving orders.

Linnet, at least, recognized he was, but his approach was

such that neither Gerry nor his men had their noses put out of joint. Command was her forte, yet she looked on with reluctant appreciation as Logan asked questions, clearly valuing the men's knowledge, then made suggestions, which the men therefore saw the sense in and immediately implemented.

The mantle of command rode easily on Logan's shoulders, very much second nature to him, something he didn't have to think to do.

As she skirted the herd, wondering how she felt about that, she noticed the herd's matriarch had been hemmed in by their shepherding. She pointed with her whip, yelled, "Clear her way—get her to lead them."

Logan was closest to Linnet. He looked, and changed his previous orders to implement her direction.

She continued to ride nearby, and he continued to defer to any countermand she made.

By the time they drew within sight of the herd's destination, she had to admit he knew what he was doing in this sphere of command as much as in the bedroom. He was one of those rare men who was so settled in his own skin, so confident in his own strengths, that he didn't have any problem deferring to others; he didn't see others' status as undermining his own.

He didn't see taking orders from a female as undermining his masculinity.

Thinking of his masculinity, of its innate strength, made her shiver.

Damn man—he really had got under her skin.

As Gerry and his men turned the herd through the gate into their winter quarters, Logan drew near. "Back to the house?"

She nodded, waved to the others, then turned Gypsy's head homeward. Logan settled Storm to canter alongside.

They rode through the morning, the rising wind in their faces. One glance at his face told her he'd returned to wracking his brains, trying to remember his present, and his recent past.

Unbidden, Mrs. Corbett's words echoed in her mind. Prophetic in a way; if he was an apple fate had dropped in her lap, she'd already taken a bite. And intended to take more. Until he remembered who he was, and left.

The thought effectively quashed the budding notion that, as he seemed a man capable of playing second fiddle to a female, she might, just might, be able to keep him.

She couldn't regardless, because he wouldn't stay. Almost certainly couldn't. His nighttime lessons stood testimony to considerable experience in that sphere; for all she knew—all he knew—he might have a wife waiting for him in England.

No thought could more effectively have doused any wild and romantic notions that might have started germinating in her brain. She had to be realistic; he would remember and go . . . and that any wild and romantic notions had even occurred to her proved that her wisest and most sensible course was to do all she could to help him remember. So he could leave before she started yearning for things that could never be.

She glanced at him. "Torteval—the village—isn't far. We should ride over and see if anyone there has learned anything more about the wreck."

He met her gaze, then tipped his head. "Lead on."

She did, wheeling east, determinded to find some clue to ressurect his memory so he could be on his way.

They rode into Torteval, a village just big enough to boast a tiny tavern. Leaving their mounts tied to a post, Logan followed Linnet inside. The locals greeted her eagerly; she was clearly well known, well liked, well respected. She introduced him, and eagerness instantly gave way to curiosity.

Those seated about the tables were old sailors and farmers; none were young.

"You've the luck of the devil," one elderly seadog informed him. "Coming from that direction, if you'd missed Pleinmont Point, you'd have washed into open sea—next stop France."

Logan grimaced. "I was hit on the head, and I've yet to remember where my ship was bound."

Stripping off her gloves, Linnet sat on one of the benches at the long wooden table about which everyone was gathered. "Has anybody found anything—learned anything—around here?" She looked up at the innwife, bustling out from the kitchen. "Bertha, have you heard of any pieces of the wreck being washed up?"

Bertha shook her curly head. "No, miss—and I would of if there had been. We'd heard there'd been a wreck, so those 'round about have been looking, but no one's even seen bits and pieces."

Grimacing, Linnet glanced up at Logan. "It was worth a try." Looking back at Bertha, she said, "Now we're here, we'll have two plates of your fish stew, Bertha, and two pints of cider."

Bertha bobbed and hustled back to the kitchen. Understanding they were lunching at the tavern, Logan stepped over the bench and sat beside Linnet.

One of the old sailors leaned forward to look at Linnet. "No sign of debris in Roquaine Bay?"

She shook her head. "My men have checked, but no one's found anything."

"Then seems likely the ship broke up on the reefs well out from the bay, north and west of the point. Given the direction of that last blow, if things didn't fetch up in your west cove, they'd miss our coasts altogether." The sailor looked at Logan. "If that's the case, there's not going to be anything to help you get your memory back, not anywhere on the island."

The other sailors all nodded their grizzled heads.

Bertha appeared with two heaped and steaming plates, which she placed with a flourish before Linnet and Logan. "There you are! That'll warm you up before you head out again. Wind's whipping up. I'll fetch your ciders right away."

The talk turned to the perennial sailors' subject of the day's likely catch. Logan applied himself to the surprisingly tasty fish stew and let the chatter wash over him.

He was ready to leave when Linnet rose and bade the company good-bye. He was reaching into his pocket for his purse when he remembered.

Linnet waved to Bertha, telling her to put the charge on the Mon Coeur slate. Logan followed her from the tavern, frowning as they walked to their tethered horses.

He lifted Linnet to her saddle, then held her there, caught her gaze. "If I was wearing Hoby's boots, I must have money somewhere. When I remember where, I'll pay you back."

She arched her brows. "I was thinking you could pay me back tonight."

Lips thinning, he held her gaze. After a moment said, "That hardly seems sufficient recompense."

Releasing her, he turned, grabbed Storm's reins, and swung up to the saddle.

"Then make it sufficient." Linnet caught his eye. "I'm sure, if you exert yourself, you'll manage."

With that, she set her heels to the mare's sides and surged out into the lane.

Logan held Storm in, prancing on the spot, while he stared at Linnet's back. Then, frown converting to a scowl, he eased the reins and set off after her.

Returning to the house, Logan insisted on doing what he could to help about the estate—which that afternoon meant helping the other men erect a new enclosure to protect a small herd of deer Linnet had imported to breed and raise for meat.

He threw himself into it, blotting out his frustration with not being able to remember—and with her. He hadn't liked her suggestion that he repay her hospitality with sex the first time he'd heard it, and he was even more annoyed that he'd let her override his scruples and lure him into playing her game last night.

Her continuing insistence on casting their nighttime interludes in that light made him . . . he didn't know what, but spearing a shovel into the dirt to dig out a post hole felt good.

He was aware of his wound, of it pulling, skin tugging, but as long as he protected his left side, he wasn't too restricted. His strength had largely returned to what he thought it should be, and as he was right-handed, he could wield a mallet with more force than any of the other men there.

So he dug, and thumped, and with the other men heaved posts into place, railings into grooves, and ignored the female critically watching.

Linnet stood under a nearby tree and watched her deer pen take shape. The pen itself met with her approval; it was just the right size, in both acreage and height. She wasn't so sure about her latest stray, but she could hardly complain. Constructing enclosures was not her forte, yet he, apparently, knew enough to direct Vincent, Bright, Gerry, and their respective staffs. From the respect they'd immediately accorded his "suggestions," he was, once again, firmly in charge.

He pulled his weight, literally. Despite the chill wind and the gray clouds scudding overhead, all the men had stripped off their coats and were working in their shirts, with or without waistcoats. In Logan's case, without; she watched the way his muscles, visible through the fine cotton of one of her father's old shirts, bulged and shifted, contracted and released as he lifted a huge post into the last hole.

Immediately he grabbed a shovel and started filling the hole in. Young Henry ran to help; even from a distance Linnet could detect a certain awe in the lad's expression.

She humphed. All very well, but . . . was this Logan's way of balancing the scales with her, rather than obliging her in her bed? In her view, there was no real debt—she would do the same for any man in his situation and expect nothing beyond sincere thanks—but their liaison had been established, more through his doing than hers, and in light of that, her request that he educate her in matters in which he was expert was entirely reasonable. Yet although he wanted to lie with her, neither last night nor this afternoon had he been at all eager to fall in with her script.

Indeed, after today's exchange, her earlier challenge, he'd insisted on coming out here and building her a deer pen.

Folding her arms, she frowned, as the last section of fence in place and secured, negligently swinging a mallet it would take her two hands just to lift, he walked to where Vincent and Bright were assembling the gate.

The message was clear. He wasn't going to cease his exertions until the pen was complete.

She narrowed her eyes on his back. She knew the male of the species found her significantly more than passably attractive. Logan was, in that respect, typical of his kind. So why wouldn't he accept her proposition?

Presumably because he didn't like the language in which it was couched.

Last night his reticence had sprung from a sense of honor. While she might not agree, *that* she could respect. And the more he recalled of the man he was—cavalry commander, gentleman—the more his code of honor would become entrenched. However, if *she* didn't have the excuse of allowing him to repay her by teaching her of things she, at her age, really ought to know, things she patently wouldn't be able to learn from, or with, anyone else, then what reason would *she* have for indulging with him?

What other excuse could she have for wanting to lie with him?

She felt like Queen Elizabeth worrying about Robert Dudley. At least she judged Logan more trustworthy, and less power-hungry, than Dudley had been.

But like Elizabeth, she felt she was grappling with a relationship that was threatening to develop in ways she didn't want.

Ways that could only lead to heartache.

So no. Logan would have to toe her line, and accept her proposition as it stood; it was safer that way. While their interaction remained on such a footing—a near-commercial exchange—neither she nor he was likely to forget that what happened in her bed had nothing to do with her heart.

And neither would develop any deeper expectations.

The men finally lifted the gate into place and secured it. As a group, they stepped back and looked at it—surveyed the pen, admired their handiwork, then congratulated each other on a job well done.

The lads gathered up the tools. Parting from the other men, Logan bent to retrieve his coat from where he'd tossed it over a log—and Linnet saw the bandage around his torso shift and slide.

Lips thinning, she stepped out from beneath the tree and waited on the path as, shrugging on the coat, he walked toward her.

As he drew near, he arched a brow.

"Thank you for your help. Now come inside and let me check your wound and retie that bandage."

Spinning on her heel, she stalked ahead of him back to the house.

Lips tightening, Logan followed.

After pausing to wash his hands under the pump near the back door, Logan ambled in Linnet's wake into the downstairs bathing chamber. Without a word, he shrugged off his coat, drew off his shirt, then sat on the bench beside the sink and let her have at him.

He'd largely worked off his earlier frustration, but was curious as to what was gnawing her. As she shifted back and forth in front of him, unwinding the long bandages, he studied her expression.

When she next went to step past, he caught her about the waist, held her between his knees. He examined her forehead, then lifted one finger and rubbed between her brows.

She jerked her head back, stared at him. "What was that for?"

"There was a furrow forming there."

The furrow promptly returned. He raised his finger again. She batted it away. "Stop that."

"You don't have any reason to frown, so why are you frowning?"

She met his eyes, hesitated, then said, "You're making things too complicated. Just . . ." The last bandage fell free and she scooped it up. "Just sit there and let me check your stitches."

Linnet shifted his arm, held it back, and focused on the stitches. She breathed in, steeled herself against being this close to him. *Just concentrate on the stitches.*

She examined, gently prodded. Thought again of how he must have got such a wound. Seized on the distraction. "Some man faced you with a sword—someone who knew how to wield one. Right-handed, like you. He went for a killing stroke, but you pulled back just enough, just in time. You must have been fighting on deck during the storm—you could only have just taken this wound when you went into the water. You lost some blood, but you would have lost a lot more if you hadn't been immersed in icy water."

"There were two of them."

She glanced up to see his gaze fixed in the distance.

"No." His eyes narrowed. "That's not right. There were *three*, but I killed one . . . after they leapt on me as I came out of the forward companionway. I came up to see what was happening with the storm."

Carefully straightening, she held her breath. His words were coming slowly, as if he were literally piecing the memory together.

"I didn't know them . . . I can't remember who they were. I'm not even sure I knew at the time. I can't see their faces."

When he fell silent, she whispered, "What can you see?"

"Beyond the storm, beyond the flash of blades . . . nothing." Suddenly focusing, his gaze shifted to her face. "But I know they were after something I had. That was why they wanted me dead, so they could take . . ." He paused, then, face and voice hardening, continued, "The only thing of potential value I had on me at the time. They must have been after the wooden cylinder."

He tensed to stand.

Slapping her hands on his shoulders, she held him down. "No! The cylinder is where we left it. You can get it in a minute, but first I need to finish checking these stitches, then I need to wash, dry, and rebandage. With stitches you can't go out without a bandage yet."

The look he bent on her should have withered steel, but she was adamant and gave not an inch.

With a disgusted humph, he settled back on the bench.

Logan let her finish tending his wound while he struggled to make sense of what he'd remembered. The facts were sketchy, disjointed, some visual memories, others just random bits of *knowing*.

When he added them up . . . his blood ran cold. He didn't know who his opponents were, or why they wanted the cylinder, but of their viciousness, their utter disregard for life, their callousness, their unrelenting evil, he had not a shred of doubt.

He might not remember who they were, but he knew what they were.

The thought that such evil might have followed him there, might even now be tracking him to this isolated, windswept, and so beautifully complete little corner of the world— Linnet's corner, her domain—shook him.

"I need to leave." He met Linnet's eyes as she turned from setting a washcloth aside. "They might follow me here."

"Nonsense." She frowned at him. "You heard the old seadogs—if they didn't wash up in our coves, then they almost certainly perished."

He frowned, shifted as she dabbed along his damp side with a towel. "Others might have been waiting ahead and now be searching—they might hear there was a survivor and come looking here."

Linnet blew out a dismissive breath. "If they're waiting ahead, then they're either somewhere in England, or somewhere even farther away—we assumed your ship was heading north, but it might just as well have been going the other way." Opening a pot of salve, she dabbed two fingers in, then—trying not to notice whose chest she was tending, or indeed anything about that chest at all—she smeared Muriel's potent cream down the still red, but healing, wound.

"And," she continued, doggedly stroking, "no one other than locals knows you're here. How could anyone—especially off-island—learn you're here?"

She glanced up, saw his jaw clench. Setting aside the salve, she reached for the roll of clean bandage she'd left ready.

"Matt and Young Henry went to the market with the cabbages the second day I was here—they would have mentioned it to someone."

"No, they wouldn't. Trust me—they know better than to gossip about something like that." As she shifted around him, bandaging his chest again, she looked into his face, saw his disbelief. "If you need more reassuring on that point, both lads are ex-buccaneer brats. They know to keep their mouths shut about anything that washes in from the sea."

Logan gave up arguing. He didn't have enough facts to win, or even to make sense of his burgeoning fear. His pursuers were people any wise commander would fear—of that much he was now sure. And in that vein, the fear he felt wasn't personal. All his fear was for her and hers.

He didn't know why—couldn't formulate a rational argument—but he knew what he felt.

Later, standing before the sideboard in the parlor and turning the wooden cylinder over and over in his hands, he still couldn't say why he felt so strongly, but the premonition of danger, of impending threat, was impossible to deny.

After dinner, he sat on the parlor floor with the children and taught them another card game.

Linnet sat in her armchair and watched, not the children but him.

She could almost see the connections forming, the intangible links. Brandon and Chester he'd held in the palm of his hand from the moment he'd opened his eyes, but Willard—

Will—was both older and more wary. Although friendly, Will had initially held back, hesitated to commit to the near hero-worship the younger boys had so enthusiastically embraced. But Will was now a convert, too.

All three asked questions—about this, that, male-type questions—all of which Logan either answered or used to gently steer their thoughts in a more appropriate direction.

The girls, too, Jen and Gilly, enjoyed his company, and while they didn't take the same advantage of his presence, they, too, were benefiting simply from having a large, strong, adult male about with whom they could interact freely, and trust implicitly to care and watch over them.

Children knew. Her children—her wards—certainly knew. She, Muriel, and Buttons hadn't raised them to be anything but quick and bright. Enough to be wary of strangers, ready to be suspicious, ready to react to any even minor detail that wasn't quite right.

All of them had looked at Logan, looked at him and seen, and known he was trustworthy.

And in that they were correct. He was good with them, instinctively knowing when to be firm, when to laugh and tease. When to be kind. He was good with them in ways neither Edgar nor John, both of whom were fond of the children, could emulate. Where the older men struggled to find the ways, Logan simply knew.

She doubted he was even aware of it; his reactions to the children were immediate, innate. It occurred to her that while he might still be wrestling with what sort of man he was, she and her brood could fill in many traits—all the important ones, certainly.

He was good, kind, considerate without being overwhelming. He was commanding, yes, but only in spheres in which he was experienced. He was trustworthy, caring, strong, able, and, after his response to his latest recollection, she could throw loyal and protective—highly protective—into the mix.

She also suspected he could be recklessly brave.

And on that note, she decided she would stop—she was making him sound like a saint, and he was definitely not that.

Underneath his protectiveness and caring lay a dictatorial possessiveness she recognized all too well; she carried the same trait. That was one reason he and she would never be compatible beyond a certain point. For a few days, even a few weeks, they could brush along well enough, but eventually the inevitable clash would come—and she would win. She always did, and then he'd leave—if he hadn't remembered and left already.

"Time for bed." Pushing out of the armchair, she rose, let her skirts fall straight as she fixed the children with a direct look that slew their protests before they uttered them.

Edgar and John had already retired. Buttons was struggling to stifle her yawns. Muriel looked up from her knitting and smiled over the top of her spectacles. "Indeed. It's grown late."

Within minutes, Linnet was alone with Logan in the parlor, with only a single candle burning and the sound of footsteps retreating up the stairs. She arched a brow at him, wordlessly asking why he'd remained.

"I recall last night you said something about 'doing the rounds.' "

She might have known. "I check all the doors and windows on the ground floor—a habit my father instilled in me." Shielding the candle flame, she started for the back door, smiling wryly when Logan fell in behind her. "At one time, pirates, then later buccaneers, used to lurk in the southern reaches of Roquaine Bay."

"I'd always heard that folk from the Isles were descended from pirates."

"You heard aright—we are."

"Are there any pirates—or, for that matter, buccaneers—remaining in these parts?"

She smiled. "Nearer than you might suppose. But they're no threat to you, much less to this household."

128 Stephanie Laurens

Reaching the back door, she slid the twin bolts home; as she led the way on, she pretended not to notice that he checked, then tried, the door.

Her "rounds" done, she parted from him on the first floor and headed upstairs to check on her wards. Logan watched her go, imagined her bending over the small beds, tucking hands beneath covers, dropping kisses on foreheads.

Doing all the little caring things women—mothers—did, even though she wasn't their mother.

He still wasn't sure what to think of this household, but the longer he spent within it the more he realized that for all its unconventionality, it worked. It provided those who lived there with all they needed for a full, happy, and contented life.

A safe life, too, as far as Linnet could guarantee.

Reaching her room, he went in. Closing the door, he crossed to the window, and as he'd done the night before, stood looking out. He'd thought, last night, that he'd been drawn to the view because that way lay England, but in reality, it was the sense of peace, even in the face of the strafing winds and beneath the roiling skies, that drew him. Held him.

Outside the window, nature ruled over a raw, rough, elemental landscape, yet people had lived there for centuries— possibly longer than they'd lived in England. The rawness, the roughness, reminded him of Glenluce, yet here the elements were harbingers of excitement, adventure, and exhilaration, lacking the bleakness, the grayness, that characterized Scotland.

This was home yet not, familiar yet different, and somehow more welcoming. Perhaps that was why he felt so intensely about protecting it, defending it, from any threat.

Such a depth of innate protectiveness wasn't something he'd felt before—not anywhere, not for anyone. His memory might still have holes, but he was indisputably sure of that.

Just as he knew that Linnet herself would deny he had any right to feel so. There was no logic or rationale behind his unbending conviction that he was, somehow, protector and defender of these innocents, of this small realm. As if he'd fallen under some spell—the house's or hers. Perhaps both.

Regardless, Mon Coeur increasingly felt like the lock his key fitted.

The door opened. He turned his head as Linnet came in.

Locating him, she set the candlestick on the tallboy and walked deliberately, with certain intent, toward him. She was wearing another of her fine woollen gowns, a plain, modest creation in smoky green, yet the sleeves outlined the graceful lines of her arms, the scooped neckline drew his eye to the swells of her breasts, while the clinging skirts flirting about her long legs teased his senses.

Fixing his gaze on her face, he steeled himself to hear her push to continue their "arrangement," with him repaying his obligation to her by educating her, tutoring her, in the ways of the flesh.

Her flesh, and his.

He didn't want that—didn't want to, couldn't bring himself to, treat her like that, to view her and her body as part of some bartered exchange. He, body, mind, and soul, would be delighted to make love to her if she wanted him—if, freely, she wanted to lie with him, to explore that side of paradise with him without any hint of obligation or coercion.

He wanted to deal with her on a different plane—man to woman, gentleman to lady, lover to lover. He wanted nothing, no other consideration, tainting what they shared, coloring it, corrupting it.

As she halted before him and looked into his eyes, he wanted to tell her, to find the words and rescript their relationship, nudging it onto the simple, direct, conventional path, one he'd followed with no other woman but wanted to follow with her.

He knew what he needed to say, but he didn't have the words.

Regardless, he couldn't speak them. Uncertainty, lack of memory, forced him to silence.

He didn't yet know his recent past—didn't know if he had a wife waiting for him. He didn't think he had, yet the possibility was there.

Making love to Linnet at her instigation, more, at her insistence, was one thing—something his honor didn't approve of but could live with given he had no real choice. That she would leave him no choice. But to speak, and lead her to believe there could be more between them when he didn't know if that were so, would be the action of a cad.

He looked into her eyes, lucent in the moonlight, and knew he wasn't going to like where she would lead him. Yet until he knew all about Logan Monteith, the man he was now, the commitments he'd made and had yet to fulfill, he was helpless to, on her own turf, take the reins from her.

Linnet studied his eyes, examined what she could see in his face, in the chiseled angles and planes. "You're thinking too much." He was thinking of ways to argue, to discuss their situation. She trapped his dark gaze. "Stop resisting. You know there's no point. Your obligation to me is mounting, so how are you planning to balance the account?"

She felt utterly brazen—and just a touch guilty—holding to such a line, compelling him in a way she knew he didn't like, yet that way would keep her firmly in control, dictating their relationship.

Ensuring it remained superficial.

Ensuring she did nothing to encourage him to think it might be more. Could be more. That she might ever wish for more.

His eyes narrowed on hers. "What do you want of me? What lesson am I supposed to teach you tonight?"

His voice had lowered; she hid a smile. He was, it seemed, going to fall into line. "I want to learn more—I want you to show me more beyond what we've already shared."

His lips thinned. "You'll need to be more specific."

Her own eyes narrowed. Perhaps she'd been too quick to assume his capitulation. How could she be specific if she didn't know? . . . she smiled. Smugly. "I want you to treat me as you would a slave—a pleasure slave."

His eyes widened.

She let her smile deepen. "As a female given to you to do with as you wish—*specifically* for you to indulge your most potent desires." Boldly, utterly brazenly, she arched a brow. "Is that specific enough?"

His lips tightened to a grim line. His eyes were deepest midnight. "You don't know what you're asking for. Try again—you don't want that."

She raised her brows higher, haughty and assured. "I know what I want—your desires unfettered. I want to know—to experience—what meeting those desires means. What fulfilling your most potent desires feels like."

Logan stared into her witchy green eyes, took in her prideful, arrogant expression—and felt everything within him quake.

He felt like a predator about to pounce. To be offered such a sexual feast, to have it forced on him . . . but he shouldn't. She shouldn't. Desperately he sought some way to deny her.

She tilted her chin and stared back at him, stubbornness in every line of her face, of her body. "Tonight," she stated, her tone a ringing challenge, "that's my price." Her gaze held his. "And I believe you're obligated to pay."

He struggled not to react. All but shook with the impulse to seize her and devour. How had he got into this? Every time he thought he'd be able to control her, she took another step into deeper waters—and effortlessly dragged him with her.

If he did as she asked. . .

You don't know what you're asking for.

Truer words he'd never spoken—he knew to his bones she had no idea. Compared to him, she was an innocent. Why she was pushing him in that particular direction he didn't know, but given said innocence, if he complied, even half complied . . . perhaps she wouldn't push him again. At least not along such a dangerous path.

The last thing he wanted was to see fear in her eyes, yet just a lick, a suggestion, would with luck have her shying from any further dangerous games—not with him or anyone else.

God forbid she tried this with anyone else.

That thought sealed his fate. Better him than any other. If he wanted to protect the damned witch, then picking up the gauntlet she'd just flung at his feet was the right course.

To make sure she never flung it again.

"All right." He nodded. "You're my pleasure slave for the night. You don't speak unless asked a question, and you obey every order I give instantly—without hesitation."

Her lips curved in subtle triumph as she inclined her head.

"Fetch the candlestick."

She turned and walked back to the tallboy. He flung himself into the armchair angled before the wide window. She returned, candlestick in hand.

"Put it on the table by the bed."

She did, then looked at him.

He pointed to a spot a yard before his feet. Obediently, she crossed to stand there. Cloud-veiled moonlight and starlight washed through the window, combining with the candle glow to illuminate her while leaving him largely in shadow.

He met her gaze. "Take off your clothes."

Her lips curved, and she obliged. She patently understood enough of her role to do so without haste, yet without unnecessary hesitation.

He watched as she revealed herself, the long lines of her limbs, her delectable curves, all encased in alabaster-white. He debated, but didn't instruct her to let down her hair; the rippling mass would conceal too much of her body, and he was leaving her no modesty tonight.

That was part of his plan. As he watched, he worked out more.

When she tossed her chemise aside and it floated down to join the rest of her clothes scattered to one side on the floor, he openly examined her, ran his gaze slowly over the white curves and hollows, over the full peaks of her breasts, the indentation of her waist, the flare of her hips, the thatch of redgold curls at the apex of her thighs. Long, sleekly muscled thighs, sculpted knees, svelte calves and delicate feet.

Slowly, still blatantly assessing, he ran his gaze back up, to her face. "Put your hands on your breasts. Cup them."

She blinked, but obeyed, supporting the white mounds in her hands.

"Fondle them." He gave her directions, watched as she complied—watched the arrested expression in her eyes. He debated how far he might take that tack, but the activity wasn't making his life any easier.

His gaze on her breasts as they overflowed her hands, he reached up and unknotted the kerchief about his neck, slowly pulled it free, knowing she'd noticed and was watching.

Slowly, he stood, then walked toward her. "Keep fondling." Unhurriedly he circled her, then halted behind her, with less than a foot between her back and his chest.

He draped the kerchief over her shoulder, clearly intending to use it later. For what, he left her imagination to supply, for now.

Then he curved his palms about the ends of her shoulders and began.

Linnet fought to stay upright, to keep her spine rigid while his hard hands and long, strong fingers commanded her senses and suborned her will.

His hands roved her body and possession seared her skin.

Until her nerve endings sparked, until every inch of her skin came alive, delicately flushed, heating.

Abruptly he pushed his hands under hers, still loosely cupping her breasts.

"Leave yours on top of mine."

The rough command fell by her ear, then he closed his hands and kneaded, much more firmly, more devastatingly knowingly, than she had. His fingers found her nipples and squeezed, squeezed until she came up on her toes, head tipping back as her spine bowed and she gasped for her next breath.

He drew his hands away, pressed hers to the now swollen and aching mounds. "Like that."

An order, one she bit her lip and tried to obey.

As his hands slid down to her waist, then back and over her hips.

To caress her bottom. To explore, flagrantly possessive, to examine.

The night air turned cool as her skin fevered and dewed.

Without warning, he clamped one hand about her hip, with the other reached beneath the globes of her bottom and touched her—stroked once, long and sure—then he thrust one finger into her, penetrating deep into her sheath.

Her lungs locked; she couldn't breathe. She closed her eyes—and felt her own hands on her breasts, felt her awareness heighten, felt sensation streak like lightning through her.

She closed her hands, sucked in a tight breath as he eased his hand back, but only to push a second finger in alongside the first.

He stroked, deep, hard, the pressure nothing less than an intimate invasion.

Her heart raced. Desperate, she trapped her nipples and squeezed as he worked his fingers relentlessly within her, his fist flexing beneath her bottom, pushing her on.

The tension built, soared. Head back, she gasped. His iron grip on her hip guided her as she helplessly rode his invading fingers.

As release drew closer, brighter, as her nerves tightened and coiled.

His fingers slowed, then left her.

Eyes snapping open, lips parted and dry, she fought to stand steady as her senses reeled.

He walked around to face her. His face a mask carved in stone, he met her gaze. "Pleasure slaves have to earn their pleasure." His gaze fell to her hands, still locked about her breasts. "Hold out your hands, wrists together."

Dragging in an unsteady breath, she obeyed. He lifted his kerchief from her shoulder and lashed her wrists together, tightly enough so she couldn't part them but could swivel her hands back and forth.

"On your knees."

She felt heated but empty, and deliciously, fascinatingly, out of her depth. Excitement flickered through her as she lowered herself, settled on her knees, then looked up at him.

His eyes were dark pools. "Open my breeches and take my member in your hands."

She knew enough—had heard gossip enough—to know where this was leading. She tried not to be too eager, to keep to her role of slave as she freed the buttons at his waistband, pushed open the placket of his breeches and took his straining erection between her hands.

It wasn't the first time she'd touched him there, skin to skin, yet she couldn't hide her continuing curiosity, her avid fascination. Without waiting for any instruction, she traced the length, circled the empurpled head, then closed one fist and lightly squeezed.

Heard his breath hitch, catch.

Felt tension leap and snare him. Sensed the muscles all over his body tighten as beneath her palms his erection turned to steel. Rigid steel covered with skin the texture of fine satin; such a contrast, such a strange softness.

Forgetting to wait for orders, she played, explored, learned.

Felt his hands slide into her hair, glide beneath the heavy chignon that hung low on her nape, fingers spreading into the coiled tresses as he gripped.

"Take me into your mouth."

She complied instantly.

Greedily.

Logan closed his eyes on a groan, one he only just managed to hold back as her lips slid over his engorged head, then lower, and her hot mouth engulfed him. He tightened his grip on her skull to guide her, only to have logical thought suspend as she licked, laved, then sucked.

Where the hell had she learned . . . ?

Even as she set about shredding his control, he realized she was improvising. That she didn't really know but was doing as she wished. . . .

God help him.

As if in answer to his prayer, she eased back and released him, but only to demand, "Tell me how to please you."

Opening his eyes, he looked down.

Just as she glanced up, met his eyes. "Master."

She purred the word, her sinfully wicked lips brushing skin so sensitive he felt it like a burn.

Looking into her green eyes, all he could think was: Master? Who was master here?

But then she licked, broke the spell, and his hands tightened on her skull and pressed her back into servicing him, to which she enthusiastically devoted herself as, in a voice hoarse with passion, he instructed her.

As he told her how to raze every defense he possessed against her and bring him to his knees. . . .

Realizing, he looked down, saw her red head at his groin, felt the silk of her hair brush his exposed skin . . . felt his control sliding. Dragging air into lungs locked tight, he forced himself to act—to slide a thumb between her lips and withdraw his throbbing erection from the haven of her mouth.

She complied with his implied directive. Sitting back on her ankles, she looked inquiringly up at him—undaunted, uncowed, undeterred.

All he saw in her eyes was desire and brazen willfulness.

Delight and the unalloyed anticipation of pleasure.

His own lips tightened. Clamping his hands about her shoulders, he lifted her to her feet—and slanted his mouth over hers. Kissed her—devoured her. Passionately, possessively demanding, commanding, then ravishing without quarter. As he wished, as he wanted.

As she wanted, too.

She met him in a clash of tongues and rapidly escalating desire.

He couldn't get enough of her, the taste of her like this, wild and wanton, and so patently, potently, his.

Surrendered, but joyously, gladly, eagerly.

Dangerous, so dangerous . . .

He was supposed to be teaching her about what she didn't want, what she shouldn't invite. . . .

Wrenching his mouth from hers, he spun her around to face the side of the bed. Her hands were tied; grasping her waist, he lifted her. "Kneel on the edge."

She did. The mattress brought her hips to the perfect height; her knees spread for balance, she glanced over her shoulder.

"Face forward. Keep your gaze fixed directly ahead."

His words were little more than a guttural growl. Linnet deciphered them well enough to obey, breasts aching, pulse thrumming, as she waited for what came next.

A hard, hot, masculine presence, he stood close behind her, between her calves, and touched her again, but differently.

He showed her how force could be wielded against her, taught her how feeling helpless could add a sharp edge to passion, how through nothing more than touch her senses could be razed, how desire could be honed into a whip to lash her until she sobbed.

Until she moaned.

Until desperation sank to her bones.

He showed her how waiting for his touch could make her quake, how receiving it could make her gasp, then moan. Then sob, then scream.

Showed her how passion could build, and build, until it grew claws and raked her, then shattered her.

Taught her how pleasure could flay her, how raw need could beat her from the inside out, how pleasure could become a raging fire that consumed her.

His hard hands moved over her with unveiled intent. Harshly, compellingly, driving her on. If he'd pressed possession on her before, now he gave her fire and conflagration—gave her no choice but to take it in and let it rage. Let it have her. Consume her.

Eyes closed, giddy, she fought to keep upright, to keep her head from tipping back. Tried not to notice how her breathy pants converted again to moans, then to hitching sobs.

Greedy passion again leapt high, flared cometbright, then raced over her skin, spreading beneath, then building like a fever.

Until she burned again.

Until primitive passion ran molten in her veins.

Until visceral desire was an empty furnace in her belly and she ached with the need to feel him within her. Had to fight the compulsion to writhe under his hands.

His wicked fingers continued to knead, to squeeze and explore, to possess every curve, every intimate hollow. From behind, he probed her sheath again, but purely to confirm that she was ready, wet and hot and slickly prepared to receive him.

Gasping, sensually reeling, she felt him move closer. Between her thighs, he slid his fingers further forward, with the broad tip of one circled the delicate nubbin throbbing behind her curls, sending sensations spiraling and rising, pushing her arousal to even greater heights.

"What do you want?" The words were a guttural whisper by her ear.

"I want you inside me." Eyes closed, she licked her lips. "Deep inside me. Now."

"Good."

She felt him at her back, then one hand flattened and pressed between her shoulder blades, forcing her down.

"Bend over. Put your elbows on the bed."

Her skin crawling with need, she did. His hands clamped about her hips, gripped.

She had an instant of warning—an instant for her nerves, every sense she possessed, to seize with expectation, then he drove himself into her—hard, deep, powerful and sure.

Into the weeping furnace of her sheath.

She couldn't hold back a moan as he filled her, then he withdrew and thrust powerfully in again, pushing deeper still, and her moan turned to a strangled sob.

The fabric of his breeches rode against the sensitized skin of her bottom, reminding her that he was all but fully clothed while she . . . was bent naked and helpless before him on her bed, her wrists tied, her sheath flagrantly offered for his use.

Another layer of arousal, a deeper possession.

She sobbed, panted, unable to do more than shake her head from side to side as he pounded into her, and she gladly—so gladly—received him. As she tightened and clung, embracing the fullness of his shaft as he pressed deep and filled her, as she desperately clung to sanity as he drove her ever higher up the peak of sensation.

She wanted every last moment, every senses-shattering instant of pleasure.

She fought to shift, to ride his thrusts and prolong the engagement—and discovered she couldn't. Discovered just how helpless she was as he held her immobile and repeatedly, relentlessly, filled her.

As over and over he worked his erection, all steel and fire, deep in her sheath, until the friction felt like living flame.

Logan held her in position, refused to let her buck, let her move her hips at all as he stroked repetitively, pressing deep, as he felt her instinctively clamp and cling, the most primitively intimate caress of all.

Her head threshed as he drove her harder, higher up the peak; the sounds falling from her lips were gasping sobs of entreaty and surrender.

He felt her muscles clench, closed his eyes, and thrust forcefully deep—heard her scream as she came apart, her sheath clamping hard, pulling him in.

Jaw tight, he hung on, pumped steadily through the powerful, rippling contractions, until he felt them slowly ebb, then fade.

Opening his eyes, he looked down at her. Her hair had come loose; a rumpled red curtain, it flowed over her shoulders and veiled her face as she lay slumped, panting, still gasping, her cheek on the covers as she struggled to catch her breath.

Her skin glowed like a pale-rose-tinted pearl, flushed with desire, sheened with spent passion.

He still held her hips clamped between his hands, was still sunk to the balls in her bounty.

He'd slowed his thrusts while he'd looked. He picked up the pace, worked his erection deeper into her surrendered body, enjoying the sensations of having her so open, so intimately exposed and conquered.

He stroked deep, felt sensation shiver through him, long, luscious, a lingering sense of triumphant possession.

He'd planned to let go and plunder her body anew, to finish like this, in this position, reinforcing what he hoped was the lesson she'd learned—that she could be made helpless by passion, then taken, conquered, and used in whatever way her conqueror desired. . . .

He'd thought that was what he would want, but . . . no.

She'd demanded he use her to satisfy his most potent desires.

There was no reason he shouldn't.

Withdrawing from her, he stepped back, and stripped off his clothes.

Lifting her, he laid her on her back in the middle of the bed, her body flat, her head barely touching the pillows, her arms extended above her head, her hands, still tied, between the pillows. Her limbs were still lax; she struggled to lift her lids, tried to frown. Naked, on his knees, he grasped her ankles and spread them wide, then moved between and let his body down on hers.

Came down on his elbows, wedged his hips between hers,

caught her gaze as her lids rose to reveal dazed green eyes.

He thrust powerfully into her.

Watched her eyes flare, heard her breath catch.

Then he bent his head and took her mouth.

Rapaciously, ravenously plundered, sinking deep and claiming both her mouth and her body.

Felt her rise beneath him as he did.

Felt her join with him and ride the uninhibited crest of unleashed passion, of unfettered desire.

This was what he wanted—his most potent desire—to have her spread beneath him, his to plunder, yet with her with him, an active participant, every heated inch of the way.

He filled her forcefully, repeatedly, unrelentingly. Yet even as he reached for her knees, she lifted her legs, wrapped them about his hips and tilted hers, inviting him deeper yet, luring him further yet, riding him as he rode her in an unreservedly primitive consummation.

Taking unreservedly.

Being taken unreservedly.

But as he sensed their climax roaring down on them, as the wave of release reared, about to crash, as her body clung to his, abandonly enticing, he realized . . .

Then she screamed his name and shattered, and her release brought on his own, and all thought was drowned beneath an orgy of sensation.

Bliss rolled in on a heavy wave of aftermath.

In the instant before he succumbed, he acknowledged defeat.

She hadn't drawn back. She hadn't been frightened—not the faintest lick of even reticence had touched her.

She'd loved every minute, every intense second.

On a long-drawn groan, he slumped on top of her.

He'd achieved the opposite of what he'd intended—and more. Worse.

Only one thought, one reaction, managed to surface in his exhausted brain. *How the devil had it come to this?*

* * *

He should have guessed she'd revel in the power, the passion, the intensity. She was like no woman he'd ever known, ergo . . .

Some untold time later, when he'd managed to lift from her and settle them in the bed, with her curled beside him, he lay staring at the shadowed ceiling—thinking. Of what, beneath all the heat and fire, courtesy of the power, the passion, and the intensity that had undeniably ruled, had actually occurred.

Had happened.

There was no going back.

It had definitely not been what he'd intended—almost certainly not what she'd expected, either. But she'd stubbornly brought it on, engineered the encounter, and it had happened, come to pass, and so here they now were.

Somewhere they hadn't been before.

He'd thought that being so dominant a personality, she'd recoil from being dominated—that she wouldn't like it, would draw back from it. Instead, she'd gloried in his possession, welcomed and embraced it, and him, and wrapped him in something akin to heaven—an angel's embrace. He'd thought she'd run screaming, at least figuratively. Instead . . . he was the one conquered.

The one now addicted.

She'd satisfied every dream—every potent desire—he'd ever had.

Even if he dreamt up more, and he could—definitely could—he felt certain, now, that she would happily fulfill them.

After what had happened . . . things between them had changed. Irreparably, irretrievably. He wasn't going back, could no longer step back. Not now he knew what it was like to touch heaven and come to rest in an angel's arms.

Even if she was, very definitely, no angel at all.

Seven

December 14, 1822
Mon Coeur, Torteval, Guernsey

*L*innet woke, once again, to the sensation of being filled, of being swept away, smoothly, irresistibly, on a tide of pleasure and quiet passion, of being taken, whisked high, and shattered, drained, then suffused with indescribable glory as she sank to rest, sated and bliss-filled, in her lover's arms.

As she slipped, helplessly, back into slumber, Logan slumped by her side, and felt his lips curve. His new direction was irrefutably right. Satisfied, reassured, he surrendered to the combined lure of her warmth and his satiation and let sleep have him again.

He woke as Linnet slid from the bed. Opening his eyes, he raised his head, looked at her. Arched his brows.

Linnet stared into his dark blue eyes—into the smug, distinctly masculine, self-satisfied expression inhabiting them—and nearly panicked.

She never panicked.

"Don't get up—it's early yet. You should rest." *After your amazing exertions of the night. And the morning.* Desperately ignoring her naked state, she walked to where she'd dropped her clothes, swiped her chemise from the top of the pile, and tugged it on.

Better. She could still feel his gaze—all over. The flimsy chemise didn't dull its edge. Donning her shift helped, gave her a touch more confidence.

Enough to ignore him as he rolled over the better to watch her dress.

She'd told him to go back to sleep, so she wasn't going to talk to him. Talking could wait until her mind was working again.

It was early, earlier than usual, but she had to get away. Had to get out of sight of him, out of reach of him, before she did something stupid.

Like grab him again, demand he make love to her however he wished again.

Foolish, *foolish*, but how could she have known? No one had ever told her "making love" could be like that—something that seized you, sank claws so deep you couldn't escape, then turned you inside out with need.

Before satisfying every last iota of that need with mind-bending pleasure.

Her mind had definitely been bent. She didn't think she could trust it to work again, not where he was concerned.

She kept herself facing away from the bed. Yet—damn it—she was already thinking, mentally flirting, with notions she shouldn't. Like imagining what it would be like to keep him in her life. To have him there to satisfy . . . all he'd shown her, the deep cravings she'd never known she had.

Now she knew, and she couldn't undo the damage. She would know she craved that—preferably with him—for the rest of her life.

Her lonely, largely solitary life. The life that stretched before her, much as the life she'd had to date—the one without a large, naked, entirely capable man in her bed.

Without a man by her side to share the day's burdens . . . oh, this was not good.

On a personal level, she was alone, and always had been.

She'd survived before, and she would again—once he'd left and she'd recovered her equilibrium.

Annoyance and irritation came to her aid. Annoyance at him for being all she'd never known she desperately wanted, irritation at herself for wishing for something that could never be.

Pulling a dark navy gown from her armoire, she yanked it over her head, tied the laces as she headed for the door. She was almost surprised to reach it without some comment from him, but she told herself she was inexpressibly grateful. *Don't look back.*

She put her hand on the knob—and glanced at the bed.

Arms crossed behind his head, like a dark Adonis he lay watching her.

"I'll see you at the breakfast table." Opening the door, she stalked out, and shut it carefully behind her.

Any day—perhaps today—he would remember the missing pieces of the jigsaw of his life, and then he would leave.

That was the one thing above all others she had to remember.

The one thing she couldn't afford to forget.

Logan lay in her bed, lips slowly curving in a knowing smile.

It might not have been obvious, but his angel who was no angel had been flustered—that's why she'd beaten such a hasty retreat. He doubted she approved of having her senses, let alone her will, suborned so easily.

He hoped this morning's interlude had given her something more to think about, another perspective on what they'd shared last night. The same possessive passion, but a gentler, less blatant version.

Gradually, his smile faded as the challenge that lay ahead of him solidified in his mind.

He didn't think he was married. He was starting to feel sure enough of his reactions to believe he couldn't be; if he had been, his Calvinistic upbringing would have him writhing with guilt, regardless of whether he could remember or not.

He was almost certain he didn't have a wife, almost certain he could ask Linnet to fill the role.

He was even more certain that when the time came, he could convince her to agree.

One trait that became clearer, more pronounced, every day, was that he wasn't the sort of man who gave up. Not when he'd set his mind on something, on attaining something.

And he wanted Linnet with a passion beyond anything he'd felt before.

In a few short days, she'd made him—forced him to—face his future, to understand and accept that she and this place of hers were elements he couldn't do without. That they fulfilled him in ways, and to a depth, he hadn't before thought possible. That his place there, securing it, was vital—that he had no choice but to incorporate her and all that was hers into his life.

She would be the lodestone around which the rest of his life would revolve.

How to make that clear to her, how to persuade her to accept the inevitable consequences . . . of that he wasn't quite so sure.

Tossing back the covers, he rose and stretched, feeling more alive, more energized, than he could ever recall feeling before. Lowering his arms, he glanced at the door. Regardless of what Linnet might think, he already had a place in her life, one he was currently filling. No matter what she thought, he wasn't going to surrender it, wouldn't give it up.

He wasn't going to let her go.

When he joined her at the breakfast table, he decided he might as well start as he meant to go on. After taking his usual seat on her left, and smiling and thanking Molly, who came rushing up with a plate piled with sausages, ham, and kedgeree, he looked at Linnet, met her eyes. "So what are we doing today?"

She stared at him, then repressively replied, "I haven't yet decided what I need to do."

"Whatever you decide, I'll come with you."

"I was thinking it might be better for you to rest after your disturbed night—perhaps help Buttons with the children."

He held her gaze for a second, then glanced at the windows, at the gray day outside. "The weather's closing in—the children will most likely stay indoors. I think it would be more useful for me to go with you."

He returned his gaze to her face, scooped a forkful of kedgeree into his mouth, chewed, and kept his gaze leveled on hers.

Eyes narrowing, Linnet baldly stated, "I believe we should do whatever we can to prod your memory, but I'm not sure what else we can do."

He nodded, finally gave his attention to his plate. "There must be something. I'll think about it."

Linnet bit her tongue against the temptation to reply; if he'd decided to stop baiting her—she was fairly certain that's what he'd been doing—then she'd be wise to let sleeping dogs lie.

From across and down the table, Vincent asked Logan about cavalry mounts and stabling. While Logan answered, Linnet glanced around the table, confirming that none of the others had seen their exchange for the clash of wills it had been.

Head down, she finished her meal, absorbing the conversations bandied about the table, hearing more the sounds than the words. Buttons and Muriel chatting at the far end, their voices brisk, but light. Edgar, John, and Bright discussing something about the crops, voices low, while the boys' bright, eager voices joined the conversation Vincent had started. Even Gilly piped up with a question. Logan's deep voice was a rumbling counterpoint running beneath all the others, balancing and connecting the others into a harmonious whole. . . .

She inwardly shook herself, wrenched her mind from that track. No matter how well Logan *fitted*, he wouldn't stay.

Exasperation tinged with frustration bloomed. She might

want him to remain, might want that, and him, to a degree
she hadn't mere days ago thought possible, but realistically,
she knew it wouldn't work. If he stayed, there'd be problems.
He'd want to lead, he was that sort of man, while she would
never consent to handing over the reins—to stepping aside
from the position she'd been born and raised to fill.

She ignored the niggling fact that he'd already shown
a certain sensitivity over not stepping on her toes, that he
might be intelligent enough to see and accept the need for
compromise on the who-was-leader front. If he stayed they'd
have to make their relationship formal, and that was where
the intractable problems lay. This was her place; she would
never leave it, but his home was in Scotland. And then there
were the issues of gentility and expectations of ladylike
behavior. He was a gentleman, an officer, yet while she'd
been born a lady, certainly qualified as gently bred, she had
neither the inclination nor the training to play the role of
lady-wife.

And she certainly didn't have the temperament.

With one last, dark glance at Logan's black head, she
pushed back from the table, rose, and followed Muriel into
the kitchen.

She felt Logan's dark gaze on her back, but he remained
at the table, chatting with the other men while Buttons gathered the children preparatory to herding them upstairs for a
full day of lessons.

Mrs. Pennyweather, Molly, and Prue were busy in the scullery. Muriel, a cup of strong tea in her hand, stood at the
window looking out over the kitchen garden. Pouring herself
a cup of the fragrant black brew from the pot in the middle of
the big table, Linnet sipped, then went to join her aunt.

Her gaze on the garden, Muriel murmured, "I'm not going
to ask, and you're not going to tell, but . . . you're fond of
Logan."

Looking out on the brown beds, Linnet sipped. Took the
instant to consider her words. "Fond is as fond might be,
but regardless, once he remembers the rest—the missing

pieces—he'll leave." She hestitated, then added, "I'd rather that was sooner than later."

So she could limit the hurt, the disappointment that she, and the children, too, would feel.

Muriel nodded. "Yes, that's wise. Not a pleasant prospect, but inevitable."

Linnet said nothing, simply sipped and fought to keep that looming prospect from dragging her spirits down.

"Smell."

Linnet glanced at Muriel, saw her aunt frowning in concentration.

"I heard somewhere that smell is the most potent trigger for memory."

Before Linnet could respond, heavy footfalls had her turning.

Logan halted in the doorway. "The others suggested we check in L'Eree to see if anyone or anything from the wreck turned up there."

In terms of finding something to jog his memory, it was a reasonable suggestion, but of course he'd need her to introduce him to the locals, and ask the questions, too. She didn't want to spend more time alone with him, but the sooner he remembered and left . . . the sooner this—her restless, chafing, disaffected mood—would end.

Setting down her cup, she nodded. "Very well—let's go."

Muriel stood at the window and watched Linnet and Logan, cloaks flapping, stride toward the stables. Behind her, Mrs. Pennyweather came out of the scullery, wiping her hands on her apron.

"Pennyweather," Muriel said, her gaze still on the figures walking to the stable yard, "what spices do you have in your pantry?"

Alongside Linnet, Logan rode back into the Mon Coeur stable yard in the early afternoon. The ride had been refreshing, exhilarating in parts, but their hours in L'Eree had been disappointing. In more ways than one.

No one in the small town had even realized there'd been a wreck, so they'd made no advance of any kind on that front.

A drizzling rain had settled in during the long ride back. After leaving their mounts with Matt and Young Henry, he and Linnet strode swiftly, heads down, to the house.

In the small hallway inside the back door, he shrugged off her father's cloak, hung it on a peg, then reached for hers. As he lifted the cloak, heavy with damp, from her shoulders, she shot him a sharp, irritated glance, then stiffly inclined her head. "Thank you."

He swallowed a snort. Her politeness was so thick he could whittle it.

That was the way it had been between them all day, a battle of sorts in which neither would yield. As far as he could manage, he'd seized every opportunity to underscore—to make plain to her—his view of her vis-à-vis him, and she'd been just as relentless in holding firm to politeness and her "arrangement," depressing his pretensions with haughty distance.

He followed her into the parlor as determined as she to prevail, equally irritated and, he suspected, a touch more grumpy. The rest of the household were already gathered, passing around delicate cups and mugs of tea and a plate of—he sniffed—some sort of spiced biscuit.

Eschewing the armchairs, he joined the children on the floor before the hearth. Buttons handed him a mug of tea, which he accepted with thanks, along with the plate of biscuits Muriel handed him. He set the plate down before the hungry children. "So what did you learn today?"

Accepting a cup of tea from Buttons, Linnet sat in her usual armchair and doggedly kept her gaze from the large male sprawled a few feet away. Their recent interactions reminded her forcibly of a battering ram thudding on a pair of castle doors—unrelenting force meeting unbending resistance.

From the moment they'd left the house, his attention had

been constant. His gaze had rarely left her, his awareness of her had never faltered—any more than had hers of him. That hyperawareness irritated, but there seemed nothing she could do; the curse seemed an inescapable outcome of the heated engagements in which they'd indulged.

The sooner he left, the sooner her nerves, her senses—and her foolish, wanton heart—would recover.

Disinclined to make conversation, she found herself listening to the children, to their interaction with Logan. . . .

Damn! How the devil had he drawn so close to them so quickly?

Shifting, she studied the group, and a chill touched her heart. Not only because of the happy, engaged look in Will's eyes, and the eager hero-worship on Brandon's and Chester's faces, or the settled content in Jen's—but more than anything because of the outright adoration in Gilly's innocent eyes.

She was supposed to be their protector. It was unarguably her duty to protect them as best she could from the disappointment, the distress, that would come when Logan left.

Glancing at Buttons, then at Muriel, Edgar, and John, she realized her entire household had, each in their way, fallen under Logan Monteith's spell.

Throwing a glance at the clock, then the window, she stood. "I'm going for a walk along the cliffs."

As she'd expected, Logan looked up. "I'll come with you."

"As you wish." As she wanted. Better that only she be devastated by his leaving. Turning, she met Muriel's surprised eyes. "We'll check the western coves for any further wreckage—according to the experts, that seems the only place there might be more to find."

"Be careful if you go down to the rocks," Edgar said. "Tide's on its way in."

Linnet nodded and strode for the door.

Behind her, she heard Muriel ask Logan, "Did you like the biscuits?"

Linnet could feel his gaze already locked on her as he replied, "Yes, thank you, ma'am. They were delicious," then he followed her.

Muriel watched Linnet and Logan leave, then sighed. She looked at Buttons. "I don't know. Perhaps not the right spice."

Rising, Muriel headed for the kitchen. "Pennyweather?"

Linnet stood at the top of the path leading down to the west cove. It was the third and last of the coves on this narrow face of the island, and like the other two, it was devoid of anything but the smallest slivers of debris.

She scanned slowly one last time, then shook her head. "If anything other than you and those two bodies was washed in this direction, the waves battered it to smithereens on the rocks before it had a chance to reach shore."

Logan stood beside her, his hands in his pockets as he looked out to sea. "I gathered there are submerged rocks out there." With his chin, he indicated the choppy, broken sea well out from the headlands.

"There's reefs aplenty, and when the waves are high and the troughs between them deep, they stick out like jagged teeth. They've ripped the hulls of more ships than anyone will ever know." Turning away from the surging sea, Linnet started back, electing to take the longer route through the wood southwest of the house.

Logan fell in on her heels, his eyes on her cloak's hem, his mind retreading their conversations through the day, dissatisfying as they had been. Being subtle wasn't working. She could too easily deflect any point he tried to make. He needed to be more forceful. More direct.

Silence descended as they walked beneath the first trees. Registering the lack of even bird calls—with the scent of a storm in the air, animals and birds had already sought shelter—Logan looked around, noting the relative stillness after the building ferocity of the wind out on the cliffs.

The trees were old, their branches entwining, with saplings pushing up wherever they could, filling in the gaps where their fellows had fallen or been harvested for firewood. The tang of the sea was countered by the scent of cypress, of fir. Shadows pooled to either side of the path, at one with the gloomy day.

Linnet strode on, her stride even and sure.

Further along, deep in the wood, a clearing opened to one side of the path. The roughly circular space hosted a pair of flat stones surrounded by splintered wood, now damp.

No one would be coming to chop wood, not today.

He caught Linnet's arm, halted her. When she faced him, he released her, locked his eyes on hers. "We can play games, circle the subject forever, but it won't change anything. Won't achieve anything."

Comprehension showed clearly in her green eyes, but she wasn't going to help him. He searched for words, for the right tack forward. "There's no point in pretending that what is, isn't."

She tensed slightly, faintly arched a brow.

Drawing breath, he held her gaze—took the plunge. "To me, you're a drug, an addictive ambrosia—I'm not giving you up. I might have to leave, to deliver that wooden cylinder to whoever or wherever it's supposed to go, but I will be back." He paused, let every ounce of his determination color the statement "I'll come back for you."

Green flashed as her eyes narrowed. "You can't know that—you can't say that. You absolutely cannot promise that."

He felt his jaw clench, felt temper stir. "I know what I want—*you*. I know what I'll do to get you."

"Do you, indeed?" Her tone was sharp, incisive, and as hard as her darkening eyes. "If you think you'll return here, to me, to us, after you recall what you haven't yet and go back to continue your life in England, then you know yourself less well than I do."

He opened his mouth, but she held up a hand. "Don't argue! You're the type of man who makes commitments and sees them through. Am I right in that, or not?"

Lips compressed, he could do nothing but nod.

"Exactly." Looking down, she folded her arms, took one step off the path, then turned and paced back, crossing before him. "What do you think it would take to make you walk away from a commitment made, a vow solemnly sworn?"

He gave no answer.

Swinging around, she inclined her head; his silence was answer enough. "You won't break a vow, an undertaking. That would run counter to everything you are." Halting before him, she looked up into his face. "So how can you swear you'll come back when you have no idea what commitments you already have on your plate?" She gestured. "Back in England, or wherever you've been?"

She met his gaze, his determination, toe to toe. "You already know you're on some sort of mission—you're a courier for someone, taking that cylinder somewhere, doubtless for some excellent and very likely important reason. And once back to your previous life, who knows what other commitments you'll discover you already have? Commitments that take precedence over any you can make here and now."

Holding his gaze, she drew in a deep breath, her breasts swelling above her folded arms. "So *don't* tell me you'll be back, don't swear, don't you *dare* make me—or the children—promises you have no idea if you can keep."

Inwardly railing, he met her irate gaze. He wanted to sweep the past aside, to declare that *she* and *here* took precedence, regardless, over anything that had gone before . . . but he couldn't.

She wouldn't believe him even if he did.

His jaw was locked so tight, he was grinding his teeth. "So . . . what? We go on as we have been, and wait and see?"

"No. We go on as I stipulated at the outset. In return for my material aid, you teach me what I want to know." She tipped up her chin, looked him in the eye. "That's all that exists between us—a barter. That's all it was supposed to be—all it can be." Her eyes flashed. "That's all I'm offering you."

Violent reaction surged. Fists clenching, he quelled it. Searched her eyes, saw that she meant every word. He forced himself to nod. Once. "Very well. If that's all you'll allow . . . I'll take it."

Before she could move, he seized her elbows, pulled her to him. Bent his head and kissed her. Dipped his head, forced her lips wide and tasted her.

Backed her as he did.

When her spine met the bole of a tall tree, she pulled back on a gasp, eyes wide. "What?" She glanced to either side, then met his eyes as he released her arms, grasped her waist, and stepped closer.

"Another lesson. Alfresco." He wedged one thigh between hers.

Her hands gripped his shoulders, whether to hold him back, or to her, she didn't seem sure. "Here?"

"Right here." Locking his eyes on hers, he pushed her cloak wide, reached down, and drew up her skirts. "Right now."

"But . . ." She licked her lips, stared into his eyes.

Lifting her skirt and shift out of his way, he reached beneath, slid his hand under the hem of her chemise, and found her curls. Reached past, and found her.

He watched her lips part, heard her breath hitch, felt her tense as he cupped, stroked, and stoked her passion. Watched her gaze grow unfocused as her all but instant response coated his fingers in slick heat.

With his other hand he undid his breeches, then withdrew his fingers from between her thighs, pushed aside her clothes, and reached beneath to close his hands about her bottom and lift her.

To just the right height.

Linnet gasped, braced her hands on his shoulders, eyes wide as she looked down into his eyes, at the hot blue flames flaring in their depths. She struggled to breathe, to assimilate the sensation of the hard head of his erection poised at her entrance.

To assimilate just how ready, how wantonly willing her

body was, how eager to receive him. To have him fill her and stretch her, pound into her and pleasure her.

His eyes held hers; she couldn't look way. His hands kneaded, his grip shifted, tilting her hips. She surrendered to impulse, raised one leg and curled it around his hip.

Brazenly, she licked her lips, looked at his.

Wordlessly dared.

His lips twisted, half grimace, half acknowledging smile. "This won't be slow, and it won't be short. You can scream as much as you like—no one's going to hear." He shifted his hips, teasing her with the promise of the rigid rod riding at her entrance; anticipation shivered through her, sharp as any knife. He repeated the movement and her eyes closed; her breath caught. Her fingers slid over his shoulders and dug in.

Logan leaned closer, angling his head to whisper as he pressed into her just a little way, "I'm going to take you thoroughly, and I guarantee you'll scream."

Opening her eyes, she looked into his. "All right. Show me." She arched her brows. "It's the least you can do."

He shut her up. Filled her mouth with his tongue and silenced her.

Ravished and took, knowing it was precisely what she wanted. That she would revel in the heat, in the passion and the hunger.

He thrust deep and filled her, and simply let go—let all he was free to engage, unfettered, unleashed, with her. It was what she wanted—and after her little lecture on him and commitment, it was what he needed.

He needed to imprint himself on her soul.

Linnet clung and let his passion take her. Felt her own rise to meet it, to taunt and challenge and boldly mate, to give and take in a storm of sensations.

Felt heat and desire surge and merge in a fiery wash of grasping, greedy need.

Hungry need.

Frenzied greed.

Their lips clung, mouths mating as thoroughly and completely as their bodies. She held him to her, moved against him as they raced for the distant peak.

As he'd promised, it wasn't a short ride.

But it was fast. Hard, powerful, exhilarating.

He took her breath and gave it back. She arched against him, demanding more.

Commanding more. Whipping him on, driving herself as much as he drove her.

Pulling back from the kiss, she tipped her head back, gasping, struggling to find enough air to breathe. Fighting to expand her senses to take it all in.

To fully appreciate the heavy bucking thrust of his hips between her thighs, the forceful repetitive surges that rocked her against the tree. Pinned her there as he filled her, and took his fill of her.

The tempo built, and built. She caught his nape and locked her lips on his—and gave. Gave.

Felt the rush as they reached the last stretch, the surging power as they raced up the rise.

Higher and higher, faster and harder.

She flung back her head and breathlessly screamed.

In the indescribable moment of brain-scrambling glory as together they crested and flung themselves high—over the precipice and into the void.

Linnet knew the engagement had been at least partially fueled by anger—his that she hadn't believed him, perhaps that she hadn't begged him to return, hers because he was all she'd ever wanted and yet knew she could never have.

She didn't care.

Head back against the tree, eyes closed, she wondered when she'd be able to fill her lungs again. He lay against her, slumped, his head on her shoulder, his shoulders pinning her chest, his hands still beneath her bottom, supporting her.

He didn't seem able to move any more than she could.

So she let her lids rest closed, let her lips ease into the satisfied smile they wanted to form, and savored. Absorbed.

Stored up all the little details of having him out there, in the wild. In her wild, in her wood.

He'd surprised her, yes, but at no point had she been averse to another of his lessons. She needed to—should—take all he would give her while he was still there.

She had a strong premonition his time there, with them, with her, was coming to an end.

The winter's dark had closed in by the time they made it back to the house; they'd had to wait in the clearing until she'd been able to command her limbs enough to walk.

He'd offered to carry her. She'd declined. Quite aside from seeing no need to feel that helpless again so soon, she worried that his recent exertions might have harmed his stitches.

When she'd said as much, he'd looked at her, then reminded her that *he* hadn't screamed.

She glanced at him as they stepped free of the trees, pulled a face at him that he didn't see. Damn man—he annoyed her so much by the way he made her feel.

He was looking grim. Grim because she hadn't let him sweep her away into his impossible dream. What irritated her most was that, even though she knew how futile and unutterably stupid it would be, she felt ridiculously tempted to let him do just that—just to see him smile.

Just to make him happy.

That she could contemplate such an action, even knowing it was pure delusion and would only lead to emotional devastation far worse than anything she would, as things now stood, feel, was a real measure of just how dangerous to her he'd grown.

Never had she imagined feeling for a man as she already did for him; never had she imagined that her emotions could be this deeply involved.

They entered the house through the kitchen door. No one used the front door; she'd never known why—the back door had been *the* door for all her life. As they paused in the small hall to remove and hang up their cloaks, a rich aroma of blended spices wafted out from the kitchen.

She breathed in; the exotic smell made her mouth water. "Pennyweather hasn't made curry for months."

She glanced at Logan—and froze.

He'd frozen, too, caught in the act of hanging his cloak on a peg. Arm raised, he stood stock-still, his eyes unfocused, his expression not blank so much as not there.

Her heart thudded, one painful thump. She waited a moment, then, her mouth suddenly dry, asked, "What is it?"

But she already knew.

Slowly, he returned, animation reinfusing his features, then his gaze refocused on her face.

Eventually he met her eyes, and he said the words she'd known were coming. "I've remembered. All of it."

It was like floodgates opening—a roiling, tumbling powerful river of facts and recollections rushing in. Logan felt overwhelmed, close to drowning, at first.

Seated at the dinner table surrounded by the rest of the household, all eager and excited to hear his news, he started with the most important—most pertinent—facts. "I'm Major Logan Monteith, late of the Honorable East India Company, operating out of Calcutta under the direct orders of the Marquess of Hastings, Governor-General of India."

Absentmindedly eating the curry-stew and rice placed before him, he frowned. The missing pieces had arrived, but not in any order; he had to sort them, fit them into the right blank spaces, before he could see a cohesive whole.

At the foot of the table, Muriel was beaming, thrilled that what had apparently been her stratagem to use smell to jog his memory had worked. He was sincerely grateful, yet he'd sorted through enough to know he didn't need to burden them—the innocents of this household—with all he knew.

After one searching glance at him, Linnet waved the children, all bubbling with questions, back. "Let him remember it all first. The faster you clean your plates, the sooner we'll go into the parlor. Logan can tell us what he's remembered then."

The children looked at him, then applied themselves diligently to their plates.

He was grateful to them all. There was so much to slot in, to realign and confirm.

To acknowledge.

His instincts hadn't been wrong in presaging approaching danger. He'd been right in thinking that the assassins who had attacked him on the ship were part of a greater whole, and that their colleagues wouldn't have given up.

The more he remembered, the grimmer he felt, but he forced himself to go through it all, to examine and verify that each segment of memory was now clear, consistent, no longer had holes. That what he remembered rang true.

The memory of his last sight of his friend and close colleague, Captain James MacFarlane—the sight of James's body, of the torture he'd endured at the hands of Black Cobra cultists before he'd died—that, above all, was blazoned in his mind.

That, and the knowledge that he and James's three other close friends, Colonel Derek Delborough, Major Gareth Hamilton, and Captain Rafe Carstairs—all of whom Logan regarded as brothers, having fought alongside them for more than a decade—were ferrying vital evidence to England, evidence that would bring the Black Cobra cult's reign of terror to an end.

That—his commitment to that—took precedence over all else.

Movement around him had him refocusing. Discovering that he, like the children, had cleaned his plate, not just of the main course but also of the coconut-flavored blancmange that had followed it, he laid down his spoon as Molly and Prue arrived to clear the table.

He glanced at Linnet.

She caught his eye. "Let's go into the parlor." Pushing back her chair, she rose. "And you can tell us what you've remembered."

He nodded. Hung back as she, Muriel, and Buttons went

ahead, trailed by the children, heading for their places before the hearth. He followed them in, Edgar and John, equally curious, on his heels.

Setting foot in the parlor, his gaze went to the wooden cylinder lying on the sideboard. The scroll-holder it was his duty to ferry to the Duke of Wolverstone. Walking across, he picked up the holder and carried it to the armchair he'd occasionally occupied—the one facing Linnet's across the hearth. The place that, in just a few short days, had come to feel like his.

The children swung to face him as he sat. They watched, eyes growing round as, with confident flicks, he opened the six brass levers in the top of the cylinder in the correct order, then lifted the cap of the cylinder free.

Reaching inside, he drew out the single sheet the scroll-holder contained, unrolled it, and glanced over it, verifying that that, too, was as he remembered.

It was. He'd got his past back, every last bit.

The good news was that there was no impediment to him returning to Linnet, and remaining with her for the rest of his life.

The bad news . . .

Looking across the hearth, he met her green gaze. "I have to get to Plymouth."

Eight

*T*hree hours later, Logan followed Linnet up the stairs. During those hours, he'd talked and answered questions, satisfying as much of the household's curiosity as he could. The only elements he'd omitted were the grim details of the atrocities the Black Cobra cult had committed, presumably was still committing, in India; those were the stuff of nightmares.

The children had gone up after the first hour, chased to their beds by Buttons, who had later returned to sit with Linnet, Muriel, Edgar, and John as he'd outlined his mission, which explained why he had to reach Plymouth as soon as possible. According to the orders he'd memorized months ago, he was already two days overdue.

Linnet had, too calmly, assured him she would help him arrange his onward journey tomorrow. He would have to cross the island to St. Peter Port, the deepwater port on the east shore where oceangoing ships put in, and hire one to take him to Plymouth.

He brooded on that, on the part she'd have to play in arranging his departure, how his leaving so abruptly—having to leave immediately now he'd remembered all—sat with their earlier discussion in the wood, while he trailed her to the children's rooms, propping in the doorways to watch as, exactly as he'd imagined, she tucked them in, kissing them even though they were asleep.

As was now his habit, he'd followed her on her rounds downstairs, assuring himself that all was indeed secure, doubly important now he'd remembered who was after him. He hadn't again mentioned his concern that cultists might follow him there; Linnet would only dismiss it as she had before. The best way he could protect the household was to leave as soon as possible.

Which was why he'd followed her to the upper floor, knowing this would be the last chance he would have for some time to watch her tuck her wards in. His last chance—until he came back—to watch the softer side of her that she only allowed to show around the children.

He'd wanted that memory to add to his stock, to balance out some of the horrors.

To remind him why—give him a specific reason why—his mission was so important, why his unwavering deter-mination to see it through was the right and proper course. Why James's death had to be avenged, why evil—a real and present evil—had to be defeated.

So the good could live.

So women like Linnet could tuck children who weren't theirs into bed at night.

So those children could grow up safe and secure, never knowing terror, never seeing evil's cold face.

Linnet straightened from Gilly's bed, then, picking up the candlestick, came toward him. He straightened from the doorjamb, stepped back into the corridor to let her past, then followed her down the stairs to her room.

Leading the way in, she set the candlestick on the tallboy, then crossed to her dressing table and sat before it.

Closing the door, he paused, watched as she reached up and started unpinning her chignon. It was the first time he'd seen her tend her long hair; when the mass of rippling tresses fell loose, veiling her shoulders and back in red-gold fire, he drew in a breath, then walked to stand behind her.

Sinking his hands into his pockets, he watched as she plied a brush, drawing it through the silky strands, then he met her gaze in the mirror. "Tomorrow. I'll have to hire a ship, but, as you know, I don't have any funds here. I'll need to contact London, but that will take days."

Her lips curved lightly. "Don't worry. I know a captain who will take you on account."

Logan wondered what he was supposed to make of that. Was this unnamed captain a rival, or simply another of Linnet's male acquaintances? He'd noticed that, presumably because of her peculiar status as queen of her realm, her interactions with men—the vicar leapt to mind—were different, as if she were more lord than lady.

She'd refocused on her hair, on the soothing, repetitive motion of the brush down the long tresses.

Unable to help himself, he reached out, closed his hand around hers and lifted the brush from her fingers. Ignoring her questioning look, he settled behind her, settled to brush her hair.

Another memory he wanted—of the brush sliding smoothly down, the black bristles stroking the gleaming curtain of fire, making it gleam even more.

Another image to hold on to, to know he would return to.

Linnet watched him, watched the concentration in his face as he steadily worked through the heavy mass, laying each brushed strand down as if it were in truth the red-gold it resembled.

She tried to ignore the gentle rhythmic tug, the subtly soothing, almost hypnotic caress.

Felt her lids grow heavy, seduced nevertheless.

He'd be on his way tomorrow, and although she would be going, too, this would be the last night they would share here—in her bedroom, at Mon Coeur.

No matter what he said, she knew he wouldn't be back.

Reaching up, she caught his hand, took the brush, and set it down on the dressing table. Then she rose, stepped around the stool, and turned.

And boldly went into his arms.

He was waiting—waiting to close his arms around her, to bend his head and take the lips she offered.

To kiss her long and lingeringly, deeply and possessively—as she wished, as she wanted. Tonight she was determined to claim one last lesson, and she knew what she wanted to learn.

Logan sensed her intent, her focus. Felt her determination when she pushed his coat open, then down his arms. Breaking off the kiss, he let her go and drew his arms free of the sleeves, tossed the coat aside. By the time he had, she'd opened his waistcoat and fallen on the buttons closing his shirt.

He wasn't averse to letting her undress him—to a point.

Somewhat to his surprise, with his shirt dispensed with, she pushed him around to pick at the knot securing the bandages around his chest.

"I need to examine your wound." She tugged, and the bandages loosened.

As she unwound them he almost sighed in relief. The long wound, the stitches she'd so neatly set into his flesh, had been itching like fire all day. A good sign, he knew, but he was more than happy to lose the constriction, the restriction.

She freed him of the long bands, then tugged him to a position where the candlelight played over his side. He shifted his left arm out of her way as she poked and prodded, swiftly scanning down.

"Good." She straightened. "It's good." She met his gaze. "It'll be some days yet before the stitches can come out, but you can do away with the bandages, at least for tonight."

Her hands had come to rest at his waist. Eyes locking on his, she slipped the buttons there free.

He sucked in a shallow breath and took a step back. "Boots." He took two more steps back and sat on the end of the bed.

Eyes narrowing, she followed, her navy skirts flicking about her legs, her stride reminding him of a stalking cat.

"All right." Hands going to her hips, she watched him ease off the tight boots. "Just hurry. I want you naked on my bed—now."

He nearly laughed. She thought he'd argue? But . . . he glanced up at her. "What about you? Are you going to take off your clothes, too?"

She frowned, obviously not having worked out her scenario to that extent. "Possibly. Probably."

After a moment's cogitation, during which he tossed first one boot, then the other, to the floor, she stepped between his knees and turned, giving him her back. "Help me with these laces."

He did, swiftly undoing the laces at her back. By then she'd undone the ones at the side of her waist.

She stepped away. Waved a hand at him. "Now strip and lie on the bed."

Pulling her gown up and over her head, she moved away.

Watching the show, he rose and unhurriedly complied with her orders. Settling—naked as requested—on his back in the middle of her bed, his head and shoulders on the mound of pillows, he crossed his arms behind his head and watched her pull off her warm shift, lay it aside with her gown, then roll down her stockings, removing her garters and slippers, too.

Finally, in just her chemise, the cotton so fine it was translucent, she returned to the bed, came to stand at its end. She looked at him, surveyed him with a proprietorial air guaranteed to have him standing at full attention, then she smiled and climbed onto the bed.

Crawled up it to his side. The candlelight struck through her chemise, revealing every svelte line, every luscious curve, every tantalizing hollow.

She stretched out, propping on one elbow and hip beside him. She resurveyed his body, then lifted her gaze to his eyes. "I want you to lie there, your hands where they are, and let me . . . satisfy my curiosity."

He studied her face, read the not-so-subtle challenge in her green eyes, nodded. "All right. I will. But first . . ."

In one smooth surge, he had her flat on her back, his chest held over hers. "Before we get started, there's a few matters I'd like to get clear."

Once she commenced her game, he'd be in no state to discuss anything, and she would be in even less state to hear.

Her brows had flown high, her gaze coolly haughty. But she inclined her head slightly. "Very well. I'm listening."

He had to smile, but the expression faded as he looked into her eyes. As he marshaled his arguments. "I'm not married." That was his first point. "But I can't offer to share my life with you until I know I'll have a life to share." Point two, his only hesitation. "The mission I'm involved in is deadly dangerous. Those opposing me would be happy to see me dead—as my wound so eloquently illustrates. And as you rightly foretold, I have an outstanding commitment, one I can't break, to see the mission through to a successful end— or die trying." The reason behind his hesitation.

"*But*"—he held her gaze—"my commitment to completing this mission is the only commitment of any sort I have. Once the mission is over, assuming I survive, I'll be coming back here. To claim you."

He saw her lips tighten, saw not refusal of the prospect but refusal to believe cloud her eyes. His own lips thinned. "I can see that for some reason—which I don't comprehend— you don't believe I'll return. But one thing I can and I will swear to you: If once this mission is over I still have a life worth sharing, I'll be coming back here to lay it at your feet."

She blinked once, twice. She studied his eyes, then an unusually gentle smile curved her lips. Raising a hand, she laid it along his cheek, but the disbelief didn't leave her eyes. "I value your words—don't think I don't. But I've been me, myself, for too long not to face reality, and my reality is that no matter what you say, in the end, you won't be back."

He opened his mouth—

Placing her fingers over his lips, Linnet silenced him. Stopped him from saying anything more to wring her heart even more than he already had. She spoke as strongly, as decisively, as she could. "No—this is our last night together here, and I don't want to waste it arguing."

Lowering her gaze to his lips, she drew her hand away, then boldly raised her eyes again to his. "I want to spend tonight loving you. I want you to lie back and let me."

One hand on his shoulder, she pushed.

Openly exasperated, he held her gaze for an instant longer, then sighed through gritted teeth and rolled back to lie as he had before.

Letting her come up on her elbow and hip alongside.

His dark eyes glittered as he crossed his arms behind his head. "So what now?"

She looked down over his large body, over the expanse of delectable male flesh, solid muscle, heavy bone, taut skin. Crisp, crinkly, black-as-night hair scattered across his chest, arrowing down to his groin. Where he was still fully erect.

She smiled, raised her gaze to his eyes. "Now you lie there, and let me feast."

He obeyed. She had to give him that. Even when she pressed him to the very brink of breaking, he fought to remain supine and let her have her way.

Let her caress him, first with her hands, spreading them wide to sweep over his shoulders, over the bunched muscles of his upper arms, then down over the contours of his chest, lovingly outlining the broad swath before heading lower, over the rippling strength of his abdomen, over the concave hollow of his waist, over his flat belly to the rock-hard mucles of his cavalry officer's thighs, the solid length of his calves, and his large feet, before returning, sweeping up his body again to take his member between her hands and caress, fondle, stroke.

Examine, weigh, assess.

She continued to touch him there, where he was most sensitive, where he most liked to be touched, while she rose up over his chest, found his lips with hers, and kissed, long, lingeringly, as openly possessive as he was with her, before drawing back and sending her lips to trace the path her hands had already forged.

Outside, the storm that had been threatening all day finally rushed in. It rattled the windows, lashed at the house, pelted rain in drumming fury on the glass. She heard it, but distantly, too wrapped in the warmth, in the pleasure as, finally, she rose up on her knees and straddled him, and, with his help, his direction, took him in.

Her head fell back on a gasp at the sensation of him filling her. Excitement skated over her skin as she realized that this time, all—everything she felt—was under her control.

That this time he'd ceded the reins to her and was letting her drive them both.

Her breath tight in her chest, she opened her eyes and looked down at him. His face showed the strain—the battle he waged not to seize control—as, his hands clamped about her hips, he urged her up, showed her how.

How to ride him.

How to pleasure him and please herself.

"Your chemise—take it off."

The guttural words cut across her concentration, her inward focus on all she could feel. She considered them. Eyes closed, she rose up, sank down, down, down again, then reached for the chemise's hem.

Opening her eyes, she drew it off over her head, flung it away.

Smiled down at him as she used her thighs and rose up yet again.

Closed her eyes as she slid down.

Felt his hands caress, then claim, her breasts, felt his long fingers close about her nipples.

She rode and he paid homage. There was no other word for the way his hands moved over her body, reverent and sure.

Too soon, she was panting, flushed and heated, her hair a mane of living fire writhing about her shoulders, lashing her sensitized skin, sending sensation lancing through her, flashing down to where the exquisite friction built and built between her thighs.

Eyes open yet near blind, she rode on in increasing desperation, searching, wanting. The peak was so close, but not yet within her reach.

Beneath her, he shifted, then drove upward into her, timing his thrusts to her downward slides so she felt him higher than before, sparking a furnace deep inside.

One hard hand captured one of her breasts, gripped and framed the swollen flesh. She glanced down, through her lashes saw him prop himself on one elbow and bring his mouth to her breast.

He licked, laved, then he took the ruched aureola and nipple into the hot wetness of his mouth. The sensation of scalding heat closing about the excruciatingly tight peak had her gasping.

Then he suckled and she screamed.

He suckled harder and she shattered. Flew apart in a long agony of bliss that went on and on and on. His mouth feasting at her breast, his hips pumping beneath her, he drove her through it, through the raging fire, over the precipice, and into ecstasy's waiting arms.

She was barely aware when he gripped her hips, held her down as he thrust high and hard one last time. He held rigid for a fractured instant. Then on a long-drawn groan, he collapsed back on the pillows.

Boneless, she sprawled atop him.

Logan lay there, his heart thundering, feeling her heart beating against his chest. Waited for both to slow.

Eventually, he raised a hand, brushed back the rich fall of her hair enough to tilt his head and look down at her face. "I meant what I said. You can't seriously imagine I won't be back for you."

She stirred, but didn't seem able—didn't seem to have the strength—to lift her head to look at him. "No matter what you say, once you get back to your normal life . . ."

Weakly, she waved. "You'll fit in there, and you'll realize that's where you belong." She paused, then went on, "What can I offer you that you won't have—and have in greater abundance—there?"

He knew the answers—the many answers. A ready-made family, the home of his dreams. A place he belonged. Her. Those many answers burned his tongue, yet he didn't give them voice. Other than she herself, he couldn't make a strong case for any of those things meaning as much as they did to him without revealing his birth—his bastard state.

And that he wasn't yet ready to mention. He would, would have to, but not yet—not until he had set the stage.

Telling the lady you wanted to marry that you'd been born a bastard, albeit a well-born bastard, was something that needed to be handled with care.

Linnet wasn't surprised by his silence—what answer could he give? She wasn't the sort to undervalue herself, but in this she was simply stating fact and clinging to reality by her fingernails.

In order to protect her silly, foolish heart.

She couldn't afford to believe his almost-promises.

Because her silly, foolish heart had already commited that most wayward of acts and fallen in love with him.

But he didn't love her; he might desire her physically, but she wasn't wife material, as he would realize once he returned to England. And he would soon be on his way, and that would be the end of this. Of them.

He shifted, reaching for the covers, dragging the sheets and quilts over them, then settling her more comfortably on him. She sensed an instant of hesitation, then he murmured, "No matter what I say, you're not going to believe I'll come back, are you?"

"No." Spreading one hand over the spot beneath which his heart beat strongly, she pillowed her cheek on the thick muscle of his chest. "I'm a realist."

He sighed. "You're a bone-stubborn witch, and I'm going to take great delight in proving you wrong."

December 15, 1822
Mon Coeur, Torteval, Guernsey

"I. Am. Driving." Linnet glared at Logan, then, the disputed reins in her hand, stepped back and waved him to the wagon's seat. "You can sit beside me."

Logan glared back, but as Edgar and John were coming up the path from the cottage beyond the stable to join them in the yard, he reluctantly climbed onto the wagon's step, hoisted his bag—the one Muriel had given him to carry his few possessions—into the wagon's tray behind the seat, then turned and held out his hand for the bag Linnet held.

As if suddenly remembering she had it, she huffed and handed it over. Stowing it beside his, he noted the strange sound as the bag connected with the wagon's bottom. He wondered what had caused it—what she was carrying that sounded like a scabbarded sword.

Edgar and John came up as he swung around and settled on the seat. They grinned at him, tossed bags similar to Linnet's into the tray, and climbed up to sit in the bed of the wagon, facing rearward, legs dangling over the tray's edge.

Logan turned to watch Linnet take her leave of Vincent and Bright. They'd already farewelled Muriel, Buttons, and the children in the house. When he'd come downstairs that morning, Linnet had, in a low-voiced aside, asked him not to mention returning to Mon Coeur to anyone else. Given he knew he'd be waltzing with death in the next days, he'd reluctantly complied.

So the rest of the household thought he was leaving for good, but they'd all, each and every one, pressed him to return.

He'd told them the truth, that he would try.

They'd believed him, at least.

So they wouldn't be surprised when he turned up again—not like the witch who climbed up to the seat, sat beside him, and flicked the reins.

The four donkeys between the shafts pricked up their ears, then started to trot.

He'd never been in a donkey-drawn vehicle before. Sitting back, he folded his arms and took in the scenery as they rattled along.

They joined the main road that Linnet had told him ran along the island's south coast, eventually turning north to St. Peter Port. The journey, apparently, would take three hours or more.

A mile or so later, she murmured, "We're just crossing out of the estate."

Considering that, he felt a curious tug—both back and ahead at the same time. Now he'd left Mon Coeur, he was impatient to get on and finish his mission so he could return. The compulsion was real, a palpable force inside him.

He glanced at Linnet as she sat alongside, her thick wool cloak wrapped about a dark red gown, kid gloves covering the hands that held the reins, competent and confident as she lightly wielded a whip and kept her donkeys trotting along. He was tempted to ask what she was carrying in her bag, but after that scene in the stable yard, she'd probably bite off his nose before telling him he had no right to pry.

An assertion he might well respond to, yet she did have the reins in her hands. Along with a whip.

Edgar and John wouldn't appreciate ending in a ditch. The donkeys probably wouldn't, either.

Aside from all else, he had to mind his tongue because he needed her help to get to Plymouth. That was the principal reason he'd quashed the impulse to filch the reins from her back in the stable yard. He needed her to introduce him to this captain who would, she insisted, be willing to take him to Plymouth, apparently just on her say-so.

He didn't know that much about oceangoing vessels, yet it seemed odd that such a ship would simply be standing by, her captain amenable to what would almost certainly be a rough Channel crossing for no other reason than to oblige a friend.

But he had to get to Plymouth as soon as possible.

Shifting, he looked at Linnet. "If the captain you mentioned can't put out immediately, what are the chances of finding another ship?"

She glanced at him, then her lips curved. "Stop worrying. The *Esperance* will take you—I can guarantee that. But it won't be tonight."

Before he could say anything, she tipped her head back and called to the two in the rear, "Edgar, John—I'm thinking the tides will be right for the *Esperance* to leave harbor tomorrow morning. About eight o'clock?"

"Aye," John called back. "Eight o'clock'd be about right."

Linnet glanced at Logan again. "Even if a ship beat out of harbor under oars, the coast is such that she would have to remain under oars, driving against both wind and tide, until she rounded the north tip of the island, and that's simply too far. So you won't be able to get out of the harbor, not on any vessel, until tomorrow morning."

Logan pulled a face. He couldn't argue with wind and tide.

He did, however, wonder what it was that Linnet was so carefully not telling him.

They reached St. Peter Port a little after noon. The town faced east, overlooking a roughly horseshoe-shaped bay delimited by slender, rocky headlands. A castle and associated buildings lined the right shore, with gun emplacements guarding the narrow channel linking the bay to the sea.

"Castle Cornet," Linnet informed him. "It's still garrisoned."

Logan nodded. Looking down the precipitous, narrow cobbled streets leading to the wharves built below the town, he understood why there was such great demand for donkeys in St. Peter Port.

Yet instead of driving her four beasts and the wagon further down, Linnet turned into the yard of an inn on the high ground above the town proper.

Sticking his head out to see who had arrived, the innkeeper immediately beamed and came to welcome her.

Logan watched while Linnet exchanged greetings, then

turned to include Edgar and John, who had hopped down from the wagon's tail. Unsure what was planned, Logan listened. When Linnet made arrangements to stable the wagon and donkeys for a few days, he climbed down and hefted both his bag and hers from the tray. He stepped back as three ostlers, summoned by the innkeeper's bellow, came rushing to take the wagon; once it was pulled from between them, he walked across to join Linnet and the innkeeper just as Edgar and John touched their caps to Linnet and, bags swinging, headed down into the town. Inwardly frowning, Logan watched them go.

Linnet glanced at him, then turned back to the innkeeper. "This is Logan."

He inclined his head to the innkeeper, pleased she'd remembered his insistence that they say as little about him as possible to others, the better to ensure no Black Cobra minions learned he'd been staying at Mon Coeur.

"I was thinking," Linnet continued, "that Logan and I would let you feed us luncheon before we get on with our business below."

"Aye—come you in." Beaming, the innkeeper waved them to the inn. "The missus'll be delighted to see you. She's got pies just out of the oven."

Linnet smiled and fell into step beside Henri, very conscious of Logan at her back. She always left her donkeys and wagon with Henri and his wife, Martha, until she needed the wagon to fetch goods from below.

"So is the *Esperance* putting out again?" Henri glanced at her. "The weather's turned, and there's storms to the north."

Linnet smiled easily. It wasn't surprising that Henri would be curious about what might take the *Esperance* out in this season. "I expect she'll be going out for a short run—some unexpected business to attend to over there."

Reaching the door to the inn, she passed through. Not needing to look at Logan to know he wouldn't want to invite further questions, she paused and told Henri, "We'll wait in the parlor for our lunch."

"Yes, of course. There's a good fire in there. I'll send Martha in."

Collecting Logan with her eyes, Linnet led the way into the neat—and at this time of day, deserted—little parlor.

Logan followed. He had curious questions of his own, but Linnet gave him no more than she'd given the innkeeper. Apparently she had business to attend to in town. What with the innkeeper's wife popping in and out, and the serving girls, and Linnet's chatter about the town, and the remarkably delicious pie, the meal was over and he was following her from the inn before he'd learned anything to the point.

Carrying their bags, one in each hand, he followed her down the steep streets, noting the many donkeys and the busy industry of the people all around. They descended past houses built cheek by jowl, propping each other up; all looked well-cared for, neatly painted, the stoops scoured and swept. Further down, they came to shops and businesses of all types. As St. Peter Port was the center for all commerce on the island, it hosted banks and merchants of every conceivable sort.

At last they emerged onto the long quay fronting the harbor. With mooring for ship's boats, mostly pinnaces and barges, on the seaward side, on the town side the quay was lined with shipping company offices and warehouses.

Sparing barely a glance for the many ships riding at anchor out in the bay, their masts a small forest of bare poles tipping this way, then that, with the swell, Linnet strode confidently on, then turned into the entrance of a solid, prosperous-looking stone building.

Following, Logan glanced at the brass plaque on the wall flanking the entrance. *Trevission Ships.*

He was still absorbing that as he followed Linnet through the swinging wood-and-glass doors, the glass again announcing Trevission Ships in gilt lettering, with a logo of a ship under sail in a braided circle etched beneath. Halting behind her, wondering if she was related to the owner—perhaps an uncle or cousin—he watched as various clerks behind desks looked up, saw her, and smiled, and a well-dressed man, a senior manager by his dress and deportment, came hurrying out from an office to bow in greeting.

"Miss Trevission. Delighted to see you, ma'am."

Linnet smiled. Drawing off her gloves, she inclined her head. "Mr. Dodds. And how are things here?"

"In prime shape, as usual, ma'am—although I must say I'm glad you dropped by. I have a number of issues I would like you to consider."

"Of course." She turned, and Dodds bowed her on, then, with just one curious glance at Logan, fell in at her shoulder.

As she reached a pair of handsome wooden doors, Dodds reached around her to open one. "I've left some of the papers on your desk." Dodds stepped back. "Shall I fetch the rest?"

Pausing in the doorway to glance Dodds's way, Linnet nodded. "Yes. And I also need to know if there's any cargo the *Esperance* might take to Plymouth. I find she needs to make a quick trip there, so we might as well make what we can out of it."

"Of course, ma'am. I'll bring the cargo register in right away."

Dodds hurried off to fetch his papers. Linnet turned and stepped into the room. Logan silently followed.

Pushing the door closed, he looked around, and saw confirmation everywhere that, yes, she—Linnet—was indeed the owner of Trevission Ships. The room was dominated by a large, long, rectangular central table, the far end of which she used as her desk. Reaching that end, dropping her gloves by the blotter there, she sat and picked up the papers awaiting her and read.

Setting down their bags, Logan grasped the moment to survey the place—her place, her space. A pair of long windows looked out over the quay to the harbor and beyond. The looming bulk of the castle, also built of stone, sat perched to the right, limiting the view in that direction. Velvet curtains framed the windows. The room was well appointed—richly appointed without being ornate—from the gilt frames of the paintings on the walls, to the glowing colors of the subjects, to the royal blue carpet beneath the highly polished table, to the fine etched glasses of the lamps upon it.

Numerous multidrawer cabinets lined the paneled walls below the pictures. A rather fine bust of Nelson sat on a pedestal by the door.

Hands sliding into his pockets, Logan finally moved, commencing a slow circuit of the room, studying the paintings. Most were of ships under sail. One along the wall was titled *The Esperance*, which explained Linnet's certainty that the captain of that vessel would happily do as she requested. Naturally he would; she owned the ship, a fine-looking, three-masted barque, square-rigged on the fore and middle masts and with an aft sail on the mizzen. The ship was depicted as all but flying over choppy waves. He spent a moment considering the picture, then moved on.

Irresistibly drawn by the portrait that hung in pride of place behind Linnet's chair. As he passed behind her, she picked up a pen, checked the nib, then flipped open an inkpot, dipped, and signed some of the papers she'd been perusing.

Shipowner at work, Logan wryly thought. His passage to Plymouth would be yet another thing he owed her. Halting to one side of where she sat, his back to the room, he gave his attention to the portrait—to the man who looked down the length of the room. He had a humorous twist to his lips, a devil-may-care glint in his green eyes, and hair the color of burnished red-gold.

Logan read the title, set into the base of the frame, unsurprised to learn that the man was Captain Thomas Trevission, of the *Esperance*.

Without turning, he murmured, "Your father?"

"Yes."

He glanced at Linnet; she was still bent over her papers. Turning back to the portrait, he felt a number of pieces of the puzzle that was her and her household fall into place.

Her taking in orphans whose fathers had been sailors, lost presumably from Trevission ships. And all the men attached to the household, including Vincent, Bright, and even the younger lads, now he thought of it, had that distinctive rolling seaman's gait.

The door opened and Dodds returned, his nose in a ledger. "By way of immediate cargo for the *Esperance*, Cummins has a shipment waiting that he would, I judge, pay extra to get to Plymouth this side of Christmas."

Linnet looked up. "That's precisely the sort of cargo I'm looking for. Send a message to Cummins that if he's willing to meet our price, and can have his cargo to the ship before we sail, we'll take it. And you may as well spread the word—any smaller consignments that need to get to Plymouth, we'll be taking on cargo until the morning tide. They can speak directly to Griffiths."

"Indeed, ma'am." Dodds noticed the papers she'd signed, smiled. "Excellent. The only other items pending are these three queries." He offered a sheaf of papers. "If you can tell me how you'd like them handled, I can take care of them."

Linnet took the papers, rapidly scanned, then handed them back. "We are, as usual, not interested in selling any ships or warehouses to anyone. Please thank Messrs. Cartwright and Collins for their inquiries, and politely decline. As for the query from the Falmouth shipyard . . ." She paused, then said, "Tell them we'll be interested in discussing taking their barque, but won't be commissioning new fleet until March next year, at the earliest."

Rising, she shook her head. "It never fails to amaze me that they think we might buy a new ship just as the shipping season ends. Anything else?"

"No, ma'am." Dodds shut the ledger. "That's it."

"Good." Linnet pointed to the ledger. "Get moving on lining up cargo for the *Esperance* first. The rest can wait."

"Indeed, ma'am. Right away." Dodds bowed, spun around, and departed.

Linnet looked at Logan. "We can leave our bags here for the moment. There's somewhere else I need to go before I can take you to the ship."

He inclined his head and fell in behind her as she led the way around the table and back out of the door.

Stepping out onto the quay, Linnet turned right. Pulling her cloak, whipping in the rising breeze, more tightly around her, she headed toward the castle. Lengthening his stride, Logan came up alongside her.

When she turned onto the walk leading up to the castle's gate, his pace faltered. "Don't worry," she murmured, exchanging a nod with the guard, who, like all those at Castle Cornet, knew her at least by sight, "I won't mention your mission." Raising her voice, she addressed the guard. "Lieutenant Colonel Foxwood?"

"In his office, I believe, miss."

"Thank you."

Giving Logan no chance to remonstrate, she swept on, striding confidently through the main doors and on through the echoing corridors.

Logan had to keep pace, wondering, debating. There were too many others around for him to stop her and demand to be told what she was about. But . . . as he saw a pair of guards flanking a door at the end of the corridor ahead, he gripped her arm and slowed her. Lowering his head closer to hers, he whispered, "Don't tell anyone of my rank. I'm just a friend of the family you're helping out by arranging passage to Plymouth."

She flicked him one of her haughty glances, but said nothing in reply. He released her as they neared the guarded door.

Halting, Linnet smiled at the guards. "Please inquire whether the Lieutenant Colonel can spare me a few minutes."

With an abbreviated salute, the elder guard nodded, rapped on the panel, then opened the door and looked in. "Miss Trevission, sir, come to see you, if you've a moment."

From his position beside Linnet, Logan heard from within the room, "Miss Trevission? Yes, of course, man—show her in."

"You can wait here if you like."

At the soft whisper, Logan looked down into Linnet's green eyes. "Not a chance."

She inclined her head. "In that case, just let me do the talking." To the guard, she said, "He's with me."

The guard obligingly held the door for them both. Following Linnet through, Logan swiftly scanned the room, then focused on the two occupants.

The elder, Foxwood judging by his uniform's insignia, was lumbering genially to his feet behind a substantial, exceedingly messy desk. Logan instantly pegged him as a career soldier, sent there to see out his last years. The second man, a youthful captain, clearly Foxwood's aide, stood to one side of the desk, his openly eager and appreciative gaze fixed on Linnet.

As Linnet halted before the desk, Logan grimly took up station at her shoulder, between her and the overeager captain. What the devil was she doing there?

Nodding amiably, Linnet extended her hand. "Good morning, Foxwood." She ignored the captain.

Beaming, Foxwood reached over the desk to clasp her hand in both of his. "Delighted as always, my dear. Please, do have a seat."

Foxwood sent an inquiring gaze at Logan. Mindful of Linnet's instructions, he didn't respond.

Neither did she. "No, thank you. I merely dropped by to inform you that the *Esperance* will be putting out tomorrow morning, bound for Plymouth. A quick round trip, but as there's cargo to be delivered, and possibly to be brought back, it might be a few days before she returns."

"Indeed, my dear? I wouldn't have thought the weather . . ." Foxwood trailed off, smiled. "But you would know more about such matters than I, so I'll wish you Godspeed and safe journey."

Linnet inclined her head, briskly took her leave—still ignoring the all-but-adoring young captain—then turned and led the way out. Puzzled, with a polite nod to Foxwood, Logan followed her.

He waited until they were out of the castle to ask, "What was that about?"

"Preserving the courtesies."

After a moment, he asked, "What is there in this that I'm missing?"

She cast him a sidelong glance. "You need to get to Plymouth—I'm arranging it. Don't rock my boat."

Somewhat grimly, increasingly convinced he was not in possession of all the relevant facts but unable to guess what it was he didn't know, he followed her back to the Trevission offices, where he reclaimed their bags and Dodds gave her an update on cargo both for the run to Plymouth and the return trip, then, once again, they walked out onto the quay. This time Linnet turned left.

Hefting their bags, he followed. When he'd picked up her bag, he'd again felt the shift of something very like a scabbarded sword. It was an item with which he was so familiar that his senses immediately identified it. Had the bag belonged to any other female, he would have dismissed the notion as nonsensical and asked what it was that had confused his senses . . . only this was Linnet, and he didn't think his senses were confused.

His gaze locked on her back, he was trying to think of some innocent way to phrase his query—something that wouldn't result in her tartly telling him that what she chose to carry was none of his business—when his feet hit the thick wooden planks of the wharf.

He looked around, surveying the vessels, most of which were anchored out in the harbor. He searched for the ship in the picture, but many of the ships were three-masted barques, and the painting had been from too great a distance to provide identifying details.

Linnet continued to stride along. He was about to ask her to point out the *Esperance* when two sailors leaning on the side of a vessel hailed her—not as Miss Trevission but as something else Trevission. With the quickening breeze whipping their words away, Logan didn't catch what title they'd used, but Linnet smiled and raised her hand. And continued marching on, briskly turning left to continue down a pier along which several larger vessels were berthed.

The pier was busy, with sailors and navvies loading and unloading holds. Several more sailors saw Linnet and waved, but none again hailed her. At her heels, Logan realized she had to be making for the last ship in the line. Looking ahead, he saw a sleek, undoubtedly swift three-masted barque that, from the activity on deck, had come in to the pier only minutes before.

Sure enough, when they stepped free of the chaos before the ship one berth in, and into the relatively clear space alongside the sleek barque, he saw the name stenciled on the prow—it was indeed the *Esperance*.

The name, he knew, meant "hope" and "expectation" in French, the base language of Guernais, the patois of the island. Linnet strode straight for the gangplank; he followed, trusting her to lead him safely while his gaze drank in the sight of her ship.

Like her owner, the ship was a beauty. Not new—all the woodwork had gained that glowing patina of lovingly tended oak—yet she was clearly designed for both power and speed. With lines more pared down, more sculpted, than the other barques around her, she sat lightly on the waves, gracefully riding the harbor swell, a princess among the bourgeoisie.

Very like her owner.

Linnet swung onto the gangplank and climbed swiftly up, not even bothering to reach for the rope rail. Closing the distance between them, Logan was directly behind her when, without waiting for any assistance, she jumped lightly down to the deck.

"Ahoy, Capt'n!" A large sailor dropped down the ladder from the stern deck and snapped off a jaunty salute.

For an instant, everything in Logan stilled, then he stepped, slowly, down to the deck, and turned to stare at Linnet.

Who, ignoring him, returned the salute. "Good afternoon, Mr. Griffiths."

"Indeed it is, ma'am, if what I hear is true." Griffiths halted before her, beaming fit to burst. "Welcome aboard, ma'am. Edgar and John seem to think we're off somewhere."

∽ Nine ∼

ogan stared at Linnet in increasing horror as she grinned at Griffiths.

"Yes, we're heading out." She waved at Logan. "Major Monteith must reach Plymouth urgently, and I've volunteered to take him."

She started toward the rear hatch; Griffiths fell in beside her. Logan followed, still struggling to take it in—feeling very much as if he'd been hit over the head again.

"We'll go out on the morning tide," Linnet continued. "Please summon the crew and have everything made ready. And Dodds said Cummins has cargo for us to take, and there may be more as well. If they have it here in time to load before the tide turns, I've agreed to take it—I told Dodds to have the merchants report direct to you."

"Aye, ma'am. We'll have all ready to sail on the tide." From the corner of his eye, Griffiths was eyeing Logan in the same measuring manner as Edgar, John, and the men at the house had.

"Excellent." Pausing by the companionway hatch, Linnet glanced at Logan. "Major Monteith will have the cabin next to mine. We'll be spending the night on board. Tell Jimmy and Cook we'll have dinner in my cabin." She turned to go down.

"One moment." Logan was still grappling with the news that Linnet—*Linnet*—was the captain of the *Esperance*, but . . . he fixed his gaze on her face as she turned back, brows rising a touch haughtily. "There's something I intended to tell the captain—whichever captain you inveigled to ferry me across the Channel." Apparently her; every instinct rebeled at the thought. His lips thinned. "It's possible we'll meet resistance somewhere between here and Plymouth."

She frowned. "From the cultists chasing you?"

"They're not skilled sailors, but they have deep pockets, enough to hire captains and crews who can sail and are willing to engage, even with a peaceable vessel." He glanced at Griffiths, who he took to be her first mate. "You can't count on them behaving rationally—they're dangerous because you simply can't predict to what extent they'll go to seize what they want."

"And they want you?" Griffiths asked, eyes narrowing.

"They want the document I'm carrying," Logan replied. "It's crucial evidence to bring down a villain—an Englishman who's been wreaking havoc in India—and he, of course, doesn't want it to reach the authorities."

Griffiths snorted, looked at Linnet. "Well, he won't catch the *Esperance*, that's for certain."

She nodded. "Give the orders and have the crew armed and ready to sail by dawn. We'll put out the instant the tide turns—the others will give way to us. What winds are expected?"

"For Plymouth, fair. We should be able to catch a good breeze once we're round the point."

"Good." Linnet stepped through the hatch. "I'll be below. Make sure the others report as they come aboard—from the sounds of it, we'll want a full complement for this trip."

"Aye, Cap'n."

Logan stood and watched her descend. He wanted to put a halt to the insanity; just the thought of her facing cultists made his gut clench sickeningly. But . . . how to do that without trampling on her toes—or, worse, her pride? Still wrestling with the ramifications of this latest twist in who and what she was, feeling strangely helpless as if awash on a tide he couldn't control, he hoisted their bags and followed her down the narrow stairs, then along the tight corridor to the cabin door through which she'd passed.

Ducking, he stepped through the open door. Filling the space across the stern, the cabin was large and, like her office on the quay, beautifully appointed, all polished oak paneling and furniture, the latter anchored to the floor. To one side stood a desk, with an admiral's chair behind it and two smaller chairs facing it. In the center of the room was a round table, with bench seats attached, while in the far corner a good-sized bed was built out from the wall, with storage below and racks above. A sea chest sat at the foot of the bed, with an armoire along the wall, while the inner wall played host to a built-in washstand with every necessary amenity.

A lamp was set into the table's center; there were holders for cups and candlesticks at suitable positions around the room.

It was the best, most comfortable cabin Logan had ever seen.

Tossing her cloak on the bed, Linnet started pulling pins from her hair. "Shut the door—and I'll have my bag."

Pushing the door closed, Logan set down his bag, then crossed the cabin and put hers on the bed. With her hair loose, tumbling about her shoulders, she set her pins down, opened the bag, rummaged inside, and drew out a long-sleeved white shirt. Nudging Logan aside, she went to the sea chest—from there she pulled out a pair of leather breeches, a waistcoat, and a coat.

Logan blinked. When she tossed the clothes on the bed, he reached out and touched the breeches—and found the fawn leather butter-soft. The image taking shape in his mind did not bode well. "Linnet—"

"Help me with these laces." She gave him her back.

He frowned. Muttered, "This must be what King Canute felt like."

"What?"

"Never mind." He swiftly undid the laces while evaluating his options. "Linnet—I appreciate all you've done and are doing for me, but . . ." Having freed the laces, he stepped back, sat on one of the bench seats, his back to the table. Leaned his forearms on his thighs and clasped his hands the better to keep them from her. Locking his gaze on her face as she glanced inquiringly at him, he said, "Frankly, I'd be much happier getting some other ship."

She considered him for a moment, then smiled, almost secretively, and stripped off her gown. "No, you wouldn't be. Happier, that is. Let me tell you why."

He frowned, found himself watching in curious fascination as she pulled off her shift, then, drawing a long linen band from her bag, set about binding her breasts. He knew women sometimes did that, for hard riding or similar violent exercise . . . shaking off the distraction, he forced his gaze back to her face. Recalled her last words. "So tell me."

Her faint smile suggested she knew very well to where his mind had wandered. But then she grew serious. "At this moment, completing your mission is your highest priority, and rightly so. It's important—the outcome will be far-reaching, affecting many lives in a positive way. The choices you make must be those that give your mission the best chance of succeeding—and if that means you must put personal feelings aside, then that's what you'll do." Tying off the band beneath her left breast, she met his eyes. "You're that sort of man."

Lips thinning, he couldn't disagree, but . . . "Be that as it may, there's plenty of ships in the harbor here, and surely one of them—"

"No." She pulled on the shirt; it billowed about her slender arms. Settling the neckline, then lacing it, she continued, "Of all the ships in the harbor, the *Esperance* represents your best chance by far of reaching Plymouth safely." Toeing off her half boots, she picked up the soft breeches and stepped into them. Tucking in the long tails of the shirt, she buttoned the waistband. "And contrary to what you're imagining, the prospect of pursuit and attack, of action, only makes that more so."

Logan felt adrift, cut free of the moment again. The soft leather clung lovingly to her long legs. As she shrugged into the waistcoat, buttoned it, then pulled on the loose captain's coat, all he could think was that the masculine attire only made her look more intensely feminine.

More blatantly female.

Also more dangerous.

"We have superior capability, unmatched speed, and a highly experienced crew." She went to the armoire, reached inside, and drew out a pair of long boots. Pausing to button the closures at the ends of the breeches' legs, she glanced at him. "Believe me, if that weren't so, if I didn't believe the *Esperance* was the best ship for your mission . . ."

Stepping into the boots—high boots in gleaming black leather that reached above her knees—she tugged and stamped, then, straightening, looked him in the eye. "If I didn't know the *Esperance* was the safest ship for you to take, I'd set aside my own feelings and find you the best ship and captain, and twist his arm to make him take you instead."

Reaching up, Linnet parted her hair, then set about swiftly plaiting it. "As matters stand, however, you're going to have to accept that, in this, I know best, and, judged on all the criteria that matter, the *Esperance* is the best ship to take you and your letter to Plymouth."

Eyes narrowed, his face like stone, Logan sat and watched her; she could all but see him searching for a way to counter her arguments. Tying off her braids, she walked to the small mirror set in the armoire door and wound the plaits coronet-style about her head, then set about pinning them.

In the mirror, she glanced at Logan, studied his face.

She'd known he'd be difficult over her being there, captaining the ship, which was why she'd avoided telling him, had been careful to let no hint fall prematurely. Yet she'd told him the truth; the *Esperance* with her at the helm was his best chance of reaching Plymouth safely—there was not one soul on Guernsey who wouldn't tell him the same.

Of course, she'd yet to divulge the most pertinent peculiarity of the *Esperance*, the one that sealed the argument beyond doubt, but some niggling need wanted him to accept her word, her judgment—to understand and acknowledge that in this arena she not only knew best but was also commander enough to make the right decision with regard to his mission and his safety. Her decision to take him on the *Esperance* was based on what was right, what should be, not on a personal whim.

Her hair secure, she reached into the armoire and retrieved her captain's hat with its jaunty cockade, then returned to the bed to pull a kerchief from her bag and knot it about her throat.

Then she reached into her bag and drew out her sheathed cutlass.

Instantly sensed Logan's tension jump.

"Yes, I can use it." Pushing back her coat, she slung the leather belt about her hips. Buckling it, she looked up and met Logan's eyes. "How do you think I could read your wound so accurately? I was right, wasn't I?"

The question distracted him, diverted his attention as he thought back, then, with obvious reluctance, lips tightening, he nodded. "Yes."

A tap on the door had them both glancing that way. "Come!" she called.

The door opened and her cabin boy, Jimmy, poked his head around it. "All right here, Capt'n?"

"Yes." She could never keep back her smile, not with Jimmy. "How's things above?"

"All hands have reported for duty. Mr. Griffiths has everyone scurrying. Truth is, we'd'a been ready to sail tonight if the tides were right, but they aren't, so we'll just have to wait 'til tomorra, but we're all keen as ever to get out. Wasn't expecting any adventure this late in the year—like a Christmas present, it is."

"I dare say." Jimmy had been throwing curious glances at Logan. Linnet waved at him. "This is Major Monteith, and he, or more correctly his mission, is the reason we're doing this dash to Plymouth, so it's he you should thank."

Jimmy grinned at Logan, bobbed his head. "Major. You won't hear any grumbles from the crew. It's a pleasure to be of service."

Logan, not quite succeeding in keeping his lips straight, inclined his head. "Pleased to be of service in return."

"Jimmy—the major will use the cabin next door, and we'll dine here this evening. Usual time. And now . . ." Collecting Logan with her gaze, Linnet picked up her hat and started for the door. "I'm going to do a round of the decks."

Logan followed her up, trailed her as she circled the decks. Listened as sailor after sailor hailed her as "Capt'n," the light in their eyes, the expressions on their faces, testifying to their eagerness and the respect and confidence they had in her as their leader. He'd seen successful generals who'd inspired less devotion.

And the more he listened to her question each man about his family, about his home or whichever of the island's small communities he hailed from, the more he saw of her eagle eye and her attention to detail, the more he heard of her quick, decisive orders, the more he understood that, even if she'd in some ways inherited the rank from her father, the respect that came with it in such abundance was something she herself had gained.

Yet just how that had come about—how she had risen to fill such a position in such a way—mystified him.

He got no real chance to pursue the issue when, with night shrouding the now quiet ship, they repaired to her cabin to sit around her table and dine; Jimmy was constantly in and out, often standing to attention behind Linnet's chair and chatting nineteen to the dozen, mostly filling Linnet in on the latest gossip among the crew.

Logan quickly realized that Jimmy saw no need to censor the subjects on which he reported on the grounds Linnet was female.

The more Logan thought of it, the more he suspected that her crew saw her as . . . not male, definitely not that, but as a different category of female, one demonstrably capable of leading them.

Her comparisons between herself and Queen Elizabeth seemed even more apt.

After dinner, he followed her up on deck, again trailing behind her as in the weak moonlight she checked this rope, that furled sail. Finding themselves at last alone, he murmured, "I thought sailors were superstitious about having women on board."

She laughed. Reaching the prow, she swung around, hitched a hip on a coil of rope, and looked up at him. Studied him through the shadows, then faintly smiled. "Most of the crew, certainly those years older than I, have sailed with me since I was a child. The *Esperance* usually does relatively short trips, so my father often brought me along." She glanced around, affection in her face. "I ran wild on this ship as a toddler, as a young girl. And from when my mother died—I was eleven at the time—I sailed on every voyage." She met his eyes. "I was even on board when we assisted with the evacuation at Corunna."

Logan shifted to lean against the side, studying her in return. "So you were a seaman's brat, and when your father died, you inherited his captaincy?"

"More or less. The rank is, of course, honorary, but you won't find anyone in Guernsey quibbling." Her lips twisted wryly. "Just as no one, not any harbor master here or in England, or even in France, or any other maritime authority, would question my right to take the helm even though, as a female, I can't hold a master's ticket." She tipped her head back along the ship. "There's two others aboard with master's tickets who could captain the ship, but they're content to leave that to me. Experience tells, and on the sea there's much less tolerance of mistakes."

How far had she ranged? Had she seen any naval actions? How much time did she spend aboard in any year? Did the *Esperance* ever put to sea without her? Logan asked his questions and she answered, directly, honestly.

The confirmation that she had seen real action, that yes, she'd wielded her cutlass and killed when necessary, was both reassurance and horror combined, although the information that she'd carried her sword for more than a decade provided some relief.

By the time his curiosity was satisfied, he had a much better understanding of who she was, and how she had come to be Captain L. Trevission, owner and captain of the *Esperance*.

As those mounting the nightwatch came up on deck, Linnet rose, quirked a brow at Logan. "Are you feeling more resigned to letting me take you to Plymouth?"

He looked at her for a moment, as if only then realizing that easing his mind had been her intention, then he looked across the deck to where most of the other larger ships dipped and swayed in the weak moonlight. "I suppose I am." He looked back at her. "If you're the fastest, the surest . . . then I suspect I should stop arguing and thank you."

Lips curving, she inclined her head regally. "Indeed." Glancing pointedly at the men on watch, she looked at him, smiled. "You can thank me below."

She led the way, feeling deliciously brazen. He pushed away from the side and followed without a word. Down the companionway stairs, along the narrow corridor and into her cabin.

He shut the door, turned, and she was on him, stretching up, winding her arms about his neck and pushing him back against the wooden panel. She pressed her lips to his, felt his hands fasten about her waist. She kissed him boldly, determined to keep the reins, to remain in control, to have him offer his thanks under her direction.

This was their last night together. Her last night with him, almost certainly forever. She would do her duty and get him to Plymouth tomorrow; by the time night fell again, he would be gone from her life. She was sure that was the way fate would have their liaison end—he would go, and she would never see him again.

Blindly reaching with one hand, she fumbled, found the bolt on the door, and slid it home. Then she framed Logan's face and kissed him, kissed him with all the passion he'd shown her she harbored in her soul.

How? Where? She was struggling to think when, in the blink of an eye, in one surging heartbeat, he took over the kiss.

Simply filched the reins from her grasp—as he hadn't that morning in the stable yard.

As he steered her back, back, until the back of her thighs hit the edge of her desk, she fought to regain the ascendancy, their battlefield the ravenous mating of mouths their simple kiss had become—but there he held the upper hand. Experience told.

Wrenching back from the kiss, eyes closed, she tipped her head back, gasped, "My ship. I'm captain here."

"But I'm the captain's lover." As if to prove the point, he closed one hard hand possessively over her bound breast, palpating, then rubbing his thumb over her tightly furled nipple. "Regardless"—wrapping his other hand about her thigh, he eased her hips up and back onto the desktop— "last night was yours." He caught her gaze, boldly pushed his hand between her thighs and through the buttery soft leather, rubbed her there. "Tonight's mine. Tonight I get to dictate. Tonight I get to have you my way."

His head swooped and his lips came down on hers and he captured her again, captured her wits and her senses and waltzed them into the fire.

Into the heat she'd come to know so well, into the flames she'd learned to delight in. One hand at her breast, the other working between her thighs, he pushed her on until she was panting and desperate, then he flicked open the buttons at her waist, worked his hand inside her breeches, and his fingers found her. Stroked, then delved, then penetrated her.

His tongue filling her mouth, his hand at her breast, his fingers buried in her body, he sent her spinning, dizzyingly rapidly, over the edge into ecstasy.

Wits whirling, she slumped back, bracing her arms on the desk behind her. Eyes closed, head hanging back, she struggled to breathe, to think, to anticipate. Yet as he drew his fingers slowly from her sheath, all she could think about was having him replace them with his erection. She wanted that, ached for it, as if she were hollow inside. But how? Where? Her breeches were too tight—she needed to get them off before—

One hand on her midriff, he pushed her down, until she gave up and fell on her back across the desk. He worked her breeches down to her knees. She felt the cool wood, the ridges of the desk, against her bare bottom. Then he grasped her knees, pushed them up and as wide as the breeches would allow and bent to taste her.

Thoroughly.

Until she lost her breath so completely that she could only sob and wordlessly beg, entreat, implore. Hands clenching tight in his black hair, she arched helplessly beneath his too-knowing ministrations. Desperately dragged in a breath. "For God's sake, Logan—just fill me. *Please . . .*"

He obliged, but with his tongue, stroking so deeply, so roughly that she climaxed in a shattering, shuddering rush of sharply glittering pleasure.

As it waned, she only felt emptier still.

Cracking open her lids, she focused on his face, took in his expression of pure masculine gloating as, straightening, he looked down at her. His slow smile stated he knew exactly what she wanted, what she needed, and how to deliver it.

"Up." Grasping her hands, he pulled her up and off the desk, steadied her when she wobbled, then turned her and steered her, guiding her unsteady steps toward the table. It was difficult to walk with her breeches about her knees, but before she could think to do anything about it, his hands tightened about her hips and he halted her. "Lean forward and grip the edge of the table."

She did, her knees against the edge of the bench built out from the table's base.

Even as the vulnerability of her position registered, she felt his hands roam her bare bottom, sending sensation and dewed heat washing beneath her skin, then his boots bracketed hers, keeping her feet, her braced legs together. His splayed hands caressed slowly, savoringly, upward over her hips, pushing her shirt and her chemise up over her waist, exposing even more of her, then one hand settled heavily over the back of her waist while the other swept down and away.

Her heart was still cantering, hadn't slowed from before. Anticipation kicked it into a full-blown gallop.

She'd barely started to work out what he planned, hadn't truly caught her breath, when she felt the thick rod of his erection push into the hollow between her thighs, felt the marble head nudge between her folds—and he thrust home, pushing her forward, onto her toes, making her breath stutter, her hands grip tight.

He withdrew and thrust in again and she nearly mewled with pleasure. He held her hips steady and filled her repeatedly. She could feel his groin meeting the smooth skin of her bottom, feel the rasp of crinkly hair, the evocative pressure of his balls against the backs of her thighs. She clung to the table, head bowing as the sensation of him filling her over and over, deeper and yet deeper, rolled over and through her, and claimed her mind.

His hips pumped powerfully in a primal beat. He reached around her, hands working, then she felt a tug. He leaned forward, pushed deeper into her. A darkly whispered order in her ear had her complying by releasing one clenched hand, then the other, letting him strip off her coat and waistcoat, then reaching beneath her shirt, he loosened her bands, drew them down, and closed his hands about her breasts, screened only by her fine chemise.

He kneaded, filled his hands and played, possessed, while his body possessed hers in the most flagrant way.

Then he leaned closer yet, one hand leaving her breast to skate down her front, to stroke her curls, then reach further and stroke her, then cup her there, steadying her as he changed the angle and pushed her on.

She shook her head in desperation, started rocking her hips, riding to his rhythm.

Glorying in the sensations that crashed through her as he rode her deeply, thoroughly, unrelentingly, until she shattered again. Came apart on a cry she fought desperately to smother.

Felt her legs, her arms, fail, heard his deep, dark chuckle as he caught her against him, held her to him, still sunk in her body, hard and full.

She felt a moment's indignation that he wasn't as desperate as she.

But she knew him, his ways, well enough by now to know that he would seek his own release only after reducing her to boneless helplessness with bout after bout of blinding ecstasy.

Her wits were so enthralled in glory she was only distantly aware of him shifting her bands, unpicking the knot, then unwinding them.

Then he drew off her chemise, withdrew from her, shuffled her the short distance to her bed, and tipped her onto it.

She could barely summon the strength to lift her lids, and through her lashes look up at him. He stood for an instant looking down at her, his smile holding equal measures of primitive possession, unalloyed pleasure, and simple content.

The latter clutched at her heart, but she pushed it aside. He would undoubtedly be just as content with some other woman, some other lady, later. After.

Logan couldn't help smiling at the sight of her, his fierce captain, sprawled mostly naked on her bed, her skin rosy, flushed with sated desire, the marks of his possession showing faintly on the fine skin of her breasts and hips. He would probably mark her more before the night was out, but as he'd informed her, this was his night, his way.

He saw the glint of green beneath her lashes. Before she could think to say anything, he reached down and tugged off her boots, rolled down her stockings, and drew off her breeches.

Leaving her totally naked, still sprawled, letting him look his fill as he swiftly dispensed with his own clothes, then, naked, let his body down on hers, covering her, with one hard thrust mounting her, feeling her arch instinctively beneath him, then wriggle to more comfortably accommodate his harder bones, his different angles.

Clamping one hand about the worked head of the bed where it attached to the wall, he looked down at her beneath him and let the reins fall, let his body surge.

Again and again, he moved powerfully over her, thrusting deeply into her, smoothly, rhythmically, taking her, possessing her. Imprinting the feel of him deep within her.

He didn't stop when she dragged in a huge breath, thrust a little faster as she raised her arms, ran her hands down his sides, over his back, then helplessly clung.

And started riding with him, her body undulating beneath his, actively receiving him.

Giving him all, everything he wanted.

All of her, every last gasp, every moment of passion he wrung from her. With his free hand, he reached down and gripped her thigh, raised it. She lifted it further, wrapped that leg, then the other, around his hips, opening herself even more.

So he could fill her even more deeply, take even more of

her luscious heat, bathe even more deeply in her scalding glory.

Eyes closing, he rode on, harder, ever more powerfully pushing her on. He could feel his grip on reality fracturing, feel the siren call of her body as it tightened around his, inexorably racking the wheel of passion to the last degree.

He raised his free hand, blindly searched and found her face, framed it, then bent his head and sank into her mouth. Filled it to the same primal rhythm with which he filled her sheath.

Swallowed her scream as she climaxed beneath him, as bucking and straining she fractured, and ecstasy took her, racked her, raked her.

As she pulled him with her, hands clutching, her sheath a velvet fist clamping around him until he surrendered, until, on a long, hoarse groan, one she drank in, he gave himself to her.

Sometime later, Linnet awoke, immediately reassured by the weight of the heavily muscled leg entwined with hers, by the warmth of the hard chest wedged beside hers. Opening her eyes, she saw Logan propped on one arm alongside her. The narrow bed forced him to lie half over her—no bad thing in her opinion.

The moonlight had strengthened, pouring through the stern portholes to bathe his face, limning the chiseled angles in silver. Revealing his expression, the firm set of his lips, but drowning his blue eyes in shadows.

A long moment passed, then he said, his voice deep, low, but definite, "I meant what I said. I can't believe you can conceive of anything in this world powerful enough to make me give you up. Make me not return. Only death, or something close to it, will stop me coming back for you."

She said nothing; there seemed nothing she could say. In this, their views were diametrically opposed, and no amount of his loving was going to change that. But . . . "I believe you believe that." She had to allow him that. "I don't think you're just saying it, a sop to your conscience or mine. But—and yes, there is a but—I don't have your faith that, once back in your real world, away from my world, you'll still see things the same way."

The twisting of his lips told her clearly what he thought of her lack of faith, her inability to believe. But after searching her face for a moment more, he shifted, then slumped over her shoulder, laid his arm across her, holding her half beneath him.

If their minds weren't in accord, their bodies were. Sleep drifted over them, inexorably drew them down.

Before it captured them completely, he murmured, his voice a dark, faintly Scottish rumble by her ear, "One of us is wrong. Bone-stubborn witch that you are, it's going to be glorious when you realize it's you."

Linnet fell asleep smiling.

Close to midnight
Shrewton House, London

Daniel strode into the bedroom he and Alex had been sharing, brushing lingering snowflakes from his coat. By the flickering firelight, he saw Alex rise to prop in the bed, brows arching in question.

Closing the door, Daniel headed for the bed. "The snow's coming down heavily. I'd forgotten how wet snow here is. The roads are slush."

"I thought you and dear Roderick were off to deal with Hamilton in Surrey."

Daniel grimaced, and sat on the bed to pull off his boots. "So we'd thought, but by the time we reached the area, he—or those with him, guards like Delborough had, according to the few of ours left to tell the tale—had removed those of our men sent to trail their party, and before you lose your temper, the party split into four, so there were only two men at most following any group." Boots off, he stood and stripped off his coat. "With our followers dispatched, the devil and his henchmen went to ground. But all is not lost."

Tossing his coat aside, he started on his waistcoat. "Roderick and I managed to track our men well enough to get a reasonable idea of the area in which Hamilton's bolt-hole is. We've left men enough to trail him whichever way he runs, and they'll send word as soon as he does."

"Hmm." Alex resettled in the bed. "I still think it's close to certain he'll head in the same direction—toward the same ultimate goal—as Delborough. Somewhere in Cambridgeshire, northern Suffolk, or Norfolk, to whoever is the puppetmaster pulling all their strings."

Daniel tugged his shirt from his breeches. "Did you have any luck with finding a new base closer to the action?"

"Yes. Creighton proved most useful. From his description, the house he's found in Bury St. Edmunds will be just the thing. I've organized for our removal there tomorrow."

Undoing his breeches, Daniel nodded. "You've sent word to all our scattered commanders?"

"I have. I thought it best to get the word out before the weather closed in."

"So what's happened with Delborough?"

"Larkins is, apparently, confident his little thief is terrified enough to deliver Delborough's scroll-holder to him—he seems very sure, but I'd rather Roderick went up there tomorrow to make certain nothing goes amiss." Alex rolled over as Daniel lifted the pale blue silk covers and climbed into the bed. "As for Monteith and Carstairs, we've had no further news."

"With any luck, both are already dead."

Alex grimaced. "Much as I'd like to believe that . . . Delborough and Hamilton, too, were supposed to be dead by now. Yet they live, and still have their scroll-holders, and what's more, are steadily getting closer to their goal—wherever that is. Regardless, our cultists are having a harder time of it here in England. Not only do they stand out, but they're also having difficulty comprehending that they can't simply kill, torture, and intimidate as they do at home in India."

"Sadly true. And they can't gain access to places like Grillon's." Daniel turned to Alex, smiled through the shadows. "I suspect we might have to take a hand ourselves." His smile widened. "I know how much killing distresses you, m'dear, but you'll simply have to grin and bear it."

Alex laughed and reached for Daniel. "I will. For you, I will. Still, I just hope we've brought enough assassins to assist."

Ten

December 16, 1822
St. Peter Port, Guernsey

The day was overcast, dense clouds in myriad shades of gray blocking out the weak sun. A cold wind strafed low over the sea, sending whipped gray-green waves spraying in plumes over the rocky breakwater.

Standing beside Linnet at the helm, with the wind raking chill fingers through his hair, Logan watched the gun emplacements of Castle Cornet slide away to starboard as, under limited sail, the *Esperance* rode the tide out of the harbor.

The Channel swell lifted the prow high. Linnet held the wheel, held course, her gaze locked on the breakwater to port. The instant the stern cleared the line of tumbled rocks, she snapped out orders, relayed by her bosun down on the main deck. Sailors leapt to obey, many already hanging in the rigging above. Her gaze now following their movements, as more sails unfurled, Linnet turned the wheel, hand over hand, and steady and sure, the *Esperance* came around.

As the prow came onto the heading she wanted, she called out more orders, setting sail to run north along the island's coast. Once they rounded the northern headland, she'd turn northwest for Plymouth.

Sensing the sheer power of the ship beneath his feet, of wind and waves expertly harnessed, Logan looked up, admiring the taut sails, square-rigged on the fore and main masts. At the top of the main mast, the Guernsey flag flapped and snapped in the stiff breeze.

Beside him, Linnet called out another order, and a young sailor dashed to the mizzenmast. Logan watched him operate the lines of some other flag; shading his eyes, he looked up to see . . . squinted. Blinked and looked again.

He was army, not navy, yet he recognized one of the various Royal Navy ensigns now flapping high above the *Esperance*'s deck.

Stupified, he turned to Linnet, gestured. "What the devil does that mean?"

She grinned, corrected the wheel a trifle, then handed it over to Griffiths. "Straight north, then northwest. We'll take the most direct route unless we see anything that suggests otherwise."

Griffiths nodded and settled behind the wheel.

Turning to Logan, Linnet waved him to the starboard side of the stern deck. "That"—with her head she indicated the ensign above—"is the strongest plank in the argument that the *Esperance* is the best ship to carry you to Plymouth."

Logan stared at the ensign, then looked at her. "I don't understand. How can the *Esperance* still be sailing under a Letter of Marque, much less with you as captain?"

Leaning on the stern railing, looking out over their wake, Linnet smiled. "The Trevission family has held an extant Letter of Marque for literally centuries." She cast Logan a glance. "Englishmen forget that the islanders are more allied to the English Crown than they are. We—the Channel Islands—have been part of the Duchy of Normandy for untold centuries, and still are—your King is our Duke. We're a property of the English Crown, not of the British state. As such, we've fought the French for just as long, if not longer. We've been a bastion against the French, and the Spanish, too, in centuries past, and in more recent times through the Peninsula Wars, we played a crucial part in England's defense, specifically in imposing naval supremacy.

"As I mentioned earlier, the *Esperance*—this version of her, there have been four—played a role in the evacuation of Corunna. Later we guarded your troop ships when the army returned. The Guernsey merchant fleet in particular has always provided a bulwark against direct attack on the Channel coast from any of the ports in Brittany, all the way to Cherbourg. And because we're usually out and about, traveling the western reaches of the Channel, we've often provided early warning of any attack from further afield, to the west and south. Without us patrolling those waters, covering so many of the sea lanes, Plymouth and Falmouth wouldn't have been able to concentrate their fleets on the Channel itself, on discouraging Napoleon from launching his invasion from Boulogne, and then later supplying and protecting the army when you returned for Waterloo."

She met Logan's eyes. "English naval dominance owes no small debt to the merchant ships of Guernsey. And the commanders at Castle Cornet, and at Plymouth and Falmouth, know it."

"Which explains why you informed the castle before sailing—your courtesy call to Foxwood." Logan studied her face, saw the passion behind the history. "Does the Admiralty know that Captain Trevission of the *Esperance* is a woman?"

Her lips twisted in a cynical smile. "They do, but you would, I suspect, never get them to admit it. Not in any way."

He considered, then said, "What you've told me explains why your family held a Letter of Marque until your father died. What it doesn't explain is why it was renewed after his death, presumably with you as holder, and why it's still in force so long after the end of the war." He glanced up, then looked back at her. "I'm assuming you are legally entitled to fly that?"

She chuckled and turned, leaning back against the rail to

look up at the ensign. "Yes, indeed—I'm fully entitled to claim the right, might, and protection of the Royal Navy." She met his eyes. "Which is why the *Esperance* sailing under marque is the perfect vessel to carry you to Plymouth. With that ensign flying up there, any captain would have to have rocks in his head to even challenge us."

Logan shook his head. "I can't argue that, not anymore, but you still haven't answered my questions."

Linnet met his eyes, then looked ahead, along the ship. "My father died in '13. I was seventeen. You know how things were in the Peninsula at that time—you were there. The navy desperately needed the *Esperance* sailing, and more, sailing under marque—she was, still is, the fastest ship of her size in these waters, the best armed, most agile, and her crew the most experienced and best trained. The navy couldn't afford to lose the *Esperance*, not at that juncture. The Admiralty received urgent petitions from the island, as well as the fleet commanders at Plymouth and Falmouth.

"No doubt the Admiralty sputtered and paled, but the admirals of the fleets and the then-commander at Castle Cornet all knew me. They knew I'd been trained to sail the *Esperance* by my father, that I could, and frequently did, take command. They knew I'd already seen more battles than most of their own captains, that I'd been sailing these waters since I could stand." She glanced at Logan, smiled cynically again. "Basically the Admiralty had no choice. They renewed the Letter of Marque exactly as it had been for centuries—to Captain Trevission of the *Esperance*.

"So I took over in my father's place, and the *Esperance* continued sailing, patrolling, fighting the French. Mostly to hold them at bay. Other than certain special missions, our role was to ensure no speedy French frigate tried to spy on Plymouth or Falmouth, and then race home to report. As you might imagine, the *Esperance* is well known. The instant any French frigate lays eyes on us, it piles on sail and flees."

She paused, eyes instinctively checking the sails, the

wind, the waves. "As to why the Letter of Marque is still in effect, the fleet commanders at Plymouth and Falmouth recommended it remain in effect permanently, essentially because they have no faith that, should their need of the *Esperance*'s services arise again, they'll be able to convince the Admiralty to issue a new letter to a female captain—at least not quickly enough."

Pushing away from the rail, studying the sails, she strode to the forward rail of the stern deck and called a sail change. Again, the crew sprang instantly to carry out the order. After considering the result, she spoke with Griffiths, then, leaving him with the wheel, swung down the ladder to the main deck. Logan followed more slowly as she strolled to the prow, looking over the waves as she went, constantly checking the breeze and the sails above, reading the wind and the sky.

It was as if, now they were out on the sea, it called to her. She seemed to have some connection with the elements that commanded this sphere, some ability beyond the norm to interpret and anticipate. Even he could sense that, see it. A commander himself, he didn't need to ask the men, her experienced and well-trained crew, what they thought of her; their respect, and more—their unshakable confidence in her to the point they would unhesitatingly obey her orders, would follow her into battle with total conviction that she would guide them in the best way—shone in every interaction.

The crew trusted her implicitly. It wasn't hard to see why. Her competence—and that certain, almost magical ability—were constantly on show. As the deck rolled and pitched as the ship neared the northern point and Linnet called more sail changes, trapping the wind as she prepared the *Esperance* to come about onto a northwest heading for Plymouth, Logan felt the power beneath his feet, felt the rush of the wind, the lifting surge of the ocean, and fully understood the crew's eagerness to sail on this ship, with her.

He watched as, satisfied for the moment, she strode swiftly back toward the helm, then followed more slowly.

This—the unrivaled, unquestioned female captain of a privateer—was another part, a large part, of who and what Linnet Trevission was.

It was, he could admit to himself, an awesome part, one that boggled his mind, yet also filled him with honest and true admiration. Not an emotion he'd expected to feel for a lover, let alone a wife. Yet she was proving a lady of many parts—and each and every one called to him.

And that, he suspected, as he climbed the ladder to the stern deck where she had once again claimed the helm, was something she didn't yet understand.

But she would.

Smiling to himself, he settled against the stern railing to watch his lover, his sometime-soon-to-be wife, send her ship racing over the waves to Plymouth.

With her ship smoothly heeling around the northern tip of Guernsey, Linnet set sail to best capture the brisk breeze for a fast run to Plymouth. Setting course for Plymouth Sound was something she could do in her sleep in any weather; Plymouth was the port to which she and the *Esperance* most frequently sailed.

Although Cummins and his men had been on the wharf at dawn, as had a number of other merchants, even with their collective goods in her hold, the *Esperance* was still running light; no need for full sail to streak over the waves.

Beside her, his large hands curled about the rail, Griffiths nodded. "That's a good pace. If the wind keeps up—and no reason it shouldn't—we'll be in Plymouth well before dusk."

"That's what I'm aiming for." Leaving the wheel in Griffith's capable hands, Linnet stepped down to the main deck and set out on a circuit—a habit when underway. She ambled down the deck, exchanging comments with the crew members she passed. Logan, she'd noticed, had halted in the prow. Hip against the rail, arms crossed over his powerful chest, he stood looking down into the waves.

Lifting her face to the breeze, she briefly closed her eyes, savored as always the inexpressible thrill of being at sea, of flashing over the waves, the wind tugging her hair, the salty tang of the ocean sinking to her soul. She was a child of sea and ship, of wind and wave. She loved the familiar, reassuring roll of the deck beneath her feet, the creak and snap of spar and sail. Loved the sheer exhilaration of speeding beneath the wide open sky.

Opening her eyes, she continued on, taking stock as she always did. She'd taken Logan's warning to heart and given orders she hadn't had to give for some years—not since the end of the war. A Royal Navy ensign might be flapping over her head, signaling to all others on the waves that any vessel seeking to impede the *Esperance* would, in effect, be taking on the English navy—the navy that currently ruled the seas—yet while she found it hard to believe that anyone would engage, she'd nevertheless given the order to have the crew armed, and the guns made ready. Two words from her and the cannon would roll out, primed and ready to fire.

She'd rarely uttered those two words. The *Esperance*'s guns were especially deadly, and she'd never liked seeing such graceful creations as ships smashed, broken, and sent to the deep. Nature's wrecks were bad enough; only if the opposing captain gave her no choice would she fire. She'd been forced to do so on more than one occasion, and knew she would again if that was the only way to protect her ship and her crew.

Threaten either, and she would act; safeguarding ship and crew was her paramount duty as captain.

Her circuit had led her into the prow. As she joined Logan by the rail, other ships came into view.

He nodded toward them. "Company."

She scanned the sails, but could tell little from this distance. "Hardly surprising. This is the Channel—we're traversing the busiest shipping lane in the world."

Leaning on the rail, she glanced at him, realized he was looking at the gun port below.

"I went down onto your lower deck, took a look at your

guns." He met her gaze. "They're not positioned in the usual way."

She smiled, shook her head. "My father built this vessel, the fourth to carry the name. He was always looking to make improvements, and one he designed and implemented was a different sort of platform for cannon, at least of the caliber barques of our size carry. The platform allows a greater degree of swivel than found in other ships. Through using it, and changing the position and structure of the gun ports accordingly, the *Esperance* is able to fire effectively well before we've attained the customary broadside position, which puts us one up on the opposition from the first."

"You can still fire fully broadside as well?"

"And even angled sternward. It gives us more freedom in any engagement, whether the other ship is coming up on us or we're chasing them."

"What's the largest cannon you can carry?"

Somewhat to Logan's surprise, she knew the answer. An almost disconcerting discussion of ordnance ensued, one he would never have imagined having with any female.

After that, a comfortable silence enveloped them. With her leaning on the railing alongside him, they looked out to sea, at the sails of the seven other ships they could see crossing the waves under the gray sky.

They'd been watching for some time when three ships changed course, some sails furling while others were released to billow and catch the wind.

Slowly, Linnet straightened.

Logan glanced at her face, saw the intentness of her expression as she tracked the three ships.

Then her lips tightened. "Damn!" She watched for a moment more, then glanced at him. "The idiots! They're coming for us." She glanced back at the ships, exasperation in her face. "Perhaps once they get closer they'll remember what the ensign means . . . but they would already have seen it, and I'm not taking the chance they'll rediscover their brains."

Whirling, she strode, bootheels ringing, back up the ship. "All hands on deck!" Fully raised, her voice carried clearly. "All stations!"

Thunder rolled below, then erupted as men pounded up the stairs, pouring out on the deck, buckling on swords and bandoliers, checking pistols and knives, short swords and cutlasses, tying back long hair, yanking on coats. Many swung straight up into the rigging, climbing with focused attention to specific positions on the spars above.

Everywhere Logan looked, men rushed with single-minded purpose. Every man knew exactly where he needed to be, what he had to do. Not one questioned why they were summoned; like an excellently drilled company, they swung into battle-ready formation.

Following Linnet as best as he could, he caught the glance she threw over her shoulder. "You'd be best up with me at the helm."

He knew she meant that there he'd be out of her men's way, but he wasn't about to argue. Catching up, he stayed on her heels as she ducked and wove unerringly through the organized chaos that filled the *Esperance*'s main deck.

Jimmy, Linett's cutlass and belt in his hands, popped up at the bottom of the stern ladder just as Linnet reached it. She grabbed them and went up the ladder faster than a monkey, giving Logan a glimpse of the sailing brat she'd been.

Giving thanks for the impulse that had seen him buckle on his saber before he'd come on deck, he followed. His dirk was, as usual, in his left boot.

By the time he reached Linnet, she'd buckled on her sword and reclaimed the helm. Taking up a position behind her right shoulder, Logan saw with surprise that the deck that an instant before had been a sea of rushing bodies was now the epitome of calm preparedness, all the men standing ready at their stations.

With one eye on Linnet, the crew watched the three approaching ships; that they were approaching was no longer in doubt. Griffiths, standing off to Linnet's left, had a spyglass to his eye. "The buggers are circling to come up astern. They've pitch-dipped arrows ready, and braziers on deck, archers standing by—looks like they think to slink close, within range, take out our sails, slow us, then board us."

Linnet snorted, an eloquent sound. After a moment, she said, "They're smaller and faster than us, but they don't have what it takes to take us. Here's what we'll do."

She'd spoken in a clear, decisive, but even tone; she paused to let Griffiths repeat her words loudly, then they were bellowed by the bosun, Claxton, standing amidship, so all the crew could hear.

When Claxton fell silent, Linnet continued, pausing every now and then for Griffiths and Claxton to relay her words. "There's three enemy ships out there—all frigates and as quick as frigates can be. No flags, so we can't know how experienced they are in these waters. Regardless, two are circling to come up astern, to get within arrow-range and take out our sails, then presumably they think to flank us, and wedge us between for boarding. Of course, we're not going to let that happen. As they pull close, we're going to put on all sail—as they'll expect us to do, as if we think to outrun them. They'll chase, and put on all sail, too, to run us down. But we're not going to run—at just the right moment, we're going to veer hard port, and cut across the bow of the ship on that side, raking her with our guns as we go. Our sail changes are going to have to be slick, we'll be at full speed, so be ready.

"Once we're past her, we'll be in position to go after the third ship, the one presently hanging well off to starboard—most likely the one with their senior commander aboard. If they give us the chance, we'll board his ship and capture him, but meanwhile, we'll need to keep an eye on the other ship, the one we'll have left to come around. By the time she does, we need to be clear of the commander's ship, so if we do board, we keep it fast. This will be a raid—we go in, we do what we came to do, and we get out *tout de suite*—do you hear me?"

An instant later, when the question was relayed, a re-sounding "Aye!" rose from the decks.

"Good." Linnet kept speaking, her words fed down the line. "The instant we're all back, we pile on sail for Plym-outh and race the bastards there. I don't think they'll give chase, but who knows? If they do, we might turn and savage them, but"—she slid her gaze to Logan—"today our duty is to get Major Monteith into Plymouth, so as far as possible, we'll stick to our course."

Logan stepped closer. "Tell them that if they come up against dark-skinned men with black scarves about their heads, they'll be Indian cultists, and they shouldn't hold back. The cultists won't. They'll be eager to kill anyone any way they can."

Linnet glanced at Griffiths, nodded. The first mate relayed Logan's words.

"Good luck," Linnet called. "Now stand ready!"

The crew shifted again, some going below to the guns, others taking up fresh positions, waiting for Linnet's order to change sail as, far to the rear, the two unflagged frigates completed their circling manuever and fell in on either side of the *Esperance*'s wake.

As she'd intimated, Linnet called for all sail. Overhead, canvas was released; it billowed for a few seconds, then the wind rushed in and filled it—and the *Esperance* leapt.

The pursuing frigates at first fell behind, but then fresh sails blossomed in their rigging, pulled taut, and they came on.

Pushing, pushing, surging to get nearer, they reminded Logan of pursuing hounds. Further back, the third frigate was forced to set all sail to keep up.

"Bosun—message to the gun captain." Linnet held the wheel lightly, steady on her course. "He can fire the port guns at will after we start the turn."

"Aye, ma'am." Claxton pointed at Jimmy, who raced off below to deliver the order.

An odd silence fell, broken only by the waves splashing against the hull, the caw of an inopportune wheeling gull.

Logan recognized the lull, the universal nerve-racking hiatus before battle was joined—that moment when no one wasted even a breath.

"They've taken up our challenge and are coming up fast." Linnet glanced at Griffiths; he relayed her words. "They won't be able to change direction as fast as we can. You know what to do, which sails to furl, which to trim. Which angle we need to catch the wind. We've drilled often enough, so stand ready now . . . on my word when I give it, hard to port."

They waited. The entire crew held still, expectant and ready, barely breathing. To Logan, it was exactly like waiting for the order to charge. Battle-ready tension sang in the air, yet every man stood reined, poised, all but quivering.

He waited, too, fist resting on the hilt of his saber as he stood beside Linnet, facing astern, watching the ships draw nearer and nearer—and still nearer. And still Linnet held to her course. She glanced over her shoulder, once, twice, gauging distance, but still she held the wheel steady.

Jaw clenched, he swore behind his teeth. He was about to appeal to her—if she didn't move now, surely the ship on their portside would cleave the *Esperance* in two—

"*Now!*" Linnet swung the wheel hard.

Griffiths helped her haul and haul.

The ship heeled to the left so violently Logan had to grab the rail to keep from being thrown. The instant the turn, a tight one-hundred-and-eighty-degree turn, was commenced, sailors aloft were hooking and trimming sails, hauling in others, changing angles of spars as the ship swung around.

Logan held his breath, hand fisting on the stern rail as he felt the changes take hold, felt the force of the wind in the sails combine with the pressure on the rudder to push the *Esperance* smoothly through the turn at maximum speed.

He saw how close Linnet had judged things, and wondered how she'd dared. From his position in the stern, he could clearly see shocked faces on the sailors and, yes, the cultists crowded on the frigate's deck.

Then the *Esperance*'s stern slipped past the oncoming frigate's bow, and he—along with many others, he was sure—exhaled.

Then the *Esperance*'s port guns boomed, once, twice, a raking, staggered volley that ripped a long, jagged hole right on the waterline of the frigate.

Pandemonium erupted on the frigate's deck. If they'd had guns prepared, they would have been on the wrong side. Their archers with their pitch-arrows and braziers were also facing the wrong way, and with the cultists milling in the middle of the ship, they couldn't reposition—not in time. The *Esperance*'s speed and the frigate's even greater speed combined to rapidly widen the distance between the ships.

Then Linnet and Griffiths fully righted the wheel and the *Esperance* straightened. "Full sail!" Linnet yelled.

Even as the order was relayed, sails were being unfurled and reset. In seconds, the *Esperance* leapt forward again—streaking away from the stricken frigate.

Logan looked back. A few burning arrows came belatedly whistling their way, but fell well short, fizzling out in their wake.

Linnet had just sunk an enemy frigate without sustaining so much as a scratch, not to her crew or her ship. The realization was stunning.

He dragged in a breath, felt a sense of exhilaration streak through him. Turning away from the crippled frigate, he looked at Linnet.

Her eyes locked on the sails above, her hands steady on the wheel, she called orders, Griffiths and Claxton relayed them, and sailors leapt to obey.

Most of the sailors were grinning. Logan realized he was grinning, too. The speed and power of the *Esperance* under full fighting rig—under an expert captain's hands—was breathtaking.

Even if those hands were delicate.

He had no experience of naval battles, but having a cap-

tain who knew precisely which sail needed to be where
at any time, to the square inch, was clearly a significant
advantage—and Linnet, with her years of experience from
childhood on, knew this ship, and these waters, these winds,
as few others could. Her knowledge was all but instinctive.

It was no longer any wonder that she was so widely accepted as Captain Trevission, that even the old fogeys in
the Admiralty turned a blind eye to her gender. Underneath
their gold braid, they were sailors to a man, and Linnet was
a sailor of the most exhilarating sort.

But their battle wasn't over.

With the disabled frigate slowly sinking behind them,
Linnet exchanged the wheel for Griffiths's spyglass. The
second frigate, the one that with the first had tried to come
up on the *Esperance*'s stern, had started to follow when
she'd turned hard port, but the cannon volley had sent it
shying away. Now its captain seemed to be dithering, probably signaling to the third frigate, the one she assumed was
the command ship, for direction.

The command ship itself seemed unsure what to do. Her
unconventional manuever appeared to have given the captain second, even third, thoughts. As the situation stood,
both frigates were still heading toward Plymouth, although
they'd trimmed their speed, while the *Esperance* was heading the other way, picking up speed as it passed the command ship at a safe distance.

With their original attack plan in tatters, the frigates were
waiting to see what she would do.

Closing the glass, she returned to take the wheel. "We'll
turn to port and come about again—let's get back on course
for Plymouth, then see what these idiots do."

She rapped out orders, and the crew responded as she
steered the *Esperance* through another turn, this one much
wider than the last, coming full circle. When they were once
more on line for Plymouth Sound, all three ships were sailing in more or less the same direction. The second frigate

was well off to port and a good way ahead, too distant to pose any immediate threat, but the command ship, also now off the port side but much nearer, was scrambling, angling as if to intercept the *Esperance* rather than slink away.

"They can't be serious." Linnet shook her head. "We're coming up astern and they've just seen what our guns can do."

"The other frigate's turning." Griffiths had the glass to his eye.

Lifting her gaze, Linnet watched, then frowned. "That's too big a turn to come directly at us—looks like he plans to circle and come up astern again."

Slowly, Griffiths nodded. "Looks that way. They don't want to come broadside and risk our guns."

"The command ship's running." Linnet watched as the command frigate suddenly angled away and put on more sail, drawing ahead and apart. She watched for a moment, then snorted. "What does he think I am? Blind?"

The *Esperance* was still traveling faster than either of the frigates. Linnet called for sails to be trimmed, slowing the *Esperance*, and, as if helpfully falling in with the command ship captain's plan, turned slightly off course as if to follow.

When Griffiths glanced inquiringly at her, she smiled tightly. "He wants to engage, and assumes, after our last manuever, that I want to, too, but he wants to lead me a dance until the other frigate can come around and assist. I can't just leave him and run for Plymouth; we're still too far out—they'd catch us again, try coming up astern again, but I won't be able to play the same trick twice. I suspect their new plan is for me to get distracted chasing the command ship, then suddenly discover the other frigate coming up hard astern and to starboard. When I react and try to run, the command ship will spill wind enough to swing close alongside the port bow. While we're distracted at the stern, they'll send men over the bow."

Logan asked Griffiths for the glass, trained it on the command ship. What he saw made his blood run cold. Lowering the glass, he caught Linnet's eye. "I'd say your reading is correct. There are cult assassins on board the command ship. They'll be the ones wanting to come over your bow."

Linnet nodded. He stood beside her as she continued to follow the command ship as it tacked this way and that, much like a fox before a hound.

"He keeps trying to slow us," Linnet said, "but has to, at least at the moment, stay far enough ahead so I don't simply overrun him."

Logan looked up, trying to judge how much sail she'd had taken in. "Could you overrun him?"

"At his current speed, easily, but I don't think he realizes that. The *Esperance* is significantly faster than other ships of her class. In these conditions, the speed we're doing now is more typical."

"Which suggests the captain doesn't know the *Esperance*, which means he's from further afield—not these waters."

"It certainly seems that way."

Logan watched as she called another set of sail changes; he couldn't follow the purpose behind them all, but assumed she was setting the stage for the upcoming engagement.

Sure enough, once the *Esperance* was riding steady again, going nowhere near as fast as it could, she left the wheel to Griffiths, took the spyglass from Logan, and trained it on the other frigate, now attempting to sneak up on their rear.

Those on the frigate saw her looking. The captain immediately put on all sail and came on as fast as the wind allowed.

Linnet smiled. Lowering the glass, she gauged the distance between the ships, then strode to the forward railing and leaned over to yell, "Tommy, Burton, Calloway! Get your bows, arrows, and a brazier, and get up here—but keep everything hidden from the ship in front, and below the rail up here."

"Aye, Capt'n!"

Two minutes later, three young sailors came clambering up the ladder. Logan helped the first lift a brazier of glowing coals up, carefully setting it near the stern rail. The three slid long bows across the deck, then climbed up, each carrying arrows with ragged heads dipped in pitch in one hand.

Leaving the arrows with their bows, the lads looked at Linnet. She joined them, her gaze on the frigate coming up hard on their stern. "They have arbalests standing ready to light our sails, but your bows have greater range. How soon before you can take out most of their sails? Doesn't have to be all, but we need the main sails alight."

With the *Esperance* slowed, the frigate was closing the distance quickly.

The lads narrowed their eyes, pursed their lips.

"Just a little more . . . ," one of them said.

"As soon as you're ready, then—fire at will." Linnet turned and walked back to the helm.

Resuming his position more or less at her back, Logan watched as, with no further instruction, the youngsters waited, muttering between themselves about distance and wind, then as one they bent and, screened by the high side of the stern deck, fanned the brazier. With one eye on the frigate, each found his bow, notched an arrow and lit it, then, in perfect concert, the trio stood, smoothly drawing back the long bows, and let fly.

They didn't even wait to see fire blossom on the sails, but bent again. In less than a minute they sent another three arrows flying. They were fast and accurate. Using just nine arrows in all, they set nearly all of the rear frigate's sails ablaze, sending the frigate crew frantically scrambling.

All but instantly, the frigate fell away.

Linnet returned to clap the three lads on their shoulders. "Perfect!" Behind them, the frigate was all but becalmed. "Excellent work—now get below. We've one more frigate to fry."

Logan looked back at the frigate rapidly falling behind. They hadn't enough sail to even limp along, yet how soon before the cultists on board reached shore? And which shore?

And while the first frigate they'd engaged had almost certainly sunk, it had gone down slowly; plenty of time for all those aboard to abandon ship.

"Full sail again!"

Linnet's call had him putting such concerns aside. Beneath his feet, the *Esperance* leapt like a hound unleashed. What would she do with the third frigate, the one carrying assassins? Returning to his position beside her as she stood alongside Griffiths, presently managing the helm, he followed both their gazes to the last frigate—and saw it swing very definitely away.

Linnet watched, eyes narrow, lips thin, then humphed. "Ten points starboard." Griffiths obeyed, and the *Esperance*'s bow swung elegantly north. Linnet called several sail changes, then regauged the distance to the frigate, still some way ahead to port. "That will take us past at a safe distance. If they've finally come to their senses and want to scrurry out of our way, we'll let them go."

The sails caught more wind on the new heading; the *Esperance* picked up speed, swiftly moving away from the last frigate.

Logan watched, inwardly cursing, yet . . . "A magnanimous gesture."

Linnet shrugged. "That misbegotten captain must by now realize that taking the *Esperance* is beyond him."

She'd turned to look at Logan as she spoke.

Griffiths's shout had her turning back. "Blimey! Will you look at that."

The three of them stared. Most of the crew stopped what they were doing and stared, too.

Rather than slink away, as it had definitely and sensibly started to do, the frigate abruptly changed course again, as if to engage—but then the masts dipped wildly and the ship nearly keeled.

"What the devil's going on there?" Linnet grabbed the spyglass she'd set down and refocused on the frigate's deck.

A second passed, then, her tone disbelieving, she reported,

"There's fighting on board. Some men—men with dark skins and black scarves about their heads—are fighting the captain and his mate, and the rest of the crew, too. They've seized the wheel and are trying to steer the ship our way . . . but the idiots are simply forcing the wheel over without changing sails. In this wind, they'll capsize the ship."

Grimly Logan stared at the frigate. To his admittedly inexperienced eye, the space between it and the *Esperance* was already great enough to ensure the frigate wouldn't be able to come up with them, certainly not if manned by cultists and not sailors. "All we can do is hope the captain and his crew win the battle."

And toss the cultists, especially the assassins, into the briny deep.

Linnet lowered the glass. "Indeed." She looked at Griffiths. "Keep all sail on. Let's leave them to it and race for Plymouth."

Setting the glass back in its holder beside the wheel, she headed down the ladder to talk to her men.

Logan watched her go, then picked up the spyglass, walked to the stern rail, and trained it on the frigate, now dwindling to their rear.

He'd been prepared for a battle, but his saber hadn't even cleared its sheath. He felt frustrated and stymied, especially over having to leave cultists, and even more assassins, alive to tell their tales. To report to their superiors, as they inevitably would.

Yet there'd been no help for it, no legitimate way around it. The battle had been Linnet's to command; she'd made her calls and got them clean away, crippling the opposition while her own men remained unscathed.

The hallmark of an excellent commander.

Asking her to turn back and attack the other ship, to put the *Esperance* and her crew at risk again to satisfy his wish to ensure no cultist who knew he'd been on the *Esperance* remained free to report . . . that wasn't in the cards.

She'd done the right thing every step of the way.

Lowering the glass, he stared at the speck the last frigate had become. Rubbed a hand over his nape.

Like any good commander, Linnet had rescripted her plans on the run, rejigging them to best save her ship and her crew.

Now he would have to do the same. He'd have to meet the challenge of rescripting his plans to see them all safely home.

Later that afternoon, still out in the Channel but with Plymouth not that far ahead, Logan arranged to meet with Edgar, John, Griffiths, and Claxton in the cabin he'd been given next to Linnet's. She was still on deck, more or less above their heads at the wheel.

When Griffiths, the last to join them, came in and shut the door, Logan waved him to a perch on the narrow bunk, and from his position leaning against the wall beside the small porthole, began, "Edgar and John already know about the Black Cobra cult and my mission, of my role, and those of my three colleagues and numerous others, in attempting to bring the fiend to justice. But what none of you can have much idea of is the reason our mission's so vital."

In stark detail, he described some of the cult's atrocities, enough to have the four sailors blanch. "That's what these people are capable of."

He tipped his head toward the sea beyond the porthole. "You all saw the cultists aboard the last frigate—most were cult assassins, the deadliest group, the most fanatical. You saw how desperate they were to reach this ship—they'll do anything to reach me, and, now, Captain Trevission. She, a woman, defeated them. Her gender will make the defeat sting unbearably. I doubt they'll come after the *Esperance* herself—they don't think of ships in that way—but they will come after her captain—to punish her. When I escape them, as I must once I reach Plymouth, those remaining on the coast will be desperate to—as they'll think of it—redeem themselves in the eyes of their leader, the Black Cobra, by killing Captain Trevission in the most gruesome and painful way they can devise."

He paused, scanning their faces; their expressions were as grim as he could wish. "To a lesser extent you and the crew will be in danger, too, but it's Captain Trevission they'll focus their vengeful hatred on."

Shifting, he straightened. "When we left St. Peter Port, my plan was for the *Esperance* to carry me to Plymouth, where I'd leave the ship, meet with the guards waiting for me in town, and carry on with my mission. I've already told Captain Trevission that on completion of my mission, I plan to return to Guernsey and Mon Coeur. If I survive, I intend to ask her to be my wife and live on Guernsey with her, but I won't, can't, make any offer until I know I've survived hale and whole."

The men blinked at his open declaration, but Edgar's and John's expressions lightened, and they nodded with both approval and relief.

"However," Logan continued, "if after today's action I continue as I'd planned and leave Captain Trevission on the *Esperance* in Plymouth, the cult will target her."

Griffiths and Claxton frowned. "We can rally the crew—we'll keep her safe."

Logan inclined his head. "I've no doubt that, while she's on board, you'll be able to do that. But I seriously doubt that, after today, the cult will come after her while she's on the *Esperance*. They'll wait until she leaves and heads home—to Mon Coeur." He paused, scanned their faces as the potential for horror sank in. "And we all know what's at Mon Coeur. The cultists aren't much good on the waves, but tracking on land—at that they excel. They'll follow Captain Trevission to Mon Coeur, scout the place, gather their forces—and they do have considerable numbers—and pick their time. I know there are men at Mon Coeur capable of fighting, but even if you can persuade Linnet to allow some extras to go home with her, it won't be enough. Not enough of you will realize the savagery and fanaticism you'll face, not until it's too late."

Again he paused, then simply said, "There are too many innocents at Mon Coeur to risk it."

None of the four disagreed; he could see their rising protectiveness in their faces. Griffiths fixed his shrewd eyes on Logan. "What's our alternative?"

Logan met his gaze. "I can see only one. If you could keep your captain on board the *Esperance*, under constant guard and in Plymouth Sound, until my mission is complete and the Black Cobra is no more, I believe she and everyone associated with her would remain safe. The cult might, in desperation, try to attack the ship in harbor, but from what I've seen of your crew—and you'd be surrounded by other navy and army, more or less at call—I can't see even assassins succeeding. In addition, most of the assassins will follow me—it's reasonable to assume those are their standing orders."

He paused, noting that all four men were nodding, following and agreeing with his assessment thus far. "The problem with that scenario is that I can't see you—any or all of you—managing to keep Captain Trevission in Plymouth. The instant she realizes the potential danger, as indeed she might already have done, she'll insist on returning to Guernsey and Mon Coeur with all speed, to make sure all's safe there—to be there to defend it and her household when the cult come calling. She'll reason that as the *Esperance* is flying the Guernsey flag, is so well known, and as her captaincy is an open secret, the cult will be able to identify Mon Coeur as her home even without her leading them there, and seek to harm her by harming her family."

He grimaced. "In this instance, that reasoning is wrong, but neither you nor I will be able to convince her of that. The cult would delight in butchering her family, but they'd want to do it in front of her. That's the sort of fiends they are. It's her they want—she's their target—and they'll remain fixated on her. Only if she's in the immediate vicinity will family or associates be used as tools—to draw her out, weaken her, or cause her pain. For all their brutality, the cultists are simple—acting at a distance isn't their way."

He studied the four men, raised his brows. "As I see it, the only way you and the crew could keep her on board, here in Plymouth, is by committing mutiny—she is, after all, Captain Trevission of the *Esperance*, holder of an extant Letter of Marque. I won't even suggest that—I think it would be an equally bad disaster, just in a different way."

The four men exchanged glances heavy with meaning, then Edgar looked up, grimly nodded. "You're right. We couldn't do it. This is her ship, and none of us would stand against her. She's our leader—it's been that way since her father died."

"And so it should remain." Logan pushed away from the wall, but the cabin was too small to pace.

Griffiths eyed him measuringly. "So what's your solution? Your new plan? We'll do whatever's necessary to keep the capt'n and her family, and the ship and crew, safe."

Logan looked at the other three, saw agreement and the same resolution in each face. "It's simple." In a few brief words, he outlined his plan.

They opened their mouths to argue, closed them, opened them again, then, accepting there was no real option and that he'd countered all their objections, they slowly nodded and agreed.

Logan leaned on the stern rail alongside Linnet, once again at the wheel, and watched the shores of England rise on the horizon.

It had been so many years since he'd last seen them, so many hard, dusty years—the last, spent in chasing the Black Cobra, the hardest of all.

For long moments, he simply stared, let his soul drink in the green. The lush, vibrant fields of Devon—even with the louring sky above, the sight welcomed, soothed.

He was conscious of the glances Linnet threw him, but didn't meet them. She didn't speak, didn't question, but left him to his quiet homecoming.

And it was that. This time he was home for good. He wouldn't be setting out on any more adventures, any more campaigns. Now, in this moment, and he felt it in his bones, he was stepping beyond that phase of his life—and into the next. Whatever it would be.

Whatever he made of it.

Wherever he made it.

He glanced at Linnet, then looked ahead. Home, his uncle had told him, was wherever you chose to make it.

If fate allowed, he would choose to make his home with her.

With that certainty sinking to his bones, he stood beside her and watched her steer her ship into Plymouth Sound.

One thing he knew about was command. As the last of the daylight waned, and she sent the *Esperance* gliding past Drake Island, tacking through the many naval vessels riding at anchor in the protected waters, he harbored not a shred of doubt that Linnet was a natural leader. She could probably even teach him a thing or two about inspiring men— Tommy, Burton, and Calloway, the three young archers, would, he judged, be hers for life.

In that, they would only be joining the rest of the *Esperance*'s crew. To a man, they were devoted to their captain.

Linnet steered the ship directly into Sutton Harbor, Plymouth's principal basin. She called orders; once again at her elbow, Griffiths relayed them. Sails were furled, still others hooked in as the ship slowed, slowed, then, on the last gasp of wind spilling from canvas, was expertly turned to slide smoothly into an empty berth at Sutton Wharf.

The sandbags slung over the ship's side bumped once, then again more softly as the *Esperance* settled. Straightening, pushing away from the rails, Logan swung down to the main deck, then went down the companionway to the stern cabin. He paused only to seize the handles of the two bags he'd left waiting there—Linnet's as well as his—then headed back.

He felt no sentimentality over leaving the *Esperance*—no need to look around and fix anything in his memory. He would be back. As soon as his mission allowed. Of course, he might be, very possibly would be, groveling at Linnet's dainty heels as she strode back on board, but he would be back. He hoped, he prayed.

Emerging on deck, he saw Linnet standing by the railing midship, watching the gangplank being rolled out. The ship had been secured and was now bobbing lazily on the swell. He glanced around, then out at the town as he walked to where Linnet waited, arms folded, beside the gap in the railings. The light was fading fast. Running lights flickered on many ships. In the town, lamps already glowed in many windows, and streetlamps were being lit.

Shadows were lengthening, deepening, prime concealment for watchers and assassins alike.

Halting at the head of the gangplank, directly in front of Linnet, he brought his gaze to her face—only to discover she'd noticed her bag in his hand.

She frowned, stabbed a finger at the bag. "That's mine. Put it down." Raising her eyes to his, she scowled. "You're going on to complete your mission, and I'm sailing home on the *Esperance*. I'm not going ashore with you, not even just for the night."

He dutifully set down the bags, both of them. Faced her, eye to eye, and said, "Today you foiled the Black Cobra's men, and they got a good look at you. By now they know that Captain Linnet Trevission of the *Esperance*, a woman no less, defeated them, took on three ships and left them wallowing in her wake. Their master is not going to be happy—and they won't be, either. For the safety of this ship, your crew, your household, your home—and most especially you yourself—you have to come with me."

The truth, nothing but the truth.

Eyes narrowed, arms crossed even tighter, a barrier be-
tween him and her, she tartly—entirely predictably—replied,
"I'm more than capable of taking care of myself and mine.
All of mine."

He heaved an exaggerated sigh and shifted closer. Lowered his voice so no one else could hear. Held her gaze as
he said, "And who's going to take care of me while I'm distracted, worrying about you?"

Another very real truth.

"What?" She looked genuinely surprised.

Which had him narrowing his eyes. "You heard. If you're
with me, I'll know you're safe. If you're not . . . I'll most
likely fail in my mission because I'll be distracted, concerned over you."

Her eyes slitted to green shards. "No." They were trading
forceful whispers. "I am not falling for that. I don't mean
that much to you—not that much. Nothing you can say will
convince me otherwise. I am *not* coming with you."

He held her gaze. "That's your last word?"

Linnet searched his eyes, trying to find some clue as to
what he was up to. She saw nothing in the midnight blue
beyond his usual relentless determination. She raised her
chin. "Yes."

"Very well." Stepping back, he nodded to Edgar and
Griffiths, standing to one side behind her. "I'll send word."

She was wondering what he meant by that—what word
he would be sending to them—when, turning back to her,
Logan ducked.

He angled his shoulder into her midriff and, before she
could react, cleanly hoisted her over his shoulder, anchoring her legs against his chest with his right arm, in the same
sweeping movement swiping up both of their bags in his
other hand, then he turned and strode down the gangplank.
Fast.

"What . . . ?"

For one definable instant, she was speechless—utterly
dumbfounded.

How dare he?

He swung off the gangplank and turned along the wharf, and she found her tongue. Cursed and swore using every invective, every colorful expletive she'd ever learned in all her years on board—an extensive litany that had no discernible effect whatever.

He actually chuckled.

She threatened him with castration, and he only lengthened his stride, rapidly crossing the wharf toward the old town and its narrow streets.

Fisting her right hand, she thumped on his back, hard. "Put me down this instant, you moron—I am *not* going with you."

He jiggled her on his shoulder. "Watch out for my wound—you don't want to burst your stitches, not after all your hard work."

She swore, switched to her left hand, and thumped his other side. All but screeched, *"Logan!* Enough! Put me *down*—or I'll make it my duty to make the rest of your misbegotten life a misery!"

He halted, heaved a gigantic sigh, then, dropping their bags, finally grasped her waist and eased her down, sliding her down the front of his body until her toes neared the ground.

Before they did, he kissed her.

Kissed her in a way he never had before, with passion, yes, but it was passion leashed, held back so he could . . .

Woo her. Plead, persuade.

Beg.

Her hands came to rest on either side of his face, gently cupping. She couldn't pull away, couldn't stop herself from sensing, savoring, knowing.

When he finally lifted his head, hers was swimming, previous certainties fading, new questions rising.

He stared down into her eyes. "My life is already yours to do with as you please—to make it a misery, or even a living hell. Just as long as you're alive to do that, I don't care."

His gaze lifted, scanning the wharf behind her, then he set

her fully on her feet, seized her hand, and their bags. "Now behave, and come along."

He towed her on, into a street she recognized as Looe Street. "Do you even know where you're going?"

"Yes. I think." He glanced back at her. "I haven't been in Plymouth for years. The Seafarer's Arms—it's this way, isn't it?"

"Yes." She grimaced as he pulled her along. As she let him. Resisting, knowing he'd only hoist her up again, didn't seem worthwhile. But she did want to escape him . . . didn't she?

Frowning, she glanced around. "This is nonsensical." Night was closing in; there were few people around. "You can't keep me with you against my will."

The glance he shot her was dark—too dark to read. "Possibly not." Jaw tightening, he looked ahead. "But I can change your mind. There's no reason for you not to come with me, and every reason that you should."

She knew better than to encourage a madman, but . . . "Why?"

"I told you why." Forging on, he spoke through clenched teeth. "Because I can't function properly without knowing you're safe. And while you're safe, all the others are, too. I know you don't believe that—any more than you believe that I'll return to you when this mission is over—but whether you believe or not doesn't change reality. That is my reality—my truth." Reaching an intersection, he halted, met her eyes as she halted beside him. "The least you can do is give me a chance to prove it."

She held his gaze, in the light from a nearby street flare searched his eyes, saw that he truly was asking for that, a chance to prove he meant what he said. And no matter how hard she looked, the midnight blue of his eyes showed nothing but an unshakable veracity, and beneath that an unshakable belief.

It wasn't a belief she had any confidence in, any faith in, but he did.

She heard herself sigh. "All right." She looked around, pointed. "The Seafarer's Arms is that way, if that's where we're truly headed."

He nodded; scanning the shadows, he grasped her hand more tightly. "Come on—we need to get there. We'll definitely have been spotted by now."

❧ Eleven ❧

*L*innet didn't ask, *Spotted by whom?* She kept her eyes peeled as she took over the lead and steered them to the ancient inn, one of the oldest in the old part of town.

She wasn't certain just what she should do, but leaving Logan at this point wasn't an option. She was still wearing her cutlass, and he his saber; she felt certain he would have his dirk on him somewhere, and she had two knives, one in each boot.

They reached the Seafarer's Arms without challenge, but her instincts were pricking, and by the way Logan looked around before ducking in the door behind her, his were, too.

She paused inside the door. The tap room opened out to her left, a low-ceilinged room with massive oak beams hanging low to strike unwary heads. Lamps bathed the long oak bar with golden light. Five old tars sat enveloped in smoky haze at a pair of tables before the fire. An old woman nodded in the inglenook.

A man in a heavy coat and well-polished boots was sitting at the bar, large hands cradling a pint pot; as the door clicked shut, he turned his head and glanced their way.

And slowly smiled. Leaving his mug on the bar, he stood and walked unhurriedly to them.

He had thick, curling dark hair, and much the same build—much the same dangerous presence—as Logan. Dark, heavy-lidded eyes passed over her, noting and taking in, but as he neared, the man fixed his smiling gaze on Logan and held out his hand. "St. Austell. Monteith, I presume?"

"Indeed." Logan gripped the offered hand with very real relief. He was inexpressibly grateful that St. Austell had been kicking his heels, waiting. That he and Linnet would have to spend the night at the Seafarer's Arms, waiting for his contact to show in the morning, when the cultists had almost certainly already followed them there, had been looming as his worst nightmare. "Thank you for waiting."

"Well, of course." St. Austell's gaze shifted to Linnet. "Paignton and I are keen and eager to start our part in this adventure." Then he arched a black brow at Logan. "But what happened to you?"

"The cult spotted me the instant I disembarked in Lisbon, so I had to take ship immediately, earlier than planned. Unfortunately, I was shipwrecked off Guernsey. More fortunately, I survived and made it to shore. This is Captain Trevission, captain of the *Esperance*. Her household found and tended me until I recovered enough to come on." Logan glanced around. "If you don't mind, I'll explain the rest later. Captain Trevission's ship was attacked en route here, and we were almost certainly followed from the docks."

"And the cult now has even greater reason to want you"— St. Austell's shrewd gaze flicked to Linnet—"both of you, dead?"

"Precisely." It was a relief to work with quick-witted people, but from all he'd heard of the legendary Dalziel, Logan had expected his operatives to be top-notch.

"In that case, I suggest we repair to the carriage I have waiting to whisk us to Paignton Hall and safety." St. Austell waved them toward the rear of the inn. "We can go out the back way. Here"—he took Linnet's bag from Logan—"let me carry that."

They went down a narrow corridor and out of the inn's rear

door. St. Austell led the way across a tiny yard and into the
lane beyond. "This is the oldest part of town—it's a maze of
lanes too narrow for a carriage. Best if we keep silent until
we're through it. It's not that far, and then we'll be—"

The lane they'd been following opened into another
yard; when St. Austell broke off and halted, Linnet peeked
around him—and saw men in an odd mixture of Eastern
and English clothes materializing out of the gloom. All
wore black scarves wrapped around their heads.

All held naked blades in their hands.

She, Logan, and St. Austell had no real option but to
stand and fight. Their only retreat was the narrow runnel at
their back, and they'd never make it. But there were . . . she
counted nine cultists. She hoped they weren't the assassins
Logan had mentioned.

St. Austell shifted to her right. A sliding hiss had her
glancing his way. The edge of a saber like Logan's glinted
in the weak light; he held it in his right hand, hefted her bag
in the other.

She felt Logan brush past, glanced the other way and saw
him take up position on her left, likewise with saber drawn,
his bag in his other hand.

Dragging in a breath, she took a step back and drew her
cutlass from its sheath.

The unexpected movement, the appearance of a third
defending blade, made every man— the two flanking her
as well as their attackers—hesitate. She didn't need to look
to sense the swift exchange of glances that passed over her
head between St. Austell, his black brows raised high, and
Logan, who grimly nodded and refocused his attention on
their attackers.

Slightly crouched, Linnet kept her gaze on their opponents as they spread across the small yard, cutting off any
way forward. Suddenly realizing their vulnerability—the
runnel at their back—she could only applaud when St. Austell stepped further to his right. She shifted smoothly, too,

as did Logan, circling as one, enough to get their backs to solid wall.

Their attackers suddenly realized they'd lost a possible advantage. Savage whispers passed back and forth, then one raised his sword, yelled something incomprehensible, and rushed at St. Austell.

He held his ground until the last minute, then jerked Linnet's bag into his attacker's chest, neatly followed with his saber, and that was one attacker less.

Even before the first man fell, Logan had accounted for another with the same move, the same efficiency, but the other seven followed in a concerted wave.

Sabers flashing to Linnet's right and left, Logan and St. Austell held them back—but just. From her position between the men, Linnet had hoped to have a chance to slip her blade in, but they each had three blades to counter, and that left one cultist to smile a ghastly smile and come directly for her.

She met his first strike, beat it back with one of her own, sensed his surprise that a woman could actually wield a blade. But that wouldn't last; surprise wouldn't save her.

She didn't like to kill, but she'd been taught, schooled, and had learned her lessons in time of war, in the heat of battle. She'd learned to suppress everything but the instinct to survive, to forget about fighting fair and fight to live.

Fit and active though she was, most men were stronger than she. Plucking one of the knives from its sheath in the high top of one of her boots, she countered the cultist's next strike with her sword, then tempted him to strike high. He did, and she met his sword with her own, held it high, stepped forward, and slid her knife between his ribs.

Stepping back, she let him fall, her attention immediately going to the cultist to her right, who, seeing his comrade fall, uttered a shriek and came at her.

She already had her other knife in her hand; all she needed to do was deflect his crazed thrust, step inside, and place her blade. The second cultist slumped on top of the first, creating a barrier. One glance to her right and she saw St. Austell drop one of his remaining opponents, leaving him fighting one on one. From what she'd already seen of his handiwork, he'd be finished shortly.

Unsurprisingly, the strongest and most able cultists had gone for Logan. She watched, picked her time, then pushed in and forced the one nearest her to shift his attack to her.

Logan quickly palmed his dirk and dropped the cultist on his left, then with two swift, powerful cuts, brought down the other who had stayed to parry with him.

Without hesitation, he swung his saber and ruthlessly cut across Linnet's engagement—a dangerous undertaking, but not for her. The cultist who'd been jabbing at her, trying to find a way through her dogged defense, tried desperately to readjust to a stronger and taller opponent, but too late. He joined his fellows on the cold cobbles—just as St. Austell felled the last.

St. Austell held up his hand, enjoining silence. Breaths sawing, bloody blades in their hands, both Logan and Linnet crouched and retrieved their knives.

Then they heard the running footsteps coming from deep in the maze behind them. Without a word, Logan grabbed his bag, St. Austell grabbed Linnet's, and the three of them ran.

Of necessity, St. Austell led the way. Linnet followed, Logan at her heels. She didn't have breath to spare to even think as she pushed herself to keep up with the longer-legged men.

But St. Austell knew his way, and he'd spoken literally. They burst into a wider yet still minor street, and the carriage was there. St. Austell yanked open the door, held it while Linnet, then Logan, piled in, then he threw Linnet's bag in and followed, sprawling on the opposite seat.

Even before the door swung smartly shut, the driver had flicked his reins. The carriage rumbled off—quickly, yet smoothly.

Panting, struggling to catch their breath, they all listened. When the carriage rumbled into one of the main squares, then on down a main street, they all drew in long breaths, righted themselves, Logan and Linnet on the seat facing forward, St. Austell and their bags on the other, and finally relaxed.

St. Austell bent and rummaged beneath the bench seat. Pulling out a rag, he reached for Linnet's bloodied cutlass. "Allow me, captain ma'am."

Linnet's lips quirked wryly. She handed over her blade. "In the circumstances, after what we've just shared, I believe first names are in order. Perhaps we should redo the introductions. I'm Linnet Trevission of Mon Coeur, Guernsey, owner of Trevission Ships, also captain of the *Esperance*."

"Also holder of an extant Letter of Marque," Logan put in.

St. Austell looked suitably and sincerely impressed. "Yet another aspect of your quite astonishing talents. You're also no mean wielder of a blade. I'm one of your two appointed guards." He flourished a half bow. "Charles St. Austell, Earl of Lostwithiel, at your service, but please call me Charles." He handed Linnet's cleaned blade back, beckoned for Logan's.

Logan handed it over. "Logan Monteith, as I assume you're aware ex-major with the Honorable East India Company. And you're no mean wielder of a blade yourself. The Guards?"

"Originally." Handing back Logan's wiped saber, Charles picked up his own. "But Royce—Dalziel as he then was—recruited me within months. After that, I spent most of the war years behind enemy lines. Most at Toulouse."

"You must have seen some difficult times there," Logan said. "Were you in place when we came through?"

Linnet let her attention wander as Logan and Charles compared experiences of the taking of Toulouse while Charles cleaned their knives.

They'd rumbled out of Plymouth and were heading—she consulted her inner compass—east. She didn't know England well, not beyond the major southern ports, but she assumed they were on the road to Exeter.

She was shivering, fine tremors coursing through her.

Without breaking off his conversation, Logan reached for her bag, set it on his knee, opened it, reached in, and drew out her traveling cloak. Returning the bag to the opposite seat, still chatting with Charles, he shook out the cloak, then held it for her, helping her drape it about her shoulders.

She accepted the additional warmth glady enough, allowing the fiction that she was shivering due to the increasing chill stand. But it wasn't cold that had her muscles so tense that they were trembling. Nor was it exhaustion or simple shock; she'd been in far worse and longer battles, seen death at closer quarters, had had to fight for her life, had had to kill before.

But she'd never before fought alongside someone she cared about as she cared for Logan. Never stood beside someone with whom she'd shared that degree of intimacy and known their opponents were fixated on killing him.

A deeper, more icy shiver shuddered through her.

Raising her head, she shook it—as if by doing so she could shake off the lingering emotional panic. She glanced at Logan, sure he'd noticed. Beneath the folds of her cloak, his hand closed warmly about hers, squeezed gently, but otherwise he gave no sign, for which she was grateful.

His gaze remained on Charles. "What news do you have of the others?"

Charles handed back her knives and Logan's dirk. While they tucked them back into their boots, he said, "Delborough's in England. He landed at Southampton on the tenth of the month. There was a spot of bother there, apparently, but he got away cleanly and has been in London for several days, although I suspect he'll have moved on by now. It sounds as if he'll be the first to reach Royce. Hamilton's in Boulogne, or was a few days ago. We're expecting Royce to send word that Hamilton's landed and is on his way to him, but any message will take a while to reach us down here."

"Carstairs?"

"We've had no word of him, but that doesn't mean Royce

hasn't. Our ex-commander has a tendency to share only what he feels one needs to know."

"We heard that he—Dalziel—is now Wolverstone."

Charles nodded. "He was Marquess of Winchelsea all through his years of service, not that we ever knew. It was one of those twisted, only-in-the-British-nobility tales."

"Regardless, his reputation is all but legendary. How long were you under his command?"

Logan and Charles settled to discuss wartime espionage. Linnet's attention drifted. Soothed by the steady rocking of the carriage, she focused on the now black night outside, the wind raking the trees bordering the road.

No icy drafts penetrated the carriage. Registering that, she looked more closely, despite the enfolding dimness noted the superb craftsmanship, the luxurious trim. This wasn't just a carriage—it was a very expensive carriage.

Presumably Charles's—the earl's.

She was out of her depth socially, but she'd already heard enough of Charles's exploits, seen enough of him, to know he was a man very much like Logan. A man of action and adventure, doubtless infinitely happier riding into battle than doing the pretty in some hostess's drawing room.

She could manage Charles, deal with him and any like him. Which was just as well.

She hadn't made any final, reasoned decision to fall in with Logan's insistence that for her safety, and that of those connected with her, she should travel on with him.

Yet here she was.

The rush from the inn and the battle in the narrow yard had made any further arguing moot. After seeing the cult's members face-to-face, seeing Logan trying to defend against three simultaneously—something no swordsman, no matter how brilliant, could be certain of doing and living to tell the tale—she was no longer focused on rejoining the *Esperance* and setting sail for home. Not yet.

Given the icy fear she'd experienced in that poky little

yard, given the aftermath still fading from her muscles, from her very bones, she would stay with Logan and travel on with him until his mission was complete.

Not for her safety, but for his.

That she could tip the scales in engagements such as the one in the yard—the most likely type he would encounter in winning through to his goal, wherever in England that was—owed nothing to starry-eyed, foolhardy optimism but was simple fact. Men never expected a woman to fight. They discounted her presence, her ability, and that instantly gave her, and the side she fought on, an advantage, one she was well equipped to exploit.

She paused, pressing her mind to rationally examine her decision—an impulsive one, yet all her instincts screamed it was right. No matter which way she twisted the facts, she came up with the same answer—the same best plan.

She would continue on with Logan, guarding him while he guarded her, until he reached his goal and successfully concluded his mission. Then she would bid him farewell and return home to Guernsey, to Mon Coeur, leaving him to the life he would live—would choose to live—once he returned to the world in which he belonged.

Glancing at him, then at Charles, she gathered her cloak closer and settled into the well-padded seat.

Minutes later, the carriage slowed, then turned right. Looking out, she glimpsed a signpost, managed to decipher Totnes. "Where are we heading?" She looked at Charles, remembered. "Paignton Hall, I think you said."

Charles nodded. "It's south of Paignton itself, on the coast beyond Totnes. It's Deverell's—Viscount Paignton's—family seat."

"My other guard?" Logan asked.

"Indeed. There were four of you coming in, and Royce could call on eight of us, so you each have two guards to conduct you to our erstwhile leader's presence. You'll be relieved to learn that for the occasion he's wintering on his estate in Suffolk, and not at his principal seat, Wolverstone

Castle, on the border in Northumbria." Charles glanced at Linnet, smiled reassuringly. "Paignton Hall is our refuge for the moment—a safe place to take stock. The Hall is built into the husk of an old castle—quite neat. They have the views, the position, the outer walls and the bailey, but not the drafts."

His gaze slid over her; his expression, his smile, what she could see of it in the dimness, turned decidedly wry. "Penny, my wife, and Deverell's wife, Phoebe, are going to be utterly thrilled to meet you. If I could just mention, if you could avoid giving them too many ideas, Deverell and I will be forever grateful."

Linnet stared at him. She was tempted to ask exactly what he meant, but . . . he'd just informed her she was going to be staying at an aristocratic residence—part castle, no less—in the company of ladies, and all she could think was that she had only one gown—and that a traveling gown—with her.

Still smiling, Charles shifted his gaze to Logan. "I meant to mention—we have a connection of sorts through our fathers. Along the lines of my father the earl knew your father the earl. Apparently they first took their seats in the Lords on the same day and remained acquaintances ever after— connected via a shared ordeal, you might say."

Slowly, all but unable to believe her ears, Linnet turned her head to stare at Logan. He was an *earl's* son?

His gaze on Charles, he shrugged lightly. "My father died some years ago—he never mentioned the acquaintance, but we weren't close."

He asked about Charles's home, which was, apparently, Lostwithiel Castle—a real castle, drafts and all—in Cornwall.

Linnet heard, but wasn't truly listening. Traveling on with Logan was leading her into waters far deeper, and more strewn with reefs, than she'd foreseen.

As if to emphasize just how out of her depth she was, their arrival at Paignton Hall went entirely counter to her expectations.

The Hall itself was everything Charles had promised. But from the moment the carriage halted in what was clearly the old inner bailey and she followed the men out onto the cobbles, in a nod to feminine decorum allowing Logan to hand her down, nothing went quite as she'd expected.

For a start, a beautiful, willowy blond in a simple woollen gown came rushing down the steps to fling herself into Charles's arms. He caught her with a laugh, kissed her soundly—but then she pulled back and pinned him with a narrow-eyed look. "You've been fighting. I can tell. Have you been wounded?"

The quality of Charles's smile as he slung an arm about the lady's shoulders was breathtaking. "Such confidence in my swordwork. But no—I didn't take so much as a scratch." He looked up as another couple descended the steps to join them, the gentleman dark-haired and distinguished looking—a somewhat less obvious version of Logan and Charles—the lady on his arm with dark auburn hair, and a kind, openly welcoming smile on her face.

They proved to be their host and hostess, Viscount and Viscountess Paignton. Charles made the introductions.

While the men shook hands, Paignton—who went by the name of Deverell—expressing his disgust that he'd missed the action, both ladies, far from turning up their aristocratic noses as Linnet had fully expected, smiled delightedly and welcomed her eagerly, touching fingers, then turning to flank her as they escorted her up the front steps. "You truly are most welcome," Phoebe, Viscountess Paignton, assured her. "I had no idea Monteith was bringing a lady with him, but I'm delighted he did."

Linnet looked from one delicate face to the other, sensed sincerity and a certain determination behind both, and felt curious enough to admit, "The truth is, *I* had no idea I would be traveling on with him. I found him shipwrecked on my land on Guernsey, my household cared for him until he regained his strength and his memory, then I brought him to

Plymouth on my ship, but I expected to leave him there and sail home—"

She broke off as they halted in the lamplit front hall and Lady Penelope waved her hands to halt Linnet's words. "Wait, wait! I'm already dying with envy. First let me say that along with Phoebe here, I am most sincerely thrilled to see you, because you clearly know something about this mission all our men are about to embark on, so you can tell us—give us a feminine view of the matter. However, my head is reeling, filled with avidly green jealousy."

In the better light, along with Phoebe, Lady Penelope ran her shrewd gaze down Linnet, taking in her jacket, leather breeches, high boots, and her cutlass still riding at her hip, then she pointed a delicate finger at the cutlass. "Don't tell me they allowed you to fight alongside them?"

Linnet looked from one openly amazed face to the other, but could detect not a single hint of censure. "I didn't actually ask their permission."

Lady Penelope blinked, asked of no one in particular, "Why didn't I ever think of that?"

Intrigued, Linnet added, "I have two daggers in my boots, as well."

"Did you account for any of the attackers?" Phoebe's eyes had hardened, her chin firm.

"Two. But we didn't wait to check if they were dead. It started off as nine to three, and once we'd accounted for the first nine, there were more coming, so we ran."

"May I?"

Linnet turned to find Lady Penelope with a hand hovering by her—Linnet's—thigh, fingers waggling, wanting to touch her breeches. Bemused, already fascinated by these totally unexpected gently bred females, Linnet nodded. "Of course."

The Countess of Lostwithiel ran her hand over the fine, butter-soft leather, felt its quality, and heaved a long, wistful sigh. "Please call me Penny—and I would really love a pair like that. Can I inveigle you into telling me where you got them? On Guernsey, or farther afield? Not that I care—I'll send Charles anywhere."

"Actually, they're from much nearer to hand." Linnet grinned at Penny's eager expression. "Exeter—there's a leathermaker there I convinced to make them for me. I can give you his direction."

Penny clasped her hands to her bosom, her face alight. "Wonderful! I've just decided what Charles can get me to make amends over me having to miss the action in this latest adventure."

"I'm still working on what to wring from Deverell," Phoebe said. "But I have another question. You said you conveyed Monteith to Plymouth on your ship. You own a ship? Do you sail it?"

Her lips curving irrepressibly, Linnet snapped a jaunty salute. "I'm afraid I left my captain's hat on board, but I'm Captain Trevission, owner of Trevission Ships, and in particular, the barque the *Esperance*." She glanced over her shoulder at Logan, lightly frowned. "Mind you, I'm not, at this precise moment, exactly sure where my ship is. My crew were seduced into letting me be carried off it, but I suspect the *Esperance* is currently riding in Plymouth Sound, safely tucked among His Majesty's warships."

The men had followed them into the hall. Logan heard her comment, smiled crookedly, and inclined his head.

"I think," Phoebe said, tucking her arm in Linnet's, "that you and I, Penny, should escort Captain Trevission to a nice guest room, and learn just how she's achieved such things in no more years than we've had."

"Indeed." Penny took Linnet's other arm. "Clearly there's much here we can learn."

When Phoebe paused to give instructions to her kindly butler and her efficient-looking housekeeper, Linnet glanced back at the three men, and saw Charles's and Deverell's faintly concerned expressions—remembered Charles's comment about not giving their ladies ideas—and finally understood.

Smiling, she looked ahead and allowed Penny and Phoebe to sweep her up the stairs. "Actually, there is one thing you could help me with." Reaching the head of the stairs, she glanced at Penny, confirming, as they started along the corridor, that they were much the same height and not dissimilar in shape. "In return for the direction of my breeches maker."

"Anything!" Penny declared. "At the moment, I would even gift you with my firstborn—he's been a handful all day, wanting to follow his father, of course."

Linnet laughed. "Thank you, but I have one of those— well, not mine, but one of my wards. But I really do need some gowns."

"My wardrobe is yours." Penny smiled intently. "Just as long as you tell us all you know."

"All," Phoebe said, halting at a door along the main corridor, "that our dear husbands are keeping to their chests."

She set the door swinging wide, then ushered Linnet in. "Now—how about a bath?"

She had, Linnet decided, landed in some strange heaven.

She'd never had feminine companionship like this—freely offered, from ladies of her own class, her own generation. It was . . . a revelation.

Under Phoebe's direction, a bath had been prepared, and Linnet had luxuriated, then Penny had arrived with a selection of gowns, all of which she'd insisted Linnet take, assuring her, "I always pack so much more than I need."

While Linnet had dressed, then dried and combed out her hair, the other two had perched in the window seat and they'd talked. They'd shared bits and pieces of their lives openly with her, and she'd found herself reciprocating.

She and Penny had exchanged tales of horses and riding, shipwrecks and sailing, and she'd listened with rapt attention while Phoebe had explained about her agency, then they'd listened with real interest while she'd described Mon Coeur and explained about her wards.

Phoebe had instantly volunteered her agency should any of Linnet's brood ever want to find work in England. "I can always place well-educated young women, and even young men, as companions or personal secretaries."

Linnet had had no idea aristocratic ladies were so engaged and active.

When she'd said so, Penny had pulled a face. "The sad truth is, a lot aren't, but we are, and all those you'll meet when you reach Elveden—the end of your journey—are like us, too. We have the position, the wherewithal, and the ability, and so we do. Sitting and embroidering is definitely not for us."

Phoebe had laughed. "In fact, not many of us can embroider. Minerva, Royce's wife, does, beautifully, and perhaps Alicia might. But most of us are not, as one might say, accomplished in that direction."

Linnet had grinned. "In that respect, at least, I'll fit in."

By the time the three of them went downstairs to join the men for dinner, Linnet was, to her very real surprise, relaxed, at ease, and indeed, in that moment at least, enjoying herself.

Not that she didn't have a bone or two to pick with Logan, but that would have to wait until later.

Over dinner, the others were eager to hear about Logan's mission thus far, from its beginning in India to when he and Linnet had arrived at the Seafarer's Arms.

Reassured that all was well with Linnet—very aware that it was at his insistence that she'd been forced into a world she wasn't accustomed to, and that any consequent unhappiness would lie at his door, and thus relieved and cravenly grateful to Penny and Phoebe for smoothing her way—Logan set himself to succinctly but comprehensively satisfy their curiosity.

Linnet listened, too, no doubt adding flesh to the bare bones he'd previously revealed to her, but she left all questions to the others. Charles and Deverell were experienced interrogators; they knew what to ask to clarify his story.

When it came to Linnet's part in it, he didn't hold back. She blushed at his compliments, his very real praise, tried to deflect attention by claiming it was no more than anyone else would have done—which argument none of the others accepted.

Penny waved Linnet's words aside. "There's no help for it—you're heroine material. No point trying to clamber off the pedestal. You'll just have to get used to the height."

Which shut Linnet up. Logan thought she was dumfounded, which in his admittedly short experience was a first.

He took pity on her and quickly summed up their time in Plymouth, which brought them to the present and Paignton Hall.

They paused to allow the empty dessert dishes to be cleared.

When the footmen had withdrawn, Deverell asked, "So your mission's a decoy run?"

When Logan nodded, Charles said, "From the way Royce is managing the four individual threads of this action, I suspect Delborough's most likely a decoy, too. Hamilton I'm not sure about."

Logan thought of his comrades, of Gareth, and especially Rafe, about whom he'd yet to hear definite information. He stirred, looked down the table at Deverell, then across it at Charles. "So what now? Where to from here?"

Deverell raised his brows at Phoebe, at the other end of the table. "Shall we repair to the drawing room to make our plans?"

Phoebe nodded decisively. "Yes, let's. Aside from all else, we ladies aren't about to leave you gentlemen to swap secrets over the port. If you want any spirits, bring the decanters with you."

Deverell checked with Charles and Logan, but as none of them felt the need for any further bolstering, they left the decanters on the sideboard and fell in on the ladies' heels as they led the way to the drawing room.

A minor distraction occurred when the respective nannies ushered in the Deverell and St. Austell children to say their goodnights. Logan watched as Linnet smiled and shook hands with Charles's two little boys, and Deverell's eldest daughter and his son, admitting that yes, she really was a ship's captain, that yes, her ship was a big one with lots of sails, an oceangoing vessel, not a sailboat, but that as yet she hadn't ordered anyone to walk the plank.

Satisfied, the children smiled huge smiles, bobbed bows and curtsies, and chorused their goodnights.

Penny and Phoebe handed their youngest children— Penny's daughter, Phoebe's second girl—to their husbands to jiggle, kiss, then return to the nannies' waiting arms.

When the door finally shut behind the small cavalcade, Penny fixed her eyes on her husband's face. "Right. Now cut line, and tell us what your orders are."

Charles arched a brow at Deverell.

Subsiding beside his wife on one chaise, Deverell said, "I've already sent a messenger to Royce to report that Logan's reached us hale and whole, and with his scroll-holder still in his possession. However, Logan was late in to Plymouth, so Royce has already sent us our orders for the next leg. We're instructed to reach Oxford by the evening of the nineteenth, traveling via Bath, where we're to stay at The York House. Further orders will await us at the University Arms in Oxford. Our ultimate goal is Royce's house, Elveden Grange, just short of Thetford in Suffolk, but he'll want us coming in on a specific route, on a particular day. Presumably we'll learn which route and what day once we reach Oxford."

Lounging beside Penny on the opposite chaise, Charles said, "Given the enemy knows you're in England, and will almost certainly trace us to Totnes, I suggest we remain here in safety before doing a dash in the minimum number of days required to reach Oxford on the nineteenth."

Deverell nodded, his gaze going to Logan. "We're safe

here—it's close to impossible to successfully attack this house."

Logan inclined his head. "So what's the minimum number of days on the road to get from here to Oxford?"

"Two," Deverell replied. "With the days so short—and we certainly won't want to be traveling through the night, inviting attack—then it'll take us one long day to reach Bath, and then a shorter day's journey to Oxford."

"That should allow us some flexibility as to which roads to take," Charles said, "although I assume we'll stick mostly to the main highways."

Deverell leaned back. "Unless we have reason to do otherwise, that would be my plan."

"All right," Phoebe said. "It's the sixteenth today, so that leaves you tomorrow to make preparations and get everything arranged, then the day after tomorrow, you leave for Bath."

Everyone nodded. Charles looked at Phoebe, then Penny beside him. "I still can't believe Minerva invited you and the children—and the other wives with theirs, too—to join us at Elveden."

"Minerva," Penny stated, adding for Logan's and Linnet's benefit, "she's Royce's duchess, is an eminently wise and sensible lady. And she's now one of the grandest of the *grandes dames*, so of course we can't possibly decline the invitation."

"Especially not when that invitation so perfectly aligns with your own wishes," Deverell rather acerbically remarked.

Phoebe struggled to keep her lips straight as she patted her husband's hand. "Indeed. Especially not then." She looked at Penny. "If they're leaving the day after tomorrow"—she glanced at Deverell—"and I expect you'll be away at dawn?"

Resigned, he nodded. "We should leave at first light, if not just before—if there's any surprise to be had, we want it on our side."

"Well, then"—Phoebe looked at Penny—"I can't see any reason why we couldn't set off within an hour or so."

Logan shifted, frowning as he imagined it. "If you can, it would be wiser to wait a few hours at least." He met Deverell's, then Charles's, eyes. "We have to work on the assumption that the cult will locate us here, that they might be watching. If we leave, they'll follow us, but it would be preferable that they get no hint that anyone else might be leaving shortly after."

"In case they think to take hostages?" Charles asked.

"No point taking chances." Logan looked at Phoebe. "Don't start making preparations—any that might be seen from outside the Hall—until we've been gone for at least two hours. If there's others waiting for us further up the road, those watching might mill about for a while when we leave, but if there's nothing happening here, they won't stay—they'll fall in on our tail."

Charles and Deverell both nodded emphatically.

"That's what you'll need to do." Charles looked at his wife. "Where had you planned to stay on the road?"

Penny exchanged a look with Phoebe. "We'd planned to make Andover on the first night, which we still should be able to do." When Phoebe nodded, Penny went on. "There's a very large hotel there—what with our guards around us as well, we'll be perfectly safe. On the second day, we'll travel through London to Woodford."

"Another very large hotel, again with lots of other people around," Phoebe put in. "Which means we'll reach Elveden easily on the third day. We'll be there to welcome you when you get there."

Charles glanced at Deverell, grimaced. "I suppose, as neither of you will consent not to go, then the best we can do is surround you with guards."

Penny smiled resignedly. "We'll take however many you want to send, but if I might point out, we're already resembling a royal procession."

Charles grunted.

Linnet asked a question about Elveden Grange, and the talk veered into less fraught waters.

Leaving the three men reminiscing about the war and their respective parts in it, Linnet climbed the stairs with Phoebe and Penny, very ready to rest. The day had been beyond eventful; quite aside from recouping physically, she had a great deal to review and digest. Parting from the other two at the head of the stairs, she found her way to her comfortable chamber and what promised to be a very comfortable bed.

Undressing by the light of a small lamp some maid had left burning, Linnet let her mind range over all she'd learned that day—the true danger of Logan's mission, the reality that she could, and now looked set to, play a part, in her mind as his guardian, his keeper, regardless of what he might think. The abrupt shift in her view of aristocratic ladies, the realization that, at least in terms of Phoebe's and Penny's world, she might indeed fit in; they thought like her, had so much in common, shared so many attitudes, and had no more patience with social pretense than she did. She had a shrewd suspicion that, given the circumstances, they could both be as bold and as brazen as she.

She found Charles's and Deverell's attitudes to their wives interesting, too. Revealing, intriguing—their marriages were definitely not the norm, or at least not the norm as she had previously understood it.

There was a lot to assimilate, a large number of her views to reassess and rescript in light of what she'd observed. Yet one topic, one piece of news, increasingly filled her mind, increasingly captured her thoughts. Increasingly commanded her entire attention.

Logan was an earl's son.

What did that mean with respect to her?

In a nightgown Penny had loaned her, wrapped in the counterpane for warmth, she was standing by the window staring out at the restless sea and wrestling with that question when the door opened and Logan came in.

She glanced at him. "I wondered if you'd come. I've no idea which room you were given."

With a quirk of his brows, he sat on the end of the bed and bent to ease off his boots. "I could tell you it was my superior tracking skills that led me to your door, but the truth is my room is two doors further along, and going down to dinner I passed this door and heard your voice." Setting his boots aside, he looked at her. "Regardless, I would have found you. I wasn't about to stay away."

She faced him, but didn't venture closer. "Wasn't about to sleep alone?"

Logan studied her face in the lamplight; the set of her features was uninformative, her eyes shadowed. "No." He had no interest in sleeping alone ever again, not if he could help it. "However, if you're wondering if that was part of the reason I insisted you came with me, the answer is no—that consideration didn't occur at the time, and weighed not at all in my decision. Yet now you are here, with me, I can't imagine not lying with you, sleeping with you in my arms."

She seemed to hear the truth in his words. Yet still she hesitated, her arms wrapped over the counterpane, her gaze on him.

Then her lips firmed, and her gaze grew sharper. "An earl's son?"

The question was quiet, yet loaded with intensity. With intent.

Mentally cursing his luck, he baldly stated, "My father was the Earl of Kirkcowan."

"Was? He's dead. So who's the earl now?"

"His eldest son." Standing, he shrugged off his coat, tossed it on a nearby chair. Started unbuttoning his waistcoat.

"From which curt description, I take it you're estranged?"

He nodded. "I'm . . ." *A bastard.* "The black sheep of the family." He had to tell her, and surely this was the perfect opening, but he hadn't yet got all in place. He was too good a commander to charge in when his troops weren't ready. Jaw tightening, he said, "You don't need to worry about my . . . elevated connections. In every sense, they're irrelevant."

"Are they?"

"Yes." Laying aside his waistcoat, he turned as she came closer, but she halted more than a yard away, studied his face as, raising his chin, he unknotted, then unwound, his cravat.

From her stance, arms still folded, from her increasingly determined expression, from the frown tangling her brows, she was preparing for battle.

Sure enough . . .

"Originally you swore you'd return to me. Instead, you've managed to whisk me away with you." Her green gaze locked on his eyes. "But you can't keep me with you. You'll have to let me go in the end."

Meeting her challenging gaze with adamantine stubbornness, he started unbuttoning his shirt. "I am not going to walk away from you." *Stubborn witch.* "I won't be letting you go. Not now, not later. You'd best get used to that."

The scoffing sound she made stated she was far from that.

"Just how do you see that working?" Temper snapping, Linnet swung out an arm, encompassing the pair of them and the bed. Inside her roiled panicky fear—and the fact she felt it scared her even more. The desperate fight in the narrow yard, the race through the maze with enemies in pursuit, the knowledge that those enemies were still there, lurking beyond the Hall's thick walls to fall on him again . . . her reaction to that, and to what that reaction meant and might mean, shook her to the core.

She'd fallen in love with this stubborn, irritating, impossible man, and she'd never be the same again.

Her heart would never be the same again.

That didn't mean she would let him trample it, cause her more pain—more pain than she would feel anyway when they came to part.

She stepped closer, locked her eyes on his. "I refuse to allow you to keep me with you. I will not be kept." Raising a finger, she pointed at his patrician nose. "I will not be a kept woman. I will not be your mistress, sitting waiting for you at your house in Glenluce."

Something flared in his eyes, some emotion so powerful that her unruly heart leapt and her nerves skittered, but then he locked his jaw, reined it, whatever it was, in.

All but ground his teeth as, eyes burning darkly, he stated, "I don't want you as my mistress."

She held his gaze. "What, then?"

"I want you as my *wife*, damn it!"

Slowly, she released the breath she'd been holding. Commendably evenly stated, "Wife." She'd assumed he'd meant that, but . . . "You never said anything about marriage. You didn't mention a single associated word—like *wife, bride, wedding*." Belligerently stepping closer still, temper rising as her emotions churned, even more out of control than before—God, how did he make her *feel* so much?—she deployed her finger again, wagging it under his aristocratic nose. "And don't you *dare* suggest that me not jumping to a wedding-bell assumption is in some way a slur on your honor. I can't read your damned mind—and it's not as if scions of noble houses don't keep mistresses. It's a time-honored tradition for earl's sons!"

The point that had been preying on her mind for the past hours. Folding her arms, a barrier between them, she glared at him from close quarters.

Somewhat to her surprise, he didn't glare back.

Hands fisted at his sides, jaw clenched, Logan held his fire—because she was right. He'd spelled out his intentions to her men, but he hadn't told her, not clearly. He'd sworn he would never give her up, had insisted that once he was free, he wanted to share his life with her, but he hadn't mentioned marriage.

He'd omitted stating what to him had been the obvious. He'd assumed she had, as he had, come to see their relationship as something any sane man would seek to formalize, that, indeed, being a very sane woman, she would view it in the same light . . . but she hadn't.

Clearly she hadn't been thinking along those lines. Marriage lines. Vows and permanency.

Which was both a blow to his pride, and a sudden, jolting disappointment—more, a threat. A threat to what he now wanted, nay, needed his life to be—a threat to his dreams for the future.

Yet he couldn't fault her—she'd always stated that in her view their liaison would inevitably end. She'd expected it to end in Plymouth. Instead, he'd all but kidnapped her, and now . . .

His eyes locked with hers, he dragged in a slow breath, filling his lungs, fighting to clear his head while he grappled with how to forge a way forward. Her description of a mistress sitting and waiting in a house in Glenluce . . . the vision had rocked him, pricked him on the raw as nothing else could have. The thought that he would ever subject her to that . . .

That had been his mother's life. It would never be Linnet's. Not while he breathed.

Forcing his fingers to uncurl, his jaw to ease, he slowly lifted his hands and gently closed them about her arms, simply held her and looked into her eyes. "You're irritated, annoyed—and you've already countered any argument I might make that you ought to have guessed what my intentions were, any righteous assertion that as a gentleman I'd never have slept with you—continued to make love to you— if my intentions hadn't been honorable—"

Eyes sparking, she opened her mouth—

"No—it's your turn to listen."

Reluctantly, all but smoldering, she subsided.

"You countered those arguments before I made them because you've already thought back and realized that, all along, I *could* have been intending marriage—you just assumed I wasn't." He held her gaze. "But I was. As God is my witness, I never thought of making you my mistress—I don't want you as that. I want you in my bed, but I also want to have breakfast with you, to spend my days, my time, with you. I want to dine with you, to follow you on your rounds and check the doors after you, and follow you up the stairs to your bed.

"I want that as my life, my future. I told you I wanted to share my life with you, but I didn't say anything about marriage because the fact that I might die, or be too seriously wounded to have a life to share, precludes that. You saw what I'm facing—the cult is determined to kill me and seize the scroll-holder. Until we reach the end of this, I can't—in the traditional, honorable way can't—make any formal offer for your hand."

He dragged in another breath. "But I can tell you this—*you* are the woman I want to share the rest of my life with, whether you consent to marry me or not. I won't willingly let you go, and while, as you're so relentless in telling me, I can't force you to stay with me, I can, and will, do everything I can to change your mind."

Still holding her gaze, he drew her to him, slid his hands slowly around the silky comforter in which she was wrapped. Quietly stated, "I want you as my wife, to have and to hold, and never release from the day we exchange our vows."

She blinked up at him. Watched as he bent his head to hers, but didn't pull back, away.

He sensed in her gaze, in the uncertainty of her stance— her uncharacteristic indecision over whether to sink against him or hold rigid in his arms—that she was caught in emotional turmoil, too.

Unexpected turmoil. Matters between them were not proceeding as, apparently, either of them had thought.

The realization lent a grim edge to his voice as, letting his lips cruise her temple, he murmured, "I want you. I want a life with you, a traditional, time-honored married life with you—and I would prefer not to settle for anything less." He paused, his breath fanning her cheek, then added, "I've been a soldier, a commander, all my adult life, and I'm going to fight for you. And win. I will push to win. Because, for me, there's no other choice." He bent the last inch and his lips brushed hers. "You are my future, the only future I want."

He kissed her, pressed his lips to hers and caressed. Gathered her closer, inexpressibly relieved when she permitted it—more, when she came. When she sank slowly against him and let him settle her there, her hips to his thighs, her taut belly cradling his arousal.

Arousing him even more.

He wanted her with a power, a force, a raw need that ripped at him. A need their discussion, her miscomprehension of his intentions, had only whipped to more raging heights.

But this wasn't a battle that could be won with force and might, not with power. Only with persuasion.

So he set himself to persuade, to hold all the power, the force and raw might of his need in check—let her see it, sense it, know it was there, but that it was, for her, held at bay.

Held back so he could show her, demonstrate and reveal how real and vital, how vibrant and deep, was his ardor. His passion, his desire, his fathomless need of her, something that welled from his heart, not just his loins, that lived in his soul, not just his mind.

Linnet sensed the difference, his intent. Felt it in the heavy thud of his heart beneath the palm she placed, braced, on his chest. Sensed it in the way his lips moved on hers, enticing, beguiling, not seizing, not taking.

Knew it in the strength, masculine and demanding, yet tonight not commanding, that closed around her, surrounding her, but gently.

All but reverently.

And yet the passion built, the heat and the flames, until her own need rose. Until their lips turned greedy, hungry and needy, until their bodies yearned.

He released her and shrugged out of his shirt. She dealt with the buttons at his waist, then, as he stepped back to strip off his breeches, she dropped the counterpane, quickly flicked the ties at her throat free.

Naked, he gripped the nightgown, with quiveringly restrained care drew it off over her head.

Then he flung it away, reached for her, and she went into his arms.

Caught her breath as he lifted her, wound her legs about his waist, her arms about his neck and gasped, head back, as, slowly, he filled her.

Filled her until she was full and complete.

Held her in his arms while they both, for that magical instant, savored.

Then he tipped his head up and his lips found hers, and he kissed her and she kissed him back and clung as he moved her on him.

As he lifted her, drew her down, thrust in.

Their bodies strained to race, to plunge and plunder, yet he held them back. Even though the drumbeat of their mutual desire had escalated, even though, steady and relentless, it pushed them on, he still took his time, held their rhythm to a rigidly reined cadence, and showed her.

More.

Lavished feeling and sensation and delicious delight on her, on her body. Fed her whirling mind with another type of joy, communicated by his hands as they held her securely, by his body as he used it in myriad ways to please and pleasure her.

And she couldn't fight this—couldn't resist his lure. Couldn't pretend she didn't see, didn't know, didn't understand what he was doing, what he wanted her to see.

What he wanted her to want.

Him. Like this. For the rest of her life.

She could have told him she did, that that very need was a barb buried deep in her heart, in her soul. But she didn't.

Head back, breathing labored, she shook free of all thought, gave herself up to the moment, and rode on through a landscape colored by sensation. He found her, snared her, pushed her up, quick and hard, to the peak of jagged desire, and she shattered in bright incandescence.

Even as, tumbling her back on the bed, he followed her down, then came inside her, hard and fast, deep and powerful, again, she couldn't find the words, couldn't grasp the essential meaning of what she should say.

What she could say, could tell him.

Instead, she let all inhibitions fall, joined with him and let him drive them on into a landscape richer, more vibrant, more brilliant, more intense—let all she felt free to well through her and meet all the passion, the desire, the need he let her see.

In that moment she accepted what lay between them— what he felt, what she felt, what together they had somehow created.

This was real.

Powerful, intense.

That reality was etched on his face as, head rising, he groaned as his body clenched, then shuddered with release.

She went with him, let the potent pleasure have her, shatter her, clung as together they flew. . . .

They drifted back to earth, locked in each other's arms.

As he slumped, wracked and spent, upon her, as her arms closed around him and held him close, as her body welcomed his weight, his warmth, savored that incredible moment of closeness, she acknowledged this was right, that this was truth, that above all, this was their reality.

For tonight, knowing that, recognizing that, was enough.

Tomorrow, in the harsh light of a winter's day, she would weigh, assess.

She would have to adjust.

Because this, and he, would never leave her. That much, she now understood.

Late at night
Bury St. Edmunds, Suffolk

"So where do we *really* stand?"

In the bedroom Alex had chosen as theirs in the temporarily empty house tucked into the arches of the old abbey ruins into which they'd moved that day, Daniel watched his lover pace.

They'd just parted from Roderick, who had reported that, with heavy snow now blanketing the region, the boy-thief Roderick's man Larkins had inserted into Delborough's household—now quartered at Somersham Place with the Cynsters—would have to wait for the drifts to decrease before delivering the scroll-holder to Larkins at nearby Ely Cathedral.

"Why so agitated?" Daniel bent to warm his hands at the fire. The house was still cold. Their people had been in residence for less than a day, not enough time for the fires to dispel the winter chill. "Delborough's not going anywhere in this snow, and Larkins seems to have set up a reasonable scheme to get his hands on the colonel's scroll-holder. We'll just have to wait and see on that front. There's nothing you or I can do to improve matters."

Frowning, Alex bit a nail—never a good sign.

Inwardly Daniel sighed, and continued, his tone steady and reassuring, "Hamilton's gone to ground and—given the weather—is unlikely to move north for a day or so. But when he does, we'll know of it before he crosses the Thames. As for the other two . . . a rider just came in with news."

As he'd known it would, the information captured Alex's immediate attention.

Inwardly smiling, Daniel went on, "Monteith's ship, the one he took from Lisbon, has failed to reach port. It's believed to have been lost in a storm in the Channel." Catching Alex's pale eyes, Daniel smiled coldly. "I think we can assume that, one way or another, Monteith is feeding the fishes as we speak."

Alex flashed a chilly smile in response, but didn't cease pacing. "We've heard nothing more about Carstairs?"

"No, but that may be to the good. It gives us time to deal with the others without having yet another on the doorstep."

Alex grimaced. "True."

Daniel waited, quietly pointed, for some explanation of Alex's continuing concern.

Alex waved. "It's this notion of a puppetmaster. More than a notion—there *is* someone behind this, driving the entire scheme, and we don't know who he is. That, my dear, is what's worrying me. I *hate* not knowing who our opposition is."

Halting, Alex met Daniel's eyes. "As I said earlier, this puppetmaster is someone with real power."

"You're sure it's not St. Ives?"

"Yes. If what Roderick says is true, it won't be him. St. Ives is . . . a lieutenant, if you like. Which only underscores our puppetmaster's standing. He commands at a very high level, and he's somewhere around here." Alex sat on the bed and frowned up at Daniel. "It's worrisome, to say the least, that we now have someone of that caliber involved."

Daniel left the fire. Halting before Alex, he wondered what the correct thing to say was.

Alex could be difficult. Against that, Alex was rarely wrong.

"Perhaps," Daniel ventured, "either Delborough or Hamilton might lead us to this puppetmaster—after we relieve them of their scroll-holders, of course."

"Of course." Alex sighed and fell back across the bed. "I just wish I could feel more confident that Delborough is the one carrying Roderick's letter. That way, once we seize it, we can depart this drab, dreary, and oh-so-damp place, and never need to tangle with the puppetmaster."

"I thought"—Daniel leaned over Alex—"that you reveled in taking on challenges."

Alex smiled up at him, pale eyes like winter ice. "Only when I'm sure of winning, my dear. Only then."

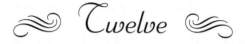

Twelve

December 17, 1822
Paignton Hall, Devon

innet was late down to breakfast. When she reached the breakfast parlor, she discovered that the cause of her lateness had already broken his fast and gone out riding with Charles and Deverell.

"Of course," Penny said, "while they carefully did not say so, they're eager to see if they can find any cult people who might be watching this place."

From her position at the head of the table, Phoebe smiled at Linnet. "Did you sleep well?"

The question might have been innocent, except for the twinkle in her hostess's eye.

Luckily, the question was one Linnet could answer with perfect truthfulness. "Yes." Sitting opposite Penny, she shook out her napkin, turned to thank the butler as he set a rack of fresh toast before her. Turning back to her newfound friends, she said, also perfectly truthfully, "I was so worn out, I slept like the dead."

Penny chuckled. Phoebe grinned.

After completing the ritual of nibbling on toast and sipping tea—a ritual not that much different from Linnet's habitual breakfast at Mon Coeur—Phoebe and Penny declared they would help her pack, and then she could help them pack for themselves and their children.

They and their children kept her engaged and amused for most of the day, yet despite her involvement, again and again Linnet found her mind drifting to other matters. Personal matters.

Hardly surprising. Her impossible man was determined to marry her.

She hadn't consciously thought of what his intentions had been, not until yesterday when the specter of him wanting her as his mistress had risen out of the revelation of his being an earl's son, yet, contrary to what she'd allowed him to think, unconsciously she'd assumed marriage had been his goal.

Regardless, she hadn't spent time considering the prospect because she'd been so sure they would part when he left Guernsey to pursue his mission, and the consequent separation would see the connection, and his impulse to marry her, wither and die. But now he'd taken her with him, and she'd decided—felt compelled—to remain by his side, no immediate separation was likely, and far from withering and dying, what had grown between them was deepening and burgeoning and growing ever stronger.

Sitting polishing her knives and cutlass on the window seat in her room while Phoebe and Penny sorted through the clothes—mostly theirs—they felt she should take, Linnet grappled with that fact. With the direction Logan had reiterated that morning in forceful, undeniable, senses-scrambling fashion. He was fixed on marrying her, and wasn't merely in earnest, but determined, dogged, and as stubborn as she.

Most ladies would be in alt, delirious with delight, yet . . . she was who she was, and she'd given up all thoughts of marriage, laid all hope of it aside years ago. She was, after all, the virgin queen in her domain; she'd seen no way of marrying while retaining both the responsibility and the ability to act that was her birthright.

And it was that—the difficulties that arose from being a virgin queen—that Logan was challenging. She suspected he knew it, too. It was a question of power and command, and the wielding of both was something he understood, something of which he had long and real experience.

He was, in effect, challenging her. To reassess, to rethink. To explore.

To take the risk.

What if she married him? Could a marriage between them work?

How could she know? How could she tell?

Yet the answer was vital, and not just to her. Her whole household, her wards, all who sailed for Trevission Ships, would be affected if things went wrong.

That was one great unknown. Another hurdle was, to her at least, utterly obvious. She might have been born a lady—indeed, she could correctly claim to be the Honorable Linnet Trevission—yet her life had never been that of a lady, certainly not the sort to marry the son of an earl. . . .

Even as her mind stalled, Penny came over, Linnet's leather breeches in her hands.

"I am still insanely jealous, but at least I'll shortly have a pair of my own. I wasn't sure if you roll them or fold them to pack."

"Roll." Linnet took them and showed her. "The fewer creases you put in them, the longer they'll last."

They chatted for some minutes about the care of fine leather, what to do, what to avoid, then Phoebe called.

"Linnet, come and decide what gown you'll wear tomorrow." Staring at the options laid upon the bed, Phoebe frowned. "I was wondering if there's any way you might wear your cutlass, but disguise it."

Even as they assessed the possibilities, Linnet's reservation over not being the right sort of lady for Logan resonated in her head.

Finally, she sat on the bed and looked up at Phoebe and Penny. "Tell me—before you were wed, was there ever any time when you wondered if you were . . . I can't think how to put this, but *enough* of a lady for him?"

Both Phoebe and Penny looked at her, then, sobering, sank down onto the counterpane.

"For me," Penny said, "it wasn't so much that. I'm the daughter of an earl, and I've known Charles all my life. We moved in the same social circles and our families were close. It wasn't anything social that was my problem—it was more if I was woman enough to accept all of him, all the parts he'd kept hidden from us all, not just me, but his whole family. It was like trying to embrace a man where half of him remained permanently in shadow. I wondered, at the time, whether I could be strong enough to see him all, know him all, and yet continue to love him all—not just the laughing buccaneering adventurer that anyone with eyes can see, but the devoted and deadly spy beneath." She paused, and an expression Linnet could only define as serene joy passed over her features as she smiled. "But I discovered I was strong enough, and I'm still reaping the rewards."

"Hmm." Phoebe tapped her chin. "I did wonder at the time if I was suitable—suitably suitable, I suppose you might say. I was already immersed in the agency, it took up most of my time, and I'd convinced myself that marriage was not for me." She smiled, the expression as joyous as Penny's. "Deverell convinced me otherwise, but I can see parallels with your situation." Phoebe met Linnet's eyes, understanding in hers. "The thing one needs to remember is, while *we* may not be the most conventional of ladies, they are, indubitably and indisputably, not conventional gentlemen."

"That's entirely correct." Penny nodded sagely. "Our gentlemen are more. And as such, it's been my observation that conventional ladies are not to their taste, and further, are highly unlikely to be able to handle them." She gave a more decisive nod. "That's my tale, and I intend to adhere to it. However"—she rose—"you might want to consider that not one of Royce's ex-operatives, no more than Royce himself, has married a conventional lady."

She paused, head tilted, then said, "Minerva is probably the most outwardly conventional, and Letitia and Clarice— you'll meet them all at Elveden. Yet even those three . . . once you learn of their backgrounds, and if you give them a challenge, a problem, or heaven forbid threaten anyone they hold dear, then you'll uncover something quite outside the realm of the conventional."

Phoebe snorted. "Oh, yes. Those three of us all—they would without a blink take on the Lord Chancellor himself and reduce him to quaking. As for Prinny, they'd likely send him gibbering."

Both Phoebe and Penny smiled as if relishing the thought.

A gong sounded in the distance. Phoebe glanced at the clothes neatly folded on the bed. "Come on—let's set aside your things for tomorrow and pack everything else. Then after lunch, we can start on the children's things."

With much to think about, and a still, as she thought of it, questing heart, Linnet readily fell in with her hostess's directions.

After lunch, she followed Phoebe and Penny up the stairs to the big nursery, which took up most of the upper floor of one of the house's irregular wings. At one end was a large circular chamber filling one of the old castle's towers. With wide windows giving wonderful views out to sea and along the coast, it was the perfect place for the children to play.

It was instantly apparent that the best way in which Linnet could assist with the children's packing was to distract the four older children. Pulling rank as captain of the *Esperance*, she had no difficulty luring them to the wide window seats beneath the tower room's windows. Ensconced there, they played spot the ship, then spot the bird. As there were plenty of specimens of the latter readily visible, and as the children's fascination with ships had yet to wane, they happily pointed and displayed their knowledge, arguing, then listening as Linnet explained and corrected. Eventually, at her suggestion, they started making up stories about the ships they saw—about their voyages, their captains, and crews.

Relaxing against the window frame, Linnet smiled, laughing and encouraging their flights of fancy. The three boys were especially inventive, describing pirates and treasure and sea battles.

Phoebe's daughter, Jessica, tiring of such nonsense, climbed up to sit alongside Linnet. Reaching up a hand, she touched Linnet's loose chignon, face lighting at the silken feel. "Can I braid it? I sometimes do Mama's hair."

Linnet smiled into green eyes much like her own, and even more like Phoebe's. "If you like." Shifting so Jessica could kneel at her back, Linnet reached up and pulled out the pins anchoring the mass. When it cascaded over her shoulders, Jessica oohed, then ran her small fingers through it.

"One big braid," Jessica decided.

Smiling, Linnet left her to it and gave her attention to settling a discussion over the relative merits of swords or knives in dispatching scurvy pirates.

Jessica was gentle, carefully using her fingers to comb out Linnet's long hair, then doggedly plaiting; she had to go back and forth a number of times, unraveling the braid to redo it tighter or straighter, but eventually she slipped from behind Linnet, scurried out to the main room, then returned a moment later with a ribbon.

Climbing back beside Linnet, Jessica frowned with concentration as she tied the end of the braid, then she sat back on her ankles, surveyed the result, and smiled. A big, beautiful smile. "There you are." Laying the fat braid over Linnet's shoulder, Jessica patted it. "That will keep it neat."

"Thank you." Linnet leaned forward and dropped a kiss on Jessica's head. Drawing back, she squinted down at the slightly lopsided braid. "It's lovely, but you mustn't be upset if later I have to brush it out and put up my hair for dinner." She met Jessica's eyes confidingly. "It's what ladies have to do."

Jessica nodded back solemnly. "I know. Mama has to do that, too."

"So does our mama," Penny's boys chorused.

Linnet laughed. Opening her arms wide, she managed to hug them all. She rocked them for a moment, an armful of warm, trusting, energetic bodies, bodies who laughed and giggled, then she released them—slowly.

Slowly straightened, staring blankly across the room, then she blinked, turned her head to look outside. "Look—is that a rowboat all the way out there? Or a fishing boat?"

The children swung back to the windows, kneeling and peering out to see, arguing once they'd located the boat she meant, bobbing on the waves in the bay.

Dragging in a breath, Linnet let them good-naturedly bicker, seized the moment to find her mental feet again.

She wanted children.

She'd forgotten how much. She'd buried that want so long ago she'd forgotten how much it had ached, and for how long, when she'd made her decision not to marry.

At the time, she'd already started gathering her wards. She'd told herself that they would do, would be enough to absorb and satisfy any maternal instinct she possessed.

But it wasn't maternal instinct that ached inside her, that made her press her fist to her breastbone, fight to draw a full, even breath.

In the instant the boys had chorused, she'd been struck by a thought—out of nowhere, yet not—a stray thought of what it would be like to look into midnight blue eyes that held that degree of mischief. To see such eyes laughing up at her out of an innocent face.

She'd wanted, for that waking instant had dreamed of, Logan's child. Son or daughter, her vision hadn't been specific, but the thought of a little Logan running wild . . .

Had made her heart ache.

Had reopened the empty, hollow cavern below her heart.

Dragging in a longer breath, forcing her lungs to function,

she blinked again, straightened on the seat, then leaned to look out of the window. After a moment, she said, "It's a fishing skiff. Can you see the nets dragging behind it? Look at the way the wake is churning."

Linnet was very ready to accompany Phoebe and Penny downstairs when they declared it was time to attend their own packing. Penny stated that her packing was merely a matter of repacking everything she'd brought to Paignton Hall—no decisions to be made—so she and Linnet accompanied Phoebe into her dressing room.

The next hour and more passed swiftly. Linnet put aside her private cogitations and gave herself up to the novel experience of laughing and enjoying the company of like-minded ladies. Then the first gong sounded and it was time to dress for dinner.

Back in her room, she washed and changed into one of the gowns Penny had lent her. Standing before the dressing table, she unwound Jessica's braid. Instead of summoning a maid, she elected to brush out her hair, then plait it again, this time into two tight plaits, which she could wind about her head and pin to fashion a gleaming, gilded coronet.

Being alone gave her time to think, to look back over the day, and consider all she'd felt, all that had surfaced while she'd been with the other two, already married ladies, and their children.

Most especially the children.

For all she knew she might already be carrying Logan's child. As her earlier forays into intimacy had been so very brief, she'd ignored the risk of pregnancy, and with Logan . . . had forgotten to remember it. Yet their liaison had extended far beyond a single occasion, and indeed would continue. . . .

No matter how she tried, she couldn't make herself view falling pregnant with Logan's child as anything other than a blessing, a joy.

That left her feeling even more unsettled.

She went down to the drawing room early. Penny and Charles were already there, as was Deverell. Logan arrived not long after, then Phoebe came bustling in. As they chatted and exchanged stories of their day, she watched and observed—took closer note of how Charles and Deverell interacted with Penny and Phoebe, and vice versa.

Now she knew them better, she could see, detect, the very real connection that flowed between each couple. Easy affection, a touch of pride, protectiveness, and yes, even in this setting, a hint of possessiveness from the men, and a reciprocal but more open affection from the women, an acceptance and a bone-deep confidence in all their men were and would provide. If she'd needed any demonstration of what constituted a sound basis for marriage between people like them, it was there, before her nose.

As Logan fell in beside Linnet as they followed Phoebe into the dining room, he studied Linnet's face, wondered what she was thinking. He'd noticed her watchfulness; she'd been quiet, quieter than he was used to her being, but she'd been fully absorbed and listening avidly. As if she was studying what was going on.

Holding her chair while she sat, he settled her, then sat beside her. Gave his attention to the soup that was placed before him.

Conversation waned while they all supped.

He didn't know what was in Linnet's mind. Didn't know what he should or shouldn't say at this point. They were in a hiatus—a frustrating interlude during which they couldn't go forward, couldn't make decisions, but had to wait for external issues to resolve before they could do anything at all.

Indeed, his whole day had been one of frustration. On horseback with Charles and Deverell, he'd ridden a wide swath around Paignton, but had found no traces of the cult. No watchers, either cultists or hired locals, no hint from the villagers around about of any sightings of unknown men.

They might have temporarily lost the cult, but, as he'd assured Charles and Deverell, they'd be watching the main roads to the north and east, knowing he'd make a dash in that direction sometime.

While they'd ridden down the lanes and over the fields, he'd had time to reassess his personal strategy, to reaffirm that showing Linnet the man he was, the man the years had made him—giving her the chance to see for herself what manner of man he was, what he'd made of his life thus far, giving her the facts on which to judge what he would bring to her and Mon Coeur—before he told her of his bastard state was the right and proper course of action.

The course most likely to succeed.

Her inclusion in the party for this last dash to Elveden meant she'd have a chance to see with her own eyes and gauge his standing, his circle of friends, his past achievements, his capabilities, even get some idea of his wealth.

He could tell her all that, recite a catalogue, but he'd much rather she saw and made her own assessment. Faster, more direct, more certain that way.

Especially as he didn't know exactly how she would react to the revelation that he was a bastard, albeit a noble one. In wider tonnish society, he would be accepted as the man he was; he wasn't in the same boat as the average bastard whose mother hailed from the lower orders. In his case, his mother, too, had been from one of the highest families. His position was more like that of old Lady Melbourne's children, all of whom where widely regarded as having different fathers, none of whom was Lord Melbourne.

Society accepted him, always had, but would Linnet? Some people had more difficulty overlooking a bastard birth than others.

He didn't think Linnet would consider his birth a problem, but as he set down his soup spoon, he inwardly admitted that, cravenly, he didn't want to take a chance.

He'd faced guns and cannon, led charges in battle, yet she

was now so important to him that he didn't want to take even the slightest risk of her rejecting him, not if it was in any way avoidable.

So he'd wait until the end of the mission to break that news to her. Aside from all else, from tomorrow morning on, his mission would take precedence, and he and she would necessarily put all personal matters aside.

Phoebe looked down the table at her spouse, then glanced at Charles. "Well, I expect you two better explain the arrangements you've put in place for our journey to Elveden."

Logan inwardly grinned as Deverell and Charles obliged.

The three of them had spent the afternoon making the necessary preparations—selecting the coachman who would travel with them, provisioning the carriage they would take. Then Charles and Deverell had turned their attention to the two other carriages that would carry Penny, Phoebe, and the children on their journey east, organizing drivers, guards, and weapons.

He'd been impressed by Charles's and Deverell's arrangements. Relieved and reassured. He couldn't imagine even the cult overcoming the heavily, if discreetly, armed cavalcade they'd organized. Their guards were experienced, loyal, and knew their work. Penny, Phoebe, and the children would be safe.

The thought niggled. He glanced at Linnet, on his right; she was absorbed with the discussion, silent but watching. He let his gaze linger on her face, on the delicacy beneath the determination.

Something in him stirred; he looked away before she felt his gaze.

She should be kept safe, too—he should keep her safe, just as Charles and Deverell were so focused on keeping Penny and Phoebe safe.

Inwardly frowning, he couldn't help but wonder if keeping her with him—and so knowing she was safe, thus relieving his anxiety on that score—was the best arrangement for her—or only the best arrangement for him.

He was still inwardly frowning when, dinner concluded, he rose with the other two men and followed their ladies to the drawing room.

They all retired relatively early. Their plans for the morrow called for a departure before dawn, at least for the three men and Linnet. Penny and Phoebe would be up and about, too, to fuss over their husbands, then wave them all on their way.

Linnet stood by the window in her bedchamber, consciously seizing the moments before Logan joined her to take stock—to fix in her mind just where he and she stood before they embarked on a journey that would be, she suspected, akin to running a gauntlet. They would run, and the cult would attack; from all she'd heard of the men's assumptions, that was how they expected the next days to unfold.

No time, not the right time, to make any decisions about him and her, yet she didn't want to fetch up at journey's end with no clear idea of where they were, what questions still loomed, what next she needed to do.

He'd declared he wanted to marry her, that that was his adamant intent. Her initial reaction had been that she could never be the sort of wife he needed, yet after spending time with Penny and Phoebe and watching Charles and Deverell, seeing and sensing how such marriages worked, she'd jettisoned that stance. She could, if he wished and she wished, be a suitable wife for him.

Assuming she could meet his ultimate expectations, his specific requirements; that was an issue they hadn't discussed, but would have no time to address now.

Staring out at the night, she pulled a face. Indecision wasn't a state she appreciated, but she couldn't decide if she could fill a position without knowing what the specifications were, before she understood what said position entailed, yet any such discussion would have to wait until his mission was concluded.

Aside from that caveat, as far as she could see there was only one hurdle remaining, and while it was a major one, on multiple levels, addressing it before deciding to accept his suit was pointless.

The one thing she could no longer do was refuse to seriously entertain his suit. Not after today, not now that she knew—to her bones and her soul finally appreciated—all he would offer her.

Quite aside from the virgin queen no longer having to remain an all but virgin into her old age.

Children. She had never considered having children with any other man. Still couldn't imagine it. Only with Logan. With Logan . . . she could, and if she married him, God willing would, fill that aching, empty hollow that resided below her heart.

She heard his footsteps outside the door, swiftly reviewed her thoughts. Inwardly nodded. As far as she was able, she knew where she stood.

Reaching up, she drew the curtains across the window. Turning, she waited while he came in, saw her, closed the door, then crossed the room to her. She'd left a candle burning on the dressing table; in the soft light, she saw he was . . . not exactly frowning, yet the expression was there in his eyes. "What is it?"

He looked surprised that she'd asked, then allowed his frown to materialize. "I was just thinking . . ." Halting before her, he grimaced, then slipped both hands into his breeches' pockets and looked down. "I was thinking perhaps you would be safer going with the other ladies."

She blinked. She might well be safer going with Penny and Phoebe—but what about him? "No." Lips setting in what she'd been told often enough was a mulish line, she caught his gaze as he looked up, and shook her head. Decisively. "Absolutely not. I'm going with you."

His lips thinned. "But—"

"No." Turning, she stalked toward the bed. "No, no, no." Swinging around, she pinned him with her gaze. "*You* carried me off my damned ship, in full view of my crew, for heaven's sake—and yes, I know you bent them to your misguided will by convincing them it was safest for me to go with you—but that doesn't change the fact that it was *your* idea that I come with you, travel with you to your mission's end. And so now, *no*. You do not get to change your tune." Lifting her chin, she held his gaze. "I'm staying with you, traveling with you, until your mission ends, and that, as far as I'm concerned, is that."

He studied her for a long moment, then his brows rose. Drawing his hands from his pockets, he walked slowly toward her.

Halting before her, he looked into her face.

His eyes were still troubled.

"You're absolutely certain that's what you want—to face whatever risks we might have to run?"

She searched his eyes, hearing inside the resonance between his mission and their lives—their putative future that yet lay unresolved. *Whatever risks we might have to run.* The same question applied in that sphere, too.

Was her answer the same?

She didn't know, but she knew her right answer here and now.

"Yes. I'm absolutely sure."

Slowly, he nodded. "All right."

His expression didn't ease.

In a flash of insight, she understood his problem. "Stop worrying." Reaching up, she wound her arms about his neck, stepped closer. "This is my decision, and you'll be there, by my side all the way, in case I need rescuing."

Stretching up against him, feeling his arms instinctively rise and close about her, she looked at his lips, let her own curve, then, looking up through her lashes, met his eyes. "Just remind yourself of how grateful I might have to be if you do indeed rescue me."

He sighed, gave in. Bent his head. Whispered across her lips in the instant before his brushed them, "As long as you're safe."

"I will be," she whispered back. "You'll be there."

She kissed him on the words, and he let her, let her for once lead the way. Let her please herself by pleasing him, then he gently took the reins and returned the pleasure.

In full measure.

Reiterated, not in words but in deeds, in devotion, with passion and desire fueled by hunger and need, the truth of all he'd told her, that she was the woman he wanted, the one above all he coveted, that she was, to him, all.

All he wanted, all he would ever need.

Much later, when she lay sated and boneless beneath him, her fingers idly riffling his black hair, she saw deep inside a truth she had until then overlooked.

He was everything she had ever wanted, and all she would ever need.

Thirteen

December 18, 1822
The road from Paignton Hall to Exeter

They encountered the first ambush five miles from Paignton Hall. Thick fog blanketed the coast. The carriage's sudden appearance out of the murk surprised eight sleepy cultists camped beyond the ditch; they scrambled to form up across the road, a human barrier waving short swords.

The coachman, David, whom Linnet concluded Deverell and Charles had chosen for his reckless enthusiasm, whipped up his horses and drove straight for them. Yelling, screeching, the cultists scattered, leaping and tumbling back into the muddy ditch.

Linnet saw open mouths and stunned faces as the carriage rocketed past.

"Well, that was uneventful." Charles resheathed his sword, settled back into his corner, and closed his eyes.

Inwardly shaking her head, Linnet tucked her cloak more snugly over her red traveling gown, and with her cutlass riding comfortingly against her hip, settled in her own corner, diagonally opposite Charles. Deverell sat across from her, Logan alongside.

They'd left Paignton Hall in the icy chill an hour before dawn. Phoebe and Penny had stood on the steps and waved them away; the pair's absolute confidence as they'd fare-welled their husbands with assurances that they would all see each other shortly at Elveden had been infectious.

A good omen when heading out to face villains.

"I counted five on this side," Deverell murmured.

Linnet glanced at him.

"Three this side," Logan said.

"Which," Charles concluded without opening his eyes, "makes eight—which just might be cause for concern."

"If they had eight men to set watching a minor road like this . . ." Deverell met Logan's eyes. "Another group before Exeter, do you think?"

Logan nodded. "More than likely."

"In that case, we'd better make ready to start reducing the enemy's numbers." Opening his eyes, Charles stood, reached up to the rack above Linnet's and Logan's heads, and lifted down four small hunting crossbows and a handful of quarrels. "That, after all, is the main purpose of a decoy mission—to draw out and weaken the enemy." Handing the bows around, he asked Linnet, "Can you fire one of these?"

She took a bow, examined it. "We have arbalests, big ones, on board, and I can fire those when they're mounted, but this"—she tested the weight—"is light enough for me to hold, so yes." Accepting the small winch used to load the bow, and a few quarrels, she raised her brows. "I might even be able to reload it."

Resuming his seat, Charles loaded his. "We shouldn't need to reload immediately, not unless they manage to halt the carriage. If they hunt in packs of eight or thereabouts, then if we each down one, that should be enough to get us through their next roadblock."

"They won't know it's us, not until they look into the car-riage." The carriage was one of Deverell's, built for speed as well as comfort, but anonymous and unmarked. Deverell set his loaded crossbow on the floor. "If we obligingly slow when they wave us down, wait until they're close enough, then drop the windows, fire, and David springs his horses immediately, we'll be through."

Linnet looked at the windows—glass in wooden frames that slid down into the carriage's sides and secured with a latch at the top.

Logan nodded. "I can't see any holes in that."

Deverell rose, opened the hatch in the carriage's roof, and gave David his latest orders.

As Deverell resumed his seat, leaving the hatch open, the carriage slowed, then turned right onto the highway between Plymouth and Exeter.

"This is the road they'll expect us to be on." Logan peered out of the window, searching ahead. "The Black Cobra— Ferrar—is clever, and he's had time to send his cultists to all the main ports on the south coast. We know he had men in Plymouth. He wouldn't have missed Exeter."

"And knowing you fled Plymouth in this direction but have yet to reach Exeter, they'll be waiting." Charles smiled in anticipation.

The carriage bowled on as a gray and mizzling dawn spread across the land.

"Heathens ahead, m'lord." The words floated down through the open hatch. "Nine of the bastards with swords in their hands. I guess I'd better smile and look innocent." The carriage slowed.

Deverell beckoned to Linnet. "Change places with me."

She didn't argue, just obliged.

Like Logan, Deverell angled back in the corner, gaze fixed through the window. They all had their crossbows in their hands. The coach rocked to a halt. Linnet shrugged off her cloak, reached her hand to the window latch. Saw the men slowly do the same.

"Now!" Deverell flipped his latch.

The sound of the four windows slamming down startled the approaching cultists, three on each side.

Logan's and Deverell's bows twanged. Two cultists fell.

Linnet angled her bow around, sighted a dun-colored tunic, a black scarf dangling over the shoulder; she pulled the trigger. Instantly drew back, raising the window as the carriage jerked, then surged.

She relatched the window, glanced out and saw two cultists who must have been standing by the horses sprawled on the ground.

Then they were past. Through.

"Four down." Charles set his bow on the floor. "I wonder how many more we'll meet?"

Minutes later they were passing the outer abodes of Exeter.

"They're following, m'lords," David called down. "Three of 'em. But they're hanging back, not looking to close the distance."

"Let them follow." Deverell looked at Logan. "I assume they're unlikely to mount any attack in town?"

"That's not their style, especially not if we're traveling through. Hard to stop a carriage without anyone else noticing." Logan settled back. "They tend to prefer more isolated surrounds, but not because they care about breaking any laws—to them the violence they employ is the only law that matters. They don't care about witnesses, either, but while they'll happily kill anyone who gets in their way, people getting in the way distracts and hampers them, and their master is very keen on success when it comes to the tasks he sets them."

Charles nodded. "So they're following, waiting for us to helpfully drive into the next little band of theirs further down the road."

"In that, they'll be disappointed," Deverell said. "They'll expect us to head directly east, out on the road to London— where else?" He raised a brow at Logan. "What are the odds that once we're bowling along the London road, they'll send one of their number forward to alert the next group?"

"That's a certainty."

"So when we turn north, they'll have to send a second man back to alert the others of our change in direction."

"So we'll be left with one man." Logan smiled. "And he won't be able to leave us to alert anyone for fear of losing us altogether."

"Which, I must remind you, we don't actually want them to do." Charles settled back. "The trick with a mission like this is to reduce their numbers as much as we can without risking being overwhelmed."

"This is the center of town." Deverell signaled to Linnet and changed places with her again, giving her the more comfortable position facing forward. "We're now heading out and east, so let's see if our predictions prove correct." Still standing, Deverell spoke through the hatch, "David, keep to our planned route to Bridgwater, but take your time until the turnoff to Cullompton. Give them a chance to send a rider past us."

"Aye, m'lord."

Deverell resumed his seat.

Sure enough, five minutes later, when the last cottages of Exeter fell behind, Charles pointed out of the window. "There he goes."

They all looked and saw one of the cultists, rugged up in a frieze coat buttoned over a dun tunic, but with his distinctive head scarf flapping, urging his mount over the soggy field bordering the road. Eventually, he pulled ahead.

Minutes later David called down, "He's away, m'lord. Round the next bend and out of sight. The Cullompton turn-off's just ahead."

"Take it," Deverell ordered, "and drive on as fast as you safely can."

The carriage slowed, then turned left into a narrower road that ran between high hedges. As soon as the carriage completed the turn, David whipped up his horses; they surged, then settled to a steady, mile-eating pace.

"Lots of argy-bargy going on between the two heathens still with us, m'lord. Seems like one of 'em's turning back."

"Good." Smiling, Deverell sat back. "On to Bridgwater as fast as you can."

They rattled on through the morning, through wet mists that blurred the landscape. The damp chill reached deep. Linnet huddled in her cloak, glad she was in the carriage and not on horseback. They passed through Taunton without challenge, but their sole follower was still with them when they reached Bridgwater. David slowed his horses, then turned the carriage into the yard of the Monmouth Arms.

Deverell led the way in, bespoke a private parlor and the best luncheon the inn could provide. Linnet found herself bowed deferentially into the parlor by the innkeeper, then before she could swing her cloak from her shoulders, Logan lifted it away, then held a chair for her at the table.

Once she sat, the three men took their seats. Almost immediately the door opened; the innwife and a bevy of serving girls swept in, bearing covered platters and a huge tureen. With a flourish, the innwife set the tureen before Linnet. "Ma'am."

With a bobbed curtsy, the innwife turned, shooed her girls out ahead of her, then went out and closed the door.

Linnet didn't need to look at the three faces about the table to know that they, too, expected her to serve the soup. With only a slight twist to her lips, she did. The oxtail broth was delicious, as were the various roast meats and assorted vegetables and puddings provided as accompaniments.

Early in the proceedings, the innkeeper arrived with three mugs of ale for the men and a glass of ginger wine for Linnet. Once again, the innkeeper's deferential "ma'am" niggled Linnet; despite the fact that she wore no ring, everyone, Logan included, was treating her as if she were his wife.

She felt a touch off-balance, and didn't appreciate the feeling.

But she, Logan, Charles, and Deverell had more pressing concerns.

When only the platter of cheese and walnuts remained, Charles popped a piece of cheese into his mouth, gathered a handful of nuts, and pushed back from the table. "I'm going out to scout around."

Deverell nodded. "I'll come with you."

From the door, Charles looked back at Logan. "Give us at least half an hour before you send the cavalry."

Logan nodded, and then the pair were gone.

They returned twenty minutes later. Logan turned from the window as the door opened and Charles walked in, looking puzzled.

"They're here." Charles waited until Deverell came in and closed the door. "But for some ungodly reason they're gathered, all eight of them, back down the road."

Deverell halted by the table. He, too, was frowning. "They know we're here—they're keeping watch on the entrance to the inn's yard." He looked at Logan. "We checked ahead first, then circled all the way around before we found them. It looks like they're intending to follow us rather than attack, even though there are eight of them."

"I can't see how they can attack from the rear, not in this sort of country, on this sort of road, and against a fast carriage and four." Charles looked at Logan. "There's something we're missing here."

After a moment, Logan said, "I think I know what." He looked at Deverell. "Have you got that map?"

Reaching into his pocket, Deverell drew out a map, carefully unfolded the parchment, and laid it on the table. Linnet rose from the armchair to which she'd retreated and joined them. They all stood looking down at the map.

"We're here"—Deverell pointed to a spot labeled Bridgwater—"currently on the road to Bristol. Our destination, Bath, is here." He pointed to the town northeast of Bridgwater, and southeast of Bristol. "As the crow flies, it's about thirty-five miles, fifty or more by road. Five hours' drive, perhaps less. The reason we've come this way is that, from here, there are many different routes we can take to reach Bath." He traced a number of them. "None of those routes is useful for mounting an attack from the rear—so why send eight men to follow us where one, or at most two, would do?"

"Because they think we're going to Bristol, and they're not just following us." Logan pointed to Bristol, to their nor'northeast, then looked up, met the others' eyes. "We know Ferrar sent his men to the south coast ports, those being the ones we, the couriers, were most likely to come through. But the three frigates that attacked the *Esperance*? Given no one believed any captain from the south coast would fail to recognize the *Esperance* and therefore know better than to attack it, especially when it was flying the naval ensign, I asked Linnet's crew where they thought those ships hailed from. Their educated guess was from an east coast port. And if Ferrar sent men to the east coast ports, he would have sent men to Bristol, too."

Charles grimaced. "It is one of the major trading ports."

"So," Deverell said, "it's likely the group behind us have already sent someone to alert their colleagues in Bristol, and as we drive on, with the eight behind us, we're going to run into a cult welcome up ahead."

"And we'll be trapped between"—Charles looked at Logan—"sixteen or more? Those are not odds I like."

"Nor I," Logan said, "but that's how the cult operates. They smother opponents—overwhelming odds to ensure victory. Ferrar has no consideration for how many he loses, and many cultists have absorbed so much of the religious zeal Ferrar has fostered that they view death in the service of the Black Cobra as imparting some sort of glory."

"In that case," Deverell said, leaning on the table and studying the map, "we need to break up the group behind us, or step sideways out of their trap."

"Or both," Charles said. "The question is how."

They evaluated the various roads they might take.

"The problem," Logan said, "is that if we take any of these roads to Bath, in the carriage we're going to be slower than a rider from the pack behind us seeing our direction, riding hell for leather to Bristol, meeting up with the welcome committee there, and redirecting them to Bath. They'll be able to reach Bath, and even come southeast to meet us as we drive in. We'll be no better off, and might even be in worse, less frequented terrain."

They all stared at the map. "That means," Deverell eventually said, "that regardless of all else, the best route for us to take to Bath is the one that's quickest from the moment we turn off the Bristol road." He traced a route. "This one—we turn off at Upper Langford, then go via Blagdon, Compton Martin, Bishop Sutton and Chelwood to Marksbury, and so to Bath. For us, that's the fastest way."

Logan grimaced. "They're still going to reach Bath well ahead of us."

Linnet tapped a finger on the map. "Not if they don't see which way we go." She glanced up at the three men. When they all simply waited, she half smiled and looked down. "Here—just past this hamlet called Star. There's a bend in the road, and then half a mile further on, Upper Langford and the turnoff we want. And while it's difficult to stage an attack from the rear, we're in front. *We* can attack *them*. And if we do, and cause sufficient panic and mayhem, just after Star and just before this bend, then we can be on and around the bend, down the road to Blagdon and out of sight, before they catch up enough to see us turn."

Deverell was studying the map closely. "They'll realize we've turned, but they won't know to where. Just past that bend there are roads to Cheddar, Weston-Sur-Mare, Congresbury, as well as the one we want to take."

"They'll spend time casting about, trying to find which way we've gone." Linnet looked at Logan. "It might not delay them long, but it will gain us some time, perhaps enough to beat them into Bath."

Logan nodded. "That's our best plan so far."

Charles straightened. "The only alternative is to kill all those following us, and as they're all on horseback, it's too likely one of them at least will flee and ride on, so that's not a viable option."

Deverell nodded. "I vote for Linnet's plan."

"And me." Logan nodded at her.

Charles grinned and swept her a bow. "Indeed. And I've got just the thing to ensure sufficient panic and mayhem to get away unseen."

When their carriage rattled out of the Monmouth Arms yard, only Logan and Linnet were inside the vehicle. Charles and Deverell were stretched out on the roof, with two primed rifles each. Logan and Linnet each had one rifle and two pistols. The pistols were unlikely to have much chance of hitting any cultists, but the shots would add to the confusion.

David, who'd looked thoroughly thrilled when told the plan, took his time settling in his new team, galloping them along the straighter stretches, then reining them in, trotting through the small towns, before settling to a steady, but rapid, pace.

According to Charles, who reported via the open hatch, the changes in pace alone caused uncertainty in their pursuers' ranks.

Not that they stopped pursuing.

Linnet had claimed the map. She continued consulting it as they swept on. Deverell, Charles, and Logan had agreed that the welcome party from Bristol would be waiting to ambush them along a particularly empty and desolate stretch between two villages. Luckily that stretch was at least three miles further on from where they planned to turn off.

The carriage slowed, and she looked out, saw a signpost. "That's Sidcot." She checked her map, then called to the two above. "Star's about a half mile on."

Setting aside the map, she undid the ties of her cloak and let it fall from her shoulders. She'd left her cutlass in the carriage when she'd gone into the inn, but had promptly buckled it on again as they'd left Bridgwater. Although their plan didn't involve any face-to-face combat, she preferred to be prepared. Standing, she resettled the belt about her hips, then looked at the crate Charles had left on the opposite seat.

She studied the glass bottles wicked with rag that lay nestled in crumpled paper inside the crate. "Do you think these will actually work?"

Logan glanced at the bottles. "I've seen far less professional incendiaries work brilliantly."

"Star coming up." David's voice drifted down from above.

David followed the pattern he'd established when driving through smaller towns, slowing to bowl smoothly through, then whipping up his horses the moment the last cottages fell behind.

He drove on for several hundred yards, then abruptly slowed the carriage to a grinding halt.

The cultists, by then clear of the hamlet, at first came on at their accustomed gallop, then, realizing the carriage had halted, they slowed, confused . . . yet still closing the distance.

"Now!" Charles called, and both he and Deverell opened fire.

On the heels of their first volley, Logan and Linnet swung open the carriage doors, and, one foot on the carriage's steps, took aim and fired. They pulled back into the carriage as the second volley sounded from above.

Logan dropped the rifle he'd used, grabbed the tinderbox he'd left ready.

Linnet lifted one of the bottles from its packing and held it for him.

He lit the wick, seized the bottle, and passed it up through the hatch to waiting hands. Immediately lit a second and passed that up, too.

The carriage rocked as Charles and Deverell stood. Logan imagined them waiting, then the carriage swayed as they threw the small flame bombs.

"Go!"

David had the carriage rolling when Charles and Deverell dropped to the roof.

Just as the bombs hit.

Logan and Linnet hung out of the carriage windows, and saw a scene of carnage and confusion, of cultists lying on the ground, some clutching wounds and wailing, of horses milling. The bombs had landed, as intended, just in front of the cultists. Flames had whooshed and flared—the pervading damp would soon have them out, but the show was enough to have the cultists' mounts panicking, pulling free if they could and galloping away.

As the carriage started around the bend, the flames died and smoke rose in billowing waves, engulfing the cutlists, setting them coughing and choking.

The carriage rounded the bend, their horses racing on as David drove hard for their chosen road.

They reached it and turned off toward Bath.

The carriage rattled wildly along the lesser road, helpfully lined with high, unclipped hawthorn hedges. David slowed a trifle as they passed through another hamlet. Once they were bowling along again, Charles called down, "None of them got to the bend before we turned. We've lost them, at least for the moment."

They busied themselves tidying away the rest of the incendiaries, the rifles and pistols. At the next hamlet, David halted long enough for Charles and Deverell to climb down and return to their seats inside the carriage.

"It's damned cold out there." Charles stamped his feet, blew on his hands. "But at least we've made some impact."

"We've done our duty," Deverell affirmed, "at least for the moment."

They all settled back, drew their cloaks closer. Linnet looked out of the window, thought back through the recent engagement.

Reduce numbers, avoid being overwhelmed.

That, apparently, was to be the catchcry of their mission.

The best-laid plans of mice and men were, sadly, subject to the whim of the gods.

The gods' minions, in this instance, were sheep. Lots of them. The carriage was forced to a halt just beyond the tiny town of Compton Martin by a large flock being moved to winter pastures. There was nothing for it but to wait for the bleating mob to file slowly past.

When the road was finally clear, David whipped up his horses—only to have to rein them to a halt again just past West Harptree, then again near Sutton Wick.

"It's like a damned organized migration," Charles muttered.

By the time they reached Marksbury and headed toward Bath on the last stretch of their day's journey, although no one said anything, they were all tense and watchful. What advantage they'd gained by their inventive action near Star had been well and truly eaten away by the sheep.

There was every chance the Black Cobra's men had reached Bath by now; they might even be lurking along the road into town.

Dusk fell, and the shadows thickened. Their tension racked steadily higher the closer they got to the famous spa town; Logan knew little about it beyond its famous waters. They each sat back from their windows, watching, scanning, searching for any telltale black scarves.

That they rattled into the town center without spotting one didn't materially ease Logan's concern. The more deadly variety of cultist, the assassins, loomed high in his mind.

David, under orders to drive unremarkably so as to draw no especial attention to their vehicle, eventually halted the carriage outside their chosen hotel, The York House. Streetlamps had been lit, bathing the wide pavement before the hotel in warm welcome. With the hour edging toward dinnertime, there was not a great deal of other traffic about.

After all Logan's worrying, it felt anticlimactic to step down from the carriage, hand Linnet down, and find an august, liveried doorman waiting to bow them in.

"Logan."

He turned to see Charles beckoning. His hand on Linnet's back, he urged her on. "Go in—we'll follow."

Leaving her to the deferential care of the doorman, Logan returned to assist Charles and Deverell in packing the rifles

and their other weapons, and hiding the remaining incendiaries while handing their personal bags to the footmen who
swarmed out to help.

Brows arched, Linnet watched, saw, then consented to
turn and follow the doorman across the wide pavement to
the front door. She'd heard of The York House. It had long
been the favored haunt of visiting nobility. Running an eye
over the elegant façade, she cynically smiled, imagining
telling Jen and Gilly—and Muriel and Buttons, too—that
she'd stayed there. At least, thanks to Penny and Phoebe, her
wardrobe would pass muster.

The doorman had stridden ahead to pull open and hold
the heavy brass, etched glass, and polished wood front door,
bowing her regally through. Lips curving more definitely,
she glided toward the doorway—

Heard the telltale sing of an arrow.

Instinctively she ducked, curling herself into a smaller
target, then looking around. The doorman froze, eyes widening, then he whisked around the open door, taking cover
behind the thick panel.

With a gasp and a clatter, the footman who'd been following Linnet with her bag hit the ground. Eyes wide with
shock, he clutched one arm from which a crossbow quarrel
protruded.

She didn't think, just acted. She'd been in too many battles to panic, was too much a leader not to immediately take
charge.

Moving swiftly in a halfcrouch, she turned back, grabbed
her bag in one hand, the footman's uninjured arm in the
other, and hauled him to his feet—thanking her stars he
wasn't taller or all that much heavier than she. As more
arrows rained down, using the bag to cover their backs, she
propelled him through the still open front door.

Halting in the hall, she let the footman go. He collapsed
to the tiles. She turned back to the door, taking cover just
inside to look out.

The doorman picked his moment between showers of

arrows and rushed in. Shaken out of his rigid control, he nevertheless called for help for his footman, gave orders for others to man the windows, then came to stand behind Linnet, peering past her shoulder as she surveyed the scene.

"No one else is down," she murmured, for herself as much as the doorman. Logan had been in the carriage, but must have jumped down and been on his way to help her when she'd acted and got herself out of danger. He'd taken cover behind the open carriage door on this side, protected to some extent by the bulk of the carriage. Deverell had been inside and still was. He was working frantically. As she watched, he passed Logan one rifle, then another.

Logan looked toward the rear of the carriage. Called to Charles, who reached around and took the rifle, then returned to his position at the far rear corner of the carriage.

The arrows were still coming in unpredictable fits and starts. They seemed to be coming from the top of a building a little way down the street. Linnet could see all the footmen now huddled in a group at the carriage's rear, looking longingly at the front door. But David—where was he? He'd been on the box in full view of the enemy. Had he been hit? Was he even now dying?

But then she saw a shadow beneath the carriage, beneath the box itself, and realized he'd taken cover there. As far as she could tell, he was uninjured, just temporarily stuck in a cramped space.

Relief slid through her; she'd known David for all of a day, mostly as a voice and a presence guiding the horses, yet she thought of him as one of their small band. Refocusing on the continuing danger, she saw a town carriage rumbling down the street toward them. Charles stepped out, waved his arms, called orders—then ducked back, most likely swearing, as another flight of arrows rained down.

The startled coachman halted his horses, scrambled down from his box, and took cover—bobbing up by the side of the carriage to explain to his master what was happening.

After checking that all was clear in the other direction,

Logan looked back and called orders to the huddled footmen; they nodded in reply.

Then Logan eased forward, inching to the edge of the box seat, then crouching to aim his rifle—at what neither Linnet nor the doorman could see.

"This is outrageous," the doorman huffed. "Such things simply don't happen at The York House. Not anywhere in Bath!"

Linnet struggled not to let her lips curve. "Sadly, they are. Take heart—no one ever died of a little excitement, and your man"—she tipped her head toward the injured footman—"isn't badly hurt. Now step aside—I think you're about to get the rest of your footmen back."

Logan fired his rifle, then Charles took his shot, too.

In a group, the footmen raced across the pavement and in through the door as Deverell fired out of one of the carriage windows.

Logan and Charles were already tossing their spent rifles back into the carriage; they stepped back with pistols and swords. Deverell emerged, and then the three, all armed to the teeth, separated—Charles and Deverell going around the back of the carriage, then racing, doubled over, across the street. Logan glanced at Linnet, signaled that he was going to circle the cultists' position—presumably to ensure the enemy had fled.

No more arrows had come slicing down since they'd discharged their rifles.

Linnet nodded, waited, saw Logan race across the street, then, hugging the shadows thrown by the shop fronts, ghost away, out of her sight. Inwardly sighing, she turned and took up the role they'd left her. Tugging off her gloves, she swept up to the heavy desk behind which the manager, somewhat goggle-eyed, stood. She vaguely recalled Deverell saying their rooms had been arranged. "I believe, if you consult your register, that you'll find a booking in the name of Wolverstone."

The name worked wonders. Within minutes, she was ushered into one of the hotel's principal suites.

Luxurious, even opulent in its decoration, the suite had two bedrooms giving off a central sitting room; she claimed the bedroom to the left, leaving the other for the men, but when a footman carried Logan's bag into the room she'd chosen, she didn't protest.

Inwardly grimaced; there was no point.

Trailing after the footman, she was in time to stop the maid from unpacking Logan's bag; the scroll-holder was in it. She felt obliged to allow the maid to unpack her gowns and hang them up instead.

When the maid eagerly asked which gown she should leave out for dinner, Linnet arbitrarily picked one of the evening gowns—one in green silk. The question had reminded her that someone needed to order the meal.

She had little experience in choosing menus—Muriel normally handled such matters—but she had the happy thought to consult the maitre d'hotel, and he was both delighted to have been asked and solicitous in arranging an appropriate repast.

That done, she oversaw the disposition of the men's weapons, then summoned David up to report, confirmed he was unharmed and well-quartered—and insouciantly thrilled by the action—then she settled to pace—only to have a succession of the hotel's staff tap on the door to offer this, that, and the other.

By the time her three companions walked through the door, she'd been driven to the edge of distraction by the maids' offers and by an unaccustomed, yet very real, nagging worry—one that evaporated the instant Logan walked in and her eyes confirmed he was unharmed.

That he looked faintly disgusted was neither here nor there.

Dropping into an armchair, Charles explained the disgust. "They'd fled."

Arms folded, she looked down at him, then at the other two. Then she turned on her heel and headed for her room. "Dinner will be served in half an hour. I'm going to change."

In these surroundings, even in this company, she felt obliged to play the part of lady, no matter how ill she fitted the role.

The dinner was superb, and served with a smooth, silent efficiency that allowed them to concentrate first on the dishes, then, once the cheese platter arrived and the servers withdrew, on their plans.

"I don't think there were more than four archers pinning us down out there." With a tilt of his head, Deverell indicated the front of the hotel. "As there's bound to be more cultists than that around, I think we can conclude that they reached Bath before us, but then set up ambushes at all the major hotels—there's not so many of those to cover in Bath."

Logan nodded. "I think our diversion near Star worked more or less as we'd planned, and by the time they reached here, not knowing we'd been held up, they assumed we were already in residence. Those archers were posted to pick us off if we showed our faces outside. That's why they were in that position—perfect for when we walked out onto the pavement, but not so ideal when we rolled up in a carriage to go in."

Charles nodded. "Tomorrow we have an easier day—only about sixty miles in all, along larger, well-surfaced, well-populated roads." He looked at Logan. "Any insights into what they're likely to do?"

"This hotel is too solid, too secure, and has too many people in it to attack. They won't have time to organize anything complicated, like hiring someone local to break into these rooms." Logan paused, then went on, "I've been thinking that our presence here must be causing the cult members stationed in this region some consternation. It's reasonable to expect that all the cultists in England know by now that three couriers have landed, but there's one more yet to come. They don't know where Rafe is going to land, so they have to continue their watch at all the ports. Which means our group currently here—mostly drawn from Bristol—cannot afford to follow us on. They may leave a few to track us—to see where we go and later alert some other group further on, mostly likely much closer to Elveden—but the majority will have to return, might already have returned, to Bristol."

"That's a fair assumption," Deverell said. "It suggests we won't face an attack tomorrow as we set out."

Logan considered it. "Only if we try to leave very early, before there are others about. The Bristol contingent might dally long enough to see if we try to set out before dawn again, hoping to mount an attack outside town, but if we leave later, with other travelers around, I can't see them trying anything."

Deverell exchanged a glance with Charles. "No need to leave early."

"Indeed not." Charles sighed. "Let's set our departure for midmorning. Say ten o'clock. We'll still make Oxford by four o'clock at the latest. And while I would prefer to go hunting tonight, to see if we can locate and eliminate the Bristol group, such an act would make it too obvious the paper we're ferrying is a decoy. We reduce their numbers every chance we get, but we have to wait for them to come to us."

His tone made it clear that wasn't his accustomed modus operandi. Deverell, too, grimaced resignedly.

Logan eyed the pair of them and shook his head. "Wolverstone's orders made it clear we must behave as if I have the original letter."

"I know." Charles sighed. "I can see his point, but letting murderous cultists slip away unchastized goes painfully against my grain."

Logan's lips twisted wryly. "The cultists won't use firearms, so we're safe from that, unless they hire locals, which it's possible they might do. And if you find yourself facing a cultist with a blade in each hand, he'll be an assassin, so expect the unexpected. They fight to the death, to win any way they can."

"Speaking of the unexpected," Deverell said, "should we set watches?"

Logan hesitated, then nodded. "I've learned never to trust logic when it comes to the cult."

Used to rising before dawn, Linnet claimed the early morning watch, then said her good nights and headed for her room.

Suddenly weary, she stripped, put on the nightgown the attentive—frankly awestruck—little maid had left out for her, then slumped into the bed and tugged the sheets over her shoulder.

She was half asleep when the bed bowed and Logan joined her beneath the piled covers. She'd turned to the side of the bed, her back to him; he slid near, hard and warm, and spooned around her.

Through her slumberous haze, she sensed him looking down at her, studying her face. Then he dropped a soft kiss on her shoulder.

"Are you all right? You seem very . . . worn out."

Not physically, yet since he'd returned with the others, Logan had noted a certain underlying tension, a sense that underneath her competent calm, she was irritated, annoyed . . . bothered over something.

Wrapping one hand over her hip, he leaned closer, brushed his lips across her ear. "I'm sorry if the clashes today bothered you. You can't have killed that many men before—it can be unsettling."

She snorted, opened her eyes, and shot him a glare, one he felt even through the shadows. "Don't be daft. They're trying to kill us—their deaths are on their heads. *That* isn't what's worn me out." She narrowed her eyes on his. "And don't you dare try to leave me out of anything just because you think I'm about to turn into some sort of hysterical female."

He didn't; he'd suggested the excuse so he could ask, "What is bothering you, then?"

Her lips thinned. Narrow-eyed, she regarded him, then turned and settled her head back down, facing away. "If you must know, it's pretending to be a lady that's driving me demented. Having to watch what I say, what I do, how I behave—and now these sweet innocents have decided I'm some sort of heroine, and I'm not. That's not *me*." She huffed, then in an even lower tone went on, "And on top of that, they all think I'm your wife. Even Charles and Deverell have fallen into the habit of it, so even with them I feel I have to play the role, fit into some mold that's not me. Frankly, it's giving me a headache."

He looked down at her for a long moment. Then he slid down in the bed, laid his head behind hers, slid his arms around her, and gathered her close. Held her. "You don't understand—you don't have to change. I don't want you to change. The woman I want as my wife is the woman you are—Linnet Trevission, captain and all. And the staff here—the lady they now revere is the lady who, without a thought for her own safety, saved one of them. They don't care what else you are, what other traits you have—it's what they saw in that instant, the real you, that has stirred their loyalty." He paused, stared at the back of her head. "You, as you are, inspire loyalty in a lot of people."

Him included; he hoped she knew that.

She'd left her hair up. With his cheek, he brushed tendrils of flame from her nape and pressed a soft kiss there. "You, as you are, are the perfect wife for me in every way."

She wriggled, settling deeper within his arms, but all she said was, "Shush. Go to sleep. You have to get up for your watch in two hours."

Within minutes, she'd relaxed; her breathing slowed, evened out.

He listened to the sound, comforted by it, yet oddly uncertain. A touch uneasy, just a little concerned.

He wasn't sure what the problem was—not even if there was a problem at all. If she was wrestling with the mantle of being his wife . . . that was good, wasn't it?

Sleep claimed him before he could decide.

Fourteen

December 19, 1822
The York House, Bath

A t precisely ten o'clock the following morning, Logan followed Linnet out of the hotel, struggling not to grin as the staff, the patriarchal doorman included, bowed, scraped, and positively fawned as if she were royalty.

She'd exchanged her red traveling gown for a severe dark blue carriage gown Penny must have lent her. With her hair up, a red-gold coronet, she looked every inch a reincarnation of the original virgin queen. At times she had an uncannily regal air; he wasn't sure she even knew it.

She carried her cloak over her arm. Only he knew the folds concealed her cutlass. She tossed both into the carriage, turned and thanked the staff for their attentiveness, then climbed up.

He caught a glimpse of her boots as she did—her privateer boots, the knee-high ones she'd worn aboard ship. The sight of her in nothing more than a chemise and those boots, striding about the room that morning, the faint light of a candle flickering over her as she'd prepared to take her turn at watch in the sitting room, had ensured he'd got no more sleep.

With a nod for the doorman, he followed her into the carriage. Settling on the seat beside her, he found her hand, linked his fingers with hers, gently squeezed. He caught her gaze as she looked at him, under cover of the others stowing their bags, murmured, "You are what you are. It doesn't matter what you wear, whether you do something this way or that. Whether you embroider brilliantly, or raise donkeys instead. Regardless, people see you for the lady you are." Raising their linked hands, he brushed his lips across her knuckles. "You never pretend, or prevaricate about yourself—and that's good, not bad. That's reassuring and comforting. That's strong. That's why people are drawn to you." Lowering his voice, he touched his lips again to her fingers, smiled. "That's why I adore you."

Linnet stared into his eyes, mesmerizing midnight eyes, then rapidly blinked, looked away as the others climbed in.

Damn man—impossible man. He actually understood.

In her heart of hearts, she could admit that her one private vulnerability, a weakness she did her best to hide, was her uncertainty over how others, those in the wider world, saw her. She'd grown up a ship's brat, but outside her domain she had to be a lady. She had none of the right training; when outside her world, she was never confident of meeting the standards of behavior her station demanded.

Within her own world, she knew who and what she was, knew why she was that way, knew her strengths and weaknesses, and was always utterly confident.

Out of her domain, the uncertainty lingered. And she hated, *hated*, feeling uncertain.

And somehow, he understood.

That unsettled her more than the rest.

She stared steadfastly out of the window as the carriage rolled unchallenged out of Bath and headed at a spanking pace toward Swindon and Oxford beyond.

As the gray miles and the louring skies passed uneventfully by, her inner turmoil subsided. A large part of the reason she found Logan, his understanding and his comfort—that freely offered, never pushed on her, simply there, at the right time and in the right way, comfort—so unnerving was that she was always the strong one, the one who comforted others, the one others turned to for strength and support. That was her role; it always had been.

Only Muriel guessed that sometimes she needed comfort, needed strength and support. And Muriel only saw because she cared. . . .

But now Logan had seen, because he cared, too. Cared enough to look beneath her surface.

She didn't pretend, was no good at lying, but she did hide her uncertainties, her weaknesses, well. Yet he saw because he looked with the eyes of one who cared.

She dragged in a breath, held it.

He cared. And she loved him.

Not even because he cared—that was the silliness of love in all its glory. She loved him regardless of anything and everything—the impossible man who'd washed up in her cove, woken up in her bed, and changed her life.

He made her want the impossible, too.

She loved him. She was only now learning what that meant, yet given how she'd felt when she'd seen him attacked, when cultists had swung swords at him intending to kill, there was no point avoiding that inescapable conclusion—it was set in stone.

Engraved on her virgin queen's heart.

She had to face it, because now she had to deal with it. . . .

No, not now. Later.

After.

Yes, after. With a firm mental nod, she made that her resolution; she wouldn't think any more about him, her, and any potential future until his mission was over and complete.

The uneventful day was no help.

As Charles had noted, the route they took was no minor road, but a well-traveled highway. They passed through Chippenham, Lyneham, and Wootton Basset; by the time they stopped for lunch at a busy coaching inn in Swindon's main street, they were all bored beyond bearing.

However, when they paused in the busy inn yard and looked around, they spotted a number of black-scarf-encircled heads. "Three at least." Taking her elbow, Logan steered her toward the inn door. "Could be more—difficult to tell with the crowd."

Over luncheon in a private parlor, the men spread out the map again and pored over it, teasing themselves with the prospect that perhaps an ambush might lie ahead. Eventually, however, the consensus was no. Not today. The road to Oxford was too open, too clear of useful geographical obstacles, too busy—and, as Logan pointed out, too damned far from any port.

If anything, the lack of action preyed even more heavily on Charles and Deverell; both seemed positively itching to be out and doing. Logan wasn't surprised when they decided to play spy again—to hire horses and circle around to follow their pursuers.

"At least we'll get a better idea of their numbers," Charles said.

Logan would have liked nothing better than to be on horseback again, out in the fresh air, even if it carried an arctic chill. But Linnet would remain in the carriage—anything else was too problematical—and he felt compelled to stay by her side.

If by any chance their assumptions proved incorrect and an attack was mounted on the carriage, he would need to be there to defend and protect her; any other option was untenable.

With horses arranged, Charles and Deverell set out, intending to find a spot from which to watch the carriage go by, then slip behind any cultists following. Fifteen minutes later, Logan ushered Linnet back into the carriage, and they set out once more.

As predicted, they rolled briskly on through the gloomy afternoon, through Faringdon and on toward Oxford, without challenge. Without sighting any cultists, much less Charles and Deverell.

After several miles had rolled by in silence, Linnet stirred and glanced at him. "Penny for your thoughts."

He met her eyes briefly, then admitted, "I was thinking of the others—my three comrades-in-arms."

When he said nothing more, she prompted, "What of them?"

He hesitated, yet if they were to be man and wife . . . he drew in a breath, said, "Del's made it through, at least to Somersham Place, and Gareth's in Boulogne, possibly already in England. But no one's heard anything about Rafe . . . and of us all, he's the most risk-loving, the most devil-may-care." He glanced at her. "His nickname is Reckless, but more than that, he was the closest to James."

She searched his eyes. "The one who died?"

He nodded. "We all thought of James as our junior, but to Rafe he was more like a younger brother. James's death hit him the hardest."

"You're worried about him—Rafe?"

Logan half grimaced, half smiled. "You'll understand when you meet him, but all of us—Del, Gareth, and I—will be worrying about Rafe until we lay eyes on him again."

Somewhat to his relief, she nodded and fell silent again, and he didn't have to explain that part of his worry was that he didn't want to face losing another close friend, most especially not to the Black Cobra.

With all prospect of them seeing action of any sort fading with the chill winter light, Linnet found it increasingly difficult to cling to her resolution. No matter that trying to think logically about Logan with him sitting alongside her, one of his hands engulfing one of hers, his solid presence, his elemental masculine warmth constantly impinging on her senses, was a near impossible task, the impulse was a constant temptation.

In the end, she gave up, gave in. Shut her senses to his nearness as best she could, and in light of all she'd learned and now felt, tried to evaluate the pros and cons of marrying him. Until then, she'd been thinking of their marriage on a purely practical plane—how would it work?—but perhaps, with them, there were other aspects to consider. Possibly more important aspects.

She wanted him, and that in itself was unexpected. She'd never wanted any other man, yet she wanted him, yearned to keep him by her side, and not just for the obvious physical benefits. Lust played a part in her want, but it was by no means the sum of it. The prospect of having a strong, reliable, honorable man, one willing to stand at her back or by her shoulder rather than in front of her, to help in whatever way she needed—with the estate, with her wards as they grew older—was temptation beyond measure.

Companionship of a kind she'd never had, enough to banish the loneliness of her private life. A man who understood her better than even her father had—he'd appreciated her wildness, her love of challenges, her adventuring soul, but he hadn't understood her compulsion to nurture, to grow, to protect on the emotional plane as well as the physical.

Above all, a man she could trust. With her life, with the lives of those she cared about.

Logan encompassed all of that, seemed to grasp all of that—all of her. With him, she might even have a child of her own, a fundamental want she'd buried deep for so many years it ought to have died, but instead, now he was there, now the prospect dangled before her, she'd discovered that want had with the years only grown stronger. More intense, more compelling.

Logan offered her all the critical elements of a relationship, of a love she'd years ago resigned herself to doing without.

A heady temptation, a visceral yearning.

Yet against that stood her reservations. Her lingering fear, no matter what anyone said, of not being a socially appropriate wife for him. Of not being able to measure up, to manage in the ways society, and eventually he, too, would expect. He'd told her she was what he wanted, had assured her those other requirements didn't matter, but she was not yet convinced. But that was the more minor hurdle.

The major hurdle, the one she could see no simple way around, was the necessity for her to live with him, in Glenluce, Scotland. That was the way things generally happened, yet her leaving Mon Coeur would be close to impossible; she honestly didn't think she could.

He was an earl's son—he would have links, deep links, with land, with an estate somewhere; he was that sort of man. The responsibility she'd seen in him would have to have had some cornerstone, some wellspring—some place that mattered fundamentally to him. His home.

But she couldn't leave hers and share his. And despite him wanting to marry her, she couldn't see the man she knew him to be cutting ties with his home, happily turning his back on it to come and live with her at Mon Coeur.

One element in life, above all others, mattered to people like him and her—place, roots, home. Regardless of how much he wanted her, she couldn't see that want being sufficient to trump his need of his home.

Blinking, she refocused on the gray day outside, felt the numbing dullness sink to her bones.

The carriage rumbled on.

Eventually the spires of Oxford appeared, rising above the mottled brown of skeletal trees.

She stirred, and remembered her earlier conclusion, that whatever he gave her, she would take. That for however long their liaison lasted, she would give herself to it, give to him as he gave to her, take all she could and store up the memories until, with the end of his mission, he would realize the difficulties, face the insurmountable hurdle she'd already seen, and, with regret perhaps, yet regardless, he would agree that they should part.

That earlier course still seemed the wisest.

The carriage wheels hit cobbles.

Releasing her hand, Logan glanced out, then stretched. Relaxing again, he scanned the buildings and pavements as David guided the carriage to the hotel Wolverstone had nominated, the University Arms, one of the older, well-established hotels in Oxford High Street. "No sign of any cultists thus far. I can't see any reason Ferrar would have sent men to Oxford, so presumably the only ones here will be those following us."

He glanced at Linnet. He'd thought he'd made a fair stab at easing her concerns that morning, but she'd been so quiet . . . then again, so had he. An old soldier's habit, a suspension of mind and thought while on a march with no enemy in sight.

She met his eyes, yet he couldn't read her mood. Then the carriage rocked to a halt, and her lips wryly curved. "So we should be safe enough going inside—no hail of arrows likely."

"Thank God." Reaching for the door, he opened it and stepped down. After a quick glance confirming there were no cultists lurking, he moved aside and offered Linnet his hand.

He helped her down, then tucked her hand into the crook of his arm and smoothly escorted her inside.

As before, a suite had been bespoken. As he followed Linnet up the stairs, Logan wondered how the other two had fared.

Equally uneventfully, as it transpired.

"There are eight of them. They're taking it in turns, four at a time, to keep the carriage in view." Charles speared a slice of roast beef from the dish on the table. He and Deverell hadn't turned up until night had fallen. They'd walked into the suite half an hour ago, but chilled and damp, they'd gone to their room to wash and change before joining Logan and Linnet for dinner.

The servers had placed the silver dishes on the table, seen to all their needs, then withdrawn, leaving them free to speak without restraint.

"We followed them from just outside Swindon." Deverell shook his head. "The four on duty did nothing but plod along in your wake, a good distance back. All they wanted was to keep you in sight."

"When you stopped here, they halted at the corner." Charles tipped his head toward the Swindon end of the street. "They watched you go in, saw the bags taken in, then two of them left to get rooms at the tavern back down the street, leaving the other two to watch this place."

"We considered removing them permanently, but"— Deverell reached into his pocket, withdrew a folded parchment, placed it on the table, tapped it with his finger—"we knew Royce's latest orders would be waiting for us here. It was possible he might want us to lead them further on, or that it might prove prudent to give them no hint that we're aware they're following us."

Logan nodded at the missive. "Have you read it?"

"Just glanced at it. There's news that'll make more sense to you than me." Deverell nudged the packet Logan's way. "Read and explain."

Logan picked up the packet, unfolded the stiff sheets. Scanned them. "He's given us the news first. Delborough reached the Cynsters at Somersham Place on the fifteenth, managing to reduce cult numbers by fourteen between London and Somersham. Now he and the Cynsters are planning to spring a trap on Ferrar, or at least his man Larkins, at Ely"— he glanced at the date at the head of the letter—"Wolverstone says tomorrow, but this was written yesterday, so that must mean today. After said trap is sprung, Del and Devil are under orders to transport whoever they catch to Elveden."

Charles looked up. "So it's possible Ferrar's already been caught?"

Logan shook his head. "I'd be shocked were that so. Ferrar's been too clever and cautious for years to suddenly fall into some trap. I can't see that happening."

"We'll know by tomorrow morning," Deverell said. "Royce would send word hotfoot if they succeeded, because our mission's objectives would then change."

"What of your other friends?' Linnet asked.

Logan refocused on the bold, black script. "Gareth made it safely to Dover and is heading north today. He's expected at Elveden by tomorrow evening. At this point they're not sure what might come of his foray, but he and his party are expected to be at Chelmsford tonight with cultists in tow."

"That sounds familiar," Charles quipped.

"The locations are interesting." Deverell set down his knife and fork, pushed aside his plate. "Elveden is just southeast of Thetford, about ten miles north of Bury St. Edmunds, and roughly thirty miles east of Somersham Place. And between Somersham Place and Elveden lies Newmarket, where Demon Cynster and friends hold sway. So there's a line of sorts, west to east, between Somersham Place and Elveden, where Royce has a lot of troops, as it were. He's brought Delborough north from London to Somersham, removing cultists along the way—clearing the west flank. Now he's bringing Hamilton north from Chelmsford to Elveden—clearing the east flank. Now we're coming in from the west . . ." Deverell broke off, patting his pockets. "Where's that map?"

"You left it with us." Linnet rose and went to fetch it from her room.

Returning, she discovered the three men shifting the dishes and platters to the sideboard, clearing the table. Obligingly she unfolded the map and spread it out. They all retook their seats.

Deverell, a certain eagerness infusing tone and expression, traced the routes Delborough had taken, and Gareth Hamilton was taking, to Elveden.

"And now"—Deverell nodded at their orders—"Royce wants us to make for Bedford. Ferrar will have to deal with Hamilton tomorrow, or risk the scroll-holder he's carrying getting through, so the Cobra's attention is going to be fixed to the east while we're closing in from the west."

Charles was nodding. "Which suggests we shouldn't run into any substantial opposition tomorrow. The next day, however . . ." He grinned wolfishly. "Royce really is a master at planning. Ferrar will be crossing and recrossing Royce's chosen battlefield, back and forth, east to west to east, rushing to stop first Delborough, then Hamilton, then us."

Logan frowned. "Why is pushing Ferrar so important?"

Charles and Deverell looked at him, then Deverell smiled.

"Sorry—I'd forgotten you've never run in Royce's harness before." He nodded at the map. "From what we've put together, it's certain Royce was never intending to rely on your letter—about crimes committed in faraway India—to prosecute Ferrar, not if he could help it. Make no mistake—if Ferrar doesn't stumble, Royce will make the best he can of your proof, but how much more convincing if instead he, or one or more of us, captures Ferrar committing some nefarious deed here, on English soil, under straightforward English law?"

Logan's expression was a study in revelation. He waved at the map. "So all of this is really designed to force Ferrar into acting, tripping, and getting caught?"

"Exactly." Charles tapped the map. "And following that logic, I'd say it's certain that Delborough and Hamilton, like you, are carrying decoy letters. The original will come in last—with Carstairs."

Logan studied the map with new interest. "So where will Rafe land?"

Deverell pulled a face. "If Ferrar isn't caught tomorrow, then he'll have to rush west again to stop us getting through from Bedford to Elveden, but any engagement to halt us is most likely to occur between Cambridge and Elveden, somewhere on the Cynsters' patch." Deverell considered the map, then volunteered, "For my money, Royce will have Carstairs come in at one of the eastern ports—Great Yarmouth, Lowestoft, Felixstowe or Harwich."

"So Ferrar will have to hie east again . . . unless we catch him." Linnet looked at the men.

"True," Charles said. "But the thing with Royce is you never can tell. For all anyone knows, he might already have Carstairs safe and sound at Kings Lynn, just waiting for the right moment to head south."

Deverell nodded. "Will Royce play a bluff, or a double bluff? There's no way to predict which way he'll jump, or what he has planned."

After a moment, Logan raised Wolverstone's missive again,

turned a page. "There's more. Our orders. We're to proceed to Bedford tomorrow, where further orders will reach us at the Swan Hotel. He—Wolverstone—doesn't expect us to encounter any serious opposition tomorrow, but he warns we should be prepared for a major ambush the next day. He suggests we leave early and try to ensure any action occurs beyond Cambridge. The Cynsters will be holding themselves ready to assist from the environs of Cambridge on."

Charles nodded. "Just as we thought."

Logan laid down Wolverstone's letter, stared at the map. After a moment, he said, "There's just one thing. I've learned the hard way never to trust the Black Cobra. Royce is assuming Ferrar needs to be present to direct any major action, and while I admit I've never known cultists to act independently of some higher command—presumably Ferrar—in all the months we spent in the field fighting them, none of us caught so much as a whiff of Ferrar himself."

"That suggests"—Linnet continued his deduction— "that Ferrar has henchmen he can trust—some at least—to direct others in the field, so he can give orders and have them carried out even if he isn't there. So it's possible he might already have put plans in place for dealing with us— not us specifically, but any courier coming in from this direction."

Logan nodded, met Deverell's eyes. "We have eight men following us—doing nothing but following us. It's plain there's an ambush up ahead somewhere, but where? Will it be this side of Bedford, or this side of Cambridge? If I were Ferrar, I wouldn't want it to be later. And even though Del and company reduced his numbers in this area by fourteen, Ferrar has many more men than that."

"On the ships we incapacitated," Linnet said, "there were at least thirty cultists, and most of them would have survived."

"Put yourself in Ferrar's shoes." Logan looked at Charles and Deverell. "He now knows, or at least suspects, that the couriers are all heading toward Elveden, that area at least. He knows he's facing couriers coming from the south and southeast, and that chances are one will come from the west. He has unlimited men." He waved at the map. "If you were he, where would you station a body of men to stop a courier from the west?"

Both Charles and Deverell looked at the map, then Deverell pointed. "Somewhere here—*west* of Cambridge."

Charles nodded. "You're right. They won't stop us tomorrow, not before Bedford. It's only once we leave there that we become an active threat—on our last day of travel to Elveden. He doesn't want us to reach Elveden, so he'll step in and stop us decisively—*before* Cambridge." Leaning his forearms on the table, he frowned at the map. "But Royce wants us to avoid them until *after* Cambridge."

"That's not my primary concern." When the others all looked at him, Logan said, "As you noted, Ferrar will have only one aim—to stop us, crush us, before we reach Cambridge. The group he'll have left to accomplish that will be large. He'll have set it up along his usual pattern—massive numbers to smother the opposition and so be certain, absolutely certain, of victory." He met Deverell's gaze, then glanced at Charles. "As experienced as we are, we cannot face a force like that and win, not before we make contact with the Cynsters."

Charles pulled a face, looked down at the map.

Long moments passed as the four of them studied the predicament they faced. "Even if we remove those eight cultists tonight . . ." Deverell grimaced. "Unlikely we can, not without risking our lives prematurely."

Charles nodded. "Much as I hate to admit it, you're right. We can't take out all eight at once."

Her eyes on the map, Linnet leaned forward. "We don't need to. Tomorrow, all we need to do is remove the four keeping us in sight."

Deverell frowned. "The other four will simply take their place."

"Not if they don't know which way we've gone, or where we plan to spend tomorrow night." Linnet looked at Logan, then at the other two. "They can be reasonably certain we're heading to or past Cambridge, but they can't know we're going via Bedford." She placed her finger on the map. "We're here, at Oxford. Eventually, we need to pass here—Cambridge or just south of it. As you said, that's where they'll have stationed their main body of men. But we need to spend one night on the road between here and there—we could be planning to halt at Stevenage, Luton, Dunstable, Letchworth, Baldock, Hitchin, or any number of smaller towns. They don't know which, and they can't tell— which is why we have eight men just following us. They want to make absolutely certain they know where we'll be, and, most importantly, which road we'll be taking to Cambridge."

"Granted," Logan said.

"So if tomorrow we get rid of our four followers at a point before our destination becomes obvious, and get on and out of sight before the other four realize and ride hard to find us, then they simply won't know which way we've gone, and they'll have to keep their force where it is, spread out and waiting until they learn where we are, which way to turn."

Deverell was nodding. "And if we leave before dawn the next day, we'll have a chance to race past and into Cambridge before they can get their troops into position." He smiled at Linnet. "That might work."

"Indeed." Charles leaned closer, looking down at the map. "All we need now is to find the right site to remove our four faithful followers."

In the end, it was, once again, Linnet who came up with the best plan.

Late night
Bury St. Edmunds

"I still can't *believe* it!" Alex strode, all sleekly suppressed violence, into their bedroom.

Daniel followed and closed the door. He paused, then

said, "It is . . . something of a shock." He focused on Alex, now pacing before the fire. "I had no notion Roderick could be so . . . unbelievably stupid."

Arms folded, Alex paced violently. "Clearly he can—clearly he has been. I can *not* get over him using our real names—putting them on paper in black and white—and then forgetting the fact completely, focusing solely on the threat to him, on the fact he was *also* stupid enough to seal the Black Cobra's letter with his personal seal!"

His own head in a whirl, Daniel walked to the bed and sat down. Alex might think much faster than he, yet sometimes it paid to state the facts clearly. "We still need Roderick. Assuming he manages to get all four copies of the letter back, as he's promised—and he's already successfully secured the copy Delborough was carrying—"

"Thank the gods!" Alex swung around, pinned Daniel with an icy gaze. "If he hadn't, we, you and I, my dear, wouldn't have had the first inkling of the danger in which, thanks to Roderick, *we* now stand."

"True. However, he now has one of the four copies and will hie off tomorrow with enough men to make sure of seizing the second from Hamilton." Daniel inclined his head at Alex's pointed stare. "And yes, I'll be at his side to ensure he keeps his mind fixed firmly on what now must be our primary goal—seizing all copies of that letter."

"Good. You, I trust. Roderick . . ." Alex's eyes glittered coldly. "I have to confess I'm having serious second thoughts about our dear half brother."

"Let's wait until we have all the letters back—then, I admit, we need to rethink." Daniel caught Alex's cold gaze. "Just you and me . . . that would be so much easier. But eliminating Roderick now is too dangerous—not here in England. After this manic time is over and we're back in India, safe and secure in the bosom of the cult, then we can reassess."

Alex's lips thinned. The silence lengthened.

Then Alex stated, voice coldly precise, "We came here to support Roderick, thinking it was only his neck at risk. Now we discover that if anyone who knows of us, of our link with him, sees that letter, even just a copy, they'll recognize the implication and, far more than dear Roderick's, it will be *our* heads in the noose."

Daniel was still coping with that realization himself; he had no difficulty understanding Alex's fury. Barely restrained savagery seemed appropriate. But . . . he forced his mind to push through the shock, to revisit the details. "We've been careful, you and I. I can't think of anyone other than our sire likely to be shown the letter, copy or otherwise, who would instantly comprehend our part in the cult."

After a long moment, Alex slowly nodded. "True."

"If Roderick proves himself worthy of our support by retrieving all four copies of the letter, then we can be magnanimous and let him live." He met Alex's icy gaze. "For now."

A tense moment passed, then Alex blew out a breath. Nodded. "For now."

Like a puppet whose strings had been cut, Daniel flopped back on the bed. Stared at the canopy overhead.

Another moment passed, then Alex appeared in his line of vision, halting at his feet to look down at him.

Daniel arched his brows.

"When this is all over, Roderick will pay."

Daniel's smile was genuine. "Oh, he will. We'll make sure of it."

Alex nodded, eyes on his. "Take off your clothes."

Daniel's smile took on a lascivious edge. "With pleasure."

❧ Fifteen ❧

December 20, 1822

They left Oxford in good time, driving out into a constant drizzle; at least the wind had eased. As per Linnet's plan, rather than heading direct to Bedford by the road through Buckingham and Newport Pagnell, they took the more southerly route through Aylesbury. They paused in that town for an early luncheon, and to confirm they still had their eight pursuers with them. That done, they set out once again, heading northeast to Linsdale.

Linnet sat in the carriage, her cloak snugged about her, the map open on her lap. As they bowled along, she went over her plan for the umpteenth time, but could see no further improvements she might make.

She glanced at Logan seated beside her, idly watching the scenery flash past. Charles sat opposite him, slouched in his corner, eyes closed, apparently relaxed. A pile of swords—Logan's and Charles's sabers and her cutlass—lay on the seat alongside Charles, together with the two finger-thin but stout ropes they'd had David buy in Oxford that morning. Deverell, already armed, was riding on the box beside David, keeping his eyes peeled for the spot she'd chosen for their ambush.

Another minor road with a signpost flashed past; turning her head, she caught the name, looked down at the map. While she'd been fairly confident the three men—enlightened as they generally were and so thoroughly focused on winning through to their mutual goal—would see the merit in her plan, she'd been far less certain that they'd follow her orders, rather than rework them.

But no. They'd liked the plan, appreciated it, and had shown no sign of taking over. They'd accepted her orders— even, apparently, accepted the part she intended to play in the plan's execution.

They'd said nothing when, at Aylesbury, she'd taken her bag from the carriage, begged the use of a room from the landlord, and changed into her breeches. She'd wrapped herself tightly in her cloak so no one had seen the scandalous attire, not until she was safely in the coach again. Charles and Deverell had merely raised their brows resignedly.

Logan's lips had thinned, but he, too, had made no comment, leaving her to jettison her carefully prepared defense that it was simply impossible to properly wield a sword of any kind in skirts.

"Linsdale ahead," Deverell called down. "I can just see the bridge beyond it, but only because I'm up here." After a moment, he added, "It looks perfect for our purposes."

David slowed the carriage as they entered the small country town. Inside, Linnet, Logan, and Charles quickly got ready, buckling on sword belts, checking knives. Linnet doffed her cloak. Glancing out of the window, she saw the town square to one side. "It's market day."

"An added bonus," Logan said. "It'll slow the four behind us, and the other four behind them, just a bit more, which won't hurt." They'd confirmed at Aylesbury that their pursuers were adhering to the same pattern as the day before.

David had to tack through the crowded street bordering the square, but then he was through. Linnet, Logan, and Charles all stood, settling weapons, Logan and Charles grabbing up the two ropes as David followed his orders, whipped up the horses, and drove out of the small town to the bridge beyond as fast as he possibly could.

"Almost there," Deverell called down, "and I still can't see our followers."

"Good," Linnet replied. That was critical for their plan to succeed.

Abruptly the carriage slowed. Charles went out of one door, sword on his hip, rope in one hand. On the other side of the carriage, Deverell dropped down from the box. Linnet saw him come out of his crouch and run toward the pillar at the town end of the bridge's stone side.

The horses lunged forward. Linnet and Logan clung to the racks as the carriage rocked across the narrow bridge, then once again David reined the horses in.

Logan met her eyes as he turned to the far door. "Good luck."

"And you." Linnet grasped the handle of the door on her side, opened it, stepped down onto the carriage step, waited until the carriage had slowed just enough, then dropped down to the road.

The pillar at this end of the bridge was mere paces back; she raced for it as David flicked the reins and the horses leaned into the traces again. There was a curve just ahead; David would drive on as if nothing had occurred, and halt once he was around it, out of sight of the bridge.

Under the bridge, the River Ouzel ran swiftly, full and tumbling, its noise masking all other mundane sounds. The banks sloped steeply down from the pillared ends of the bridge's stone sides, but were thick with dock, bracken, and grasses. Beside her pillar, Linnet looked across the river and could barely see Deverell crouched by the pillar on the other side, and then only because he had his back to her.

A short whistle jerked her attention across the road. Frowning at her, Logan sent the rope he'd carried snaking across. She grabbed the end, and swiftly, keeping as low as she could, looped it around the stone pillar, then cinched it tight with a sailor's knot. The free end in his hand, Logan sank down out of sight by his pillar.

Linnet did the same, crouching in concealing bracken. She strained her ears, trying to hear over the river's incessant burbling.

One thing she hadn't foreseen.

But then she heard the sharp clop of galloping hooves on the bridge's flags. Immediately after came a shriek and a clatter.

Glancing up, she glimpsed a rider above her, looking back.

Knew before she saw his shocked face that the two cultists riding behind, sent flying from their saddles by the rope Charles and Deverell had abruptly raised, were being dispatched.

The first pair, already on the bridge, wanted to help their comrades, but the bridge was too narrow for them, riding abreast and now pushed on by their comrades' freed mounts, to turn. They had to get off the bridge first. As she'd predicted—hoped—they yelled and spurred their horses on.

Logan jerked the rope he'd held up and tight, just high enough to pass over the horses' heads and sweep the second pair of cultists from their saddles.

They hit the ground and their horses raced on, followed by the horses of their comrades; the cultists curled up tight to avoid being trampled.

The instant the horses were past, Logan was on the bridge, hauling his cultist up and manhandling him onto the road. The cultist yelled, struggled, but was no match for Logan. He used the hilt of his saber to knock the man out, then lifted him, swung around, and slung him toward the second cultist who, sword in hand, was facing off against Linnet.

The pair went down in a tangle of limbs. Linnet picked her moment, stepped in and with her cutlass hilt neatly clouted her cultist—the one still struggling—over the head.

Reaching the slumped bodies, Logan hefted one and turned to the river. Taking a few careful steps down the bank, he hoisted the unconscious cultist up and flung him into the middle of the swiftly moving water. The current caught the body all but instantly, swirled it, then carried it swiftly off. Turning, he found Linnet dragging the other body to him.

He lifted the limp form and sent it the way of the first. Charles and Deverell had already done the same with the pair they'd taken down. Grabbing up their rope, they came pelting over the bridge. The rope Logan had used already in her hands, Linnet turned and started running after the carriage.

Regaining the top of the bank, Logan glanced swiftly around. No blood, no mess. Nothing to trigger alarm in the other four cultists, those currently off-duty, when they shortly rode along.

Satisfied Linnet's plan had worked like a charm, Logan grinned as the other two joined him, and they set off at a run after Linnet.

They caught her up as she reached the carriage. Logan yanked open the door, held it while she climbed up and tumbled in, then followed her.

Charles and Deverell came through the other door.

David didn't wait for the doors to close before he whipped up the horses. The cultists' four horses had already thundered past; it didn't matter where the loose horses went as long as they were out of sight of the road.

Slumped on the carriage seat waiting to catch his breath, Logan knew he was grinning widely; he saw the same jubilant expression on Charles's and Deverell's faces. Even Linnet was smiling as she shook out the map, glanced over it, then raised her head to shout up to David, "Left—meaning north—at the crossroads in Leighton Buzzard, David—hold steady on the course we discussed."

"Aye, aye, capt'n ma'am," came floating down from above.

Linnet laughed, and then they were all laughing, exhilaration and exuberance bubbling free.

* * *

Their action—"the bridge outside Linsdale" as Charles took to calling it—proved a total success. As they rattled on through the fading light, they detected no hint of continuing pursuit.

Even after they reached Bedford and the Swan Hotel, and Charles and Deverell hung back to keep an eye on the road to see if the latter four cultists had succeeded in picking up their trail, no pursuers of any stripe appeared.

They were all in excellent spirits as they sat down to dine in the private parlor Wolverstone had reserved for them. They had a pair of large rooms on the inn's first floor, one on either side of a corner. One room overlooked the banks of the river, the Great Ouse, while the other boasted an excellent, uninterrupted view of Bedford High Street.

They'd opted to dine early, intending to set out before dawn the next day. Although they weren't about to celebrate what each of them knew was merely a temporary reprieve, their mood was relaxed as they satisfied their appetites with the inn's excellent fare, then, when a well-stocked cheese platter and bowl of fruit had been set before them, and the men supplied with glasses of an excellent port, they settled to discuss the orders from Wolverstone that had been awaiting them.

"So." Tonight Charles was doing the honors, reading from Wolverstone's dispatch. Sitting back in his chair, he took a sip of port, then focused on the pages in his hand. "As usual, the latest happenings first, up to this morning, when Royce wrote this. Yesterday's action at Ely resulted in Delborough and the Cynsters tripping their trap, and although Larkins, Ferrar's man, was killed, presumably by Ferrar himself, the villain got away unseen, with Delborough's copy of the letter, a decoy as we'd surmised."

Logan nodded. "As I said, Ferrar's clever, and careful never to be seen. That said, it sounds like a close call for him. It might have rattled him."

"We can but hope." Charles read further, then continued, "Hamilton and company reached Chelmsford last night, and will be heading north today with at least eight cultists bringing up the rear. Royce, Delborough, and the Cynsters plan to be in Sudbury by lunchtime to assist, assuming any major ambush will occur after that, on the more open stretch to Bury."

Charles frowned. "Royce writes that he's asked Hamilton, who is traveling with a lady, a Miss Ensworth—"

"Miss Ensworth?" Logan looked stunned.

"Who's she?" Deverell asked.

"The Governor of Bombay's niece. She was visiting from England—she was the lady MacFarlane was escorting from Poona, the reason he was there and found the letter—and she was the one who brought it on to Bombay when MacFarlane stayed behind." Logan shook his head. "What the devil's she doing with Gareth?"

Charles raised an eloquent shoulder. "Possibly the same thing Linnet's doing with you." He smiled at Linnet. "Got involved too far to be safely left behind."

Linnet pulled a face at him. She was hardly some delicate governor's niece.

"Anyway"—Charles returned to their orders—"Royce has asked Hamilton to make another copy of the decoy letter Hamilton's carrying, so that if necessary Hamilton can sacrifice his scroll-holder plus decoy copy, but Royce and the others at Elveden will still be able to study the letter and assess its contents. With Delborough sacrificing his copy, Royce has yet to read this oh-so-important letter."

Deverell grinned. "That won't have made Royce happy. An ex-spymaster denied the vital piece of intelligence."

"Indeed, but he writes that as he will have a copy through Hamilton, we can, if necessary, sacrifice our copy should there be an advantage in so doing. He notes that the Cobra appears to be behaving as expected and going after all the copies, as he can have no notion which of the four couriers is carrying the original." Charles paused, then read on, "Our specific route tomorrow is exactly as we'd expected—from here straight to Elveden via St. Neots, Cambridge, and Newmarket. About sixty-five miles, apparently, and he advises us not to halt, but to come straight on. The Cynsters will be lurking around Cambridge and beyond, but depending on the enemy's movements, we might not see them."

Charles looked at Linnet. Smiled. "We'd better order a luncheon hamper."

She raised her brows haughtily, by now unruffled by his teasing.

"That's it." Straightening, Charles tossed the missive on the table. "So it looks as if our notion to leave before dawn and go hard for Cambridge is indeed our wisest course."

They all agreed. Deverell pointed out that with their early departure, their consequently early appearance in Cambridge, about thirty or so miles on, might catch the Cynsters unawares.

Charles considered, then shrugged. "Doesn't really matter. We have to leave early—there's no question about that—but even if we fly straight through and our escort misses us, they're unlikely to miss any cultists who give chase." He grinned. "Knowing the Cynsters involved, they'll be happy to mop up."

Deverell nodded. He left to confirm their departure time with David and order the required hamper. Logan got to his feet, prowled to the window, and stood looking out.

When Deverell returned and shut the door, Logan swung back, halted by the table. "We've lost our pursuers, but the cultists will be hunting us. With luck they won't find us before we leave, but I've learned never to take the Black Cobra for granted. He always has plenty of men, and previously when pressed, he's shown a tendency to do the utterly unexpected—to act in ways so outrageous we would never think of them, much less make preparations to counter them." He met the others' eyes. "We still need to set pickets."

"Agreed." Charles pushed back from the table. "But given our early start, we only need three watches—why don't you and Linnet take the first, I'll take the middle, and Deverell can take the last?"

They all nodded in agreement.

"At least," Logan said, as Linnet rose and led the way to the door, "in such a solid building, with the general dampness plus the river so close, we don't need to fear them setting the place alight."

Bury St. Edmunds

"You do understand that he had to die, don't you?" In the drawing room of the house they'd made their headquarters in Bury St. Edmunds, Alex topped up Daniel's glass from the decanter of fine brandy Roderick had liberated from the locked sideboard.

How very apt, Daniel thought, as he took a healthy swallow. As usual, Alex was abstemious, but tonight was also sipping from a glass.

"Poor Roderick." With a shake of the head, Alex replaced the decanter on the sideboard. "So . . . sadly ineffectual."

"Indeed." Daniel took another swallow. He was still a trifle shocked, although not by Roderick's death itself—that had been coming for some time, and it was his idiot half brother's lack of thought for consequences that had landed the three of them in this mire after all. Still, he hadn't seen it coming—hadn't seen Death in Alex's eyes until the dagger had slid home.

But Alex had been right. Roderick had had to die, then and there, in that moment. Thanks to Alex's quick thinking, the pair of them had got clean away.

Daniel raised his glass, locked eyes with Alex, now seated on the sofa nearby. "To Roderick—the idiot—who was convinced to the last that our sire would always save him. He was a fool, but he was our brother." He drank.

Alex sipped. "Half brother." Alex's lips curved. "Sadly, he missed the better half—the cleverer half."

Daniel tipped his glass in acknowledgment, but said nothing. He and Alex shared a father, but their mothers had been different, so the cleverer half Alex alluded to he had missed as well. He looked at his glass, and decided he'd better stop drinking.

"But Roderick no longer matters, my dear. We do." Alex's voice was low but clear, as always compelling. "And we need to take steps to ensure our necks remain free of the hangman's noose."

"Indubitably." Setting down his glass, Daniel met Alex's eyes. "As ever, I'm yours to command, but I suspect I'd better go and check on Monteith. We need his copy of the letter."

Alex nodded. "While you're doing that, I'll organize another move. Sadly, here, we're too close to where Roderick met his end. Our opponents might think to search. I'll have somewhere else organized—not too far away—by the time you get back with Monteith's letter."

"And then we'll need to get a welcome in place for Carstairs."

"Indeed." Alex's eyes glittered. "I'll start work on that tomorrow, too. Now we know he's coming down the Rhine, and at speed, then it's all but certain he'll pass through Rotterdam. I've already sent orders to all those on the other side of the Channel to ensure he runs into a very warm reception. But given that the other three have all come this way, what are the odds, do you think, that he's making for either Felixstowe or Harwich? They are, after all, the closest and most convenient ports to this part of the country."

"He'll be carrying the original, won't he?"

Alex nodded. "Just the fact he's coming in on the most direct route . . . our puppetmaster isn't trying to draw out cultists with him, but to give him the shortest and safest road, the best possible chance of reaching the puppetmaster. That's why he's the last, and also why Monteith is coming in from the opposite direction."

"So Carstairs won't be long."

"No, but what I have planned in Rotterdam will at least slow him down, which is all we need." Alex looked at Daniel. "You take care of Monteith, and leave me to put our welcome for Carstairs in place. By the time you get back with Monteith's letter, all will be set." Alex smiled, viciously intent. "Whoever our puppetmaster is, I guarantee Carstairs will never reach him."

Daniel nodded and stood. "I'd better get going if I'm to join the men tonight."

"Where exactly are they?"

"In a deserted barn outside a village called Eynesbury. I left them with strict orders to keep watch for Monteith and make sure he doesn't reach Cambridge. They'll know where he's spending the night." Daniel smiled, envisioning carnage. "I believe I'll pay Major Monteith a midnight visit."

Alex understood what he was planning. "Very good. And who knows what possibilities tomorrow might bring? Take care, my dear—I'll see you later tomorrow, once you have Monteith's copy."

Daniel saluted. "Until then."

He turned away and strode for the door, and so didn't see the way Alex watched him.

Didn't feel the cold, piercing weight of those ice-blue eyes.

After he'd passed through the open doorway and disappeared, Alex sat staring at the vacant space.

Debating.

Several minutes ticked past.

Then Alex turned and looked toward the doorway at the far end of the room. "M'wallah!"

When the fanatical head of Alex's personal guard appeared, Alex coldly said, "Have someone saddle my horse and lay out my riding breeches, jacket, and my heavy cloak. I expect to be out all night."

Turning, Alex looked again at the door through which Daniel had gone.

Daniel was, Alex knew, entirely trustworthy.

Yet sometimes trust wasn't enough.

Alex had a very bad feeling about what was going on. About the quality of their opponents.

Pale eyes still fixed on the doorway, Alex rose, set down the barely touched glass of brandy. "I do hope I'm wrong, my dear. I do so hope I'm wrong."

Once bitten, twice shy. Alex left the room to change and ride out.

December 21, 1822
The Swan Hotel, Bedford

Linnet sat beside Logan on the top step of the main stairs on the hotel's first floor. All about them the house was quiet, settled, already in slumber. Darkness enveloped them; rather than keep a candle burning, marking their position, they'd let the night embrace them and let their eyes adjust.

The clocks in the town had tolled midnight a little while before, yet the hotel had been quiet for longer. In this season, there were no guests looking to revel into the night. Most of those she'd seen appeared to be travelers, on their way to some other place.

Like them.

In her case, however, she was no longer sure where she was going. To Elveden later that day, but after that? Where would life take her? Back to Mon Coeur to live out her life alone, surrounded by her people?

She shook free of the circling, distracting thoughts, ran her hand along her thigh, the soft leather beneath her palm familiar and reassuring. She'd changed into a gown for dinner, but then changed back into her breeches. If the cult came for them, now or later that day, she couldn't run or fight anyone in a gown. Not effectively. And while she was with Logan, fighting alongside him, she needed to be at her most effective.

Her movement had caught Logan's attention; even through the dimness she could feel his gaze.

Elbows propped on his knees, hands clasped between them, he studied her profile for a moment, then said, "Today . . . I shouldn't say it was fun, but it was. So much better than just sitting in a coach, rolling along, waiting for the Cobra to strike. Sitting and waiting isn't something that comes easily to either of us—or the other two, for that matter. Your plan was inspired, and your help with the execution much appreciated."

She turned her head and met his eyes. Forced herself to seize the moment, the opening. "I know you mean to reassure me that you're not repulsed by me wielding a sword." She put a hand on his arm, squeezed gently. "I know it doesn't matter to you—that you don't think less of me because of it. But . . ." Through the shadows she tried to read his eyes—an impossibility. "Believe me, others—lots of others, indeed, most of society—will see it differently. No—don't argue, don't try to tell me otherwise, for that I do know." She held his dark gaze. "I am not, and never will be, an appropriate wife for the son of an earl. Yes, I know Penny likes to ride wearing breeches, and she would probably love to wield a sword, but that's not the point. She's not just gently born but well brought up—she's able to do all the things I cannot. The social things, doing the pretty in duchess's drawing rooms, going to balls, knowing what to say."

Pausing, she drew breath, softly said, "I am who I am, and I cannot change—not just because I would find it hard but because to be who I need to be for all the others who depend on me, I need to be who, and what, I am now."

He'd opened his mouth once, but at her command had shut it and let her speak without interruption, had listened as closely, as intently as she could wish. He continued to look down at her, a slight frown between his brows.

Logan forced his hands to remain relaxed, lightly clasped. She'd just given him the perfect introduction to declare the truth of his birth, but . . . she hadn't yet seen all he wanted to show her before he told her the truth. She hadn't seen, so didn't know, all the factors that, to his mind, would convince her beyond all question that marrying a well-born bastard was what she should do.

He told himself he should speak now, regardless, yet . . . simple fear, for all its simplicity a cold, iron-clad vise, held him back. He couldn't risk it. Just the thought of failing to convince her chilled him. Shook him. He needed her as his—his wife—too much.

"I don't want you to change." He held her gaze with his. "I want you exactly as you are—the buccaneering female privateer, the virgin queen of Mon Coeur. I value all you are now, as you are now, and the truth, the real truth, is that I would fight anyone who tried to force change upon you."

She sighed, her lips twisting resignedly. "How's that going to work? How will I meet the needs you'll have once you take up your rightful position?" She spread her arms. "How am I, me, as I am, going to fit the mold of your wife?"

"There isn't a mold." He felt his jaw firm. "And if there is, I'll break it." Turning to her, he framed her face between his palms. Searched it, let his gaze linger on each now-beloved feature. Eventually looked into her eyes. "I'll shatter any mold and re-form it—to fit you. Only you. You are the lady I want. You are all and everything I want. All and everything I will ever need, now and forever. I know you can't yet see how that can be, how and why that—you and me, married, a team forever—will work, and I can't explain it here, now. I will once we're through and safe, and we have time at Elveden." He held her gaze relentlessly, hoping to impart his certainty, impress it on her with his gaze and his words. "Trust me—you are the lady I want. I won't have anyone else, and I'll never stop wanting you. Only you."

He searched her eyes. "I'll never stop needing you. Only you." Slowly, he bent his head, tipped her face, brought her lips to his. Whispered across them, "Like this."

Then he kissed her.

And for once let his warrior's shield fall. Let all he felt for her that he normally hid—not the passion and desire but the tenderness, the love, the yearning—rise up and be known, let those softer yet no less intense feelings color his kiss. Let them shine, glow.

Let her see.

Linnet saw. Enthralled, fascinated, she saw, and felt giddy. Raising a hand, she clasped it over the back of one of his—a necessary anchor. She sensed, felt to her bones the gentleness within him.

And, in that instant, believed.

In that instant knew she'd fight for this, to keep this—him and his love, for what else could this be?—forever.

Fathoms deep, oceans wide, she sensed it as something that knew no limits, no bounds.

That encompassed all he was, and was infinite in its promise.

Her lips moved beneath his, softly, as gentle as his had been, returning that promise. That tenderness.

That revelation of infinite, unending love.

For long moments, that reality held them in its palm.

Then a sound reached them.

They broke apart, instantly alert, both too much the warrior to resist the call for so much as a second.

They looked about, searched, scanned the shadows. Listened, intent.

Eventually, Logan breathed, "Any ideas?"

Linnet shook her head as, slowly, silently, they both got to their feet.

Again they listened, turning, heads tilting.

Scrapes—something moving against the outer walls. A thump, a soft, sibilant sound.

She frowned. "It's after midnight and icy cold. What on earth would anyone be doing outside?"

On the words, they heard a sharp crack. Then another.

Seconds later, they both smelled smoke.

Eyes wide, Linnet stared at Logan. "The cult?"

Frowning, he grasped her hand and started toward their room. "Even for them, this is ridiculous—the building's mostly stone, and what isn't is thoroughly damp. It's not going to burn down. What the hell do they think to achieve?"

As if in answer, someone outside yelled, "Fire!"

And pandemonium broke out.

≈ Sixteen ≈

From the mouth of an alley on the opposite side of Bedford High Street, Daniel Thurgood watched his assembled cultists carry out his orders with their customary zeal. Mounted atop his black horse, he watched the flurry of activity about the hotel with growing anticipation.

An hour ago, he'd ridden into the camp near Eynesbury to discover that his careful planning had borne fruit. While the men following Monteith and his guards had lost their trail, the man he'd stationed in Bedford had already ridden in to report that the major, some woman, and the major's two guards were passing the night at the Swan Hotel.

He'd brought his own guard of twelve—eight assassins and four fighters, all more experienced than the general run of cultists—with him. Although they'd lost men in their pursuit of Delborough and Hamilton, and many were still scattered along the south and southeast coasts, and Alex retained a significant number to deploy in the east, plus a personal guard much like his, he had more than enough cultists in Bedford that night to accomplish his mission—to seize Monteith and his scroll-holder.

His guard were restless, keen to join in any fun. All twelve were currently on foot behind him, concealed in the deep shadows of the narrow alley. The rest of the cultists, working in groups of eight, had surrounded the hotel, situated at the end of the block, and on the three sides—the street front, the side facing the river, and the rear that gave onto the mews—had set smoking fires flanking every door, and below every window.

Even now the smoke was thickening, billowing up to engulf the building.

He held no illusions of burning the place down—solid stone and slate wouldn't burn. But it was winter in England; there'd been plenty of split wood and coals neatly stacked in sheds at the hotel's rear. And all he and his men needed was smoke.

Enough smoke to cause panic and have everyone in the hotel rushing out.

Scenting victory in the smell now permeating the air, thin lips curving in cruel anticipation, Daniel lifted the black silk scarf he'd wound about his neck, resettling it so it concealed his features, and watched the clouds of dirty gray and dense white swell and swallow the hotel.

A hundred yards further up Bedford High Street, further away from the river and the Swan Hotel, Alex, ahorse, hugged the shadows at the corner of a lane and studied the activity along the hotel's front façade.

In jacket and elegant riding breeches, wrapped in a heavy coat, with a hat pulled low and a thick muffler obscuring all features, Alex managed the large chestnut M'wallah had commandeered without conscious thought, all attention locked on the front door of the hotel as it slammed opened and confused and panicked residents poured out.

Considering those in nightshirts and robes now flapping and coughing in the street, noting the way the smoke was rushing in through the opened front doors, Alex wondered if Daniel had stationed men at all the hotel's exits. Looking up and, despite the darkness, seeing billowing plumes rising on the hotel's other two accessible sides, Alex's lips curved approvingly. Daniel hadn't overlooked the secondary doors.

Assessing Daniel's plan, gauging the likely outcome, Alex increasingly approved. It appeared that this attack, in Daniel's more capable hands, would succeed.

Regardless, Alex's purpose tonight wasn't to assist.

Once bitten, twice shy.

Cloaked in darkness, closely observing the action, Alex's sole aim was to make certain that, this time, nothing went wrong.

It was the attack Logan had feared, yet he couldn't see the point. Not even deluded cultists could imagine they could turn the Swan Hotel into a raging inferno.

He and Linnet had raced around the first-floor gallery, knocking on doors as they'd passed. Linnet had rushed on down the corridor, knocking and yelling, leaving him to rouse their friends.

Reaching Charles and Deverell's room, he thumped on the door, yelled "Fire!" then went into the room he and Linnet had shared. Rummaging through his bag, he grabbed the scroll-holder, tucked it into his belt at the back so it rode along his spine, hidden by the fall of his coat. He already had his dirk in his boot. He buckled on his saber, loosened the blade, then grabbed Linnet's cloak and her cutlass, and strode out.

The gallery was filling with smoke and disoriented people, jostling and coughing, some shrieking. Logan turned to the others' door just as it opened and Deverell came out, followed by Charles, both fully dressed and armed.

They swiftly looked around, didn't bother asking what was going on.

Hotel staff appeared from below, while others stumbled down from the attics above. All were panicked, but did their best to hurry patrons downstairs and out of the front door.

Someone had flung the front double doors wide, allowing more smoke to rush in and up the funnel of the stairwell. Stepping to the gallery's rail, Logan squinted down through the gushing clouds, saw more smoke pouring through the doors of the dining room and the hotel's front parlor, adding to the thickening miasma now filling the foyer, and rising.

Coiling and billowing, and with every new gust of air gushing up to fill every available space.

Linnet returned, coughing, nearly choking. Glancing at the thick cloud below, she dragged her kerchief from her neck, quickly folded it, and retied it over her nose and mouth.

The others did the same, not that it helped much.

Linnet accepted her saber and cloak from Logan, buckled the first on, threw her cloak over her shoulder. "Come on." She started around the gallery.

Logan and the others followed. He was still thinking, assessing, trying to see. . . .

Reaching the stairs, Linnet went to step down, and he suddenly knew—suddenly saw the danger. "No!"

Grasping her arm, he drew her back.

Surprised, Linnet let him. "What?"

Behind his kerchief, his expression was grim. "That's what this is for—to flush us out. There's no real threat of fire—there can't be."

Deverell joined them. "They're using smoke to panic people into rushing ouside. They'll be waiting for us to appear."

"Exactly."

They looked around, listened. Most people had already gone down. A few stragglers stumbled past them and hurried down the stairs. They could hear rushing footsteps on the ground floor, and shouts and wails from outside.

"Let's take a look outside." Going to the door of a room overlooking the front of the hotel, Charles threw it open and strode straight to the window.

The smoke was roiling and boiling upward, casting an increasingly dense pall over the street.

"They must have men feeding the fires beneath that," Deverell said.

"Presumably close against the building." Logan squinted down. "We can't see them from this angle."

"No—but we can see the archers on the roofs across the street." Charles pointed. It took a moment to distinguish the shapes against the night sky, but the fluttering ends of the scarves about the figures' heads left little doubt as to who and what they were looking at.

"Ambush of a different sort," Deverell said. "We need to reconnoiter before we move. Charles?"

Charles nodded, and the pair left the room.

Linnet stayed beside Logan, peering down at the scene below. Beneath the shifting clouds, the hotel's patrons and staff were milling about in confusion. Townsfolk, roused, were bringing flares, creating an eerie golden glow beneath the thickening pall. "When they try to put the fires out, they're only going to create more smoke—at least in the short term."

Logan nodded. "That's assuming the cultists will give up their fires without a fight."

"They're actually down there, aren't they—in full view." She'd spied darker figures through gaps in the smoke.

"Yes, and that means this is an all-out assault. They're going to do anything and everything necessary to catch us and take the scroll-holder." Logan considered the scene, then tugged her arm. "Come on."

They stepped into the smokier gallery.

Charles appeared from their left. "There's no way out on this side—the hotel abuts the next building. No alley, no windows."

Deverell emerged from a room along the right-hand side of the gallery. He shook his head as he came jogging up. "They've men along the riverbank, too. Under the trees, watching like hawks, plus others feeding fires against the walls on that side."

Around them, the smoke was steadily thickening, rising and filling the upper levels of the hotel. They all coughed; Linnet's eyes were stinging.

Deverell shook his head. "Regardless of the absence of flames, we can't stay here."

"Smoke can kill just as easily as fire." Charles tightened his kerchief.

Grimly, Logan nodded. "Let's see if we can get out the rear entrance."

Coughing, doubled over, they ran around the gallery, trying to avoid the worst of the smoke. Logan found the back stairs and started down, Linnet at his back, Charles and Deverell behind her.

They descended half a flight into rising smoke, then Logan abruptly halted. He nodded at the window set into the wall beside him. "Look."

From his tone, Linnet knew what she would see when she did. He stepped down; she did, too, letting Charles and Deverell look out as well.

Cultists were ranged behind barrels and carts in the inn's rear yard. She counted ten.

Grimly shaking his head, Charles straightened and met Logan's eyes. "I don't fancy those odds. We might be able to best those we can see, but if there are more within hailing range, which seems likely, we'll be in big trouble."

And they had Linnet with them.

Logan heard the unsaid words loud and clear; they were already ringing in his head. He looked past Charles to Deverell. "Charles said the building against the fourth side abuts the hotel, so it'll have to be the roof."

No one argued.

Deverell turned around. "I think the hotel is the highest building in the area. With luck, the archers across the road won't be able to see us."

As quickly as they could, they went back to the first-floor gallery. "This way." Linnet took the lead, heading for the door through which the hotel staff had come down from the attics. Beyond the door they found the attic stairs, blessedly less smoky. They climbed quickly up and Deverell shut the door behind them.

Once in the attics, they spread out, searching. The air was clearer, but the smoke seeped steadily in. From the street below, they heard shouts, then yells, a building ruckus. Linnet tried to look out of the attic windows, but the balconies below blocked her view.

"Sounds like a melee," Deverell said. "As if the townsfolk have taken exception to foreigners setting their hotel alight."

"More power to their right arms," Charles replied. "Unfortunately, we can't risk going out and joining in."

Logan finally found the right door. "This way."

He waited until they were all assembled. "We go up and out, and with luck, there won't be any cultists waiting, but be prepared—they might have thought of the roof."

Logan turned and climbed the stairs. Linnet moved to follow, but Charles caught her shoulder and drew her back. "Ladies to the rear, this time."

He pushed past her, and so did Deverell, before she could think of any reply. With a humph, she seized the moment to swing her cloak about her shoulders and tie it firmly at her throat, then she loosened her cutlass in its scabbard, and followed.

Logan opened the door at the top of the narrow flight, gently eased it wide, giving thanks to whoever had kept the hinges oiled. Silent as a wraith, keeping low, he slipped out, through the drifts of smoke scanned the roof. It was largely flat, with no protrusions of sufficient size to hide a cultist.

And it was empty.

"All clear," he murmured, straightening as Charles joined him. The noise from what sounded like a pitched battle below would mask any sound they made.

Charles glanced back as Deverell, then Linnet emerged. He pointed to the side of the roof away from the river—the side beyond which the adjoining building lay.

Swiftly, they crossed to the waist-high stone parapet. The air was somewhat clearer, slightly fresher there, and now the thick smoke worked to their advantage, wafting up the hotel's walls and screening them from watching eyes.

Deverell had been right. The neighboring building was

shorter than the hotel, its roof lower, but thankfully not too low. And that roof, too, was empty of cultists.

"They've positioned all their archers across the street," Charles murmured.

"Luckily for us." After one glance at the archers, Logan took advantage of a thicker gust of smoke to swing one leg over the parapet, then the other, then he dropped lightly down to the lower roof.

Charles and Deverell helped Linnet to do the same, then they followed.

Keeping low—they were now at a level where, if they stood upright too close to the edge, the archers on the roofs opposite might see them—they scouted, but could find no access to the building below. No way to get down.

Logan signaled. "Next one along."

The next building's roof was lower still, but this time by barely a step. Even more carefully, they spread out and searched its roof for some way to get inside, but neither it, nor the next two adjoining buildings, all of similar height, had any direct way to get into the buildings below.

Moving on, they looked down at the roof of the next building, which was smaller and lower, two storeys but with a many-gabled roof. From above, they studied it, searched, then Linnet pointed. "There—that covered porch." A small, single-storey structure, it was built onto the back of the building. "We can go down that waterpipe from the roof, onto the porch roof, and then down into the little yard at the rear."

The building beyond the one with the gabled roof was significantly higher; climbing up to its roof would be a problem. Logan glanced back. They were sufficiently far from the hotel to risk going down into the lane that ran along the rear of the buildings. More, the small square yard into which they would drop didn't open directly to the rear lane, but was joined to it via an alley some ten yards long. Unless a cultist came to the alley's mouth and looked in, their party wouldn't be seen by the cultists watching in the lane.

And the longer they remained on the roofs, the more risk that they'd be seen.

He nodded. "Let's go."

Although the smoke was still thickening about the hotel, it was much thinner, a bare veil, where they now were. The flares in the street were largely concentrated outside the hotel, but every now and then some townsman would run past with a brand, on their way to join the fracas outside the hotel, throwing light up onto the wall down which they had to climb.

They tried to pick their times, dropping down to the roof one after another, then making their way cautiously over the gables to the pipe that let them ease down to the porch roof.

Within ten minutes, they were within reach of the ground.

Daniel cursed. "Damned meddling gits! Why couldn't they keep their noses out of things?"

None of the men at his back volunteered an answer.

Still cloaked in the alley's shadows, they watched as the fight in the street swelled to an all-out brawl. More townsmen came charging up to join in; as the minutes ticked by, more of those arriving waved weapons—pitchforks, spades, whatever they could lay hands on.

He'd overlooked the fact that the common English were not the same as the run-of-the-mill Indian—that they were more likely to react with belligerence than cower. His fault, his mistake; he knew it.

The instant the gathering townsfolk and those flooding out of the hotel had comprehended that the source of the fires threatening the building was a group of foreigners, who were continuing to diligently feed the flames, they'd cursed, bellowed, and fallen on the cultists' backs. For their part, the cultists expected anyone whose house they were burning down to cower; they'd struck back, expecting instant victory. Before Daniel could think of any way to intervene, battle had been joined.

There were enough cultists to keep the smoke billowing

and roiling up, but the ranks of the good townsfolk of Bedford were constantly increasing.

A shot rang out.

Daniel jerked his reins tight, caught his horse before it could bolt. Astride its back as it pranced, he cursed some more. The cultists hated guns—as fighters that was their one true weakness. Even the men at his back, far better trained, had flinched. Their edgy tension had ratcheted up several notches.

More shots sounded, more than likely fired over the crowd.

An instant later, three cultists fled past the alley mouth, heading away from the fight.

Daniel ground his teeth. "Where the devil is Monteith?" Despite all distractions, he'd kept his eyes on the hotel's front door. He had men stationed all around the building, watching every exit. If Monteith had gone out any other way, he should have heard of it by now.

Should have been informed that the troublesome major had been seized. Heaven knew he'd assembled enough men to be sure of accomplishing that.

Could Monteith be thinking to hole up in the hotel? As soon as the smoke faded sufficiently, Daniel would send in his assassins to scour the place.

His mount stirred, as restless as he. Another local man came running down the street from the left, a flaming brand held high, a pitchfork in his hand; the light drew Daniel's gaze.

Up above the street, the light from the brand fleetingly silhouetted an object—one that fell from one roof to the next. A man-sized object; a crouching man. Daniel stopped breathing, watched. The man didn't come to the front of the roof. He must have gone . . .

"With me!" Daniel snapped out the order. Loosening his reins, digging in his heels, he plunged out of the alley. Wheeling left, away from the melee before the hotel, he thundered up the road.

His assassins running as a group just behind, Daniel could

almost taste success as he rounded the block, drew rein, drew his sword, and turned into the lane than ran along the rear of the buildings.

Logan dropped to the cobbles in the narrow yard. He swiftly scanned the cramped space. Stacked crates and empty barrels clogged the entrance to the alley leading to the rear lane. The yard was dark and relatively quiet, the high walls all around cutting off much of the sound and fury from the street. Even the smoke had barely penetrated there.

Straightening, he reached up and helped Linnet down. While she untied the ends of the cloak she'd knotted across her waist, he checked the scroll-holder, resettled it against his spine.

While Charles, then Deverell, joined them, Logan found the back door tucked inside the porch and tried it. Not only was it locked, it was also solidly bolted from inside. No access, no even temporary place to hide.

He looked back down the alley. The walls were plain brick, unadorned, and vertical all the way to the neighboring roofs, no doors or windows. He glanced up and around. There was no other way out.

"At least the archers across the street can't see us." Catching the others' eyes, he tipped his head down the alley. "We'll have to go that way."

They nodded, resettled their coats and weapons, then he led the way forward, Charles behind him, then Linnet, with Deverell bringing up the rear.

They'd barely cleared the stacked crates and stepped into the alley proper when a dense shadow loomed at its end. As one, they halted.

The shadow resolved into a horseman in a black coat, breeches, and riding boots, astride a black horse.

Men moved behind the horse, forming up two by two and following the rider as he walked his mount slowly, clop by clop, down the alley toward them.

The sound echoed eerily off the alley's high brick walls, a portentious drumbeat.

As if responding to the drama, the moon sailed free high above; it beamed down into the alley from behind them, bathing the approaching figure and his retinue, highlighting every line in icy-cold silver light.

Silver light that glinted on multiple naked blades.

The rider wore a black scarf wound about his head, concealing nose and chin; his eyes coldly observed them from above its upper edge as he halted—just far enough away to be safe from any attack from Logan or Charles, now standing shoulder to shoulder across the entrance to the small yard. Both had drawn their sabers. Logan couldn't remember doing so; the hilt had suddenly been in his palm, his fingers locked in the grip, the blade held down by his side.

His every sense, every instinct, remained locked on the rider, even when two of the cultists moved up to stand on either side of the black horse.

Both cultists, like their fellows behind them, held naked blades in both hands.

"Those," Logan murmured, "are cult assassins."

"Ah," Charles replied, and uncharacteristically left it at that.

Linnet, behind Logan, heard the exchange. Looking over his shoulder, she finally comprehended just what had driven him and his friends to battle so hard, for so long, to face so many dangers to bring it down. To defeat it.

True evil.

It stared back at her, not from the cult assassins' dark, unflinching eyes but from the shadowed eyes of the rider. He . . . somehow, he made the hair on her nape lift, made her skin pebble and crawl; when his gaze found her, and, as if intrigued, rested on her, she had to fight to quell a wholly instinctive shiver.

An instinctive reaction.

An instinctive fear.

He wore a black coat, he rode a black horse, he had black hair. Yet it was his soul that was blackest; she knew that to her bones.

Her cutlass was already in her hand; she tightened her grip on the hilt. Not a single thought—not even a fleeting one—of fleeing entered her head. She'd come to fight alongside Logan and she intended to do just that.

Yet the odds . . . were by any estimation hopeless. That didn't mean they couldn't be overcome. She counted twelve assassins, but the biggest threat was the mounted man. He carried an unsheathed sword, held lightly balanced across the front of his saddle.

If they could get rid of him . . .

The rider had shifted his gaze to Logan. After another long, studied silence, he said, "At last we meet, Major Monteith."

His voice was educated, very English, his diction only lightly muffled by the scarf.

When Logan said nothing, the rider's eyes smiled. "I believe you know what I want. Please don't waste time by telling me you haven't got it—that you aren't carrying it on your person at this moment."

Opportunity. Possibility . . . Leaning forward, Linnet whispered to Logan, loudly enough for the rider to hear, "Give it to him. It's no use to us if we're dead."

She knew it was a decoy, no use to anyone anyway. But the rider didn't know that, and if he could be fooled into taking it and leaving, they had a chance of surviving even this attack.

Logan shifted, frowned. Made every show of reluctance, grateful to Linnet for giving him that chance. Whoever this man was, he'd know immediately that the letter was a decoy if Logan simply offered it up.

He waited, hoping that the man would make some threat—preferably against Linnet—to further excuse his surrendering the document he'd fought to ferry over half the world.

But the rider's gaze remained locked on him and didn't

again shift to Linnet. Eventually, the rider arched a brow, as if growing bored.

Who the devil was he? He wasn't Ferrar, yet from the color of his hands he'd been in India, and not long ago. He clearly commanded cult assassins, so he was, at the very least, a close associate of the cult leader. Coat, breeches, boots, and the horse were all of excellent quality, and the rider wore them, rode the horse, with the unthinking air of one long accustomed to such luxuries.

Logan allowed his frown to deepen. "Who are you?" He saw no reason not to ask.

The rider's gaze took on an edge. "My name is not something you need to know. All you need to understand is that I am, in this moment, in this place, the Black Cobra."

"The Black Cobra's Ferrar."

"Really?" The rider's smile returned; he seemed genuinely amused. "I believe you'll discover you're mistaken. However"—his voice hardened, along with his gaze—"the one thing you should note is that I am here, Black Cobra or not, to retrieve the letter that inadvertently fell into your hands." His gaze flicked to the others, then returned to Logan's face. "And I'm willing to barter for it—your lives for the letter." When Logan didn't reply, the rider drawled, "Word of a gentleman."

Logan managed not to scoff. Not to react at all. The offer was the best he could hope for, not that he believed it; he knew better than to trust the Black Cobra in whatever guise. Still . . . moving slowly, he withdrew the scroll-holder from the back of his belt, held it up for the rider to see.

The rider's gaze turned superior. "Yes, but is there anything inside?"

Letting his saber hang from its lanyard, Logan slowly opened the holder, then tipped it so the man could see the parchment inside.

The rider sighed theatrically and beckoned. "Give me the letter itself—I'm not going to cede you your lives in exchange for a plain sheet of paper. You can keep the scroll-holder as a souvenir."

Inwardly, Logan sighed, too. He didn't expect the rider to allow them to live, to call off his assassins—no one from the Black Cobra hierarchy would ever be so forgiving—but if the rider had taken the scroll-holder and ridden off, they might have had a fighting chance.

While reaching into the holder and drawing out the rolled parchment, he was planning, plotting, evaluating the closest assassins, imagining how a fight would commence; the opening minute would be crucial.

Drawing out the letter, he tossed it to the nearest assassin. The man caught it in his right hand and passed it up to his master.

Logan kept the empty scroll-holder, its brass end open and flapping, in his left hand, slid his right hand into the guard of his saber, gripped the hilt.

Beside him, he felt Charles shift slightly, also tensing for action.

The rider had, as Logan had feared he would, unrolled the parchment. He angled it to the moonlight; it was bright enough for him to confirm the letter was a copy.

The rider flipped the parchment over, confirming the absence of any telltale seal, and once again the skin at the corner of his eyes crinkled in a smile.

Logan blinked. A *smile*? It was a decoy copy. The rider, if he'd been the one directing the campaign to keep Logan from reaching Elveden, had lost countless men—and all for a copy? He should be furious.

If anything, the rider's smile lines deepened as he folded the letter, tucked it into his inner coat pocket, then he looked up, inclined his head. "A pleasure doing business with you, Major."

Raising his reins, the rider backed his horse. His men parted to let the beast through, but they didn't fall back; they held their ground, reforming as the horse retreated beyond them.

Once free of his men, the rider turned his horse; the alley was just wide enough to allow it. Then he walked the horse up the alley.

For one instant, Logan wondered . . . yet he still couldn't believe it.

The rider halted in the mouth of the alley, looked back at them, over the heads of his men saluted them. Then what they could see of his face leached of all expression, and something coldly sinister took its place. "Kill them."

The order was given in a flat, even tone.

Instinct prodded, and Logan called, "I thought you were a gentleman."

The rider laughed, a chilling sound. Abruptly he sobered. "I was born a bastard—I'm simply living up to my birth."

With that, he spurred away.

At the first clack of hooves, the assassins attacked.

Alex had been about to turn and flee the debacle Daniel's plan had degenerated into when Daniel had suddenly spurred out of his hiding place down the street, opposite the hotel, much closer to the writhing mass of cutlists and townspeople. Alex had drawn back into hiding, watched Daniel ride up and turn down the opposite half of the same street Alex hovered in. A little way along, Daniel reined in, unsheathed his sword. With his guard close behind him, he proceeded slowly down the lane behind the buildings facing the street—the lane that, Alex felt sure, ran all the way along the block to the back of the hotel.

What had caught Daniel's attention? What had he gone to take care of?

Alex hoped, sincerely hoped, the answer was Monteith.

But as the minutes ticked by with no further sign of Daniel, and the melee down the street increasingly turned the townspeople's way, the compulsion to quit the scene grew. Alex didn't want to be caught there—a stranger watching the action, and at such an hour. Difficult to adequately explain.

Alex dallied, and dallied—was lifting the reins, about

to leave, when Daniel rode out of the lane. Sheathing his sword, he looked up, but he couldn't see Alex tucked deep in the shadows across the road and further down the side street.

Alex watched Daniel walk his horse back to the High Street. Halting, he tugged down his scarf and looked back down the street at the now faltering melee. Then he smiled.

Slowly, Alex smiled, too.

Daniel, his expression tending toward triumphant, turned his horse away from the fight and rode unhurriedly out of the town.

Back in the shadows, Alex relaxed, felt tension drain from muscle and tendon. Daniel had succeeded. He'd got Monteith's letter, and that was all that mattered.

In increasingly buoyant mood, Alex toyed with the notion of riding after Daniel, catching him up, and joining him in a jubilant race back to Bury, but . . . how to explain? Daniel wasn't a fool like Roderick had been. Daniel would instantly see that Alex's secretive presence in Bedford demonstrated a very real lack of trust.

Which it did. But letting Daniel know that wouldn't serve the cause.

After several moments' cogitation, Alex realized that Daniel's guard, all twelve of them, had yet to come out of the lane. Which almost certainly meant they were engaged— which suggested Alex should leave before some worthy citizen stumbled on some grisly sight and raised a hue and cry.

Urging the chestnut into a slow trot, Alex headed up the High Street, taking the same route Daniel had.

The chestnut was a stronger, more powerful beast than the black Daniel was riding; easy enough, at some point along the way, for Alex to overtake Daniel without him seeing, and so reach Bury ahead of him, to be there, ready and willing to be graciously rewarding, when Daniel arrived, victorious, to lay his prize at Alex's feet.

Smiling in anticipation, Alex rode on.

* * *

The fighting in the yard at the end of the alley was fast, furious, bloody, and desperate.

Somewhat to Logan's surprise, he, Linnet, Charles, and Deverell were all still alive.

Cut, bruised, scraped, slashed, yet still alive, still on their feet.

They'd managed to turn the alley's narrowness to their advantage. The instant the cultists had moved, Charles and Deverell had whipped their pistols out. They'd fired at close range, and the first two cultists had crumpled.

The smoke from the pistols hadn't even dissipated—the other cultists hadn't recovered from their instinctive recoil—when Linnet had caught his belt and yanked. "Get back!"

He'd stepped back, and she'd sent a pile of crates tumbling half across the end of the alley. Charles had seen, and done the same on the other side.

Knowing it would mean death to leave the higher ground to the assassins, Logan had leapt up to the top of the crates and wildly slashed at the cultist who'd been scrambling to climb over his fallen comrade's body to claim the advantage.

He hadn't held back his swing, so that cultist, too, had joined the debris before the crates.

Charles had claimed the top of the crates on the other side, hacking at the cultist who'd come at him. Deverell had worked with Linnet to shore up the wobbling crates with others, until both Logan and Charles had had solid platforms from which to work.

The advantage was incalculable. Added to that, their longer swords, greater reach, and the narrowness of the alley, which meant that no more than two assassins could face them, come at them, at once, meant they had a chance.

They fought to make the most of it.

To Logan's utter relief, Linnet didn't try to claim a place on the crates. In such a confined space, the strength behind each blow, behind every block, was critical; she couldn't face opponents like this, in such a place.

She remained behind him, not safe but safer, yet by no means cowering. When an extra assassin pushed in along-side the one fighting Logan and slashed at his legs—with both saber and dirk engaged, he couldn't block the strike—Linnet caught the assassin's blade with her knife before it reached Logan's thigh, then her cutlass flashed forward, striking hard and deep across the cultist's exposed wrist.

Blood spurted. The cultist's blade fell. In the turmoil, Logan couldn't see what was happening to the assassin, but he doubted the man would live to fight further.

Then he took a thrown dagger in his upper arm. Deverell tapped him on the shoulder and they smoothly changed places.

Before Logan could think, Linnet grabbed him, seized the dagger, yanked it out, clamped her fingers around the wound, staunching the flow, then, wadding her neckerchief over the cut, she slid a belt—her cutlass belt—up around his arm, then cinched it tight.

He looked into her face, saw on it the same expression he knew would be on his. In battle, you stayed alert, did what needed to be done, and pushed all emotions deep.

She arched a brow at him.

He flexed the arm. As a field dressing, it would do. He nodded. "Thank you." Then he turned back to the fight.

He replaced Charles when he took a slash to his thigh, not incapacitating but bad enough to need tending.

Regaining the top of the crates, Logan dispensed with the assassin responsible. It was touch-and-go, no time for science, just quick, hard, bloody work, going for the kill in any way that offered, but with luck and skill. . . .

He and Deverell finally put paid to the last pair of cultists.

They swayed on the top of their makeshift platforms, star-ing down at the bodies tumbled and jumbled, blocking the alley.

Then Charles tapped them both on the shoulder, waited until they stepped back and down, then he went over the barricade and walked the alley with his saber in his hand, making sure none of the assassins they'd downed got up again.

His heart thundering, his breath sawing in and out, Logan slumped on an upturned crate. Deverell slowly let himself down against the yard wall.

Charles returned, clambering up and over, then he sat on the edge of their makeshift platform. "That was . . ." He paused to draw breath. "More action than I think I've ever seen—not in such a short space of time."

Deverell lifted his head, smiled the ghost of a smile. "It's the closeness—the tightness. You can't move, can't find any rhythm, get any real swing. Much harder, fighting so constrained."

Logan leaned his head back against the crates, looked at Linnet, the only one of them standing, albeit propped against the side of the small porch. The action had been so fast, so intense, he hadn't had a chance to be frightened for her. Now . . . relief had never felt so blessed, so utterly swamping. He caught her gaze, after a moment wearily smiled. "Yet we're all still alive." Almost giddy with the emotions coursing his veins, he tipped his head toward the alley. "And they're all dead."

"True." Charles heaved a sigh. "However, our night—or rather, morning, this being the next day—is not yet over." He looked at Logan. "Any idea who he was?"

There was no need to specify whom he meant. Logan shook his head. "I've never set eyes on him before." Pushing away from the crates at his back, he stretched. "That said, he may well have been what he said, or at least implied—someone who wielded the authority of the Black Cobra."

"So a very trusted lieutenant at least," Deverell said. "He was well dressed, well spoken, well educated, from his tan had been in India recently, and commanded a large body of the cult elite." He looked at Charles, then Logan. "Which means we should follow him."

Logan nodded. "He was so trusted he knew about the letter, about the seal being the important part, although why he was so pleased to retrieve a mere copy I have no idea." He got to his feet as the other two men got to theirs. "Aside from all else, although he may not be the Black Cobra, there's an excellent chance he's taking our copy—"

"To the real Black Cobra. Indeed." Charles tossed aside two crates. "Let's go."

The stables behind the hotel appeared to be deserted. From what they could hear, the fighting was continuing in the street, and less actively on the riverbank. The cultists they'd seen by the stables must have gone out to aid their fellows.

However, as they approached, they saw one lone cultist, a thin, shivering figure crouched beside a cart, clearly left to watch the back of the hotel. He was staring at the back door so intently that they were nearly upon him before he realized.

"*Aiiee!*" He leapt to his feet, brought up his sword.

He was more boy than man. His sword wavered; he was scared out of his wits.

Charles, in the lead, heaved a huge sigh, abruptly stepped and lunged, and with one quick flick sent the boy's sword flying off into the stable. Charles looked at the boy. "Boo!" The boy jerked; trembling, he just stared. Charles took another step, waved his arms, his bloodied sword. "Go! Run away! Off!"

With a strangled shriek, the boy turned and fled.

He bumped into, caromed off, another larger figure as he rounded the corner to the riverbank path. The figure halted, glanced back at the fleeing boy, then came on.

The four of them had melted into the shadows of the stable before the man—friend or foe they couldn't tell in the darkness—came trudging up. He paused just outside the stable door to peer up and down the lane, then turned inside—and found Charles's sword point at his throat.

David yelped and staggered back, but then he saw who they were and his face split in a huge grin. "You're all right! Praise the Lord." He looked at Deverell. "I'm right glad to see you hale and whole, m'lord. M'lady said she'd skin me alive if'n I brought you back any other way."

The thought—of what poor David could possibly have done to avert Deverell's death at the hands of the assassins they'd just faced—made Linnet laugh. And then the four of them were laughing. David just stood there, simply pleased to have made them smile.

When they recovered, they made plans.

They decided that delaying to explain to the local authorities just what had taken place, and their part in it, especially the carnage in the alley, would see them stuck in Bedford for days.

Logan and Linnet sneaked back upstairs to retrieve all their bags for David to take in the carriage. Deverell had already told David the route they'd been intending to follow. "Stick to that." Deverell handed over a purse. "You can pay our shot here, then go on to Elveden. Tell the manager that the horses we're appropriating will be returned safe and sound within four days, and if you run into any problems, just say you're operating under orders from the Duke of Wolverstone."

"That name," Charles put in, "is guaranteed to get you out of any tight spot."

They found four decent horses. Charles and Deverell saddled them up. "Astride all right for you?" Charles asked Linnet.

She nodded. "Please."

Charles didn't argue, just obliged. There was a lot to be said, Linnet thought, for well-conditioned gentlemen.

And then they were away. They'd got no sleep, but their blood was still up from the fight. It would be a while before any of them calmed enough for slumber; they might as well do what they could to track the one responsible.

If he led them to the Black Cobra so much the better.

They headed out of town and, under the light of the waning moon, took the most direct route to Cambridge, a secondary road that cut through the fields and fens. While they couldn't be certain of their quarry's route, they assumed the Black Cobra was lurking somewhere beyond Cambridge, in the general direction of Elveden.

A few hundred yards past the last cottage of Bedford, Logan, who had been studying the surface of the road, pointed to tracks ahead, visible where they broke through a hardening crust of frost. "Two riders, not long ago." He slowed to look more closely. "One first, then the other. Separate, not together. Both large, powerful horses going at a steady gallop."

"What are the chances one of them's our man?" Charles said.

"Excellent, I'd say," Deverell replied. "Who else would be out riding in the wee small hours in this icy weather?"

"But who's the second rider?" Linnet asked.

"No idea." Lifting his head, Logan looked across the flat, open fields. In the faint moonlight, it was a chill and somewhat eerie sight. The skies were inky black, cloudless; the cold was steadily intensifying. The morning would be crisp and clear. "A guard, perhaps. It doesn't matter. With this frost thickening, if we keep a steady pace, with luck we might come up with our man. Or even better, follow him to his lair."

They resettled their coats and cloaks, then shook their reins and rode on, buoyed by the knowledge that, regardless of all else, they were nearing journey's end.

Daniel had ridden from Bedford in wild triumph. Once out of the town, he'd let the black have its head and the first mile had flashed by. But then caution reasserted its hold. Even though it was the small hours, no one needed to remember a madman thundering past.

So he eased the horse back to a steady gallop.

He crossed the Great North Road and continued on between the flat, empty fields toward Cambridge. His most direct route to Bury, and Alex, lay via the university town, then through Newmarket beyond.

As the euphoria of relief combined with success slowly

faded to an inner glow, he reassessed, yet the relief and the jubilation of success still lingered. He wondered how many of his men had been killed or captured—taken up by the people of Bedford and handed over to the authorities. Alex wouldn't care how many cultists—assassins or foot soldiers—he'd lost, just as long as he had the letter to show for it. And none of those who'd been with him, not even his guard, knew his name, let alone Alex's.

Most had known Roderick's name, but with Roderick dead, that no longer mattered.

He glanced back once, wondering when his guard would rejoin him, but they'd doubtless be a while yet. He'd noticed the woman—had heard confused reports that Monteith was traveling with one in his train, along with a ship's captain who had caused untold problems for the cultists patrolling the Channel—but other than his two guards, Monteith had had only the woman with him . . . but she'd been carrying a cutlass, and had been wearing breeches under her cloak.

After a moment, he shook his head, shaking aside the questions, along with imagined visions of what his guard were very likely, at that very moment, doing in the little yard. He would have liked to have spent an hour or two learning more about the woman, from the woman, all in front of Monteith, but duty called. His guard would doubtless enjoy doing the job in his stead; they would report to him later.

Roderick had been vicious, but in a plebian way. He—Daniel—was much more inventive, much more imaginative.

Alex, however, could trump them both.

Their relationship, although close, was, beneath all, a battle for supremacy—they were their father's get. With the letter resting comfortably in his coat pocket, Daniel rode on through the night, lips curving lasciviously as he plotted what he would claim as his due for the night's success—what he would make Alex do to suitably reward him.

Alex hung back at a safe distance and followed in Daniel's wake. Knowing where he was ultimately headed meant Alex had little fear of losing him. Meanwhile, by keeping in his wake, Alex could watch for any signs of pursuit.

As of that moment, with the spires of Cambridge rising out of the fens ahead, dense shadows against the night sky, there'd been no hint of any followers. And the further they got from Bedford, and the more hours passed, the prospect of active pursuit became progressively less likely.

Regardless, Alex continued to play safe, to ride a watchful distance behind. No matter their relationship—and not even Alex could specify exactly what that was—no matter that Alex could rely on Daniel, appreciated him, valued him, and didn't want to lose him, nevertheless Alex would not permit even Daniel to risk Alex's neck.

When Daniel slowed, Alex slowed. From the shadows of a copse, Alex watched as Daniel unwound the black silk scarf from about his neck and stuffed it into a pocket before lifting his reins and riding on.

Alex approved. Even though there would be few awake and aware at that hour, there might be some—and no one needed to see a gentleman like Daniel sporting the cult's principal insignia.

After a moment of silent debate, Alex opted to skirt the town and pick up Daniel as he emerged again, on the road to Newmarket. Riding around via the darkened country lanes, Alex calculated that it would be some way further— Newmarket itself or better yet beyond—before an unexpected appearance on horseback could be passed off as a welcome party, as if Alex had ridden out in eager anticipation of meeting a returning, victorious Daniel.

Until then, there was little to do but hang back and watch.

Daniel halted at a tiny tavern in a village east of Cambridge, on the road to Newmarket. The tavern had just opened and he needed a hot drink to dispel the chill that had started gnawing at his bones—and he might as well watch for pursuers while he drank.

Huddled in the front corner of the taproom, low-ceilinged

and smoky, with the innkeeper poking at the fire in the hearth, Daniel kept one eye on the road through the window and sipped a mug of steaming cider. The scalding liquid warmed as it went down. As the glow spread, he turned his mind to what came next.

He wondered if Alex was still at the Bury house, or whether a new headquarters had been found. That had been Alex's intention when he'd left for Bedford; it was possible they'd already moved. Regardless, Alex would either leave word, or wait and meet him. He would wager on the latter; the letter he'd retrieved had been as much a threat to Alex as to him.

Alex would definitely want to see it as soon as possible, then would want to watch it burn.

Despite the early hour, there was traffic on the road—the occasional wagon heading to market, the occasional rider off to Newmarket, or going the other way to Cambridge. A few coaches lumbered past, one a night mail coach. There was, however, no sign of pursuit.

Somewhat to Daniel's surprise, there was also no sign of his guard. Then again, even though they would ride faster than he had and so by now should be close—even allowing for the time they would have spent torturing the four in the yard—they also knew to stay off the main roads in this area, to keep to the fields and, if necessary, rest in some barn during the day.

His guard were among the best of their fighters, surpassed only by Alex's guard; they would be along soon enough.

Draining the mug, he set it down, rose, threw a handful of coins on the table, and walked out. He looked back down the road toward Cambridge. There was no pursuit; he felt increasingly certain of that. Remounting, he rode on.

There was no reason he needed to ride through Newmarket itself. Operating as it did to the schedule of racehorse training, even though it was early, the town, the heath, and the numerous stables surrounding it would already be alive and busy. Indeed, as he approached the outskirts of the heath, he saw strings of racehorses being ridden out in the predawn light. The narrow streets of the town would already be awash with riders and gigs; it would be faster to avoid it.

He gave the scattered stables a wide berth, too.

As he rode on through the crisp, gray morning, he imagined owning a racehorse or three. The sport of kings; the prospect should appeal to Alex, and they were more than wealthy enough to indulge. Indeed, now he thought of it, once they'd destroyed all four copies of Roderick's unfortunate letter, what better camouflage than to remain here in England for a while? They could send the cultists home, dispatch their most senior men to keep things ticking along in India—arrangements could be put into place to allow him and Alex to enjoy their spoils here in England, at least for a while.

The prospect of lording it over so many, of using their wealth to satisfy all the fancies they'd had before they'd left for India but, back then, had never had the capital or the associated power to indulge, definitely appealed.

And then his horse went lame.

He cursed, tested the black's paces, but there was no going on. Dismounting, he looked around. A large stable lay ahead, in a wide, shallow dip in the heath. He was viewing it side on, toward the rear; he couldn't see the front doors, but as he watched, a long string of horses streamed out and rode away.

Out across the heath for their morning's exercise.

There would still be horses left in the stable—those of the jockeys, for a start, but almost certainly others, older racehorses, or ones being rested. The notion of trying out such a beast had him striding, as swiftly as the lame black would allow, down to the stable.

He took the black with him; the sight of a man striding about Newmarket Heath without a horse was too strange to avoid notice.

There was a set of back doors; he quietly tried them, but

they were latched and bolted. Circling the stable, he found the big front doors propped wide open and not a soul in sight.

Smiling, he walked boldly in, through a large clear space and down a long central aisle with stalls to either side. It was a very large stable, and there were, as he'd hoped, occupants in quite a few stalls, and a selection of hacks tied up at the rear—presumably the horses the jockeys had ridden in.

He tied the lame black with the jockeys' hacks, then spent some time evaluating the horses in the stalls. He'd been out of England for years, but still recognized prime horseflesh when he saw it. And some of these horses were beauties. He settled on a big roan, then fetched his saddle and bridle from the black, opened the roan's stall, and went in.

Crooning to the horse, he took a few minutes to admire the gelding's lines, then slipped on the bridle and saddled up.

He was tightening the saddle girth when a sound at the stall door had him glancing that way.

An old man, slightly stooped, with big, gnarled hands, stood in the aisle beyond the doorway, regarding him through bulging eyes. "Here! What do you think you're doing? These are private stables."

"Indeed?" Smoothly turning the roan, Daniel led the horse out. "In that case, I'll be on my way."

"Here—no! You can't just take one of our horses." The old man seized Daniel's sleeve.

Daniel lashed out and back with that arm, his forearm colliding with the old man's face. Releasing the roan's reins, he pivoted, plowed his right fist into the old man's gut, then followed up with a sharp blow to the head.

The old man went down; gasping, groaning, he fell to the straw-strewn earthen floor, curling in on himself. Daniel looked down at him, then coldly drew back his boot and kicked the old man viciously once, then again, and again in the ribs.

After gasping sharp and hard at the first kick, the old man had fallen silent.

Daniel straightened, settled his coat, grasped the roan's reins. He'd missed the fun at Bedford; he'd been owed a little violence.

Reassembling his mask of gentlemanly boredom, he walked up the aisle, paused to mount in the cleared space just inside the doors, then, with the roan shifting and prancing beneath him, clearly anticipating a long ride, Daniel lifted the reins and trotted out of the stable.

Seconds later, he was cantering out onto the open heath.

Carruthers swore beneath his breath—he couldn't catch enough breath to curse aloud. His ribs ached, his jaw throbbed. He managed to get his feet under him, then caught hold of the slats of a stall door and hauled himself up.

Hunched over, he shuffled as fast as he could, clutching the stall doors to keep from falling. Reaching the open space at the end of the aisle, he drew in a slow, pained breath, let go of the last stall, and propelled himself forward. Forced his legs to move.

Eyes locked on his goal, he made it to the side of the open door, gasped as he lunged and grabbed the rope dangling from the stable bell. It clanged as he slumped against the door frame. Clanged again as, his grip weakening, the rope tugged free and he slid slowly down to collapse on the floor.

With his ear to the ground, he heard the sound he'd hoped for—the heavy thud of flying hooves. Smiling was beyond him, but he smiled inside.

It seemed like only seconds, then Demon was there, crouching down beside him, hard hands gentle as his employer helped him up to sit against the door frame.

Demon peered into Carruthers's eyes, saw he was in pain, but conscious. "What the devil happened?"

Other horses thundered up; the string had followed Demon back to the stable.

Carruthers wet his lips. "Was in the tack room. Heard a sound. Came out and found some blighter saddling up The Gentleman. Asked him what he was about—told him he had to leave. I tried to stop him when he led The Gentleman out. He lashed out, struck me. Couple of times."

Demon took in the contusions forming under Carruthers's mottled skin.

"Then when I fell, he kicked me."

"What?" Demon stared, then swore. "Never mind—I heard. Stay here and get better. Leave the bastard to me."

Swinging around and rising, Demon pointed to Jarvis, Carruthers's lieutenant. "Take care of him." Demon was already moving, grabbing up the spyglass kept in a holder by the door; it was usually used to watch horses training.

Striding outside, he put the glass to his eye, scanned the heath in the direction the horse thief had to have gone; he hadn't passed Demon or the string coming in, so he had to have gone toward Bury.

The heath appeared flat, but in reality was full of gentle dips and rises, an ocean of green with low, widely spaced waves. A rider might be quite close but momentarily hidden, then reappear as they rode up the next rise.

Even as he picked out the smoky hide of The Gentleman, happily galloping east over the heath, Demon was inwardly connecting possibilities. What chance his horse thief had something to do with the mission he and his cousins were assisting with? Ferrar, thought to be the Black Cobra, had been found murdered in Bury just yesterday.

Demon shifted the glass, adjusting to bring the rider into sharper focus. Wolverstone and Devil would flay him— verbally at least—if he didn't at least try to get a good look at the man's face. . . .

There. Rider and horse had to turn slightly, the rider coming into full profile. For one instant, through the glass, Demon got a good view. And managed at the last to get a glimpse of the man's hands. They were deeply tanned.

Demon lowered the glass, then whirled back to the stable. "Go!" He pointed and waved the string on. "Get after him— follow him. Grab him if you can. I'll catch up."

The jockeys, shocked and furious at the treatment meted

out to their old trainer, needed no further urging. In a thunderous clatter of hooves, they set off.

Back in the stable, Demon grabbed the reins of his mount. He'd left the gathering at Somersham Place and had come over for the training session; because his wife, Flick, hadn't been able to get over for the last few days, he'd taken out her usual mount, The Mighty Flynn. The Flynn loved Flick, but would tolerate—make do with—Demon. Although retired now, the big horse was a stayer. Demon couldn't have picked a better mount for riding down a horse thief.

Yet looking at Carruthers, now in the hands of Jarvis and two stableboys, he paused.

Carruthers saw him looking and glared as well as he could. "What're you waiting for? Go get the bastard, and bring The Gentleman back!"

Demon grinned, saluted, vaulted to the saddle, and went.

Daniel was pleased with his new mount. A very good horse, with very nice paces. Despite the impulse to flee in a flat-out gallop, he was too wise to attract attention like that, especially not in a place like this, surrounded by locals on very fast horses.

Locals who, for all he knew, might recognize his stolen horse.

But keeping to a nice steady pace would soon put miles between him and the stable, and few around there paid any attention to a mounted man riding easily by. It would probably be an hour, maybe more, before the old man was found. Daniel hadn't looked back, but he'd listened intently and had heard no hue and cry.

He'd already passed two strings out exercising, and hadn't even been glanced at.

Entirely pleased—first the letter, now this excellent horse—everything seemed to be falling into his lap—he smiled and rode on.

* * *

From a vantage point on one of the higher rises some way ahead—a significant distance east, and a little to the south from where Daniel now rode—concealed by a twiggy copse, Alex watched the scene unfolding on the heath through a spyglass.

Horrified. Barely able to believe it.

All had been going so well, then Daniel's horse had gone lame. But he'd done the sensible thing and slipped into a stable to exchange it.

Alex had used the opportunity to get well ahead, then had patiently waited, and sure enough, not too many minutes later, Daniel had ridden out on a different horse.

All well and good, but . . . something had happened to alert the stable's people off exercising the horses, and had brought the trainer and his jockeys flying back to the place.

Alex had no idea what had summoned them, but the man who'd led the charge back, a gentleman by his dress, had all but immediately come out again, with a spyglass.

The man had located Daniel.

Daniel was no longer wearing his black silk scarf. His face was bare, naked, there for anyone to see.

The man with the spyglass had stood outside the stable, and looked, looked—looked for far too long to have only been interested in identifying his horse.

Alex knew without a shadow of a doubt that Daniel's face had been studied and noted.

And now a thundering herd of men and horses was charging after Daniel—and he still hadn't reacted. Hadn't glanced around, hadn't heard . . . Alex realized why. The wind, a nice stiff breeze, was blowing directly in Daniel's face, pushing his dark locks back.

Alex wanted to shout and point, but Daniel was still too far away to hear. And he'd been seen. He would be recognized.

The mob of horses was coming up fast, amazingly fast, but was still some way away; the man who had wielded the spyglass was now following, too, on a massive horse whose long strides seemed to eat the distance.

By the time Daniel heard them coming well enough to distinguish the sound from that of the other exercising strings he was passing, it would be too late.

He wouldn't escape them. He'd be taken up as a horse thief.

Bad enough, but he had the letter—copy or original—on him.

What odds that vital document would find its way into the hands of the puppetmaster, that nebulous man Alex was learning to respect, and more, fear?

Alex's mount shifted restlessly. Eyes desperately scanning the heath, Alex reined it in without thought. Had no thought to spare.

What to do? *What to do?*

There! One chance, just one, one way forward, and no other.

If Alex was game to grasp it.

If . . .

With a vicious curse, Alex set heels to the chestnut's sides and raced down the rise on a course that would intersect with Daniel's at one particular spot. A place just beyond another rise, a little higher than most, that sheltered a wide dip hosting a short line of firs and pines with thick, heavy branches—one of the few effective screens on the winter heath.

Daniel's line of travel would see him pass a little way beyond the northern end of the line of trees.

Alex reached the east side of the trees with just enough time to calm, to settle the chestnut, ease its prancing edginess. To breathe in, out, and plaster on a welcoming, expectant expression.

Daniel appeared beyond the end of the trees.

Alex hailed him and waved.

Hearing, seeing, Daniel smiled confidently and wheeled his stolen mount.

Alex waited, outwardly calm and assured, as Daniel slowed, then walked his horse nearer, eventually halting alongside the chestnut.

His knee brushing Alex's, Daniel smiled. "I got it."

"I know." Lips curving in response, Alex held out an imperious, demanding hand. "I can tell by your smile."

Daniel laughed. Reaching into his coat, he drew out the letter and laid it across Alex's palm.

Alex flicked it open, checked. "The same as the other two—a copy."

"Which means there's only one more to seize. The original Carstairs must be carrying."

"Indeed." Folding the letter, sliding it into a pocket, Alex looked up, into Daniel's eyes. Smiled brilliantly. "Excellent."

Reaching up and across with one elegantly gloved hand, Alex cupped Daniel's nape and drew his face near.

Kissed him.

Lovingly, lingeringly.

Bit Daniel's lip lightly as the blade slid between his ribs, directly into his heart.

Alex drew back, released Daniel, left the knife where it was.

Met his eyes, the velvety brown already clouding.

Saw death sliding in to claim him.

The look on Daniel's face, the utter shock and disbelief, pricked even Alex's conscience.

"You'd been seen. They're after you—can't you hear? I couldn't allow—"

Daniel slumped forward, over his saddle.

The roan shifted, getting nervous.

Face tightening, Alex grabbed Daniel's hat—it had his name on the band—stuffed it into one of the chestnut's saddlebags, gathered the big horse's reins, then paused.

Paused.

Reaching out one gloved hand, Alex gently, for the last time, ruffled Daniel's black hair.

Then, lips thinning, features shifting into a granite mask,

Alex drew back, sharply slapped the roan's rump, and sent the horse leaping.

The instant it sensed the odd weight in its saddle and found its reins free, it took off, heading south.

Alex drew in a quick breath, blew it out. Refocused and listened, gauging the escalating thud of the pursuing horses' hooves; they were nearing the rise to the west.

Following impulse, Alex spurred the big chestnut on, heading north, cutting directly across the oncoming riders.

Alex cleared the trees and was fifty yards further on when the mob broke over the rise, and slowed.

Alex kept riding north unhurriedly, outwardly unconcerned.

Heard the jockeys' voices as they circled on the rise, searching for their quarry. With luck, the trees would conceal the roan's flight for some considerable way.

Then another voice, a deeper, more authoritative voice, joined the chorus.

It took Demon a good minute to accept what his men were telling him. The Gentleman and his rider were indeed nowhere to be seen.

Another rider, a man wrapped in a heavy winter coat, with a fashionable hat pulled low and features protected from the wind by a muffler, was cantering along on a big chestnut just north of where they milled.

If the horse thief had gone this way . . .

"Hello!" Demon raised his voice, raised a hand in salute.

The other rider glanced back, slowed, raised a hand to show he'd heard.

"Did you see a man—dark coat, dark hat, dark hair, tanned features—riding out on a roan?"

The rider hesitated, then turned and pointed to the east of northeast. There was another rise that might have concealed the rider some way on.

"Thank you!" Demon swung The Flynn in that direction and thundered down the rise. His jockeys and their mounts followed.

The rider watched for a moment, then continued unhurriedly on.

Stone-faced, Alex rode on, listening until the thunder of hooves faded.

Soon, the silence of the wide and empty heath returned.

Alex embraced it.

After a while, thought impinged on the odd emptiness in Alex's mind, rose up through the unexpected shock.

Survival, after all, was reserved for the fittest.

After further cogitation a plan formed. Head north for a little while longer, enough to get well and truly out of the way of any further searching, then circle around, stop at Bury long enough to alert those left there, then head on to the new house—the new cult headquarters—that M'wallah and Creighton between them had found.

Creighton might be a problem now his master was dead, but M'wallah and Alex's guard were exceptionally good at resolving all problems Alex faced. Creighton could be left to them.

As the sun slowly rose, Alex, alone, cantered steadily on.

Just after dawn, Demon finally halted.

They'd reached a strip of heath still crisp from the frost, and it was transparently obvious no rider had crossed it that morning.

"We've lost him." Turning The Mighty Flynn, he pulled out the spyglass, and scanned all the heath that he could see.

"But how could we have?" one of the jockeys asked. "We was on his heels—well, a few minutes behind at most—and then . . . he just wasn't there."

Frowning, Demon thought back. Shutting the spyglass, he slipped it back into the saddle pocket. "You had him in sight until he went over the rise where you stopped—the rise where we asked the other rider?"

All the jockeys nodded.

Demon knew every dip and hollow on the heath; he'd

been riding there since he was a child. He closed his eyes for a moment, envisaging . . . if that other rider had been mistaken, or . . .

Opening his eyes, he wheeled The Flynn back toward Newmarket. "Let's head home, but we'll spread out in a line north-south, and go at a slow canter. Yell if you see any sign."

The horses were tiring, skittish; they needed to get back to their stable, into the warm, and be tended. The run had broken their usual routine.

Demon directed his men into a line, and they started back.

He wasn't sure what to think. He was deep in weighing up the possibilities when Higgins, to the far south of the line, gave a hie.

"Over there! Isn't that The Gentleman?"

Demon reined in, hauled out the spyglass, and put it to his eye.

And there was The Gentleman—with a suspicious-looking lump in the saddle. The Gentleman was well to the south, reins dragging as he lazily cropped coarse grass, then ambled on a little way, the lifeless lump on his back swaying with his gait.

Demon drew in a breath, let it out on a sigh. Stuffing the glass back in his saddlebag, he nodded. "That's him. Let's go."

As one, he and his men changed course, and closed on the wandering horse.

The Gentleman's head came up as they neared, but then he scented his stablemates and went back to his grass. The lump on his back didn't move.

"Hold up." Demon waved to his jockeys to rein in a little way away. Their horses sensed the wrongness of the slumped form on The Gentleman's back and grew yet more skittish.

At a walk, Demon approached The Gentleman. The Flynn was an old hand; he would trust completely and go wherever Demon steered him.

But, yes, that was a dead body. It looked like their horse thief had met his end.

Glancing back at the restless, high-spirited horses, Demon waved them off. "Go on to the stables. I'll be behind you. No more training this morning. They've had a good run. Get them inside and rubbed down."

The younger jockeys had paled; they nodded and went. The older ones hestitated, but then nodded and headed in.

Leaving Demon to draw closer to The Gentleman, lean down and grab the trailing reins, then edge nearer and, without any real hope, check for a pulse at the side of the man's neck. Finding none, he bent low and peered at the dead man's face—enough to confirm that, yes, he was their horse thief.

And judging from his hands and the tanned line at his throat, until recently he'd been somewhere sunny, like India.

Straightening in his saddle, Demon frowned at the corpse. "Who the devil are you? And what the hell's going on?"

❧ *Seventeen* ❧

*D*emon led The Gentleman and his grisly burden back to the stables. It took him and two of his men to lift the man free of the saddle; they laid him out in the back of a hay cart.

Carruthers came hobbling out of the tack room, where he'd been imbibing medicinal brandy. He looked down at the man, nodded. "That's him. Cheeky, vicious sod. Not so cheeky now. Looks like retribution caught up with him pretty quick." He glanced at Demon. "Any idea who did it?"

Demon thought of the other rider they'd seen, but could anyone slide a dagger through a man's heart, and within minutes appear so unconcerned? He shook his head. "No idea. But he was out of our sight for a good while. No saying who he might have met up with."

"Strange-looking dagger, that." Carruthers eyed the hilt that protruded from the man's chest.

"It's ivory." Demon bent and looked more closely at it, and any doubt this man was involved with the Black Cobra vanished. The hilt was the same as the daggers that had put paid to first Larkins, then Ferrar, whom they'd originally thought was the Black Cobra.

The sound of riders approaching, followed by a shout,

"Ho! Cynster!" had Demon straightening, then striding quickly out of the front doors to the area before the stable.

Logan dismounted as Demon appeared. For the first time in days, Logan grinned.

Demon's gaze reached him and his old friend's face lit. "Logan Monteith! Sorry—*Major* Monteith. You are definitely a sight for sore eyes—even if you're half covered in . . . what? *Soot?*"

"We escaped a fire, and a few other inconveniences, hence our sorry sartorial state. But I hear you've grown sober." Logan offered his hand, and it was crushed in Demon's long-fingered grip.

"Not a bit of it!" Demon thumped him on the back and wrung his hand. "As I heard it, it's you who've been getting serious these past months—and into serious danger, too."

"Sadly, that's true. Apropos of which . . ." Releasing Demon, Logan turned to the other three, who by now had dismounted and stood watching them with varying degrees of humorous understanding. "Allow me to present Captain Linnet Trevission, captain of the *Esperance*, out of Guernsey."

Linnet gave Demon her hand. "A pleasure, sir."

Grasping her fingers, Demon bowed gracefully. "The pleasure is all mine." Straightening, he eyed Linnet's breeches. "I warn you, my wife, Flick, will be after your tailor's direction."

Brows faintly arching, Linnet inclined her head, and Logan continued the introductions.

Although Demon hadn't met Charles or Deverell before, he knew of their mission.

"So," Logan asked, "what's been going on?"

"You've heard Delborough's through safe and sound, but sacrificed his scroll-holder in a trap we hoped might capture Ferrar, but his man, Larkins, got caught instead, and then Ferrar killed him and got clean away?"

When Logan nodded, Demon went on, "Yesterday, Hamilton came up from Chelmsford via Sudbury. The fiends had set up an ambush outside Sudbury, but we were there in force, too, and Miss Ensworth, who's traveling with Hamilton, managed to leave the scroll-holder and tempt Ferrar to take it, which he did. While my cousins and I dealt with the cultists at the ambush site, others"—Demon nodded at Charles and Deverell—"Wolverstone and some of your erstwhile colleagues, followed Ferrar, hoping to find his lair, but then he was murdered in the old abbey ruins at Bury St. Edmunds, and all that was found was his body."

"Ferrar's *dead*?" Logan's face, and that of the others, showed their shock.

Grimly Demon nodded. "As of yesterday afternoon." Shrewd blue eyes surveyed them. "I know you were expected in today from Bedford—dare I assume the reason you're here now, so bright and early and in such sartorial straits, is because you were chasing a man, tallish, black hair, black coat, a gentleman at first glance?"

"You've seen him?" Logan asked.

"He's dead, too." Demon tipped his head toward the stable. "Come and take a look."

Demon led them to the cart. Logan stood at the cart's foot, Linnet by his side, and looked down at the man they'd last seen riding out of the alley in Bedford.

Charles examined the dagger, the wound. "This happened recently."

"Less than an hour ago." Demon told them all he knew of the man's actions to the point where he'd found him slumped dead in his saddle.

He sent a stable lad to fetch the man's horse. While they waited, he asked, "Incidentally, how did you know to come here? Did you actually track him this far?"

Logan shook his head. "I tracked him out of Bedford, and we got sightings on this side of Cambridge, but we lost him approaching Newmarket. But when we rode into the town, it was buzzing with the news that someone had dared steal a horse from your stable. That seemed too great a coincidence—we know these people appropriate goods, horses, anything they need, as they wish. People in town pointed out the way here."

Demon waved at the black horse the stable lad led up. "The blighter left this one when he took ours."

Logan, Deverell, and Charles studied the horse; they all nodded. "That's the one he was riding at Bedford," Deverell said.

"So he was riding this way," Charles said, "not because he was fleeing us, because he thought he'd left us soon to be dead in Bedford, but for some other reason."

"Presumably to deliver the letter he took from us to someone." Deverell eyed the body. "He hasn't still got it, has he?"

"Inside coat pocket," Linnet said. "That's where he put it."

Deverell touched the man's coat, then eased it open enough to feel inside while leaving the dagger in place. "Nothing there." He patted the man's other pockets. "Or elsewhere. It's gone."

Logan frowned. "I think we can assume that whoever he delivered the letter to rewarded him with that dagger."

"We were chasing him at the time." Demon shrugged. "He might have been killed for the same reason Larkins, and presumably Ferrar, were—sacrificed because they'd been seen, and could, almost certainly would, be taken up at some point."

"And questioned." Charles nodded. "That makes sense."

Linnet glanced at Logan. "Do you recognize him?"

Eyes locked on the man's face, Logan grimaced. "He looks vaguely familiar. I might have seen him in Bombay—we were there for five months. He might have been a friend of Ferrar's. If he is, Gareth or Del would have a better chance of placing him."

Demon nodded decisively. "We'd best get his body to Elveden, then. There's a washroom if you'd like to tend to your accumulated wounds and wash off the worst of the smoke streaks while I get the horses put to, then we can ride on together."

* * *

It was midmorning when the five of them rode up to the sprawling Jacobean manor house hidden away in its extensive park; they'd ridden ahead, leaving the wagon carrying the body to follow as fast as it could. Crisped by the recent frost, snow still lay in pockets beneath the trees; Demon had mentioned there'd been a heavy fall a few days before.

Emerging from the forest into the graveled forecourt, Linnet studied the rambling house with its many gables and haphazard wings, and sensed it was ancient; an aura of permanence, of long-established peace, seemed to emanate from it. Courtesy of the dull day, lamps were lit inside; through the many paned windows, the interior of the house seemed to glow with warmth and welcome.

A warmth and welcome that came tumbling out to greet them. Phoebe and Penny were already in residence; they must have been sitting in a window somewhere, for they came rushing out to embrace their husbands, disregarding residual smoke streaks and bloodstains to exclaim over various scratches and gashes, then they whirled on Linnet and embraced her, then Logan, too.

A slender yet statuesque blond, assured and serene, had followed the two ladies outside. She proved to be Minerva, the great Wolverstone's duchess.

Introduced, Linnet would have curtsied, but Minerva prevented it, clasping both Linnet's hands instead and smiling warmly. "Welcome to Elveden, Linnet—we tend not to stand on ceremony here, so please call me Minerva. The other ladies will be delighted to meet you. And please don't hesitate to ask if there's anything I can arrange to make your stay more comfortable." She glanced back into the house as many footsteps approached. "Ah—here comes the other side of the coin."

A small army of men appeared on the front steps, led by a man Linnet instantly identified as Wolverstone. He was tallish, although not the tallest there, black-haired and lean-cheeked, with a certain predatory cast to his austere Norman features. Power hung about him like an invisible mantle, yet it was the look he exchanged with Minerva, one of male resignation overlaying an infinitely deep pool of affection, that settled it.

Smiling, Minerva introduced Linnet, then Logan.

Wolverstone greeted them with sincere pleasure and open approval, then insisted the whole party—which had swollen considerably as more and more gentlemen and ladies came out—adjourn to the warmth of the house.

In the large, wood-paneled hall—glancing around, Linnet thought it must originally have been the main manor hall—Wolverstone, who went by the name of Royce among friends, introduced them to the small army of others.

Two of the men, soldiers by their bearing, were among the first to greet Logan. Royce stood back as, with huge smiles, the three wrung each other's hands and clapped shoulders, then Logan introduced the pair to Linnet. "Derek Delborough and Gareth Hamilton. You've heard me speak of both."

Linnet shook hands, exchanged smiles, noting the closeness between the three men—that of long-standing brothers-in-arms, men who had fought shoulder to shoulder, back to back, whose friendship had been forged in the heat of battle.

Delborough and Hamilton were as surprised to see her as Logan was to see the ladies each of them had by their sides. "Miss Ensworth?" Logan shook the brown-haired lady's hand. "I heard you'd traveled with Gareth, but . . . how did that come about?"

The lady smiled sweetly, yet Linnet instantly recognized a core of steel. "Emily, please. And it's a long story." She glanced at Hamilton. "We'll tell you later."

Hamilton arched his brows.

Delborough—Del—introduced them to the striking brunette beside him. "Deliah Duncannon. Not knowing of our mission, my aunts had arranged for me to escort Deliah north, so I had to bring her with me."

"Not that he wanted to, of course," Deliah said, a definite glint in her green eyes, "but then I rescued him from certain death, and he couldn't deny me."

Del laughed. "That's a long story, too, one for later. For now, it's your story we need to catch up with."

"Let's finish the introductions first," Royce said. "Then we can get down to business."

He guided Logan and Linnet on. Within minutes, Linnet's head was whirling. She struggled to keep track of all the additional names. Gervase and Madeline, Tony and Alicia, Letitia, Jack and Clarice, Tristan and Lenore, and Kit. Letitia's husband Christian, and Kit's husband, another Jack, were apparently on the east coast waiting for Rafe Carstairs to land.

While Logan spoke with the men, redheaded Kit shifted closer to Linnet and murmured, "You are not leaving this house without telling me where you got those." She dropped bright, openly covetous eyes to Linnet's breeches.

Madeline strolled up, smiling. "I was about to ask the same thing. They look just the thing—so practical."

Linnet gave up trying to ignore what she had thought to be her inappropriate attire. "Not so much in the height of summer, but for most of the year, yes. They give much better protection than cloth, or even buckskin." Linnet glanced from one to the other. "Do you know Flick—Demon's wife?"

"Yes, indeed—and she's another who will tie you down and torture you if you don't tell," Madeline said.

Linnet laughed. "I'll tell—I've already told Penny. I get them from a leatherworker in Exeter."

"We'll extract the directions later," Kit said. "But did I hear Royce say you captain your own ship?" When Linnet nodded, Kit vowed, "I am so deeply jealous. I've wanted to sail my own ship for forever, but Jack always claims the wheel. You'd think with a husband in shipping I could have just one tiny yacht of my own."

Linnet's brain made the connection. "Jack Hendon—of Hendon Shipping Lines?"

Kit nodded. "The very same. Why?"

"I own Trevission Ships. He's a competitor."

"Just wait until he hears. He'll probably make you an offer."

"I might just make one back," Linnet said.

Kit hooted. "Oh, *please* make sure I'm there when that conversation takes place."

There'd been a knock on the door. Demon and Wolverstone had gone to look out. Now Wolverstone turned back to the room. "Hamilton, Delborough. If you would—there's a body here we need you to see if you can identify."

Naturally, within two minutes, everyone was in the forecourt again, gathered around the hay cart. Everyone looked at the body; Royce had drawn down the tarpaulin, so they could all see the dagger. Glancing at the faces, Linnet noted that while each was deadly serious, not one had paled, let alone flinched.

Returning her gaze to the dead man's graying face, she felt a sense of shared purpose, of people coming together in pursuit of a common goal. For the first time, felt a part of that whole. She'd been committed to helping Logan, but that had been personal. Now she, too, was a part of this group devoted to seeing justice done and the Black Cobra exposed.

Royce glanced at Delborough and Hamilton. "Any idea who he is?"

"He was an associate of Ferrar's in Bombay, but I never knew his name." Del glanced at Gareth. "Do you know?"

Gareth stared at the man for a long moment, then said, "Thurgood. Daniel Thurgood." He looked up at the waiting faces. "He was a friend of Ferrar, one of his circle."

"A close friend?" Tristan asked.

Gareth grimaced. "No closer than others I could name, at least in public. In private?" Gareth shrugged. "Who's to know?"

"Indeed." Royce looked at the dagger. "Same type of dagger, same style of blow—from very close. He was killed by someone he trusted implicitly."

"And that someone is still out there," Logan said.

Royce nodded. "We haven't yet succeeded in beheading

the Black Cobra. Whether they were a group of equals or a tiered hierarchy, the head, the real power, the most dangerous of these villains, is still at large."

"And not far away," Jack Warnefleet said.

Royce glanced around the circle. Many of the other men did, too. Despite the weak winter sun's valiant attempts to break through the clouds, it was still chilly and cold, and they'd all come out without coats.

"Let's go inside," Royce said. "We can discuss this latest twist and hear Logan's report in comfort. In the drawing room," he added, as if to assure the ladies they would not be excluded.

Royce stepped back; all the other men shifted as if to fall in with his directive.

But not one of the ladies moved. Minerva flapped an absentminded hand. "Wait a minute." She was studying Daniel Thurgood's face. She nudged Letitia, beside her. "Is it just my imagination, or is there a resemblance to Ferrar?"

Letitia, who had also been staring at Thurgood's face, slowly nodded. "It's the bones—the browline, set of the eyes, the chin. Imagine him with Shrewton's pale eyes and fairer hair and . . . he's very like Ferrar."

Clarice, beside Letitia, arched her brows. "For my money, he's even more like Shrewton himself."

Deverell frowned. "He—Thurgood—said something about being a bastard." He glanced at Logan. "What did he say exactly?"

Linnet, beside Logan, answered. "When he broke his word—a word he'd sworn on his honor as a gentleman—and ordered his men to kill us, Logan prodded him about being a gentleman. Thurgood laughed and said he'd been born a bastard, and was simply living up to his birth."

Everyone stared at the body. Royce murmured, "What if he'd meant the phrase 'living up to his birth' to mean behaving, not like a bastard, but like a Ferrar—one of Shrewton's get?"

"That Shrewton sired bastards is common knowledge,"

Clarice stated, "but their actual identity isn't widely known. Given the resemblance, and I do think it's strong, then Thurgood's parting shot sounds like a typical piece of Ferrar arrogance."

"Overweening, maliciously superior arrogance has been a hallmark of the Black Cobra cult from its inception," Delborough said.

Everyone looked at Royce. Gaze locked on Thurgood's body, face hardening, he slowly nodded. "I believe we should deliver this body, too, to the earl at Wymondham Hall."

"Indeed," Minerva said briskly. "You may proceed to do so after luncheon." She looked at Charles, Deverell, Logan, and Linnet. "I assume you four missed breakfast, which means you must be famished." Spreading her arms, Minerva gracefully waved everyone to the door. "Let's go in, and I'll have you shown to your rooms. You can wash and refresh yourselves, then we can all sit down to an early luncheon, and over the table we can learn the details of your adventures." She met her husband's eyes. "And add the recent revelations to all else we know, and see where we now stand."

Minerva gestured again, and everyone obeyed, moving in orderly fashion back indoors.

Royce's lips twisted wryly, then he turned to Demon. Del, Gareth, and Logan also hung back.

"I won't stay," Demon said. "If I don't return to Somersham there'll be hell to pay. I'll carry this latest news"—with his head he indicated Thurgood's body—"and the suspected connection to Devil and the others."

Royce nodded. "Do."

Demon saluted, stepped back. "We'll be ready and waiting should you need us."

Royce met his eyes. "Hold yourselves ready—I've a strong premonition I'm going to need you all before this mission ends."

Demon nodded to the other three, then headed for his horse, took the reins, fluidly mounted, then, with another salute, rode away.

"They're good men—the Cynsters," Del said.

"Good fighters," Gareth added.

"Good friends," Logan echoed.

"Indeed." Royce looked at Logan and smiled. "But you'd better get inside to be shown to your room, or my duchess will be displeased."

That no one in the house would want Minerva to be displeased didn't need to be stated.

Gareth tossed the tarpaulin back over Thurgood's body. Leaving the cart in the forecourt, the four men went inside.

Half an hour later, they were all seated around the long table in the dining room. Linnet, in a pale blue gown Penny had loaned her, and Logan, as brushed and as neat as he could be, had been steered to chairs on either side of Wolverstone's carver, so that when they spoke the whole table could hear.

They, Charles, and Deverell were allowed to assuage their appetites first, while the rest of the company nibbled and chatted about less consequential matters. Children, Logan noted, were a source of much comment.

"At least the nursery windows don't overlook the forecourt," Kit said. "If they realized there was a dead body in that cart, my eldest two would be clambering all over it." She paused, then added, "Most likely pulling out the dagger, just to see."

"Royce found them a set of tin soldiers," Jack said. "I was up there earlier, checking on our two, and your eldest two, aided by a bevy of the others, I might add, were not even halfway through Waterloo—they'll be engaged for hours yet."

From various comments, Logan gathered that Minerva, she who must not be displeased, had taken advantage of the mission her husband had undertaken to invite all the families of the ex-comrades he'd drawn into the mission to spend Christmas there, at Elveden.

The house was, consequently, awash with young children. As each family had also brought nannies and governesses, the children were not much in evidence, not least because,

as far as Logan could understand, the children were familiar with each other, and could be relied on to play together,
albeit sometimes with less than desirable results.

He'd never been a part of such a gathering—one so openly
relaxed and comfortable, with so many adults as well as
children, all at ease with one another. He glanced at Linnet,
across the table, and found her chatting with Alicia, who apparently also had older children, not hers, but brothers who
were her wards. Even as he watched, Madeline and Gervase
joined in. Madeline, too, was guardian of her younger half
brothers, and Gervase had three younger sisters under his
wing.

Letting his gaze wander the table, it seemed to Logan that
every possible construction of "family" was represented,
and all were happy and content. He noted Del and Gareth
likewise watching, listening, taking it all in; they, like him,
had yet to forge their families—this was what lay ahead for
them.

As shining examples, he felt they couldn't have found
better.

These men were like them, warriors to the core, their
ladies their equals in every way. As for the families they'd
created . . . there was so much joy, so much pride in their
faces as they talked of their children.

Even Royce and Minerva, the most august and powerful
pair present, shared the same sort of connections, with each
other, with their children, with the other married couples
around their table.

Each couple had found their way into marriage, and forged
a strong partnership and a life worth living. The prospect
dangled before Logan's nose. He glanced at Linnet, even
more determined than before to seize it, secure it. To have
this sort of future for his own.

His plate empty, he set down his knife and fork and
reached for his wineglass.

At a signal from Minerva, footmen materialized to silently whisk away the used plates.

Once the platters had been replaced with bowls of nuts and plates of cheese and dried fruits, Royce glanced at Logan, at Charles, Deverell, then Linnet. "If you're ready, might I suggest you start at the beginning." His gaze returned to Logan. "From when you left Bombay."

Logan nodded, and obliged, paring the story to the bare bones. Even so, when he described the wreck off Guernsey, nothing could hide how close he'd come to death.

He passed the story baton to Linnet for a while, then took it back once she reached the point where he'd remembered all. Succinctly he described the journey to Plymouth, the attack by the three other ships, the result, then their joining Charles in the tavern, beating off yet more cultists before taking refuge at Paignton Hall.

Deverell helpfully took up the tale, filling in the details of their journey to Bath, then Oxford, with Charles concisely outlining how they'd got rid of their followers before turning for Bedford. "But they must have had a watcher stationed in the town."

Logan nodded. "They were taking no chances." He described how he and Linnet were on watch when the smoke started outside the hotel, how they'd been trapped with the cult waiting outside to pounce the instant they emerged. He told of their escape over the roofs, then the unexpected clash in the small yard.

Recounting the incident brought the details into sharper focus; in the heat of the moment, he'd had no time to analyze. Exchanging a glance with Charles and Deverell, Logan concluded, "I've fought cultists many times, but with that number of assassins . . . we were lucky to escape with our lives."

The other two men nodded. Linnet said nothing at all.

Logan met her gaze, steady, calm, assured. He continued, "We didn't wait to see the outcome of the battle between the cultists and the townsfolk, although the townsfolk seemed to be winning."

"My coachman will be able to fill us in—he's following

with the carriage and our bags," Deverell said. "He should be here shortly."

"So Thurgood took the letter and headed this way." Royce leaned forward. "Then on the heath, his horse went lame, and he made the mistake of exchanging it for one from Demon's stable."

"Attacking Demon's old trainer when the old man tried to stop him," Charles put in. "A man old enough to be Thurgood's father."

Royce arched his brows. "Then Demon saw, gave chase . . . what then?"

"The trainer raised the alarm, Demon raced in, saw Thurgood making off over the downs." Deverell recounted the story as Demon had told it. "Demon sent his men, who were already mounted on the horses they were exercising, straight after Thurgood, but he himself paused to check that the old man was all right before going himself. He caught up with his men just as they lost sight of Thurgood. They came over a rise, and he simply wasn't ahead of them anymore. There was another rider, a man apparently out for a constitutional—well-dressed, good horse. Demon hailed him, described Thurgood and the stolen horse, and asked if the man had seen him. The rider pointed onward, and Demon and the others rode on. But they found no sign of Thurgood that way. They turned back and rode in a sweep, and that's when they discovered the horse with Thurgood's body still in the saddle."

After a moment, Royce asked, "Did they see any other rider—anyone other than the rider they spoke with—who might, conceivably, be Thurgood's killer?"

Deverell shook his head. "Demon said it *could* have been the rider he spoke with, or, given the time Thurgood was out of their sight, someone else entirely. He inclined toward the latter, because the rider he spoke with gave no indication of any hurry or concern, and—most telling to Demon—his horse didn't either." Deverell glanced around the table. "We all know how hard it is to hide emotions from our mounts. If the rider they saw had killed Thurgood, then he could only have just done so, and should have still been keyed up and tense, at the very least."

Royce grimaced. "So—we have Thurgood, like Ferrar, killed by person or persons unknown, but in exactly the same way, so we're looking at the same killer or killers." Straightening, Royce reached into his pocket and drew out a folded sheet. "Let's see how this latest information fits with what we already have."

From further down the table, Emily Ensworth leaned forward. "Is that my copy of the letter?" When Royce nodded, she said, "I'm certain Thurgood is one of those mentioned in the social chatter in the first half."

"I thought I'd read the name." Unfolding the sheet, Royce glanced at Logan. "Emily made a copy of the letter so I could study its contents—which gained greater pertinence when Ferrar was noticeably happy to seize Hamilton's copy, even though it was a copy. Now you've told us Thurgood, too, was pleased to lay his hands on a copy. More, Thurgood came after you, and set the cultists on you in an all-out attempt to wring that copy from you—all after Ferrar was dead."

Laying the letter on the table before him, Royce stated, "Clearly the threat of his family seal exposing Ferrar no longer applies." He tapped the letter with the tip of one long finger. "And Thurgood is indeed mentioned, although how we could have guessed—"

Royce broke off. He stared at the letter. "Of course. If we'd shown a copy of the letter to Shrewton, asked him if he recognized anyone named in it, anyone who might have had reason to kill his son . . ." He looked at Clarice. "I take it Shrewton is aware of his by-blows' identities?"

Clarice nodded. "He's a tyrant, so I'd say that's a certainty."

"So if, as we suspect, Thurgood is Shrewton's bastard, then Shrewton would have known to point the finger at Thurgood—"

"And given Roderick was his favorite child, his golden

boy," Letitia said, "Shrewton would have done it—handed over his bastard son—too. Thurgood was right to fear that."

Royce nodded. "Which is why he, at least, was so keen to seize every last copy."

"But you already have a copy," Linnet said.

"Yes, but the Black Cobra—whoever they are—doesn't know that." Royce flashed Linnet a brief smile. "I have three copies on their way to me—why would I ask one of my couriers to make yet another copy?"

Linnet smiled briefly back. "They didn't allow for your thoroughness."

Royce inclined his head. "However, the question we're left with is this—are the remaining member or members of the group who controlled the Black Cobra cult mentioned in this letter, too?"

"Yes," Delborough said. "They must be. One of them at least."

Royce arched a brow. "I'm not disagreeing, but why so certain?"

"Because Thurgood was taking the letter to someone. He had to have met someone on the heath—why else would he stop? He was on a strong horse, he wasn't shot—in fact, the way he was killed, given he was still in his saddle . . . he had to have approached his killer very closely."

Royce blinked. "You're right. I forgot about him being in the saddle. Whoever killed him . . ."

"They had to have embraced." Charles met Royce's eyes. "That's the only way it could have been done."

Royce nodded. "Perhaps in celebration—which, yes, given the letter wasn't left on Thurgood's body but taken, fits with the notion that at least one more person who commands the cult is named in this letter."

"In Bedford, Thurgood didn't exactly claim to be *the* Black Cobra," Logan said. "He said he was the Black Cobra at that time, in that place—as if he was a representative with direct authority, but not the ultimate head."

"So we're looking for at least one more." Royce read out the names mentioned, men and women both, then looked at Logan, Gareth, and Del. "Any ideas which one it might be?"

All three exchanged glances, then regretfully shook their heads. "We couldn't even pick Thurgood out of that," Gareth pointed out. "There's five other men named, and no way of knowing which one might be Thurgood's accomplice-turned-killer."

"If I might point out," Minerva said from the foot of the table, "in light of your inability, even if that person is named in the letter, then who is going to recognize their involvement enough to point the finger?" She caught her husband's dark eyes, arched a brow. "Who do they fear? Or is Shrewton still the key? Is he the one the true Black Cobra fears you might show the letter to?"

"An excellent question." Royce glanced around the table. "Any thoughts?"

Everyone considered, but when no one spoke, Jack Warnefleet said, "It's a place to start. And Shrewton is close at hand."

"Indeed." Royce pushed back from the table. "Gentlemen—I believe we have a body to deliver."

Royce took Charles, Gervase, and Gareth with him, deeming a duke and two earls, plus a major with direct knowledge of the Black Cobra's villainy, sufficient to impress on Shrewton the gravity of their inquiries.

It was midafternoon when they reached the earl's country house, Wymondham Hall, near Norwich. They'd been in the drawing room for less than five minutes when the door opened, and Shrewton's eldest son, Viscount Kilworth, appeared.

"Your Grace." Kilworth bowed. "I'm afraid I haven't yet heard back from those I queried regarding Roderick's friends."

Royce waved that aside. "Sadly, there's been more violence, and another death. I have more questions to place before your father, and there's another body that I believe he'll wish to see."

Kilworth, a lanky gentleman with dark floppy hair and plain brown eyes, paled. "Another body?"

Royce merely asked, "The earl?"

Kilworth shook aside his shock. "Yes, of course. He's in the library. I'll . . ." He looked at Royce, nearly winced. "I expect you'll want to come with me."

Royce inclined his head and waved Kilworth on.

He led them to a large library with high shelves stocked with leather-bound tomes. A massive desk sat across one end. The man sitting behind it looked up as they entered— then scowled from under beetling gray brows.

Kilworth gestured. "His Grace wishes to speak with you, sir."

Royce inwardly smiled a smile he would never let a sensitive soul like Kilworth see. The viscount had used Royce's honorific as a reminder to his father to toe a civil line. For all his apparent ineffectual niceness, Kilworth was a sane and sensible man. There was steel of a sort beneath the softness.

When Royce halted, waited, the earl rose to his feet, stiffly inclined his head. "Wolverstone. What brings you back here, then? I've told you all I know—which was, and still is, nothing. This is a house in mourning. Can't you leave us to our grief?"

"Would that I could, my lord. Sadly, however, matters beyond these walls continue to unfold. Matters in which your son, Roderick, was definitely involved, at least in the earlier stages."

"He's dead now." The earl looked positively fretful, unable to keep his hands still. With an ungracious wave, he indicated chairs, managed to wait until Royce took his before collapsing back into the chair behind the desk. "Can't you leave it be?"

Both tone and expression were querulous. If the death of a son could leach the father of life, of energy and purpose, Royce judged that had happened to Shrewton. The earl appeared to be noticeably diminished in presence from only the day before.

"Before you ask." Smoothly Royce introduced Charles, Gervase, and Gareth, giving each their full title, and waiting for Shrewton to acknowledge each of them. Then he sat back. "I'm here because there's been another murder related to this business. I've brought another body I believe you'll want to see." Shrewton opened his mouth to bluster. Royce calmly continued before he could, "This man was a known associate of your son's in Bombay. Has Roderick ever written to you of a friend by the name of Daniel Thurgood?"

"What?" The earl's shock was writ plainly on his face. He looked staggered. "Thurgood?"

Royce nodded. "Were you acquainted with Daniel Thurgood?"

The earl looked down at his blotter.

When his father said nothing, Kilworth, who had moved to stand behind and to the left of his father's chair, cleared his throat. When Royce glanced at him, he rather carefully asked, "Are you saying that the dead body you've brought here today is that of Daniel Thurgood?"

Royce looked back at the earl. "Yes."

Still the earl refused to look up.

The silence stretched.

Somewhat to Royce's surprise, it was Kilworth who broke it. Looking down at his father, he asked, his tone even, "Are you going to tell them? Or shall I?"

The earl slowly shook his head from side to side. From what little Royce could see of his expression, his face had set in mulish lines—lines of denial. The earl grumbled, "The man was nothing to me."

Kilworth sighed, straightened, and looked Royce in the eye. "Thurgood was my father's natural son."

Royce nodded. "So both Roderick and Daniel Thurgood were your father's sons." He made the comment a statement. While visiting the sins of the fathers on the sons was commonplace enough, the reverse operated just as well. Just as damagingly.

Neither Kilworth nor the earl responded.

After a moment, Royce continued, "We gave the body we believe to be that of Daniel Thurgood into the keeping of your servants. They should have laid the body out by now. I would ask you to view it, now, in our presence, and confirm that it is indeed the body of your natural son, Daniel Thurgood."

The earl glanced up briefly, met Royce's eyes, then reluctantly nodded. "Very well."

He rose and led the way out. Kilworth stood back and waved the others ahead of him, bringing up the rear as the earl led Royce to the old stone laundry. Roderick's body, now shrouded and wrapped for burial, lay on one bench; in the dimness behind lay the body of Larkins, likewise prepared, but less expensively wrapped.

The earl's steward had had Daniel Thurgood's body laid out on the bench at right angles to Roderick's. As per Royce's instructions, the dagger had been left in place, and the small room well lit with multiple candelabra.

The earl stood alongside the bench looking down at a face that, Royce had to admit, looked more like the earl's than even Roderick's had. A moment ticked by, then the earl dragged in a not entirely steady breath. "Yes." He nodded. "This is the body of my natural son, Daniel Thurgood."

Standing a little back from the bench, Royce asked, "Have you any idea what it was your sons were engaged in in India?"

"No. I told you. I had no idea."

"Have you any recollection of Roderick ever mentioning anyone he was particularly close to, here or in India, other than Thurgood?"

"He never mentioned Thurgood!" The earl's lips compressed; his color heightened. "Damn it—I had no notion they even knew each other. And if I didn't know that . . . clearly, I would know nothing else of consequence."

"Do you have any other sons of whom I would be unaware?"

"No." The earl waved at the two bodies. "My sons are dead." He paused, then tipped his head toward Kilworth, standing a pace away on his other side. "Well, except for him, and I've never thought he's mine."

Kilworth rolled his eyes, but didn't otherwise react to the implied insult; from what Minerva, Clarice, and Letitia had told him, Royce gathered it was an old refrain to which no one in the ton paid the slightest heed. What the earl meant was that Kilworth took after his mother in both looks and disposition, and therefore lacked the viciousness that otherwise ran in the family.

Ignoring the comment as beneath his notice, Royce drew out his copy of the letter. "Oblige me, if you will, and cast your eyes over this." He held out the letter.

The earl hesitated, but curiosity won out and he took the sheet, angled it so the candlelight fell on the page. Kilworth shifted so he could read over his father's shoulder.

Royce gave them a minute, then asked, "Is there any name you recognize? Anyone you know, or have heard Roderick mention as a friend?"

The earl continued to read. Royce watched his face harden as his eyes perused the lower paragraphs, those detailing the Black Cobra's dealings with Govind Holkar.

When he reached the end, the earl drew a deep breath. The hand holding the letter shook, although from what emotion—fury, fear, or shock—Royce couldn't tell. Then the earl met his eyes. "Is this what Roderick was doing? Why he died?"

"Indirectly, yes. It was about the money, but even more about the power."

The earl held out the letter, and he now looked truly ill. Not just shocked, but as if something inside him had broken.

Royce took the letter. "The names?"

Slowly, his gaze distant, the earl shook his head. "I didn't recognize any of the men named."

His eyes on his father's face, Kilworth looked concerned.

Refolding the letter, Royce tucked it back into his pocket, nodded to the earl, then Kilworth. "Thank you. That's all I need to know at this point."

Turning, Royce led the way out. Grooms were walking their horses in the forecourt. They reclaimed them, mounted, and rode away, leaving the earl to bury his illegitimate, as well as his legitimate, son.

≈◦ Eighteen ◦≈

t Minerva's suggestion, Linnet and Logan took advantage of the hours waiting for Royce and the others to return from Wymondham to refresh themselves and catch up on some sleep.

Retiring to the bedchamber she'd been assigned, Linnet discovered a steaming bath waiting, with a little maid laying out towels and scented soaps, and mentally blessed Minerva.

"Thank you." Her tone was so heartfelt the maid grinned.

"I'm Ginger, ma'am." The little maid bobbed. "Her Grace said as for sure you'd need this. Let me help you with that gown, and then I'll unpack your bag, shall I?"

"Her Grace is a mind reader. If you'll help with the laces, and then by all means unpack what there is—I'm afraid I wasn't expecting the journey, so have had to borrow much of what's there from Lady Penelope."

"Never you mind, miss—we're used to strange happenings in this household. Anything you need, just ask."

Linnet hid a grin as Ginger bustled about, helping her off with her gown, then flitting about the room.

"Now you just settle in there—the hot water will do you good—and then you can rest." Ginger flitted off to fetch Linnet's bag from where it had been deposited by the door.

"I take it our coach and driver—David—arrived in good

order?" Relaxing back against the tub's edge, Linnet nearly groaned with pleasure.

"Aye, ma'am. All's well there."

Linnet closed her eyes. Scented steam rose and wreathed around her. For the first time in more hours than she could count, it felt as if warmth was reaching her bones.

Ginger remained, but was quiet. The respite was just what Linnet needed. She roused herself eventually, and made good use of the soap and flannel. Ginger helped her wash her hair, roughly dry it, then wind it in one of the waiting towels. By the time the water had cooled, and Linnet reluctantly rose and stepped out, and toweled her body dry, she was warm and clean and truly relaxed.

"I'll just leave the bath until later, miss." Ginger waved at the bed, turned down and inviting. "You go on and have a nice little nap. His Grace isn't expected back until nearly dinnertime, and Her Grace said as that's to be at seven o'clock tonight, seeing as how you all had an early luncheon. Now"—Ginger paused for breath—"is there anything else I can get you, ma'am?"

"No, thank you, Ginger." Linnet smiled. "I'll ring if I need anything else."

With a satisfied smile, Ginger bobbed and departed.

Swathed in a big bath sheet, Linnet tugged the damp towel from her head. Her hair tumbled down, a riot of curls. Walking to the hearth, she raked her fingers through the damp mass of hair, then bent and let the tresses cascade almost to the floor, letting them warm in the heat from the fire Ginger had, of course, restoked before she'd left.

A large, thick rug lay before the hearth. Linnet knelt on it, the better to dry her hair. The copper bathtub stood beyond the rug, its polished side reflecting the heat thrown out by the fire, warming the air above the rug even more.

The door cracked open. Straightening, Linnet peeked over the tub and saw Logan look in. He scanned the room, then spotted her. Coming inside, he closed the door, then walked across to her.

He was in breeches and shirt, and was rubbing his black hair with a towel. "My room's next door." He glanced around. "Yours is much bigger."

"You're a man." Linnet's lips twitched. "And I seriously doubt Minerva imagined you'd be sleeping in the bed in that room."

Logan sighed and dropped down to sit on the rug beside her. "She's just a little frightening, Wolverstone's duchess."

"I have sound evidence she's a mind reader."

Still rubbing his damp hair, Logan raised his brows. His midnight eyes danced. "I'll try to remember that."

She smiled, for one long moment, lost in his eyes, rejoiced that he and she were there, alive, scathed perhaps, but yet hale and whole.

That they'd reached the end of the journey, and now . . .

His expression changed. Setting aside the towel, he drew a deep breath. "Linnet—"

"No. Wait. I need to speak first." Sitting on her ankles, she pushed back her hair, used the moment to gather her wits, her courage, her words. As he had, she drew in a breath, then lifted her chin and fixed her eyes on his. "You said you wanted to marry me—is that still the case?"

"Never more so."

"Good. Because I want to marry you." She held up a hand when he would have spoken, when, his face lighting with a joy she couldn't mistake, he reached for her. She held him with her eyes, spoke with her heart. "I want to be your wife. I want to spend the rest of my life with you, by your side. I want you by my side. I want . . . all the things I never thought I could have—and I want those things with you." She dragged in another breath, let it out on the words, "And I'm willing to do whatever I must to have them, and you."

Before he could interrupt, she hurried on, "You know I didn't believe before—not your commitment itself, but that it would prove sufficient to trump the problems I could see. I kept focusing on the practical difficulties. I didn't, at that time, understand—appreciate—that love isn't about such things. That love takes no notice, makes no allowance, for such things. Such minor impediments. Love is"—with one hand, she gestured broadly—"all emotion. It's need and want and desire." She trapped his eyes. "It's a hunger like no other, and once in love, there is no other choice but to own it and go forward."

Shifting closer, she brought her hands to frame his face, looked deep into his midnight eyes. "I knew I'd fallen in love with you, but I didn't realize, not until this morning in that little yard, all that loving you meant. If I underestimated your love for me, I barely saw my love for you—I had no appreciation of love's strength and power. I didn't realize that because I loved you, my heart had already made up its mind, given itself to you and would remain yours regardless of anything and everything. I didn't realize that I am now, already, inextricably linked with you, no matter what I say or do—that you are, now, forever and always, all I want, all I need. All I will ever desire."

The next breath she drew shook, yet buoyed by the hope, the understanding, the love shining in his eyes, she smiled mistily and went on, "So yes, Logan Monteith, I'll marry you and gladly. I'm not yet sure how our lives will work, how we'll deal with my practical difficulties, but I understand now that I have to trust in our love, put my hand in yours, and go forward together so we can find the answers."

She searched his eyes, let her love color her own. "You'll want to live in Scotland, and I accept that, but you'll understand that I can't leave Mon Coeur completely, not for all of the year. I'll have to return for at least a few months—"

"Stop." Logan grasped her hand, squeezed, then gentled his hold. He knew his expression had turned serious, sober—how could it not? She'd just offered to give up her life—her virgin queen's crown—to be with him. To be his wife. "I . . ." He searched her green eyes. "You humble me with your courage. Stagger me with your love. I want nothing more than to spend the rest of my life with you—but on Guernsey. At Mon Coeur."

When she blinked, surprised, he let his lips twist. "I love you—beyond words. I need you more than I can say. And I don't want to live in Scotland."

"But . . . ?" She looked thoroughly confused.

"My turn to explain." He took a moment to gather his thoughts, calm his heart, order his revelations. "From the beginning would be easiest, I suppose."

One brown brow arched, faintly haughty, and he fleetingly grinned. He tugged her down so she sat on the hearth rug before him, so they were face-to-face. . . . He drew in a deep breath and plunged in. "I'm a bastard. Yes, I'm an earl's son, and my mother was of good family, too, but I'm bastard-born, born out of wedlock, however you want to put it. I'm"—it suddenly struck him; his lips twisted—"just like Thurgood in that respect."

Her eyes narrowed. "You are *not* like Thurgood in any way. Regardless of your birth, you've lived a life that shows how little that distinction matters—and he did the opposite. He lived up to the worst possible expectations of his birth in every way." She shifted closer. Looked into his eyes. "So?"

He searched the clear green eyes gazing up at him, then let his lids fall. Felt an incredible weight, an unvoiced fear, lift from his shoulders. Felt giddy with relief. Opening his eyes, he met hers. "You don't care."

She flung up her hands. "Of course I don't care. You're still you, aren't you? The circumstances of your birth don't matter. The kind of man you are does. And if I've learned anything over the past weeks, ever since you washed up in my cove, it's what sort of man Logan Monteith is."

He blew out a breath. "Well, that was the point of my campaign. Good to know it was successful."

Her brows rose, haughty again. "You had a campaign?"

He grinned. "From the moment I decided I had to persuade you to have me as your consort. The virgin queen's consort. That was the position I wanted, but before I declared myself—before I told you of my birth and formally offered for your hand—I wanted to show you what manner of man I was so, when it came to this moment, you would know me so well that my birth wouldn't matter."

Reaching out, he caught a lock of her hair, flaming like fire and glinting like gold in the flickering firelight. "I wanted to show you at least enough for you to get some idea of what I'd made myself into. I started life as the bastard son of the Earl of Kirkcowan. He acknowledged me from the first, sent me to school, to Hexham, then later bought me my commission in the Guards. Beyond that, however, I have nothing from him—I have no estate, no house. No home."

He lifted his gaze to her eyes. "I fought for years in the Peninsula campaigns. Made friends like Del, Gareth, and Rafe, and later James, and the Cynsters. Then we five went to India. With the other four, aside from our pay as officers, we learned about trade, went into various ventures, and ended as nabobs. I'm wealthy, well able to afford a wife and family. Yet as I set sail for England, I knew I had no one—no family and no home—to come back to.

"Then I was washed up on Guernsey, and saved by an angel. And I found a family, and a home—one I wanted to be a part of. One I wanted to join." Raising his hands, he gently framed her face, looked into her eyes. "I never intended to ask you to leave—just to let me stay. To let me be your virgin queen's consort. To live by your side and protect you and yours. I don't even care if you'd rather we didn't formally marry—if you feel that would make things difficult for you in the community, on Guernsey, with the shipping company. I don't really care how—I just want to live the rest of my life with you." His lips twitched. "I'll even herd your donkeys."

Her face didn't just light up; her features glowed with transcendent joy. She laughed, an exuberant, glorious sound, then flung her arms about his shoulders and kissed him.

A kiss that lengthened, lingered, that unexpectedly didn't lead to a frenzy of urgent need but slid smoothly, seamlessly, into a long exchange of hopes and wishes, of shared wants and needs.

Of love.

It was she who bore him back onto the rug. He let her, smiled and helped her divest him of his clothes, then she flung away her towel and rose up and took him in, and loved him.

He held her, supported her, marveled at the way the firelight gilded her curves, shadowed her hollows. Marveled that he was there, that she was with him, that they were alive and free and able to grasp this, the future they both wanted.

Passion was there, but it no longer possessed the giddy, urgent need of a newfound, newly birthed emotion. What bound them now had grown, matured into a river that was infinitely deeper, infinitely slower, and infinitely more powerful.

The desire it fed still caught them, its ultimate need still wracked them, but now, fingers linked, gazes locked, when ecstasy shattered them and flung them into the void, they were aware to their souls of their deep and abiding union.

The togetherness. The closeness.

The reality that linked two hearts and forged a unified soul.

Later, after, when she'd collapsed upon him, her hair a warm veil spread over them both as they lay boneless and gloried, waiting for their breathing to even, their pounding hearts to slow, he shifted his head and pressed a kiss to her temple.

Murmured, "I never understood my parents before—now I think I do."

"Hmm." She shifted her head, dropped a kiss on his chest. "Tell."

"They fell in love quite young. They wanted to marry— my mother was a Gordon, her birth as good as my father's. But then my grandfather, the old earl, died, and my father inherited the title, and learned that the earldom was deep in debt. He suddenly had the responsibility for the welfare of countless people, including his younger siblings. He had to marry for money—there was no other way." He was silent for a moment, then went on, "When I was younger, I couldn't understand that—couldn't grasp how responsibility could force someone to give up something they truly wanted. Now, of course, I do."

Held safe and warm within his arms, Linnet smiled. "Your middle name could be Responsibility. I daresay you get it from him."

He humphed, then continued, "He tried to break with my mother, but she wouldn't have it. She loved him, knew he loved her, and for her, that was enough—she didn't care where she lived, that she would never be his wife, his countess. But she held his heart, and he held hers, and that, for her, was all. You've heard the phrase 'counting the world well lost for love'—she lived it. Her family disowned her, cut her off completely, but I swear that to her deathbed she refused to care. If that was the price to be able to love my father, she paid it and gladly. She never looked back. My father bought her a house in Glenluce, and he visited often. I have no idea what his wife, his other family, thought— they never intruded, he saw to that. My mother and I never wanted for anything."

"Except you didn't have a father," Linnet murmured.

"Yes, and no. In retrospect I can see that he was as good a father as circumstances allowed him to be. He spent what time he could with me—he didn't try to pretend it was normal or even the way it should be, but he did what he could. He didn't interfere when my uncle, one of my mother's brothers, decided to break with the family line. Edward eventually came to live with us in Glenluce. He was a scholar and a gentleman, and he loved sailing. He was independently wealthy by then, so could thumb his nose at the family—he was something of a black sheep, too. He filled in what my father could not—he taught me to sail, and so much more."

Moving his head, Logan brushed his lips to Linnet's hair. "My mother died shortly after I finished at Hexham—a fever. Later, my father sat down with Edward and me and asked me what I wanted to do with my life. Edward and I had already discussed the army, so I asked for a commission in the Guards. My father agreed. I think he was . . . bothered that he couldn't do more for me, but that was all I wanted, and although the earldom's coffers had recovered somewhat, he was still not wealthy.

"I lost touch through the Peninusla campaigns. When I returned to London, I learned he'd died, and by then Edward had died, too." He tightened his arms around Linnet. "So, you see, I no longer have any family to return to. But I want a family—I want to build one with you. Children . . ."

When he let the word trail away, a quiet question, she smiled and nipped his chest. "Yes, please. Lots."

He shifted so he could look down into her face. "I thought maybe you'd decided your wards were enough."

"No—they were my compensation." She held his gaze. "I'll still have wards, of course. I'll keep the ones I already have, and, I warn you, more will come with the years. And they'll still be like children in many ways to me, but they won't be, can't be, my own."

She looked into his eyes, and felt reality—the reality of their joint future—burgeon, grow, and swell with color. "I just never thought I'd have a husband to make children with me."

Reaching up, she traced a finger down his cheek, along his jaw. Arched a brow. "So you'll come and live at Mon Coeur?"

"You won't be able to keep me away." His lips curved. "As long as you and the others will have me."

"Oh, we'll have you." She spread the fingers of one hand and swept them across the width of his chest. "I'm sure we can find ways to put these broad shoulders and all these lovely muscles to good use."

He laughed, caught her hand, shifted beneath her.

She slid to the side and sat up, pushed onto her knees. She gave him her hand, tugged him up as she said, "We'll start with what we already have at Mon Coeur, and add to it. Build on it."

Sitting up, he caught her other hand, with his eyes on hers

raised first one hand, then the other, to his lips. "Marry me, and we'll make it ours—make it something more."

Her hands clasping his, she looked into his eyes, smiled mistily. "Yes."

He held her gaze. Softly stated, "You make me whole, complete, in a way I never imagined could be."

Her heart lifted, soared. "You do the same for me."

Alex sat in an armchair in the drawing room of the small manor house outside Needham Market that M'wallah and Creighton had found and commandeered. The family had, apparently, decamped for Christmas, leaving the house shut up, the furniture swathed in holland covers.

M'wallah and his helpers had been busy. The holland covers were all gone, and with evening closing in, a fire crackled cheerily in the grate.

Alex stared into the flames. The past already lay behind, done and gone if not yet buried. Ahead lay one last throw of the dice. The question was, did Alex need to play?

There were alternatives. Even if the last letter reached the puppetmaster, even if he, whoever he was, showed it to Shrewton, there was nothing to say that Shrewton, typical old tyrant that he was, would realize the part Alex had played. If Shrewton didn't point his stubby digit at Alex . . . the way lay open to take all that was left of the cult and retreat to India, there to continue to amass wealth and power, albeit in more subtle and secretive vein.

Or, if not that, there was no reason not to stay in England, to take all the money that was left and fade into the background once more.

Alex's lip curled. The thought of retreating once again into obscurity, becoming a nonentity, wasn't to be borne.

No. The only true question was whether to make a bid for the fourth and final letter, or to let it—along with the associated risk of tangling more deeply with the unknown puppetmaster and his minions—slide past.

400   *Stephanie Laurens*

Yet that decision, too, hinged on whether Shrewton could be counted on to mentally dismiss Alex as he always had, and not think to link Alex with Roderick and Daniel in any meaningful way.

The odds, when it came to it, weren't reassuring. Shrewton was a vindictive bastard who had just been dealt a major personal wound; he would be seeking to lay blame at someone's door, to lash out.

So . . . no going back. No slipping away into the shadows, not yet.

At least with the cult's reins in Alex's hands alone, there was no need to pander to anyone else's ego, and matters would proceed with greater efficiency, and commensurately greater succcess.

Despite the hurdles, the unavoidable sacrifices, three of the four letters had been destroyed. Seizing the last would eliminate any possible threat, leaving the way open to return to India and the rule of terror that delighted and satisfied on so many levels.

Alex's lips curved. Decision made.

Stretching out one arm, Alex lifted a small brass bell and rang it. A second later, M'wallah appeared. A tall, lanky man of indeterminate age, with a walnut-colored face and long gray beard, he'd been Alex's houseman for the last three years and had proved his devotion in every conceivable way.

"Fetch Saleem," Alex ordered. "I wish to go through our preparations for welcoming Carstairs."

M'wallah bowed low and disappeared without a word, reappearing minutes later with the captain of Alex's guard. Saleem was a tall Pathan, and a frighteningly vicious man; he lived to inspire fear and terror—in Alex's view, he thrived on those emotions, needed them like a drug.

Addicts were sometimes useful, especially when the addiction was coupled with rigid control.

Alex waved the pair to footstools arranged for the purpose of holding court, waited until they'd sat, waited a dramatic moment more, then commenced, "I have determined that Carstairs—unlike the three who have gone before—will not be allowed to escape our vengeance. And in that, the other three passing safely through will work to our advantage. They will expect the captain to do the same . . . but he will not."

With icy composure, Alex regarded M'wallah and Saleem. "He will not because, this time, it will be I who will marshal our troops and lead them in the field. I intend to play an active role in apprehending and torturing the captain."

Both men nodded, murmured, "This is wise."

Alex smiled coldly. "Indeed. So let us revisit what we have already put in place, and decide what more we need to do to ensure the good captain does not slip through our net."

With rigid attention to detail, they reviewed the dispositions of cult members, confirming the numbers amassed on shore nearby, in specific locations Alex had earlier decreed, and, most importantly, confirming the number of vessels already commandeered and actively patroling the waters off the east coast.

"This time," Alex concluded, "we will not wait for Carstairs to make landfall in England. We strike before, and strike hard, enough to knock him off-course. Then we follow and strike again. But once the captain lands in England, it will be me and my guards he will face—you, Saleem, will lead the elite. We will not rely as we have in recent times on the lower orders of the cult—they are not sufficiently effective in this land."

Both men inclined their heads in acquiescence; both pairs of eyes gleamed with fanatical expectation.

"The Black Cobra will be in the field tomorrow." Alex's tone was pure ice. "And we all know the Black Cobra is deadly."

Both M'wallah and Saleem smiled in clear, malevolent anticipation. Neither had appreciated being held back, restrained by the more reserved role Alex had chosen to play in England. Now, however, they were about to be unleashed, and they couldn't wait to taste blood again.

With a wave, Alex dismissed them.

Rising fluidly, then bowing low, the pair backed from the room.

Leaving Alex alone.

Entirely alone, yet being alone had its advantages.

Dwelling on all that would be gained—imagining Carstairs, and through him the elusive puppetmaster, being served their comeuppance—Alex purposely wove violent, vindictive anticipation into a cloak to keep the chill of the night at bay.

Royce sat at the head of his dining table, extended to accommodate the Cynsters, all six cousins and their wives, Gyles Chillingworth and his wife, as well as all those who had already been sleeping under Royce's roof. The Cynsters and Chillingworths had arrived en masse, possibly—Royce wasn't certain—invited by Minerva, at a time when their staying to dine was a foregone conclusion.

Certainly Honoria, Devil's duchess, had marched into the drawing room, touched cheeks with Minerva, then sat and demanded to be fully briefed on all that was going on.

It wasn't that Royce minded the company—indeed he valued the men's support, both physical and mental—but having so many independently minded, strong-willed females all together in one place, a place not that far from real and present danger, was making him edgy.

And not just him.

Still, it seemed that this was one of those crosses that had to be borne in the interests of matrimonial harmony. Over recent years, he'd grown a lot better at simply accepting what had to be.

Of his combined troops, only Christian Allardyce and Jack Hendon, already on the coast waiting for Carstairs to land, and Rafe Carstairs himself, were absent. Royce suspected the three were very much in the minds of many about the table.

Devil, seated at Minerva's right at the far end, leaned forward to say, "It doesn't make sense that the last person—whoever is what's left of the Black Cobra—isn't named in that letter."

"I also find it hard to believe," Gabriel Cynster put in from midway down the board, "that Shrewton doesn't know who that person is."

"Actually," Gyles Chillingworth said, "that I can believe. However, I do agree that Shrewton could, just as I'm sure we could, find the answer—learn who that other person was—if we had time."

"Sadly, we don't have time," Lucifer Cynster bluntly observed.

Around and around the discussion went.

Royce, Charles, Gervase, and Gareth had reported on their visit to Wymondham Hall. The result had been discussed and picked over, their suppositions reshaped, re-formed, re-phrased, yet they constantly came back to the same point, the one inescapable conclusion.

Del returned to it. "Regardless of all else, the one thing that's certain is that there *is* someone else out there, and we don't know who he is."

"More," Royce said, reclaiming control, "Carstairs is heading in. He's expected to reach our shores tomorrow." It was the first time he'd stated that—that their time frame was that tight. The meal was long over. He pushed back his chair. "I suggest we repair to the drawing room, put our heads together, and string as comprehensive a net as we can across the area."

Everyone rose with alacrity, and followed Minerva back to the drawing room. When they were all settled, the ladies on the chaises and chairs, the men lounging against walls or furniture, some with hip propped against the back of their lady's chair, from his customary position before the hearth, Royce scanned their faces. "Jack Hendon and Christian Allardyce are already in place—Jack, I understand, is haunting the harbor itself, while Christian is patrolling the town. As soon as Carstairs lands, they're primed to whisk him away into hiding, then send word here. This will almost certainly be our last chance to catch the Black Cobra committing any criminal act on English soil."

"And if we don't catch him?" The haughty question came from Minerva, sitting in her usual chair to Royce's right.

He smiled down at her. "If we don't, then we pursue him by other means." He looked at the others. "But I won't disguise the fact that such a pursuit will be more difficult, and a lot less assured of success. Aside from all else, as Gyles pointed out, identifying the remaining villain or villains is going to take time, and they're not going to wait in England while we do it."

"So putting everything we can behind capturing our remaining villain—the Black Cobra's ultimate head—is our preferred option, our best way forward." Devil arched his brows at Royce.

As Royce nodded decisively, Logan asked, "Which port is Rafe heading for?"

Royce met his eyes. "Felixstowe."

Logan was asleep, his arm around Linnet, when an unexpected sound dragged him from slumber.

The sound was distant, yet . . . he lifted his head the better to hear.

Linnet stirred, then stilled—listening, too.

The sound resolved into thudding hoofbeats. As the seconds passed, it became clear the rider was heading for the house.

Logan pushed back the covers.

"That can't be good," Linnet muttered, and slipped from the bed. Grabbing the coverlet, she wrapped it around her nightgown.

Buttoning his breeches, Logan stepped into his boots, roughly tugged them on, snagged his shirt from the chair as he went past. His face was grim as, shrugging on the shirt, he opened the door.

Linnet followed him into the corridor. Other doors were

opening, both gentlemen and ladies venturing out in various states of undress.

No one asked what was happening, or who it was. Grim-faced, they all headed for the main stairs.

No one imagined it was good news.

They halted on the stairs and in the gallery above, all looking down into the front hall. Candles were burning on the central table. As they watched, Minerva lit a lamp. Royce was already at the door, tugging the bolts back.

Hamilton, Royce's personal butler, arrived in his butler's black just in time to swing the door wide.

They all saw the rider, exhausted and worn, trudging up the front steps.

Royce spoke with him, voice too low for any of them to hear, then he drew the man inside, Hamilton closed and bolted the door, and Royce consigned the drooping rider into his care.

Everyone saw the letter Royce held in his left hand.

Minerva joined him, holding the lamp high as Royce raised the missive, broke its seal, unfolded the sheet.

Read.

They all held their breath. Waited.

Only Minerva was close enough to see her husband's face. She laid a hand on his arm. "What's happened?"

Royce looked at her, then up at all of them. A moment passed, then he said, "Carstairs has disappeared. He failed to meet his guards at Felixstowe, but two others of his party—his man and some lady's maid—made it to the rendezvous. As matters now stand, no one knows where Carstairs, and the young English lady apparently traveling with him, are."

Silence stretched.

Eventually, Charles broke it, putting their collective thoughts into words. "Carstairs is out there somewhere, and we still don't know who the Black Cobra is."